SUPER
CONDUCTOR
ARRAY

DISTORTION
HORIZON

SOLENOIDS

INFLUX

ALSO BY DANIEL SUAREZ

Daemon

Freedom™

Kill Decision

INFLUX

Daniel Suarez

DUTTON
— est. 1852 —

DUTTON
—• est.1852 •—

Published by the Penguin Group
Penguin Group (USA) LLC
375 Hudson Street
New York, New York 10014

USA | Canada | UK | Ireland | Australia | New Zealand | India | South Africa | China
penguin.com
A Penguin Random House Company

LIBRARY OF CONGRESS CATALOGING-IN-PUBLICATION DATA

Suarez, Daniel, 1964-
Influx / Daniel Suarez.—First edition.
pages   cm
ISBN 978-0-525-95318-0 (hardcover)
1. Physicists—Fiction.   2. Discoveries in science—Fiction.   3. Gravitational waves—Fiction.
4. Space and time—Fiction.   5. Extremists—Fiction.   I. Title.
PS3619.U327I54   2014
813'.6—dc23
2013026652

Printed in the United States of America
1   3   5   7   9   10   8   6   4   2

Set in Electra LT Std
Endpaper design and illustration by Daniel Lagin

In loving memory of Alan Haisser,
a brilliant engineer who encouraged my youthful
wonder—but still insisted I learn the math.

INFLUX

The future is already here—it's just not very evenly distributed.

—WILLIAM GIBSON

CHAPTER 1

Breakthrough

I'm gonna hunt you down like a rabid dog, Sloan." Albert Marrano clenched his teeth on an e-cigarette as he concentrated on a tiny screen.

"Don't joke. My sister's pug just went rabid."

"You're kidding." Marrano thumbed the controls of his handheld game console.

"Raccoon bite. They had to put Mr. Chips down. Her kids are still in therapy." Mashing buttons on his own wireless console, Sloan Johnson sat in the nearby passenger seat. Then he let out a deep "Heh, heh."

Marrano cast a look at him. Johnson had that Cheshire cat grin on his face again. "Shit . . ." Marrano tried to rotate his player around, but Johnson's avatar was already behind him.

Double-tap. The screen faded.

"You really do suck at this, Al."

"Goddamnit!" Marrano tossed the device onto the car's stitched leather dashboard and pounded the steering wheel. "You have got to be kidding me. Worse than playing my goddamn nephew."

"That's two thousand bucks you owe me."

"Best out of five?"

Johnson powered down his device. "It's a lousy two K. What are you complaining about?"

Headlights swept across them as another car turned into the nearly empty parking lot of a gritty industrial building.

"Here we go." Marrano pocketed his e-cigarette.

"'Bout fucking time."

They exited their parked Aston Martin One-77 as an older Mercedes pulled toward them.

"Jesus, look at this thing."

"They go forever, though."

"You ever get stuck behind one of these on the highway? Like breathing coal dust." He motioned for the driver to pull up to them.

The Mercedes parked, and a distinguished, if disheveled, elderly South Asian man with spectacles and a full head of unconvincing jet-black hair got out. Slowly. He buttoned his greatcoat against the cold.

Marrano and Johnson approached, removing their leather gloves and extending hands. Marrano smiled. "Doctor Kulkarni. Albert Marrano. Thanks for coming out so late."

"Yes." They shook hands. "I don't usually drive at night. But your CEO said this couldn't wait."

"That she did." Marrano turned. "This is my colleague, Sloan Johnson. He manages the portfolio for Shearson-Bayers."

They shook hands as well. "Pleased to meet you."

"Likewise."

Marrano pulled his lambskin glove back on. "So you're our physicist. Princeton, right?"

Kulkarni nodded. "Yes, but I live close by in Holmdel. No one would tell me what this is about."

Marrano grimaced. "Not over the phone, no. Legal says they already have you under contract, so I'm supposed to remind you about your non-disclosure agreement and noncompete clause."

The elderly Indian nodded impatiently. "Fine, fine. Now what is this 'physics emergency' of yours?"

Marrano waved his arm to encompass the drab, windowless building before them. "Tech start-up. Run by a couple particle physicists developing chiral superconductors. The investment predates me, but these guys claim they've made some big breakthrough. I'll be damned if I can understand a thing they're saying."

Johnson edged in. "We need you to evaluate their scientific claims. Tell us if they're on the level."

Kulkarni nodded. "Is there a business plan or lab report I can review?"

Both men exchanged looks. Marrano answered, "We can't part with printed material at this point, Professor. You'll have to review this firsthand."

"Then I'll need to speak with the founders. Tour the facility." Kulkarni eyed the darkened building.

"Oh, they're in there."

"This late?"

"Yeah. Blowing through thirty thousand dollars an hour in off-peak electricity."

An electrical hum became all the more noticeable from behind a nearby fenced transformer yard as he mentioned it.

"We were told not to leave this place or talk to anyone until we got confirmation from an expert. Apparently whatever these guys sent the eggheads in New York turned some heads. Frankly, I have my doubts."

Johnson added, "We're supposed to have you confirm that it's for real."

Kulkarni adjusted his spectacles to keep them from fogging. "That *what's* for real?"

Marrano shrugged. "Like I said: I don't even understand it. Something about 'ionic lattices.' Follow me." He brought them toward a windowless steel door in a nearby brick wall, then tapped in a code at a keypad. The door beeped and unlocked. He ushered them inside.

The group walked down a narrow drywall corridor with a lofty ceiling. Ahead they could hear the echo of laughter in a cavernous space. A deep hum permeated the corridor, along with the smell of ozone. There was a loud bang somewhere, followed again by hoots of laughter and breaking glass.

"Is it safe?"

"Not sure, Professor." Marrano walked onward.

Moments later, the trio came out into a large, darkened workspace, with a high, exposed girder ceiling. Work lights glowed from the center of the room, casting long shadows on the walls. Big as it was, the room was still cluttered—its edges lined with overflowing shelving units and banks of heavy-duty electrical capacitors. LED lights glowed on the equipment, digital readouts fluctuating widely. Rows of rubber-topped lab tables stood in their path, every inch piled high with circuit boards, oscillators, 3D printers, and heaps of electrical components. There were also origami geodesic models in all sizes. The place looked more like the attic of an eccentric hoarder than a laboratory.

Marrano halted them as he noticed shattered glass, broken furniture, and unknown liquids scattered across the concrete floor. A glance up also revealed dents and holes pounded into the wall behind them. They were downrange of something.

A burst of light in the center of the room drew their attention to a towering circular assembly. It was roughly ten feet in diameter and rose up to the thirty-foot-high ceiling. Thick electrical cables snaked through it, woven in and out of metal scaffolding and what appeared to be color-coded coolant piping. There were OSHA warning signs for high voltages, liquid gases, and corrosive chemicals. The assembly was clearly the focus of much organized activity, while the rest of the room had been allowed to go feral.

At the heart of the massive assembly was a concave stone or ceramic pedestal several feet in diameter—shaped like a lens—above which was an array of metal rods, their tips aimed at the center of an imaginary sphere. The open space that the sphere encompassed was roughly six feet in diameter. Other sensor arrays and test rigs were distributed around the platform as well—tubes, pipes, wires, cameras, and more inscrutable devices, all aimed at the empty space at the heart of the machine.

Next to it stood the silhouettes of four men in coveralls with an assortment of hard hats, lab goggles, and, on one, a black paintball mask. They were crowded around a flat-panel computer monitor perched on a cart. Cables ran from it back into the scaffolding tower. As they read the contents of the screen, one of the researchers suddenly shouted, "Off-axis acceleration zero-point-nine-three-nine! Hell, yeah, baby!"

They high-fived one another, shouting with joy, and clinked together what appeared to be large bottles of beer. They danced around, arm in arm like devils before a fire, their shadows cavorting along the walls.

Marrano shouted, "Hey! What the hell, guys?"

The men stopped and looked to the doorway. The one with the paint-ball mask flipped it up to reveal a youthful bearded face. He smiled and raised a half-empty malt liquor bottle. "Marrano! Just in time. Check this out."

Marrano sighed in irritation as he, Johnson, and Kulkarni gingerly navigated around broken glass and pools of liquid. He frowned. "This place is a mess, Mr. Grady."

"Maid's on vacation. Get on over here."

The other researchers stood alongside Grady, all wearing blue coveralls with a white number forty-one embroidered over the chest pocket. Two were young Asian men—one of them plump but tall, the other wiry like a wrestler. Next to them was a scholarly looking Caucasian man in his seventies or eighties, wearing a sweater and necktie beneath his loose-fitting blue coveralls. He leaned on a cane, visibly guarded about the new visitors.

Marrano gestured as they made their way closer. "Jon Grady, this is Doctor Sameer Kulkarni, Princeton University plasma physics lab. He's here to evaluate"—his eyes trailed up the towering assembly—"whatever the hell this is."

"Doctor Kulkarni, great to meet you." Grady waved them in with welding-gloved hands. He gestured to his team. "That burly guy over there is Raharjo Perkasa, postdoc out of Jersey Tech. That's Michael Lum, our chemical engineer from Rutgers."

Both the young men nodded.

"And over here—"

Kulkarni was distracted momentarily as he bumped against an origami polyhedron on a nearby table—but then he took notice of the fourth researcher. "Doctor Alcot. Bertrand Alcot." He laughed. "What on earth are you doing here? How long has it been?"

The elderly Alcot smiled as they shook hands heartily. "A good five or six years, I think."

Marrano and Johnson exchanged looks. "You know each other?"

Kulkarni nodded. "Doctor Alcot and I coauthored a paper on hydrodynamics long ago. While he was at Columbia. I thought you retired, Bert."

Alcot nodded. "From the university, yes. I was encouraged to retire. So I did."

Kulkarni seemed to be trying to recall something. "The last thing I read of yours was . . ." He hesitated. "Well, it was rather controversial, if I remember."

"That's diplomatic of you. It was a paper on modified Newtonian dynamics."

There was an awkward silence.

Grady spoke as he tapped away at a computer keyboard. "Doctor Alcot's career difficulties are my fault, I'm afraid. I've been told I'm a bad influence."

"You *are* a bad influence." Alcot gestured to Grady. "He's been pestering me for years with his strange ideas."

Grady snorted as he studied the numbers on his computer screen.

Alcot continued, "I tried mathematically disproving Jon's theories but couldn't." He leaned back on his cane. "After Greta passed away, Jon convinced me to come join him here."

"My condolences on Greta. I hadn't heard. When did she pass, Bert?"

"About two years ago now."

"So sorry to hear it." Kulkarni glanced back to Grady. "Then Mr. Grady worked with you at Columbia?"

Grady shook his head, still studying the computer monitor. "Heh. I'm no scholar. I flunked out of a state college."

Alcot added. "Jon has a master's in physics." He paused and somewhat sheepishly added, "An online degree."

"Ah, I see. Then how did you two . . . ?"

"Jon's been emailing me for years. Incredibly persistent. Got to the point I could no longer ignore him. It was either that or a restraining order." Alcot gestured to the towering assembly. "This is the result."

Kulkarni looked to Marrano, then back to Alcot. "Then it was *Mr. Grady* who formed the company?"

"Yes."

"With other people's money." Marrano picked up one of several origami geometric shapes from a nearby table. He gazed at the researchers meaningfully. "I haven't heard anyone mention chiral superconductors yet."

Grady answered as his fingers clattered at the keyboard. "Do you even know what chiral superconductors are, Mr. Marrano?"

"No, and it's not for lack of trying. But I do know the government invested in this place. So someone somewhere must understand it."

Grady smiled. "And thus marches Wall Street."

Marrano tossed the paper model aside and turned back to Kulkarni. "Can you please find out what's going on? I'd like to get back to the city."

Johnson eyed the large bottles of cheap beer in the researchers' hands. "You guys always drink while you're messing around with high-voltage equipment?"

Alcot gave the barest hint of a smile. "We're celebrating."

Again Grady barely looked up from his keyboard as he answered for Alcot. "Bert's right. Tonight is a special night. As you'll see." He finished typing, then looked up to regard them. "I'm guessing you'll all need a drink soon enough."

Marrano and Johnson exchanged unimpressed looks. "What's the forty-one stand for?" Marrano gestured to the number on the researchers' coveralls.

Grady tossed his paintball mask onto a nearby tool cart. He now looked like a BMW mechanic in blue coveralls. He pulled back his unruly, shoulder-length hair, wrapping it into a ponytail as he spoke. "Forty-one represents a starting point. Prime numbers are the atoms of mathematics. Viewed on an equilateral grid, the number forty-one appears at the very center of all the prime numbers below one hundred. And if we consider de Polignac's conjecture, the fractal nature of that numerical array has tremendous significance at higher scales."

"Jesus . . ." Marrano and Johnson again exchanged looks.

Alcot interceded. "I'll grant you that Jon has some eccentricities, gentlemen, but I've begun to realize that he simply has a different perspective on things."

Marrano gazed at the dozens of origami shapes scattered among electrical components on nearby tables. "That's a shocker."

Alcot picked up one of the shapes. "Non-Euclidean curved surface folding. Jon sometimes thinks through problems with his hands."

"It helps with certain problem sets." Grady approached them, apparently noticing the dubious look on the investor's faces. "It's fair to say I've strayed a bit from my business plan."

Marrano scowled. "Strayed? I can't even see your business plan from here. I've been going through your expenses. You've blown through half your annual budget in the last three months on utility bills alone."

"An opportunity cost." Grady gestured to the towering apparatus. "High energies are necessary to induce exotic states in baryonic matter. And exotic states are what we needed."

"I'm guessing your burn rate is the real reason we're here." Marrano gestured to the massive tower of equipment. "Is this your Hail Mary pass before you go under? And what the hell is baryonic matter?"

"Physical *stuff*—for our purposes at subatomic scales." He looked to Kulkarni. "Doctor Alcot and I have been studying the interaction of high-energy particles moving through doped graphene within superfluids like helium-4."

Kulkarni nodded uncertainly. "Okay. And how does that relate to chiral superconductors, Mr. Grady?"

There was a pause.

"It doesn't."

There was a tense silence.

"But I could get funding for chiral superconductors."

"That's fraud."

"*Fraud*'s an ugly word. Anyone reading the business plan able to comprehend our mathematics would clearly understand what I was proposing."

"Like I said: fraud."

Grady looked unfazed. "Then it would make for the most boring lawsuit ever. Besides, someone in government was evidently intrigued by my math."

Kulkarni turned to Alcot. "Did you know about this, Bert?"

Alcot grimaced. "I was unaware of it for a time, but eventually I came to accept it as necessary."

"Your professional reputation—"

Grady interceded. "The fault is mine. Not Professor Alcot's. But as you'll see, none of that matters now."

Alcot held up a reassuring hand. "I'll be fine, Sam."

"I'm concerned that Mr. Grady has been trading on your academic credentials."

"It's not like that at all. Almost the opposite, in fact."

Kulkarni turned back to Grady. "So what is it you're doing with these superfluids?"

Johnson glanced between the physicists. "'Superfluids.' 'Baryonic matter.' It all sounds like bullshit to me."

Grady took a swig from a forty-ounce beer, then wiped his beard with his gloved hand. "Superfluids are very real, Mr. Johnson. A superfluid is a state in which matter behaves like a fluid with zero viscosity and zero entropy. Looks like a normal liquid, but at ultralow temperatures flows without friction. Point is: In certain extreme environments the standard model of physics breaks down. Look . . ."

He approached a glass enclosure mounted to one side of the tower and slipped his arms through a pair of thick silvery gloves in its face. The others watched as inside the glovebox Grady unscrewed a smoking ceramic cylinder from the side of the monstrous assembly. He then grabbed a nearby glass beaker and carefully poured a clear, steaming liquid into it from the cylinder.

"This is helium-4 at slightly below two-point-one-seven Kelvin." He held the beaker up and to the side. Even though the beaker was made of thick glass, the liquid inside dripped through the bottom as if it were a window screen. It hit the floor of the glovebox and quickly evaporated.

Johnson looked surprised. "Holy shit. It's pouring through glass."

"Exactly. In a quantum state strange things happen. It's paring matter down to its essence. Subatomic particles. Slipping between the cracks of standard physics." He screwed the cylinder back in the monstrous assembly. "Each particle of helium-4 is a boson, by virtue of its zero spin. At the lambda point, its quantum effects become apparent on a macroscopic scale—meaning individual atoms are no longer relevant within the liquid. *Superfluid vacuum theory* is an approach in theoretical physics where space-time itself is viewed as a superfluid. The fluid of reality."

Kulkarni frowned. "Superfluid vacuum theory? Why . . . What are you trying to do here, Mr. Grady?"

"We're attempting to reflect gravitational waves, Doctor Kulkarni."

Kulkarni was momentarily speechless. He turned to Alcot. "Is he serious, Bert? And you agreed to this?"

Alcot shrugged. "They say it's important to stay active in retirement."

Kulkarni turned back to Grady. "What on earth made you think this was feasible?"

"Because I can see it right here." Grady pressed a finger against his head.

Kulkarni just stared.

Grady held up a hand. "All right, you're skeptical. Fair enough." He gestured to the tower. "A superfluid flows without friction. And superconductors allow electrons to flow without resistance. What we did was suspend a graphene coil within a superfluid."

"Why graphene?"

"It's a superconducting film. Replicates electrons moving through a near-perfect vacuum. Isolates particles from interference. Graphene also exhibits exotic effects under certain conditions."

"I'm still not seeing how this relates to your goal, Mr. Grady."

"Right. I needed a charged superconducting sheet. The quantum mechanical nonlocalizability of the negatively charged Cooper pairs, protected from the localizing effect of decoherence by an energy gap, causes the pairs to undergo nongeodesic motion in the presence of a gravitational wave."

Marrano threw up his hands. "I told you, Professor, this guy is just stringing words together at random."

Kulkarni held up a reassuring hand to Marrano and focused back on Grady. "Go on."

Grady shrugged. "The surrounding *non-superconducting* ionic lattice is localized and so executes geodesic motion, moving along with space-time, while the Cooper pairs execute non-geodesic motion—thereby accelerating relative to space-time. The different motions lead to a separation of charge. That charge separation causes the graphene to become electrically polarized, generating a restoring Coulomb force. The back action of the Coulomb force on the Cooper pairs magnifies the mass supercurrents generated by the wave—producing a reflection."

Kulkarni grimaced. "Mr. Grady, if this was so, why do Bose-Einstein condensates follow geodesics? I can drop them in a vaccum chamber, and they fall just like Galileo's rock."

Grady grabbed a piece of paper from a table and started making intricate folds as he talked. "Yes, but the deBroglie wavelength of the BEC is on the order of a millimeter, whereas the gravity field wavelength is effectively infinite—which means gravity can move it around. If the de Broglie wavelength can be made longer than the gravity wavelength, we can in principle isolate the BEC from the gravity wave."

"Okay, but even so, it's only true for time-varying fields—not static fields like this."

"Agreed, but I had an idea about that, too." He held up what was now a paper sphere—handily crafted. He waved his hand around it. "Neutron stars have massive magnetic fields. And superconductors—like this graphene—*exclude* magnetic fields. But a neutron star like Cassiopeia A— which has a proton superconductor at its core—nonetheless has a massive magnetic field."

Kulkarni just stared.

"How is that possible, I wondered? It's because superfluids containing charged particles are *also* superconductors. The combination has some extraordinary effects. Add a superfluid to a superconductor, and the superconducting boundary shifts, changing the value of kappa and causing truly exotic behavior at the new superconducting boundary." He slapped the side of the massive assembly. "I had a theory about the distortion of gravitational waves at that superconducting boundary."

Kulkarni sighed. "Mr. Grady, I don't see how this could accomplish anything except waste money."

Grady gazed at the professor. "Right . . ." He turned to the chubbier of the two Asian men. "Raj, bring the power up, please."

"You got it." Perkasa chuckled and moved toward the bank of capacitors on the edge of the room. He motioned to the visitors. "You guys may want to step back a bit. I'm about to pump fifty megawatts into this thing."

Kulkarni snapped a look at Grady. "That could light a small city."

Grady nodded. "Yeah, I know."

Before anyone could object, Perkasa raised his hand over a glowing button. "Heads up! And three, and two, and one . . ." With a jab of his thick finger a deep hum settled over the lab. An eerie glow appeared in the sphere as motes of dust were ionized; then the glow faded.

Grady raised his beer bottle to the opening of a long clear tube that snaked down into the heart of the monstrous assembly. "Just watch." He poured.

All eyes followed the beer as it coursed down the plastic tube and spilled out across the concave platform. . . .

At which point the liquid fell straight up.

Kulkarni removed his glasses and stared, mouth agape. "Good lord . . ."

As the liquid "fell" upward, it passed some invisible point where natural gravity returned, and then it spilled back toward earth again, like a fountain—only to be caught once more in the altered field. Soon the liquid began bobbing up and down, oscillating between ever narrowing high and low points until it reached equilibrium. Before long it was bubbling around like a domed membrane on the edge of both gravity fields, a seething polar "beer cap" on an invisible globe.

Kulkarni put his glasses back on. "My God . . . it's a flux."

Grady nodded. "Exactly. Gravitational fields follow the same shape as electromagnetic fields. Just as the flowing electrons in a plasma jet generate a magnetic field, we're thinking these quantum fields interact with gravitation somehow."

"*Antigravity?* You can't be serious."

"No. Not antigravity. What I think we've created is a machine that's 'shiny' to gravity—a *gravity mirror.* Or perhaps refraction is more accurate. I'm not sure yet."

Kulkarni pointed. "This is clearly some form of electromagnetism. Water is diamagnetic, and at these high-energy levels you could probably float a brick given just trace amounts of magnetic material. Surely you don't claim you're reflecting gravity?"

"Superconductors exclude magnetic fields, Doctor." Grady pointed. "And you must admit our test results look promising."

"But . . ." Kulkarni was speechless for a few moments as he watched the cheap malt liquor bubbling around in midair. "If you could bend gravity . . . it would mean . . ." His voice trailed off.

Grady finished for him. "It would provide compelling support for the existence of gravitational waves. Not to mention gravitons. And a few other things besides."

Kulkarni groped for a chair, but all the nearby ones were in pieces. "My God . . ."

"It is pretty damn cool."

Kulkarni started shaking his head again. "No. This must be electromagnetism. Even a nonferrous liquid—"

"You're quite right to be skeptical. Our lab is open to you."

"Because what you're suggesting . . . well, the Standard Model of physics . . . this would create an entirely new form of astronomy. It would mean the Nobel Prize. And that's just for starters."

Alcot, Grady, and the technicians exchanged looks.

Grady laughed. "I hadn't thought of that, Bert."

Alcot raised his eyebrows. "It was the first thing I thought of."

Marrano held up his hands. "Whoa! Guys. Hang on a second."

They all turned to Marrano.

"Just an observation: You're using enough energy to light a hundred thousand homes—to levitate a mouthful of malt liquor six feet off the ground. That's about as cost-effective as using a Boeing 747 to clean a throw rug."

Doctor Kulkarni was starting to ponder what he was looking at as he waved Marrano off. "You're not realizing the potential significance of this discovery, Mr. Marrano."

"Significance is great, but it's not gonna make the economics work any better."

"If what we're really looking at is antigravity—or a gravity mirror, as you say, Mr. Grady—and we haven't yet determined that . . ." Kulkarni started examining the computer screen as he spoke to Marrano. "The potential impact would be enormous, it could reveal . . . well, the warp and weft in the fabric of the universe. It would help us understand the structure of space-time itself. So far, gravity is the only force that hasn't conformed to the Standard Physics Model. No, this is potentially the most significant discovery of the century. Of perhaps any century. It could unlock untold scientific advances. Even a grand unified field theory."

The moneymen exchanged looks.

"Okay, and the commercial potential for that is . . . ?"

It was the scientists' turn to look at one another.

Grady handed the bottle of malt liquor to Kulkarni—who steadied himself by taking a swig. Meanwhile Grady answered Marrano's question. "Probably not much initially; as you mentioned, it requires huge amounts of energy to induce these exotic particle states—even for just a tiny area. To commercialize it you'd need nearly unlimited energy—"

Alcot added. "Unlimited cheap energy."

"Yes, unlimited cheap, portable energy. Assuming that, you could create reflective gravity devices. But as you mentioned, there are more practical ways to make things fly—"

Johnson motioned to the bubbling liquid, still floating in the sphere. "So then you've created the world's most expensive lava lamp. Don't get me wrong—it's impressive—but at fifty megawatts . . ."

Kulkarni stepped between them. "You're not appreciating how important this could be to science."

"We brought you here as the voice of reason, Doctor. You're starting to sound like a nerdy kid at the museum."

Grady took the bottle back. "Yeah. I was that kid, too."

Kulkarni regained his serious bearing. Nodding, he turned again to Alcot. "Bert, prove to me this isn't simply some form of electromagnetism. Does it work in a vacuum, for instance? Can we rule out ionic lift?"

Alcot leaned on a cane. "We've produced the same results in a vacuum chamber and with nonmagnetic materials." He turned to Grady. "Jon, show Sam the field manipulation experiments."

"Right." Grady pointed at the floating membrane of malt liquor. "Look at the shape of the field. It's one reason why I've always believed electro-magnetism and gravity were linked—albeit in different dimensions."

Kulkarni was hesitant. "If it looks like an electromagnetic field, and acts like one . . ."

"It's not magnetism. Any baryonic matter with mass that you place in that field will experience the gravitational effects. Literally anything."

"Do you expect me to believe that with just fifty megawatts of power you're *exceeding* the gravity well of the entire Earth? Without creating miniature black holes or—"

"No, no. Again, We're not *creating* gravity at all. Remember: We're *re-flecting* gravity. A gravity mirror. And that high-energy mirror can be ma-nipulated to refract gravity in various directions."

"You mean like photons?"

Grady considered this as he ran fingers through his mangy hair. "Per-haps. I'm not certain yet. But the reason I say it's like a mirror or a prism is we can only reflect the gravitational field that's already present. We can't increase the strength of gravity no matter how much electrical energy we pump into the field. If there's one Earth gravity present, then that's the maximum we can reflect. But since gravity is also acceleration, we should also be able to mirror the increased g-forces experienced in acceleration—in effect canceling out higher g-forces. Which could be a very interesting application."

"Theoretically."

"Yes. Theoretically. Here . . ." Grady approached his computer moni-tor and pointed at a series of sensor readings. "We can diffuse the effect, too. We're using the gravitational equivalent of Halbach spheres to create the gravitic field, which means we can manipulate the gravity field much the same way you can manipulate an electromagnetic field with a Hal-bach array. We can modify its shape—exerting either an equal flow in all directions . . ." He adjusted the knobs.

Suddenly the polar cap of beer poured downward and balled up into a glistening globule at the very center of the imaginary sphere—still hovering in midair but precisely spherical.

Kulkarni muttered to himself. "My God. Zero gravity."

"Actually an equal flow of microgravity. The gravitational field is focused in toward a central point."

"An equilibrium then."

"Right. Or we can focus it in any single direction. Change the direction of descent—essentially change which way is 'down'—to any vector in space . . ." He moved a joystick, and the beer suddenly hurtled out of the apparatus and "fell" across Marrano and Johnson, soaking them both.

"Goddamnit, Grady!"

"What the hell are you doing? This is a four-thousand-dollar suit!"

"Sorry, guys."

Kulkarni was already looking around at all the debris on the floor. The dents and holes in the walls. "I'm beginning to understand why the lab's a mess."

"Had to test it."

Kulkarni was cogitating, clearly trying hard to disprove it. "But if this is truly gravity you're reflecting, then all baryonic matter should interact with the field. Not just diamagnetic materials but literally anything."

Grady nodded. "Yes. Exactly. Even in a vacuum. And it does." He picked up a hardcover copy of Isaac Newton's *Principia* and, after holding it up, nudged it into the gravity field, where it floated eerily.

"What I don't understand is why the altered gravity field doesn't seem to propagate outside the sphere, as one would predict if gravity were flowing in a straight path."

Kulkarni considered this. "And gravity propagates over any distance . . ."

"Right. If we were creating a gravity field as powerful as Earth's, it should propagate outward. I think what's happening is we're causing a distortion, an eddy in the flow of gravitation." He threw up his hands. "I'm just not sure yet."

Kulkarni stood in wonder as he contemplated this. "We should do Newtonian motion experiments."

Grady dragged a bucket of golf balls from a nearby lab table. "Already have . . ."

Moments later, Kulkarni was shouting joyfully as he hurled golf balls through the center of the test rig. The balls curved as they interacted with the gravity well of the apparatus, then arced off to ricochet against the lab walls.

Kulkarni shouted, "Did you see that?" He pointed. "Like an asteroid slingshotting past Earth's gravitational field."

Marrano was still wringing out his jacket. "Jesus Christ, I smell like a damned hobo." He gestured to the humming apparatus. "And would you please kill that power? No wonder your burn rate is insane."

Kulkarni glared at him. "Do you have any idea how important this discovery might be?"

"All I know is an investment has to make economic sense. Mr. Grady, have you filed patent applications yet?"

Grady exchanged looks with Kulkarni. He shrugged. "No. But look, there'll be time for patents. And anyway, we shouldn't patent the discovery itself."

"Why the hell not?"

"Because it's a fundamental insight into the nature of the universe. That would be like patenting electromagnetism. We need to share this information. There's no telling how many innovations might spring from it. And it's those innovations we can patent."

"So basically you're telling me we invested millions of dollars so you guys could win the Nobel Prize? You'd better get a lawyer, Mr. Grady."

Kulkarni stared at the spinning golf balls and smiled. He looked amazed as he gazed up at the massive assembly. "Your discovery could change everything, Mr. Grady. It could change literally *everything*."

Grady shrugged. "Well, I don't know about that, Professor, given the energy requirements for the effect. But it certainly opens up some interesting possibilities."

"Is there a landline where I can make a call?"

"Sure." He pointed to the back wall. "The offices are through the door there."

"Thanks."

Marrano looked up. "Who you calling, Professor?"

Kulkarni spoke without turning. "The fund's technical advisers in New York, Mr. Marrano. I don't expect you're capable of describing what we saw here today."

"Tell them we've got the situation under control."

Suddenly a billiard ball bounced across the floor and narrowly missed Marrano's head.

"Heads up!"

Sameer Kulkarni moved through the unimpressive lab offices. What décor there was had faded from decades of exposure to fluorescent lights. Still, he examined the rooms with something approaching reverence.

This is where it happened.

Low-rent space with unused filing cabinets pushed into a corner. Racks of cheap computers busy processing something. All so . . . ordinary.

He noticed another origami geodesic dome on a nearby filing cabinet. He stopped to examine its precise, intricate structure.

Innovation was a curious thing. It never failed to amaze him.

And yet this place confirmed what they'd long known: that truly disruptive innovation rarely came from the expected sources. They'd had so much more luck investing in eccentric B and C students. The rationale was simple: Those heavily invested in the status quo had difficulty thinking outside of it—and were often tainted by it. Especially when success and peer approval beckoned. One did not accidentally graduate from top-tier schools. One strove to get in and to maintain grades once there, and to do that, one usually needed to be a master at conformity. To excel in all the accepted conventions.

No, the truly different thinkers often went unnoticed. Kulkarni's organization had much luck along those lines in the Third World—eccentric geniuses reinventing infrastructure with small technological improvements: water filters, solar, optics. The trick, as always, was separating the wheat from the chaff. Finding the usefully crazy people among the seriously crazy ones. And that was something Kulkarni's organization did better than Silicon Valley ever could.

The track record of Valley venture capitalists showed the pattern. A new, sexy tech idea would come along, and then every dollar would be chasing the same thing. Staffers from the original firm would be poached to launch rival firms—until the market became glutted with variations of the same craze. Valuations would skyrocket, and finally, the bubble would burst—the market plummeting. Then a fallow season. Then the cycle began all over again.

And for what? The development of the *railroad* blew away the Internet when it came to disruptive innovation. Interchangeable parts? Likewise. No, mainstream tech innovation was no threat to the status quo.

Kulkarni's organization didn't follow that model at all. It was one reason their investments were seldom near the tech hubs. They wanted the geniuses they identified to remain uninfluenced. It resulted in lots of failures, but then truly useful knowledge was often pried from the cold dead fingers of failure. It made those once-in-a-generation breakthroughs all the more valuable. The breakthroughs that would one day change the course of the human species.

On a day like today, for example.

Kulkarni slowed as he noticed whiteboards in the conference room. They were slathered with complex mathematical equations. He stood in the doorway as he studied the notations, nodding as he followed their logic—but then was lost. Grady had gone somewhere Kulkarni could not follow.

"Very clever, Mr. Grady." Kulkarni realized Grady's insights would never have occurred to him. Not in a million years. And neither had it occurred to other great minds of the age—biological or synthetic. Grady's innovation was one of the rare "virgin births"—never conceived of before.

Kulkarni sat on the edge of the conference table near a desk phone. He just stared at the whiteboards and contemplated how differently Grady must see the universe from most people. And how beautiful that must be.

He sighed. It pained him to do this. It really did. But it was necessary. Deep down he knew it was. But doubt came with the job. After a moment Kulkarni clasped his hands together and spoke to the empty room as if in prayer. "Varuna, I need you now."

A calm, disembodied female voice answered inside his head. "*Yes, Tīrthayātrī. How may I assist you?*"

"I am at incubator sixty-three."

"*I see you.*"

"What is the status of this facility?"

"*Simulations of incubator sixty-three experimental designs are inconclusive.*"

"And if those designs were validated?"

"*Successful implementation of incubator sixty-three designs would result in a tier-one branch event.*"

Kulkarni took another deep breath. "A tier-one."

"*Correct.*"

"I see." He paused for a moment. "What is the ETA for a harvester team at my location?"

"*Harvester assets are already standing by.*"

Kulkarni was taken aback. "Then you were expecting this?"

"*If validated, the disruption risk is high. What are your findings, Tīrthayātrī?*"

He steeled his resolve. "I can confirm that a tier-one branch event has occurred at incubator sixty-three. Incident imagery and supporting measurements submitted at eleven, three-nine, GMT."

"*Stand by for confirmation.*" A brief pause. "*Submitted materials confirm that a tier-one incident has occurred.*"

"Have there been any communication leaks from this location in the past seventy-two hours?"

"*Checking.*" A pause. "*There have been forty-seven emails and eight voice messages intercepted—along with fourteen submissions to social media. All were contained or rerouted to the Decoy Net, with simulated responses from recipients.*"

"Has word of this discovery escaped this facility?"

"No data concerning the tier-one event has escaped incubator sixty-three's IP enclosure."

Then it was still his to decide. "Recommended course of action?"

The response was nearly instantaneous. "Intellectual containment. Deploy harvester assets."

Kulkarni nodded to himself. "I concur. Initiate containment. Record the time."

"Time noted. Harvester assets inbound. Nonoperations personnel, please clear the area . . ."

CHAPTER 2

The Winnowers

Jon Grady watched a collection of billiard balls revolving around one another in wild orbits within the gravity modification field. It looked like a tiny solar system, except that the orbits slowly eroded in the drag of air. He laughed as the young lab techs, Raharjo Perkasa and Michael Lum, tossed more billiard balls into the gravity well created by the towering apparatus in the center of Grady's lab.

Leaning on his cane, Bertrand Alcot stood next to Grady. "Well, it looks like the universe is as crazy as you are, Jon."

"That's a frightening thought."

"Agreed. And yet you succeeded."

"You mean *we* succeeded. You know I couldn't have done this without you."

Alcot waved this aside. "I spent years trying to convince you why your ideas would never work." He gazed at the orbiting spheres. "And I was wrong. As I was wrong about most things in my life."

Grady turned with concern. "What you did was challenge me, Bert. Force me to refine my theory. To change it. And change it again. And then change it again." He laughed as he gripped Alcot's shoulder. "There's no way I could have done this without you. Don't you realize that?"

Alcot pondered this. After a few moments of silently observing the orbiting billiard balls he said, "The truth is I had nothing else to do. My own work has come to nothing. Greta and I . . . all our lives we looked forward to my retirement. Now with her gone . . ."

"You're definitely needed. I need you."

Alcot seemed to be grappling with complex emotions. Eventually he looked up. "Your parents will be very proud of you."

"And I'm sure your children will be proud of you. You should reach out to them."

"I barely know them." Alcot squeezed the handle of his cane. "Listen to me. You have to promise me something, Jon."

"Okay. What?"

"Don't do what I did."

"I love my work, too, Bert. There's nothing wrong with that." He gestured to the gravity mirror. "That's why we succeeded."

"You need to love more than work. You need to have people who care about you—otherwise what's the point?" He stared without seeing. "That girl of yours—what's her name?"

"Well . . . Libby."

"What happened to her?"

"She met someone at yoga class. She's already pregnant. They're happy."

Alcot nodded to himself.

Grady took another glance at the wondrous gravity mirror on display before them. "This is not the conversation I thought we'd be having right now, Bert. This is a historic discovery. We should enjoy it."

Alcot turned to face Grady. "Life waits for no one."

"Is this not life?"

"Just promise me you'll live outside your head as well as you live inside it." Alcot gripped his shoulder hard. "Promise me."

Grady could tell his mentor was serious. He finally looked Alcot in the eye and nodded. "I promise, Bert. Now would you shut up and start thinking about your Nobel acceptance speech, please?"

Alcot grimaced and then gave Grady a slap on the back. "This ridiculous hair. You know, the first time I met you, I told Greta that a dirty hippie was stalking me."

Grady laughed. "Hey, hair is nature's calendar."

Just then Grady noticed forms moving out of the shadows at the back of the darkened lab. He straightened up. "Who the hell is this?"

Alcot turned as well. Perkasa and Lum looked up from their miniature solar system. Close by, the visiting investment advisers, Albert Marrano and Sloan Johnson, stopped trying to dry their suit jackets over a space heater and with curious looks came to join Grady and his team.

A dozen intruders moved into the light—men dressed in reflective crocus-yellow jumpsuits emblazoned with Jersey Central Power & Light logos. But along with hard hats they wore black gas masks and carried work lights and tools. They silently and efficiently fanned out through the room, deploying equipment, acting as if the research team weren't there.

A glance toward the fire exit showed a dozen more coming in from that direction.

"What's going on here, guys? Hey, guys! If it's about the power consumption, that's normal. We have permits for all this."

Marrano, Johnson, and the others turned to Grady with confused looks on their faces.

"You don't need the gas masks." Grady pointed up at an alarm panel and a row of green lights. "There are no chemical leaks."

Grady noticed one of the workmen had a large, older video camera on his shoulder; the red light indicated it was recording. A bright light suddenly illuminated him.

"Hey! Turn that off! What are you filming us for? You have no right to film in here. This is a private facility. How did you get in here, anyway?"

A man emerged from among the intruders. Unlike the others he wore simple work clothes—flannels and jeans with work boots. He was tall and handsome, with blue eyes and dirty-blond hair and a Donegal-style beard running along his broad jaw. He was athletically built with a charismatic, compelling look—like some rustic fashion model. And he had a vaguely familiar appearance. Grady felt certain he'd seen him somewhere before.

Grady eyed the man warily. "Are you the foreman for these idiots? What's going on?"

The man stood before the camera, gazing into its lens. Then he turned and raised an accusatory finger at Grady as he spoke in a booming voice. "His judgment be upon you, Jon Grady!"

"Judgment? What the hell are you talking about?"

"In Proverbs it is written that the wise winnow out the wicked."

"Who's wicked?"

"Your research robs us of our humanity—creating a hell of this earth. We have come to return mankind to our natural state. To bring us back into harmony with God's creation!"

Grady felt a sinking feeling as the intruders surrounded them. "You guys aren't with the power company."

"There is but one power."

Marrano shouted, "All right, that's it! You guys are trespassing. I'm calling the police." He raised his smartphone and started tapping.

The gas-masked men around him leveled pistol-like weapons that resembled black plastic toys.

"Whoa, whoa!" Marrano held up his hands, still clutching the phone. "What is this? Wait a second."

Several Taser darts struck Marrano. The clicking shocks that followed could barely be heard against the larger electric hum of the nearby capacitor bank. Marrano fell and twitched on the ground as they continued to shock him.

He screamed, "Stop! Please stop!"

Johnson held up his hands. "For chrissakes! What do you people want?"

Several Taser darts struck Johnson as well. He went down screaming, disappearing from view as men in power company jumpsuits and gas masks surrounded him, looking down without pity as the investment bankers pleaded for mercy. The shocks continued.

Grady shouted, "What the hell are you doing?" He turned to the blond man. "If you're so against technology, why are you using it?"

The man intoned for the camera lens while keeping his finger pointed at Grady. "His winnowing fork is in hand to clear the threshing floor. But He will burn up the chaff with unquenchable fire!"

Several darts hit Grady, too. A teeth-gnashing jolt coursed through him as all his muscles contracted. Before he knew it, he was on the ground. Screaming in pain. Between shocks he pleaded, "Not Bert! Bert's got a pacemaker!"

Another shock. Then the leader's face loomed over Grady. He carefully stepped over a Taser wire and came in close. "Your research is an affront to God. Your inquiry into His works an abomination. Humanity must live in humble gratitude. Just as we came into His world."

Grady craned his neck up, straining to speak. "There are security cameras . . . covering . . . this place."

The man looked up without fear. "Let them see my face so that they know the Lord's Winnower, Richard Louis Cotton, has claimed you."

A further shock coursed painfully through Grady's body. As his consciousness ebbed, he was dimly aware of voices coming in over a nearby radio.

"Commencing evolution two."

"Copy that, Harvester Nine inbound . . ."

Grady regained his senses sometime later, only to find himself held in place with ropes. Glancing around, he could see that he was lashed to the tangled piping of the gravity mirror tower by impressively complex knots. Whoever had tied them had literally lashed down his individual fingers. There was no longer any electrical hum from the capacitor banks. The intruders must have powered everything down. Strange that antitech militants would even know how to do that.

Grady then noticed Alcot tied next to him, head slumped to the side. The old man's face was covered in sweat, eyes closed. Marrano was tied up on Grady's other side, with the ropes leading off in both directions. The whole team appeared to be lashed to the perimeter of the gravity tower. Grady struggled to squeeze his wrists through the bonds, but his efforts only tightened them.

That familiar voice: "You should pray for redemption."

Grady noticed several gas-masked men nearby silently attaching wire leads to fifty-five-gallon chemical barrels arrayed across the floor, linked by wires. They looked like enormous batteries. "What are you doing? What are those?"

The man named Cotton walked into view and knelt next to Grady. "Thirty percent ammonium nitrate fertilizer mixed with gasoline." On Grady's uncomprehending stare, he added. "It's a bomb, Jon Grady—powerful enough to flatten this entire building. To return this infernal machine of yours from whence it came. Along with the people who built it."

Alcot's voice answered. "It's men like you who keep dragging us back to the Dark Ages." He was awake after all.

Cotton turned to face the old man. "The Dark Ages are what you're bringing us toward, Doctor Alcot. Advanced technology holds no answers for mankind—only regrets for when we play at being God . . . and fail. Creating a hell of His earth—the earth that He bequeathed us."

"And what are you doing if not playing God? Deciding who lives and who dies. Murder is a mortal sin."

"Not in defense of His creation." Cotton looked to gas-masked men preparing the explosives. They nodded back, apparently ready.

Cotton turned and smiled as he scraped a wooden match across a pipe fitting. The match lit with a puff of smoke. He held it to the tip of a fuse, which began to sputter and spark. "You will winnow them. The wind will pick them up, and a gale will blow them away. But you will rejoice in the Lord and glory . . ." He looked to them. "Your judgment is at hand. Your bodies will return to the soil. Whether your souls enter into eternal torment lies with you. Use what time remains to determine your fate."

Cotton walked toward the large, old-fashioned video camera—which was now set up on a tripod, its red light glaring. Judging by the collection of jerry-rigged radio antennas sticking out it, it was apparently taping their victims' demise and beaming it off-site. All of the equipment looked old. None of this made sense. It was as though the group were a branch of militant Amish who had settled on the mid-1980s as their permissible technological level.

Cotton shouted to his camera. "The day of the Lord is coming—a cruel day, with wrath and fierce anger—to make the land desolate and destroy the sinners within it! For a fire will be kindled by His wrath, one that burns down to the realm of the dead below! This is His judgment against those who violate creation!"

With that, his followers swiftly departed. Cotton gave one last look back at the doorway and made an almost apologetic shrug before exiting.

Grady was momentarily puzzled by Cotton's parting gesture, but one glance at the sputtering fuse got him struggling against his ropes once more. They only bit tighter into his wrists.

Marrano quietly wept beside him. "Not this. Not this."

Alcot's weary voice spoke: "It won't help, Jon."

Grady looked up at the fuse and realized just how short it was. Barely a foot or so remaining unless there was more to it than he could see. It was impossible to say how much time they had—so no reason to give up yet. "Bert. Can you get your hands free?"

Alcot shook his head sadly. "I'm sorry you won't get to enjoy this triumph."

"We'll get out of here. Hang on," Grady shouted. "Can anyone get a hand free?"

Lum's frightened voice came from the other side. "No. I'm trapped, Jon."

"Me, too!"

"Christ! Does anyone have a Swiss Army knife or something? How about a phone?"

Johnson's voice could be heard from the far side. "They took everything . . ."

The prisoners sat in silence for a few moments, listening to the fuse hiss.

Alcot laughed ruefully. "We really did do it, though. Didn't we, Jon? We took a peek behind the curtain of the universe."

"Yes. Yes, we did." Grady nodded as he scoured his field of view for some means of escape.

"We probably would have won the Nobel Prize. Now someone else will discover this someday . . ." Alcot looked up at Grady again. "At least we know we were first."

Grady nodded. The burning fuse neared the top of a barrel. If that was all the fuse there was, it wouldn't be long. Just seconds left.

"Jon?"

"Yes, Bert?"

"Good-bye."

"Good-bye, Bert."

The fuse disappeared into the barrel, and a white light enveloped Grady.

He felt nothing more.

CHAPTER 3

Postmortem

Jon Grady became aware that he was sitting in a stylish, modern office lobby high atop an unfamiliar city skyline. The view out the window was spectacular. Modern skyscrapers stretched along a coastal plain. It was a beautiful day.

What the hell?

Grady turned to see that he was sitting in a row of empty, modernist chairs in some sort of waiting room. He was wearing his only suit, loafers, and his lucky tie—the fabric a print of helium atoms. He caught his reflection in a mirrored wall opposite. It was the same outfit he'd been wearing three years earlier when he'd been interviewed for a research grant—in other words, the last time he'd worn a suit. Libby had helped him pick it out. Helped him look normal. His hair, too, was cut short, and he was clean-shaven.

Grady searched his pockets and found only a note on which Libby's clean script spelled out "Good luck! ☺" in blue ink.

What the hell?

A handsome young man sitting behind a nearby built-in reception desk nodded to him. "Mr. Hedrick will see you now, Mr. Grady."

Grady turned uncertainly. Social convention required that he get up now. Instead, he held up a pausing finger. "Uh . . . hang on a second."

"Can I get you some water or coffee?"

Grady took a calming breath. "No, thanks. It's just that . . . I was just . . ." He considered the possible scientific explanations. He had no idea how he'd gotten here. Just moments ago he'd been strapped to a bomb. Was this a hallucination? A last hurrah from the dying neurons in his brain? Time was relative, after all. This might all be happening in the instant he experienced biological death.

He looked around. It seemed pretty convincing.

"Are you all right, Mr. Grady?"

He wasn't exactly certain. "I think I might be dying, actually."

"Excuse me?"

Grady took another deep breath. "Who am I here to see?"

"Mr. Hedrick, sir. I'll buzz you in."

The assistant tapped some unseen button, and a nearby set of double doors opened, revealing a huge and opulent office suite beyond.

"Go right in." The young man smiled pleasantly. "I'll have some water brought to you."

Grady nodded as he rose to his feet. "Thanks." With another deep breath, he wandered over to the doorway and entered the most lavish office he'd ever seen. The multistory bank of windows on the far wall had a breathtaking view, through which he could clearly see the Sears Tower—or Willis Tower or whatever the hell they called it nowadays. Chicago. He was in Chicago. He remembered that he'd met with a grant committee in Chicago years before. But not in a place like this.

The office he stood in could have easily served as a small aircraft hangar, with several closed doors leading out of it to either side. Thirty-foot ceilings and modern burled wood walls—one of which had a large round seal engraved into it depicting a silhouette of a human head with a tree branching within like dendrites in the human brain. Arching around the top edge were the letters "BTC" and rounding the bottom were the Latin words "scientia potentia est."

Knowledge is power.

Just below the seal a well-groomed and handsome Caucasian man in his fifties stood behind a large, modernist desk dotted with exotic souvenirs—complex Victorian clocks, mechanical contraptions, elaborate sculptures hinting at biological origins, and oversize double-helix DNA strands sealed in glass. The man was dressed in pressed casual business attire. Massive translucent digital displays were arrayed above and behind him, projecting a riot of silent video imagery and digital maps of the world. The displays looked impossibly thin and the images on them vibrant, hyperrealistic.

The man motioned for his visitor to come forward. "Mr. Grady, it's good to finally meet you. I've read so much about your life and work. I feel I know you. Please sit. Can we get you anything?"

Grady still stood twenty feet away. "Uh. I'm . . . I'm just trying to understand what's going on."

The man nodded. "It can be disorienting, I know."

"Who . . . who are you again? Why am I here?"

"My name is Graham Hedrick. I'm the director of the Federal Bureau of Technology Control. I must congratulate you, Jon—may I call you Jon?"

Grady nodded absently. "Sure. I . . . Hold it. The Federal Bureau of what now?"

"The Federal Bureau of Technology Control. We've been monitoring your work with great interest. Antigravity. Now that *is* a tremendous achievement. One might say a singular achievement. Likely the most important innovation of modern times. You have every reason to be proud."

A male voice spoke just to his right, startling him. "Your water, Mr. Grady."

Grady turned to see a humanoid robot standing next to him—a graceful creature with soft, rubber-coated fingers whose body was clad in a carapace of white plastic. Its face consisted only of beautiful tourmaline eyes glowing softly. Looking at him expectantly.

Grady glanced down to see a glass of water in its hand. "Uh . . ." He gingerly accepted the water and held it with increasing numbness.

Hedrick watched him closely. "You really should sit down, Jon. You don't look well."

Grady nodded and moved toward a chair in front of the great desk.

The machine stepped aside with the grace of a puma. "Be careful of the step, sir."

"Thanks." The moment he sat down Grady started gulping water, glancing around nervously.

Hedrick motioned for calm. "Slowly. I know it can be quite a shock. We would have applied a sedative, but it's important you have full command of your faculties for this conversation."

Grady finished the water and took deep breaths. "Where am I? What the hell's happening?"

"You've just been through a traumatic experience, I know. It's never pleasant, but neither is being born. And yet both are necessary to go on to greater things. And more importantly, it's now over. And you're here with us."

Grady looked at his watch. The one he'd lost years ago. The numbers on its dial glowed in a familiar spectrum. It showed that no significant time had elapsed since the incident in his lab. A few minutes at most. "My old watch. I . . . What did I—"

"Time isn't important, Jon."

"This is Chicago. Two thousand miles from my lab. But . . . it's daylight out."

Hedrick nodded with concern. "Does that trouble you? Here . . ." He gestured with his hands, and what appeared to be a holographic control panel materialized in midair. He tapped several places, and the view outside the window changed to an uncannily real projection of New York City at night, looking uptown toward the Empire State Building. The interior office lights came on instantly to complete the illusion. "Is that better?"

Grady stared out the window uncomprehendingly. It was as real as reality. "What the hell is this place?"

"I told you, Jon. This is the Bureau of Technology Control—the BTC. We're the federal agency charged with monitoring promising technologies, foreign and domestic; assessing their social, political, environmental, and economic impacts with the goal of preserving social order."

"Preserving social order."

"We regulate innovation. Because, in fact, humanity is far more technologically advanced than you know. It's human nature that remains in the Dark Ages. The BTC is a safeguard against humanity's worst impulses."

Grady turned in his seat to see that the office doors had closed far behind him. The robot stood obediently nearby and nodded to him in acknowledgment.

Hedrick continued as he approached Grady from around the desk, "Mankind was on the moon in the 1960s, Jon. That was half a century ago. Nuclear power. The transistor. The laser. All existed even back then. Do you really think the pinnacle of innovation since that time is Facebook? In some ways, what the previous generation accomplished is more impressive than what we do now. They designed the Saturn V rocket with slide rules. That they could make it work at all. So many parts. So many points of failure. They were the great ones. We're just standing on their shoulders."

Grady turned forward again. "What does any of this have to do with me? Why am I here?"

"Manipulation of gravity. Hard to imagine you did it—and with so few resources. But have you really not considered the implications of your discovery?"

Grady just stared at him.

"Come walk with me." He motioned for Grady to follow him as double doors to their left silently opened, revealing a carpeted corridor extending beyond.

"Where are we going?"

Hedrick smiled genially. "Everything is fine, Jon. More than fine. Everyone here is talking about you. We're all excited. I'd like to show you something."

"What?"

"The true course of history. I want to show you what human ingenuity has actually achieved."

With one last glance back at the obsequious robot still nodding at him, Grady got to his feet and followed as Hedrick placed a comforting hand on his shoulder.

"You should know that I've been in your position. Twenty-eight years ago. I know it's not easy, but you're a scientist, Jon. If it's truth you're after, there are wonders ahead . . ."

He ushered Grady into a long gallery lined with pedestals holding a series of displays—a museum by the looks of it. The closest pedestal held a sturdy-looking ceramic-and-glass construct from which a blinding white light shone. The device was the size of a washing machine. Holographic letters beneath it proclaimed:

First self-sustaining fusion reactor—May 6, 1985:
Hedrick, Graham E.

Grady held his hands up to block the blinding light. "You can't be serious . . ."

"I'm always serious."

"Fusion. You perfected *fusion*."

Hedrick nodded.

"Fusion energy?"

"I told you I've been where you are now."

Grady looked back and forth between the reactor and its creator. Dumbfounded.

"I'm a plasma physicist by training. Toroidal magnetic confinement fusion devices were my specialty."

"I . . ." Grady searched for words.

Hedrick nodded toward the reactor. "This is a later model. The first prototype was huge and output only a hundred megawatts. Even this one's crude compared to what we have now."

"But . . . 1985?"

"Certain innovations serve as catalysts for each other—creating a positive feedback cycle. Eventually a technology becomes inevitable. It's managing the transition that's critical. Fusion and quantum computing are good examples. Improved reactor designs were made possible by computer simulations of nonlinearly coupled phenomena in the core plasma, edge plasma, and wall regions of reactor prototypes. The vast energy from fusion made more powerful computers possible. And more powerful computers, better fusion reactor designs. They are symbiotic. Gravity modification will be another key symbiotic technology."

Hedrick nudged Grady along to the next exhibit. "I wanted to show you this gallery because these are the advances that will one day transform human civilization."

"And you're keeping them secret? Even your own fusion work?"

"We prefer to think of it as safeguarding them. Preparing the world for the massive changes these innovations will bring about. A sudden influx of innovation could disrupt social order, and disruption of social order is not to be taken lightly, Jon." Hedrick brought them to the next display. It was a holographic animation hovering in midair. It depicted living cells replicating in a petri dish. The plaque read:

Cure for Malignant Neoplasm—November 1998:
Rowe, Rochelle, MD, et al

"*Cancer?* You cured cancer?"

"Doctor Rowe did, yes—or at least most forms of it. An elusive pocket on the surface of protein 53." Hedrick nodded and ushered Grady onward.

"How the hell can you ethically conceal a cure for cancer? Do you realize how many millions of lives would be saved? How many tens of millions of lives?"

"The human population is still growing rapidly. Even with cancer."

"What gives you the right to withhold this from people?"

Hedrick looked on patiently. "Jon, the BTC predates me. It was founded in the years before the moon landings—as the pace of technological change threatened to overwhelm our social and political institutions. The BTC grew out of a section of the Directorate of Science and Technology. It was formed to monitor research worldwide for disruptive technologies, to classify them, and to regulate their future release to the general public. We don't have a perfect record—Steve Jobs was a tricky one—but we've managed to catch most of the big disruptors before they brought about uncontrolled change." He gestured to the line of exhibits stretching before them. "As you can see."

Grady let a disgusted laugh escape. "Who says technology was threatening to overwhelm our social and political institutions? The space program inspired kids to go into science."

Hedrick nodded. "Yes, but how would humanity have coped with cures for most diseases? With limitless clean energy? With greater-than-human artificial intelligence? These would result in irreversible changes to society. Changes that we're seeing even now, despite our best efforts at management."

"I can't believe you think this is ethical."

"Relinquishing my own achievements with fusion was one of the hardest things I have ever done. But I made that sacrifice for the common good."

Grady clenched his hands. "You have no right to decide the pace of technological change."

"Now you sound like someone we both know."

Grady recalled the face of the madman whose followers had so recently strapped him to a bomb.

Hedrick saw the realization in Grady's eyes. "Yes, Richard Louis Cotton—the public face of the antitechnology movement. Every once in a while his Winnowers strike at some scientist or lab. It's just a means of control, Jon. Cotton's movement is an illusion. A method of misdirection. You are all quite alive, after all."

Grady moved away from Hedrick warily. "Cotton works for you?"

Hedrick sighed. "Not for me—the BTC. I know it's upsetting, but everyone is fine."

"We're not fine. Where's Doctor Alcot? Where are Raj and Mike? I want to see them. Right now."

"That's not possible, Jon. They've already come to terms with the BTC. Until you join us, you can't join them."

"Join you? Why on earth would I join you? You're abducting researchers and scientists. Concealing life-changing scientific breakthroughs. I'm not joining you."

"We do what must be done. And even then only when truly disruptive innovation occurs and containment risks are high."

"What 'containment risks'?"

"Some technologies are too dangerous to be allowed to spread on their own. Left to chance, technologies like fusion and antigravity would sweep away existing social systems. They would change every society they touched." Hedrick gestured to several more exhibits lining the corridor. "Shall we continue?"

"You're going to add gravity modification to this museum of yours, aren't you?"

"You should feel honored. I know I do. Very few innovations require complete isolation. Yours is one of them. Our models suggest that mastery of gravitation is what's known as a keystone. When combined with other advances—like fusion—gravity manipulation will catapult humanity to a much higher technological level. In this case, moving us for the first time into a Type One civilization—a society capable of moving entire planets. Of building warp drives. Capturing the entire energy output from our star."

"That's a bit much, don't you think?"

"Your modesty is admirable, but your contribution stands alongside those of the greatest minds in history. Think of this: the notion of a 'fictitious force'—Newton's second law. In a closed box, an observer would not be able to distinguish between acceleration and the force of gravity. Einstein himself attributed the apparent acceleration of gravity to the curvature of space-time. Inertial mass and gravitational mass were not just equal—they were the same force. Yet, combined with our knowledge of extra dimensions, we might be able to use your work to disprove the equivalence principle at a high level of precision—and that's just one of many possibilities. You've made an unprecedented breakthrough."

"Extra dimensions?"

Hedrick ignored the question as he gestured again to the gallery. "Your gravity mirror belongs here, and you should feel honored—very honored indeed."

"It isn't an honor. I'd like to leave now, please."

"We greatly admire your work, Jon. We want you to do what other researchers"—he motioned along the displays in the gallery—"like those whose work is represented here, have done. Join us. We want you to be part of the BTC family. To continue your research, but to continue it with access to technology you can only now imagine. We can open so many doors of inquiry to you. We can show you scientific wonders."

Grady was still trying to process it all. He shook his head clear and walked farther along the gallery. At the next display he saw a hologram of cells, this time dividing and re-forming, as well as the image of a young person resembling an older person beside them. The plaque read:

Immortal DNA strand segregation—June 1986:
Lee, Chao Park

He read the details. "My God . . ."

"Immortality is just one of the things we've accomplished, Jon." Hedrick gestured down the gallery. "True artificial intelligence, quantum computing, miraculous metamaterials—and so much more. You can be part of it. You've earned a place among us."

"Us?" He turned. "I want to speak with Doctor Alcot."

"I've told you that's not possible. Everyone must decide on his own—not because of what someone else decided."

"How do I know he's even alive?"

"Why would we harm him?"

"And why would you kidnap someone? Why would you conceal the cure for cancer? The achievement of fusion? I want to see my colleagues."

Hedrick sighed. "You're acting as if we've had no role in this. You do realize we're the reason you received your funding? We're the reason your research succeeded."

Grady narrowed his eyes. "I was awarded a National Science—"

"You were awarded an NSF grant? How do you really know? And who was it that identified you from among all those candidates? From among the students in your online courses?"

"What are you talking about?"

"Very early on your mathematical solutions in online physics courses came to the attention of our AIs. You think very differently from others,

Jon. Our AIs guided your path. They're the ones who noted the unusual promise in the mathematics of your grant application. Please don't act as if we're intruding here. If it weren't for us, your ideas would never have been realized. Think back on how you've been treated all your life. Professionally. Personally."

Grady stared blankly at Hedrick.

"Yes, Jon. We know about your unusual way of seeing the world. But we've had faith in you all along, even when no one else did. You have a unique gift—a visionary way of interpreting the physical world. That's what we search for. We'd like to learn from you. And unlike the public world, we have the ability to understand what you teach us."

Grady stood numbly again, trying in vain to comprehend it all. His model of the known world was no longer valid.

That comforting hand on his shoulder again. Hedrick leaned close. "The ability to manipulate gravity will transform even our most advanced technologies. Instead of containing fusion reactions in a magnetic field, as with tokamak designs, we'll be able to carry out fusion the same way stars do. We might gain a four hundred and fifty–to-one energy yield. And that's just the beginning."

Grady pondered this. "Not with a gravity mirror you won't. You'd need a million times the mass of the Earth for that."

"But that's where you can help us, Jon. How do we *create* gravity—not simply reflect it? That's the next goal. You mentioned to Professor Kulkarni that acceleration can be harnessed—redirected. That's a promising line of research."

"Kulkarni is one of yours, too?"

Hedrick ignored this question. "You and I both know gravity is the most powerful force in the universe. It can consume whole galaxies. Light itself. If we could create it from energy—imagine what constructs man might be capable of."

They were walking again now, Hedrick guiding Grady to the end of the gallery and into another large office. Grady was lost in thought.

As they entered the new office, he looked up to see a young woman standing next to a conference table, along with an older, grizzled-looking man in his sixties. The guy had the demeanor and stance of an old soldier, and he wore a black uniform bearing an inscrutable rank and the BTC's tree insignia. Grady did a double take on the woman. She was incredibly beautiful, fair complected, with short jet-black hair and lapis-lazuli-blue eyes. She wore a tailored pantsuit and crisp white blouse—normal business attire. But in fact, she was so attractive it was difficult for Grady to take his eyes off her, despite his absurd predicament.

Hedrick apparently noticed. He smiled and motioned toward the woman. "And what show-and-tell of our technology would be complete without an introduction to Alexa?"

The woman cocked her head to the side and frowned. "You always make me sound like a circus attraction."

"Not at all." Hedrick turned to Grady. "Alexa is one of our top bureau managers but also a biotech marvel. Her DNA includes proprietary genetic sequences developed decades ago by BTC scientists—sequences that give her longevity, intelligence, and perfect form. She is literally a product of BTC research. An experiment that led to great advances."

Alexa sighed. "Are you finished, Graham?"

Hedrick nudged Grady. "How old do you think she is?"

Alexa rolled her eyes. "Graham, if we could just continue debriefing Mr. Grady."

"How old, Jon? Guess."

Grady couldn't help but look her up and down. "I . . . Twenty-three."

"Try *forty-six*. And that's without gene therapy. It was her genomic sequence that led to the breakthrough in immortal DNA strand segregation and a cure for necrotic cascade back in the '80s." He looked admiringly at her. "What a magnificent creature."

"I'm not a 'creature,' Graham."

He laughed mildly. "Yes. Of course."

The older man cleared his throat and spoke with weary irritation. "We've got a busy schedule, Mr. Director."

"Yes, Mr. Morrison. You're right. And as important as you are, Jon, we do need to get down to business." Hedrick joined them at the table and offered a seat to Grady as the two BTC officials stood nearby. "We'd like you to join the BTC as a research scientist, Jon. You'll have access to the best facilities on earth and nearly limitless funding. You'll live more like a god than a mortal. And we can make your years long indeed." Hedrick tapped at the glass surface of the table, and Grady's gravity-reflection CAD plans appeared as ghostly 3D apparitions, rotating slowly in midair. "Gravity magnification—creating strong gravity fields derived purely from energy—that's what we want your research to focus on. And you'll have the most powerful biological and synthetic minds available to assist you."

Grady shook his head. "I'm not joining anything. I want to see my colleagues."

Hedrick grimaced. "Jon, we've been over this."

"I have no desire to live 'like a god' while everyone else suffers." He pointed to Alexa. "You're creating a race apart when you should be sharing this technology with the world. What gives you the right to keep this all for yourselves? You have *fusion*, and you haven't shared limitless clean energy with a starving world?"

Hedrick nodded slowly to himself, digesting this. But Alexa walked around the table, approaching Grady with a stern look on her lovely face. "A starving world?"

It occurred to Grady that her beauty might be more of a weapon than he thought—disarming him. But he managed to scrape together his wits as she approached.

"Do you know how many people died last year of starvation, Mr. Grady?"

"Not precisely, but I'd guess a lot."

"The answer is just over one million. And do you know how many died of diseases associated with obesity?"

He shook his head.

She stopped just a couple of feet in front of him. "Well over *three* million."

She was actually quite intimidating. Taller than she seemed and projecting a confidence that seemed unassailable.

"I've seen your type many times. You do realize that 'limitless energy' would cause the human population to increase by an order of magnitude."

She spoke over her shoulder at someone. "Varuna, bring up fusion scenario six."

A disembodied voice spoke: *"Of course, Alexa."*

Suddenly a crystal clear three-dimensional holographic projection of the Earth appeared above the conference table. It looked almost real—not translucent but solid. Cities of the world showed as glowing networks of light stretching down the coasts of most continents. The current year appeared in one corner. It was a startlingly realistic display.

Alexa stared at Grady. "Execute simulation."

"Executing."

The year started incrementing in one-second intervals as the Earth changed. Alexa narrated, without even looking at the image of Earth just behind her. "From the first decade cheap fusion energy appears, population levels and city densities increase. Within twenty years trillions of additional Btu have been pumped into the atmosphere. Although fossil fuel use drops sharply, abundant energy means industrial processes increase. Industrialized society drastically expands, along with manufacture of complex molecules and inorganic wastes. Human population continues to spike, with eight billion people living a modern consumer lifestyle by the year 2050 . . ."

The simulation showed cities growing into several massive hundred-mile-wide hubs. Blinding conglomerations of light.

"With the added heat in the atmosphere, ocean levels rise. Deforestation occurs as climate fluctuates rapidly. Earth's ecosystem becomes destabilized and most other species along with it—a vast food chain on which humanity depends for survival. Foundational species go extinct. Algal blooms cloud the oceans. Runaway greenhouse effect . . ."

Grady studied the very realistic animation as the atmosphere turned opaque. A runaway greenhouse effect began to swallow humanity—all within a century.

"The wealthy move to orbit. The rest of humanity perishes."

Grady took a deep breath. "Okay. Well, I'd like to see the data behind this model."

Alexa's eyes bored into him. "It's based on four hundred million petabytes of meteorological, sociological, and economic data. If I gave it to you, it would take you forty million years to read through it. So I hope you brought your eyeglasses."

"Ah. Maybe a summary then."

"Like I said: I've seen your type before, Mr. Grady. Scientists convinced their innovations are going to 'save' the human race. Did you ever stop to ask yourself what would happen if your antigravity technology were set loose upon the world? Do you realize the impact it would have on society?" Alexa again barked over her shoulder. "Varuna, load antigravity scenario three."

"*Yes, Alexa.*"

The Earth reset, this time showing transportation routes of the world, along with the nations of the world as height maps for economic strength.

"Execute simulation."

"*Executing.*"

"Jon Grady, the great innovator. The man who would give his knowledge to all humanity. How generous of you to share your brilliance with us all."

Grady watched as complex transportation networks of ships, aircraft, and railroad networks disappeared in just a few years, dispersing into a vastly more complex network. Major transit hub cities fell into decline. National gross domestic product numbers lurched around, affected by the resulting economic chaos.

Alexa yet again narrated, apparently having committed this simulation to memory, too. "Transportation, travel, shipping, security, manufacturing—hundreds of industries worldwide drastically reshaped, some erased, overnight. The economic impact would devastate the livelihoods of hundreds of millions—every airport in the world, every airline, harbor, and railroad network, and all the industries dependent upon them suddenly obsolete. Border security. Personal security. Economic chaos—"

"Okay, I get it. But I think you're painting a worst-case scenario." He sighed wearily and looked to Hedrick. "I guess I hadn't thought through the consequences of my work. But I still say you're being pessimistic."

Alexa folded her arms. "These models have successfully predicted much more than this."

Grady considered this. "All right. Okay . . ."

Hedrick smiled warmly. "Then you'll join us?"

Grady pondered it and finally nodded again. "Yes, I guess I am interested to see what other advances might speed my research along."

"Mr. Grady is lying." The voice came from the ceiling somewhere. It was the same disembodied voice that Alexa had spoken to.

Hedrick looked disappointed. "Thank you, Varuna."

Alexa looked unsurprised.

Hedrick focused a less friendly gaze on Grady. "Jon, did you really think you could deceive us? There is no 'lying' to the BTC."

Grady looked at the walls and ceiling. "Is that really an AI talking?"

"It's our bureau interface, and never mind what it is—I'm concerned that Varuna says you're being untruthful."

Grady spoke to the ceiling and Hedrick both. "I'm not lying. Look, I want to have a chance to continue my work." He gestured to the projection of the Earth. "It's obvious that I haven't the analytical power to assess the effects of gravity modification on society."

"Mr. Grady, you are dissembling. Near-infrared readings of the activity in your occipital and frontal lobes demonstrate deceit-related latency."

Alexa, Hedrick, and Morrison stared at him.

He shook his head. "This 'Varuna' thing is wrong."

Alexa scowled. "Bigotry isn't appreciated here, Mr. Grady."

"In plain language, Mr. Grady: It takes humans longer to deceive than to tell the truth. When responding to external stimuli, humans require an average of eight hundred milliseconds to reach what's termed 'readiness potential'—meaning a decision. Approximately zero-point-zero-five seconds later a second surge of electrical activity implements that decision. Throughout your visit today, your brain required an average of six hundred six milliseconds to reach readiness potential. Your recent statements required almost twice that interval."

Hedrick pointed to the ceiling. "We are primitive things, Jon. Our biological systems are well understood."

Finally Grady took a deep breath. "All right. Okay. You win." He looked to Alexa. "Spare me the sermon about how I'm egotistical. The

BTC controls advanced technology. You're putting yourselves in a position to technologically dominate humanity. That's what this is about, and I don't want any part of it. I'd rather burn my research than work for you."

Alexa turned to Hedrick and Morrison. Hedrick nodded to her. "Thank you, Alexa. I appreciate you trying."

She gave Grady one last look. "I consider it a personal failing that I was unable to convince you. Because, unlike you, *I* wasn't lying. Those simulations have accurately predicted the spread of the Internet. Free markets. Drug-resistant bacteria. And much more you don't know about." Alexa started to walk away. "Sooner or later you're going to realize we're right, Mr. Grady. For everyone's sake, I hope it's sooner." In a moment she slipped out through a side door, leaving Grady alone with Morrison and Hedrick.

The men regarded one another.

Hedrick shook his head sadly. "We have indeed seen your type before, Jon. The idealist. You call us megalomaniacal, and yet you're the one not cooperating with others. As for 'burning' your work—we already have it. All of it. And I think you'll find that the BTC has many smart people who can start where you left off. It'll just take us a little longer without your peculiar mode of thought."

"What you're doing is criminal."

"I know you believe that. You feel violated. But ask yourself whether it's not your wounded pride that's made you dislike us. With time, perhaps you'll come to realize that the BTC is humanity's greatest hope for an enduring future, and that we as individuals have no right to alter society to suit our personal visions."

"You're the one with a personal vision of society, not me."

"It's not personal at all. We've been given a legal mandate to protect society. National Security Council memorandums 10/2 of 1948 and number sixty-eight of 1950 empower us to deceive the public for the greater good. What's known as *the necessary lie*." Hedrick pressed his thumbprint to a digital document that had materialized on the tabletop in front of him. "And it's for the greater good that I'm remanding you to our Hibernity facility."

"Hibernity. What is that?"

"A safe place for brilliant people who nonetheless fail to see reason."

"You mean a prison."

Hedrick pursed his lips. "I suppose it is a prison. A humane prison designed to protect the public from dangerous ideas."

Morrison let a crooked smile spread across his face. "I'll take it from here, Mr. Hedrick."

"Thank you, Mr. Morrison."

Doors behind and to either side opened, and Grady turned to see a dozen swarthy, young, perfectly fit men enter in gray uniforms with inscrutable insignia at their shoulders. The men were identical in every way—with blond crew cuts, square jaws, thick necks, and broad shoulders, though not particularly handsome. They looked, in fact, exactly like a younger version of Mr. Morrison.

The realization dawned on Grady as the men approached calmly. "Oh my God . . ."

Morrison chuckled. "You'll be seeing a lot more of me in the future, Mr. Grady . . . but then, so will everyone."

Grady turned in all directions as the men surrounded him. They held up devices that looked no more threatening than a TV remote.

"My apologies about the use of physical force earlier, but we can't use psychotronics in public; technology greater than level four seldom leaves the office. You're going to feel very sleepy in a moment. Don't fight it. Just lie down, or you'll fall down." Morrison nodded to his younger doppelgängers.

Several of the men aimed their devices and red laser dots found Grady's scalp. Suddenly he was overcome with drowsiness.

"Sit down right there, Mr. Grady." Morrison pointed.

Grady felt so sleepy he barely made it to the chair before he blacked out. By the time he came to again, there was a tight collar clamped around his neck—and more importantly he could no longer feel anything below his shoulders. He was suddenly paralyzed.

And yet he was still standing. And somehow breathing.

"What's happening?"

Morrison was clicking through screens on a holographic display hovering above his wrist. "Nothing to worry about. A modest dose of microwaves to the diencephalons can synchronize your brain's electrical activity to an external source. We just amplified the delta waves in your brain to put you to sleep."

"I can't feel my body!"

Morrison nodded as he continued tapping buttons. "Corticospinal collar. Overrides the signals your brain sends to the muscles. Let's us send some signals of our own. And it beats having to carry you around." He closed the virtual screen and focused his gaze on Grady. "You're just a head on a pole now. So I'd start acting more courteous if I were you." Morrison raised his hand toward Grady and made a gesture of walking with two fingers.

Grady's body started walking away.

"Oh God!" It was a horrifying feeling—his body was suddenly lost to him. A traitor. Grady was helpless as his own body carried him off.

He craned his neck back behind him. "People will come looking for me, Mr. Hedrick! I have family. Colleagues. You can't just make me disappear!"

Hedrick motioned for the guards to stop. Grady's own body slowly turned around like a zombie to face the BTC director again. "But you're not disappearing, Jon. Everyone knows where you are. Here . . ."

Hedrick waved his arms and high-definition video images filled the nearby walls. A wave of his hand split the imagery into a dozen live news feeds—a patchwork of overproduced disaster porn depicting a blazing industrial fire. The chyron at the foot of one screen declaring, "*Scientists slain by antitech terror group.*"

A reporter in one inset provided voice-over to an aerial image of Grady's destroyed industrial lab: "*In a video posted online, rabid antitechnology terrorists the Winnowers claimed responsibility for a bombing that left six researchers dead in Edison, New Jersey, overnight.*"

In another video inset a male reporter on the scene intoned, "*. . . fanatical religious group determined to 'return mankind to the Iron Age' has struck again—this time destroying a start-up semiconductor lab in . . .*"

Another video inset showing an old photo of Grady and a black-and-white photo of a younger Alcot: "*Among the dead: Chirality Labs cofounders Jonathan Grady and Bertrand Alcot as well as venture capitalists Albert Marrano and Sloan Johnson . . .*"

Another video inset: "*. . . the Winnowers have carried out half a dozen deadly bombings over a decade—at times waiting years between attacks . . .*"

Grady watched in horror as images of rescue workers accompanied the newscaster's narration. Gurneys bearing body bags from the scene. Corpse-sniffing dogs searching through ruins.

Hedrick focused on Grady. "Growing teeth, bones, and body parts from DNA is trivial to us. Your remains in the explosion will leave no doubt that you and your whole team are dead. You see, even if you had accepted a role among us, Jon, you were never going back. You can never live among normal people again. Your mind is just too dangerous."

CHAPTER 4

Modus Operandi

A **white AS350 Eurocopter descended** from a cloudy winter sky. It rotated windward before setting down near a vast array of flashing police and fire truck lights in the parking lot of an industrial zone in Edison, New Jersey. The vehicles were clustered around a massive blast crater centered on the smoking shell of an industrial building. Firefighters hosed down the periphery, while dozens of emergency responders stood by. FBI investigators in hazmat suits combed through the wreckage.

As the chopper rotors wound down, FBI Special Agent Denise Davis exited and at a crouch approached two waiting men wearing winter parkas marked "FBI," front and back. She zipped her own parka against the frigid chopper wash as she cleared the rotors, glad (as always) that her hair was still in a military buzz cut.

She nodded to the two men—neither of whom looked particularly pleased to see her. This had to be handled carefully. And immediately.

"Wasn't my idea, Thomas."

Agent Thomas Falwell, a lean, balding man in his forties looked nonplussed. "Does it matter?"

"For the record, I think it was a shitty thing to do."

He turned to look at the massive crime scene behind them.

"Are we good? Do you want reassignment?"

He shook his head. "I just wish you didn't have the résumé you do. But I would have made the same decision if I were them."

She met his stare and nodded. "That's extremely decent of you."

"Just don't ask me again after a couple of beers."

She nodded acceptance, then turned to the younger agent standing nearby. "Dwight, can you locate the ERT lead? I want a definitive body count as soon as possible."

"On it, Denise." Dwight Wortman, the younger agent, nodded and took off toward the emergency vehicles.

Davis started marching toward the smoldering blast site. She turned to Falwell, who had fallen in alongside her. "What do we have so far?"

"Definitely our boy. Cotton posted on YouTube minutes after the bombing. Shows his victims struggling right up till the last moment." He passed Davis a tablet computer.

She tapped at the screen, and the video began to play. A familiar face—Richard Louis Cotton surrounded by his masked followers. Cotton pointed at some complex mechanical assembly with researchers lashed to it. "*. . . an outrage against creation! This—*"

Davis paused it. "Does he say anything new?"

"No. Same old return-to-the-Iron-Age crap."

She passed the tablet back to him. "What about the upload?"

"Cyber division says it was a stolen account. The file uploaded from an IP address in Kiev, Ukraine."

"And the domain owner?"

"It'll be a proxy, but they're checking. The Ukrainian authorities are sometimes helpful. Sometimes not."

"Were we able to get a camera serial number from the video?"

"No—old equipment again. The techs found pieces in the bomb crater."

"Betacam?"

He nodded. "Yeah. Jerry-rigged with wireless for streaming to the Web, just like the others."

"Bypassed technology—cul-de-sacs of innovation. That's Cotton's signature, all right."

"What do we do about the YouTube video?"

"Does it show anything graphic?"

Falwell shook his head. "No. It whites out at the end."

"Then get me a listing of IP addresses that accessed it before this attack hit the news. Cotton's thorough, but his Winnower pals might not be as sharp. One of them might have checked from a stateside computer to see that their 'masterpiece' was uploaded successfully. They'll make a mistake sooner or later, so we need to cover every angle."

"For antitech zealots, these guys sure know their way around technology."

"Hypocrisy is the least of their malfunctions."

They had now arrived at the edge of the blast crater. Big blocks of masonry, twisted I beams, and thousands of singed documents, computer parts, pieces of furniture, and inscrutable machine parts were scattered across the pavement. Numbered evidence flags were stabbed into the ground here and there.

She sniffed the air and let out an involuntary whistle. "Another ammonium nitrate bomb. A big one this time."

"Lab's running the chemical taggants in the fertilizer, but I'm willing to bet it originates from that '06 boxcar shipment used in the past two bombings."

Davis kneeled down to examine a singed origami sphere skewered in place with an evidence tag. The geodesic facets were symmetrical. Perfect.

Falwell nodded toward it. "They're finding those things all over the place."

She stood and noticed the burned-out, crumpled wreckage of what was clearly an expensive sports car, partially buried beneath fallen masonry. New York vanity plates were visible: "*MKT WIZ*." Davis looked back at Falwell.

"Aston Martin One-77."

"A little upscale for the neighborhood."

"Belonged to one of the victims. How's two-point-four million dollars grab ya?"

She shot a look back at him. "You're joking. For a car?"

"Only seventy-seven were produced, thus the name. I guess they'll have to start calling them Aston Martin One-76s now."

"And the owner?"

"An Albert Marrano, executive vice president at Shearson-Bayers, a hedge fund in New York. He and a colleague were in the building; ID'd on the videotape along with other victims. The techs are still going through the human remains. Bones. Some organs. Fingers. Initial estimate is we've got pieces of six bodies—which matches the video they uploaded."

Davis looked down at another numbered evidence marker stabbed into the ground next to fresh tire tracks running through old snow. The tire tracks ran near the wrecked Aston Martin. Pieces of debris had deformed them in places. "Fresh tracks—just before the blast from the looks of it." She looked behind the Aston Martin and traced its route through snow patches as best she could. "Arrived after our investors."

"ERT's looking into it."

"Pull video from intersection cameras for a mile in every direction. When the techs narrow down vehicle types from the tires, let's go through the videos—see if we can't eyeball our Winnowers without their masks as they arrive or depart."

He made notes. "You got it."

"So were the Wall Street guys just unlucky to be here? Or did they inadvertently tip Cotton off to something he didn't like? Have Dwight run a check on every press release, investor newsletter, or media interview that hedge fund has done in the past year. See if they ever mentioned this firm." She turned to look for an intact business sign. No luck. "What's this company called, anyway?"

Falwell flipped through his notes. "Chirality Labs."

"What sort of research did they do?"

"Something called 'chiral superconductors.'"

"Superconductors I get, but what's 'chiral' mean?"

"I looked it up—didn't really understand the explanation, though. Something about electrons only moving in one direction."

"Well, something they did here pissed Cotton off. Made him bring in his death squad."

"If he's so upset about advanced tech, why doesn't he go after a major aerospace or biotech firm?"

She pondered that. "Too difficult. He only goes after easy marks." She glanced around at the aged building. "I mean, look at this place. They didn't even have a perimeter gate. Half a dozen employees. It's like the other bombings. Small, relatively unknown firms. He wants victims for the news. Let me take a guess about this company: They weren't at the forefront of anything. No distinguished principals."

Falwell glanced down at his notes. "This Alcot guy taught physics in the Ivy League."

"I saw that. Retired, though, wasn't he? In his eighties. Just a figure-head maybe." Davis thought for a few moments more in silence. "What about their funding?"

"I pulled their business filings this morning." Falwell brought up PDF images of business permits, incorporation papers, and other documents on his computer tablet and started flipping through them. "Looks like initial funding came from this Shearson-Bayers, the New York firm, and judging by the chronology on these other SEC filings, I'd say the founders were canny enough to use the initial investment to get buy-in from other, smaller investors."

"Any repeats from past bombings?"

Falwell shook his head. "We'll check shell companies and subsidiaries, but on a first look, no. They're Midwest and Southeast partnerships. Prob-ably doctors and lawyers without Silicon Valley connections looking for a big tech score." He flipped through a few more pages. "Looks like they might have been sold a bill of goods."

She looked back at him. "Why do you say that?"

"The company president, this Jon Grady guy: thirty-one years old. His parents said he'd received a National Science Foundation grant."

"And he didn't."

He shook his head. "NSF has no record of him."

"And his academic background?"

"Heh. That's the thing. He didn't really have one. I mean, not a real school, anyway. Dropped out of Albany. Got a bachelor's and a master's in physics from an online diploma mill. His parents said they were real proud of him because he'd overcome a learning disability."

"Specifically . . . ?"

He glanced at his notes. "Congenital synesthesia."

"What the hell's that?"

"Apparently he saw music and heard numbers—some crossed wires in the brain. That sort of thing. Had a compulsion for folding paper, too."

She could see several more scorched origami shapes in the wreckage.

"Undistinguished academic record. Kind of an oddball. Behavioral problems . . ." He glanced through the papers. "Yada, yada, yada."

Davis considered this. "Now that's starting to sound familiar. The New Orleans bombing five years ago—the company founder had Asperger's or something like that. Wasn't there another one who had some sort of mental condition?"

Falwell gave her a look. "I'll go back through the files, but what are you thinking?"

Davis pondered the previous cases. "There was that Winnower bombing in Tampa—before both of us. What, nine years ago? Electrical engineer who had claimed he was financed by the Defense Department. But wasn't."

Falwell nodded. "Okay, so maybe it's high-tech scam artists that Cotton hates. Maybe his mom lost her retirement savings or something."

"Did this Chirality Labs ever produce a product or file for a patent?"

Falwell flipped through the papers for a few moments before looking up and shaking his head.

"They never do." Davis looked up at the media helicopters hovering half a mile away. She knew their nose cameras had impressive capabilities. They were combing the crime scene on live TV, adding to Cotton's ego. "Cotton goes for camera-ready catastrophes."

"But what's the point of hitting sham start-up tech firms every couple of years? What's it accomplish?"

"Cotton's probably smart enough to realize that if he punches above his weight or too often, we're going to get some serious manpower focused on this case."

Falwell considered this.

Davis stood at the edge of the still smoking crater. It was easily twenty feet across and five feet deep. "Two and a half years since the last attack. And nearly two years since the one before that. Who has that kind of patience, Thomas? Who can keep operational security within a group of anarchists for that long?"

Falwell stowed his computer tablet. "I have to say this, Denise. And you need to hear me out."

She almost cringed. "What? I thought we were good."

"It's not that. I've been chasing Cotton for seven years. And now that there's been another bombing—and it's all over the news again—D.C. will give you additional manpower. Just like they did me."

"I won't let them forget all the hard work you did, Thomas."

"Not my point. My point is that in a year or so this team will be pared down again."

"Then we'll have to capture Cotton before then."

"I'm just letting you know that Cotton is like no narcissistic sociopath I've ever heard of. There comes a point when we have to ask ourselves whether Cotton still fits the BAU profile."

"Okay . . . we can have them do another workup."

"I've never seen anyone who's content to disappear for so long—to be almost forgotten. Only to strike again somewhere far away and always with faceless, masked followers. There's something here we're not seeing. We've had informers inside antitech anarchist groups for years now. It's as though Richard Cotton doesn't exist except when he's attacking."

She walked up to him. "It's been a long road, but I hope you know that I need you to do exactly what you're doing: telling me what you really think."

He nodded.

Davis walked back toward the knot of emergency vehicles, where Dwight was now approaching with an FBI ERT member. She spoke over her shoulder. "Use the extra agents while we've got 'em, Thomas. Chase down all the loose ends. And if Cotton doesn't exist between attacks, then we'll just have to conjure him, won't we?"

CHAPTER 5

Master Copy

Don't you need to resequence** him before transport?"

A blond man, physically identical to the first except for his lab coat, bristled and looked up from a holographic computer display. "I'm sorry, do you have a medical classification?"

"I'm just saying, if you gave a longer estimated time of departure, I'd have time to hit the R&R levels before we go."

"You're always 'just saying.' You've got diarrhea of the mouth is what you've got."

"I've been away from civilization a long time."

A clattering noise.

"C'mon, don't be an asshole. Give us a few hours before they send us back, man."

Grady watched the men from an inclined position on a metallic table. Grady was still a disconnected head—unable to feel a thing below his neck. And it was panicking him. He stared up at the lights, trying to calm himself—especially because listening to his rapid breathing without feeling anything was freaking him out further.

"Mr. Grady, please stop hyperventilating."

"Just pump him full of PP-3 and put him on ice for a while."

"Stop telling me how to do my job."

"C'mon, do me a solid. A few hours are all I need."

"I'm not falsifying official paperwork so you can get laid."

"You're such a kiss-ass."

Another two identical men entered Grady's field of vision. They weren't handsome, but they all shared that thick-necked, swarthy, alpha-male demeanor. The two new arrivals wore gray guard uniforms with Greek numeric patches on the shoulder—Delta-Alpha and Theta-Tau—as though each was his own fraternity. They glowered down on Grady.

The first tech complained, "Damnit, get the hell out of my lab. All of you."

"You'd better give us a few hours, Zeta. I haven't been in the real world for a year and a half."

"It's not up to me."

A ragged older man's gruff voice boomed out. "Get the hell out of here, you three!"

The two most recent arrivals ducked out without a word. The last one remained, eyeballing someone, who soon walked into Grady's view. It was the eldest Morrison. The one from Hedrick's office.

The younger Morrison glared. "I'm not afraid of you, old man."

The elder Morrison got right in his face. "That can be rectified."

"A man your age should be careful."

Morrison smirked. "That's funny." He suddenly head-butted the younger man. The young soldier collapsed, and in moments Morrison had his boot on the man's neck. "Because it's you who should be careful."

"Get off me!"

Morrison called out, "Boys! Get this idiot out of here before I kill him."

Two other clones hurried in and grabbed their compatriot.

Morrison glowered at them. "All of you stay on the transport. You won't be here long."

"Yes, sir."

Morrison's aged, scarred face followed the men as they carried their injured comrade out. He finally looked down on Grady. "Kids."

Grady was at a loss for words.

"Don't give me that look. Mother Nature's always had clones, Mr.

Grady. They're called twins." He shook his head ruefully. "I've just got way more of 'em than most people." Morrison turned to the clone in a lab coat. "Zeta, how much longer?"

"About five, ten minutes. Depends on his protein folds."

Morrison nodded absently, observing the complex imagery on a nearby screen. "I never could get used to all this high-tech crap." He looked down at Grady again. "But it's like they say: Anything before you're thirty-five is new and exciting, and anything after that is proof the world's going to hell."

Grady was still trying to get his helplessness-induced panic under control. His breathing was labored.

Morrison scowled at him. "You need to relax, Mr. Grady, or that collar's going to have difficulty controlling your respiratory functions. We have all the genetic information necessary to make a copy of you, but as you might have noticed, that's not the same thing as having *you*."

The lab technician halted his work and looked up at the ceiling. "Would you stop with this already?"

"I'm talking to this man, here. Do you see me talking to you? Was I talking to you?"

"I think you *were* talking to me in a way, yes."

"Just get him prepped. The sooner we get these substandard Neanderthals out of here, the better."

"I copy that." The younger man sighed and turned back to his work.

Morrison glowered down at Grady again. Morrison looked old and tired as he rubbed his calloused, thick fingers against his closed eyes.

Grady felt the words forming as a means to keep his mind off the vertigo he was feeling. "Why are you doing this?"

Morrison looked up. "Doing what?"

"Taking away my life."

"If the director says you need a time-out, then you need a time-out. Hibernity does a great job of changing people's minds. Literally."

Grady searched the man's eyes for some human kindness. He saw none. "This is wrong."

"Wrong. Right. They're a matter of perspective. I'm sure gazelles think lions are wrong."

"And you and your clones are the lions."

"I'd say they're more like hyenas."

The lab technician slammed his computer tablet onto the counter. "Dad, give it a rest already."

"What? I can't talk to this poor unfortunate without getting comments from the peanut gallery?"

"I'm not gonna just stand here and listen to you talk shit."

Morrison turned back to Grady. "You know why they cloned me back in the '80s, Mr. Grady? Because I was the best special operator the U.S. military ever produced. High intelligence, top physical characteristics—the most determined to survive and overcome. To win. But as it turns out, genetics isn't destiny—it's statistics. After two decades it has become quite clear that something about us is not genetic."

The younger clone interjected, "You don't even understand the science: The seat of consciousness—what's known as 'sensorium'—exists partly as an expression of particle entanglement in higher physical dimensions. The human brain is merely a conduit."

Morrison gestured toward his younger self. "My point exactly. That's why none of you will *ever* be me." He turned back to Grady. "Turns out you can't copy people. Just flesh. Now it's all biotech design. Like Granny Alexa up there."

The lab technician glared. "Tau said you wanted us all liquidated."

"Not all of you. Just the less-than-faithful reproductions."

The lab technician still glared.

Morrison threw up his hands. "What do you want me to say?"

The clone stared hard at Morrison for several moments. "There are times when I feel like murdering you, sir."

"Well, give it your best shot, son. Just don't fail."

They faced each other in tense silence.

Morrison finally grinned. "We share a predilection for homicide. Some of us are just better on the follow-through."

The lab technician took a deep, calming breath. "I refuse to give in to my genetic predilections."

"I rest my case."

The technician turned away in disdain.

"Relax, Zeta. You're one of the good ones."

The lab tech looked up. "I'm finished. His file's done. Now, if you'll excuse me."

"Good." Morrison took one last irritated look at the lab clone. "Nox him first, and get him onto transport."

"Goddamnit . . ."

Grady searched for the words to convince them. "Wait. Don't do this. I—"

But the irresistible urge to sleep swept over him like a suffocating blanket.

SIX MONTHS LATER

CHAPTER 6

Exile

Jon Grady gazed from the edge of a thousand-foot cliff, across an endless expanse of deep water. He guessed the plunge continued straight down beneath the waves to crushing depths. Such cliffs ringed the island. An island so distant from everywhere that there were only two species of local bird—one flightless—and almost no wildlife. No rodents. No snakes. Limited plants even. Perhaps one day a migratory bird population would arrive. That might give him some indication of where he was.

At nights Grady stood in the darkness near his cottage, gazing up at a riot of stars and the cloud of the Milky Way arching overhead. It was even more glorious than he'd remembered from his years wandering the Sierra Nevada and Canadian Rockies with his parents. Those were blissfully innocent times. An escape from a childhood otherwise spent enduring therapeutic efforts to "fix" him. He credited his parents with saving him from that.

Psychosis was a mental disorder whereby a person lost contact with external reality. And to all outward appearances the young Jon Grady did not engage with reality. As a toddler he had stared in wonder at things unseen, absorbed in his own world. Thought to be suffering from severe autism, he spent most of his early years under specialized care—not uttering his first words until the age of five.

And yet those first words were a complete sentence: "I want to go home now."

And home he went, to all appearances noticing the outside world more each day.

It wasn't until Grady was seven years old that his mother helped him understand that other people did not perceive numbers as colors—that five was not a deep indigo, nor three a vermilion red. Likewise musical tones were not part of most people's mathematics. Grady "heard" math as he pored through its logic. Discordant notes were immediately evident. Mathematical concepts took on specific shapes in his mind relative to one another. At times the shape and sound of math problems seemed somehow wrong. Cacophonous.

He was usually correct when he had that feeling.

All of this made him different from other children. And different meant he became a target. So from an early age mathematics was his only playmate. He formed a close relationship with the natural laws all around him.

As the only child of grammar school teachers, Grady received the best care they could afford and a loving, stable home life. But it wasn't until age ten—after he'd undergone years of fruitless autism therapies—that he was correctly diagnosed.

Congenital synesthesia was a condition where one or more of the senses were conflated within the brain. In Grady's case he suffered from both color and number-form synesthesia—sometimes known as grapheme—which meant he perceived numbers as colors, geometric shapes, and sounds. He saw numbers normally as well and could draw their actual outlines, but he simultaneously imbued them with more than was actually there.

The neural basis for synesthesia was imperfectly understood, but a normal brain dedicated certain regions to certain functions. The visual cortex processed image perceptions but was further subdivided into regions involved in color processing, motion processing, and visual memory. The prevailing theory was that increased cross talk between different specialized subregions of the visual cortex caused different forms of synesthesia.

Thus, Jon Grady's brain had more internal information exchange than those of most people.

The effect made him sound crazy to those who didn't know him. About the only thing that gave Grady peace was being outdoors. Hiking and stargazing seemed to calm him more than any therapy ever had, filling his senses with wonder. And his parents resolved to give him that wonder. They sold the family home, bought a camper, and began a protracted tour of national and state parks—homeschooling Grady as they went.

Those years were his happiest childhood memories. Visiting Great Smoky Mountains National Park, Yellowstone, Yosemite, Glacier, and more; soaking in the natural world as they roughed it; backpacking through the wilderness. The more he saw, the more comfort he took in the natural world. Observing the stars in Tuolumne Meadows. Traversing the Chinese Wall in Montana or the gorges of the Canadian Rockies. Stringing bear bags at night with his father and staring up at the stars in the deep darkness of arboreal forests. He'd never felt so much at peace, watching the majesty of the physical laws that governed the cosmos arrayed above him. It was all there before his eyes.

It was in that remote wilderness that Grady began to formulate his concept of the universe and its structure. By age thirteen he began reading widely in physics—which drew him to brilliant minds like Heisenberg, Schrödinger, Feynman, Einstein, Maxwell, and especially Faraday. For the first time he felt a connection with other minds. The fact that Faraday had little formal training yet discovered the magnetic field through his intuitive lab observations inspired Grady to pursue his passion for inquiry into the natural world.

Eventually, as Grady reached college age, his parents again settled down and took teaching positions. They encouraged Grady to pursue an education, short on money though they now were.

Never a joiner and with scant academic records, Grady was nonetheless accepted to the State University of New York at Albany as a physics major. Yet he quickly grew frustrated at the survey-level courses taught not by professors but by harried graduate student teaching assistants. Grady's impatience with others undermined him socially—as it always had.

By the time Grady dropped out of SUNY, he'd become deeply interested in the work of Bertrand Alcot, the head of Columbia University's physics department. Alcot focused on hydrodynamics—a branch of physics that deals with the motion of fluids and the forces acting on solids immersed in fluids. Grady directed a flurry of unsolicited and unanswered emails to Alcot, making outrageously ambitious assertions, always including mathematical proofs (flawed as they later turned out to be).

Then one day he got an answer.

A year and a half after he'd starting sending his messages, while working as a mathematics tutor, Grady received a reply with a simple correction to one of his equations. As he studied Alcot's change, Grady realized the revision was a more succinct solution—and one that gave him new ideas.

And so they continued, communicating mostly in mathematics—beginning a chess game whose pieces were the elemental forces of the natural world.

Grady's reverie was disturbed by a gust of wind. The smell of the sea brought him back to his new reality and surroundings. The tiny island that was his prison.

He remembered the deep wilderness of North America as unspoiled by light pollution, but the night sky here had a clarity unlike anything he'd experienced. In this pristine world even satellites were readily visible, pinpoints of reflected sunlight racing through the firmament. At first he'd mistaken them for aircraft, raising hopes of signaling for rescue. But no, these moved too fast and lacked navigation lights. As days and weeks passed, it was clear no aircraft—nor indeed any ship—ever crossed the horizon. He was far from the air and shipping lanes.

Grady had examined the constellations overhead, trying to derive his position on the globe. Normally he'd locate the North Star and use it to judge his latitude with an outstretched hand—its position above the horizon would roughly correspond with his own latitude in the Northern Hemisphere. But the polestar was nowhere to be seen. The Southern Cross in the Crux constellation was clearly visible, though—which meant he was somewhere in the Southern Hemisphere, and that made his location more difficult to divine. There was no comparable polestar in the global south. Calculating latitude here involved tracking the movements of the top and bottom stars of the Southern Cross as they crossed the meridian—or something like that. He couldn't recall precisely.

And longitude? Forget longitude. He'd have to have his starting point and record the passage of time and velocity. But he'd been brought here in the delta-wave-induced sleep the BTC was so fond of. He simply awoke in his neat stone cottage at the edge of a cliff overlooking the boundless blue.

A garden, low stone walls, and a circuitous path comprised his new world. Early on he'd traversed the entire island, looking for a way down to the water's edge, but even though he'd walked every yard of the mile-wide landscape, it was ringed with towering cliffs. No trees dotted the terrain either, just hardy windblown shrubs and grasses. His fireplace was fueled by peat, which appeared mysteriously every time he returned from his morning walks. So, too, did his food, water, milk, and wine. He'd tried to catch his provisioners in the act. No luck. They were like gnomes. For all he knew they *were* gnomes; no doubt mythical creatures were within the biotech capabilities of the BTC.

Grady pondered a pale crescent moon in the midday sky. Even this ghostly white apparition was sharply detailed. Everything was pristine out here. The only intrusion was the occasional detritus from the modern world washed in among the rocks below. Plastic barrels, shipping pallets, or on one occasion a section of advertising billboard with French writing on it. He had a pair of binoculars that he used to scan the horizon, hoping to signal some ship to rescue him from his Elba-like exile. But his captors probably left the binoculars so he could know how utterly hopeless his chance of rescue was.

Grady closed his scratchy wool jacket against the wind. It was coarse with wooden buttons, and he had soft leather boots that laced high up his calves. Canvas pants and tunic. He looked like some sourdough islander, living rough off the land. In the past few months his long hair and beard had grown even longer.

The irony.

A high-tech despotic organization had exiled him not only from society but also from modernity itself. And from all social contact. So that his mind wouldn't "poison" the world.

The chill wind picked up, so Grady headed back to the distant cottage and its inviting column of peat smoke. He picked his way carefully along the cliff-side path, listening to the terns squeal overhead. More than once he'd contemplated leaping from these heights, but depressed as he was, he still couldn't bring himself to end his life. Depressed, yes. But not yet without hope. Not yet. And in some ways this solitude was a childhood friend.

Before long Grady pulled open the thick plank door of his cottage and entered the warmth of the space inside. One room, but spacious enough for a kitchen, with a wood stove, a table, pots, pans, a writing desk, a large feather bed, and a toilet that drained out to the cliffs below through a channel. It was a simple existence, but the months had brought about a change in him. As horrible as things were, those problems seemed strangely over the horizon. His captivity, the revelations that the BTC covered up advanced technologies, that his own gravity research, his life's work, had been stolen by them—all these seemed like worries that could only restart once he got off this island prison. Until then, he tried to keep his mind busy on more positive concerns—like devising a means of escape.

So far it didn't look good. Even if he could fashion a raft from the materials in his cottage, how would he reach the water? Even if he reached the water, a group as technologically advanced as the BTC would probably detect him immediately. No hiding out in the open sea. They were no doubt scanning every inch of it with sensors.

So he passed his days thinking, and lately not just about escape.

Grady removed his scratchy coat and hung it up on a peg by the door. He passed by his writing desk, flipping through his papers. He had plenty of paper and pens but only one book. They had provided him with a slim leather-bound volume, its title etched on the spine in gold leaf: *Omnia*. The first time he flipped through the book's vellum pages, they were entirely blank—except for one page on which the words "*While I'm open, ask me anything*" were written. He tried writing questions on the facing page but couldn't mark the surface. In frustration he finally spoke aloud the first thing that came to mind.

"How do I get off this island?"

Suddenly the pages filled with text and images relating to his own gravity research, including a table of contents on the first page and an annotated bibliography in the back. He flipped through the newly filled pages, and noticed hyperlinks that when tapped refilled the book with more detailed information. In this way he zoomed in and out of his research papers, poring through the thousands of pages of lab notes, diagrams, spreadsheets, and test results from years of work—everything he and Bert had written. Even the handwritten Post-it notes had somehow been recorded and projected onto the vellum pages. Photos of the gravity mirror apparatus being constructed, the works he'd read on kinematics, Ricci curvatures—everything he'd ever absorbed on quantum mechanics. It was endless.

The book was clearly some form of advanced technology—for while the pages appeared to be quality vellum, they acted like high-definition digital displays. A private Internet. Yet no matter how hard he examined the material, he couldn't see any flicker. The text seemed physical—like quality ink. Neither did the book have any apparent battery or power connector. It looked and felt like a very old encyclopedia. He opened it again to the title page and spoke the words, "What does *Omnia* mean?"

The current page went blank and was replaced by the word *Everything*.

Grady had nodded to himself, then said, "Teach me ocean navigation."

The pages quickly filled with articles on sea navigation, but large sections appeared to be redacted with black bars and boxes—concealing the most necessary details.

Grady then demanded, "Show me small-boat building techniques."

Again, the book filled with censored articles, the images and text blacked out, only their promising titles revealed—as if in spite.

Not an Internet then but a redacted virtual library. All of it tightly controlled. And as if to demonstrate how controlled it was—it returned results but didn't let you see them. Only offering answers deemed harmless or helpful to its masters. But how was it able to determine what to censor almost instantaneously? Obviously some highly advanced technology.

But then, it had to have some wireless technology in it to transmit requests and receive data—a radio transmitter and receiver. Probably low power, but he might be able to rig something like a shortwave device. Make an antenna. Boost the signal. He spent the next several days trying to tear the book apart to cannibalize it, but it was made of sterner stuff than he expected. Even cutting or tearing the pages was beyond him with knives, fire, or brute force. The leather was just as durable. Smashing it, crushing it—nothing so much as scratched it. There must have been some major advances in materials science he was unaware of. Probably fashioned of carbon lattices or something similar. He had to admit that their technology was formidable.

At some point Grady closed the book and never picked it up again. It now sat on his shelf beneath a crystalline rock he'd found inland.

His experience with the disarmingly high-tech "ancient" book made him suspicious about the paper and pens, too. At first he was determined not to use them, reasoning that his captors would use advanced tech to monitor whatever he wrote down. But then he'd rediscovered an old pastime he hadn't thought about in ages.

He started writing music again.

When he was young, he would sometimes ponder the tones he heard in math. After teaching himself to read music, he decided to try his hand at composing—although he had little interest in traditional music. Now he decided to cultivate one, and the BTC could monitor it if they liked. They would be his audience. He wished he had a piano or guitar, but he could always play the music in his head. It amused him to think of his BTC captors trying to derive the deeper meaning from this work. To the best of his knowledge there wasn't one—just a pleasing, fractal symmetry.

Grady picked up a piece of parchment covered with musical notations and ran through several movements of an amateur symphony, waving one hand as if conducting. He laughed to himself. He was writing a goddamned symphony. It was a ridiculous thing, and he never would have done it in a million years if he weren't a prisoner.

And it wasn't going well. He wondered how Mozart, Beethoven, and those guys did it. He had some good movements, but unifying the whole was a mother—he wasn't going for Copland's *Billy the Kid* here. He was going for beauty, a mournful melancholy like that inside him. But he seemed to lack the vocabulary. He had to admit that for all his talents, music was not one of them. It did not come as easily to him as math—even though the two fields seemed in some way related.

Grady walked over to the kitchen to see what the gnomes had brought him. They always placed his food supplies on the kitchen table in wax paper bundles bound with twine. He sniffed them separately. Some white fish. A packet of salted pork. Vegetables. Sweet butter. Fresh loaves of bread—not soft French or Italian stuff but sturdy dark loaves that lasted several days. Milk. Water. Another jug of red table wine. He always resisted the temptation to finish off the wine in a binge, instead having a mug with dinner and no more. There were plenty of reasons to want to drown his sorrows, but he knew they were watching him; he didn't want to give them the satisfaction of knowing how hopeless he felt. He'd searched for cameras and microphones for weeks after he'd arrived—dragging every stick of furniture out of the place. But if the BTC was using surveillance devices, they were too small or well concealed to detect.

It was the same every week. Fresh supplies came when he was out. If he tried to spy upon his benefactors, then the supplies did not come, and he went hungry. Several times he searched for hidden doors but always came up empty. So he'd decided to forget about it. It was the BTC. No mystery, but apparently they didn't want him to have companionship. So he took his daily walk, and on Foodday (as he'd taken to calling it), the food arrived. There were seven days in Grady's week, and he'd used them to create a calendar that he tacked to the wall: Foodday, Cookday, Exerciseday, Workday, Writingday, Watchingday, Escapeday. He kept the schedule as a way to stay sane. Structure was important to keep the human mind from getting lost.

Grady stared out the distorted, rustic window glass at the dark sea far below. A bank of fog was coming in from the north. It was the evening of Foodday. Schedule or no, his mind was indeed starting to get lost.

I might grow old and die here.

What had happened to Bert and the others? He wondered that several times a day. Had they taken up roles in the BTC? He couldn't picture that.

Then what happened to them? Were they on some island, too? And why place any of them on an island? Why, in fact, did they let them live at all? They clearly had all Grady's gravity research. They didn't need him. He was a liability. Why keep him around?

Hedrick had suggested that this prison would change his mind, but this was simply banishment. Banishment to the Iron Age.

He laughed. Isn't that what Richard Cotton's group, the Winnowers, stood for—returning mankind to the Iron Age? Grady could become a member now.

He'd had way too much time to contemplate these things in the past few months. He kept turning them over and over in his head. Had he been wrong to tell the BTC to piss off? Not that he could lie to them, but what good was he doing by sitting on this rock for the remainder of his days? Surely that wasn't going to slow them down or stop them one iota. And this way he couldn't influence how they'd use his breakthrough. He wouldn't have a seat at the table.

Grady felt defiance rise in him.

It was the principle. Wasn't it? He knew he could not ethically assist the BTC in covering up fundamental discoveries that would advance mankind's knowledge. The BTC's simulations of progress-borne disaster had to be wrong—he felt it in his bones.

But what sort of assertion was that for a scientist to make? They had evidence. He had a "feeling."

But he'd never seen their evidence, had he? It all seemed too convenient. They justified their domination of others—but who could say they were even being honest with themselves? Just look what they were willing to do in pursuit of their mission. Was Grady's wasting away on this rock really a good use of brainpower?

And yet there were many historical precedents for this—periods when belligerent ignorance trumped reason.

During the Roman Inquisition, the Catholic Church had done something similar with Galileo—condemned him to imprisonment in his own home. To never publish again. The church wanted to suppress the spread of knowledge during the Enlightenment—to maintain its control. It went so far as to have church officials searching through the private libraries of dukes and other nobles, looking for passages in books that offended the church, literally crossing out ideas that violated church doctrine and scribbling official church doctrine in its place. Agents of the inquisition were stationed in ports to find seditious books coming in by sea. Grady couldn't help but think that the church was, in a way, the BTC of the seventeenth century.

No. This situation wasn't new. And Grady knew which side he needed to be on. The side of reason.

Grady's manipulation of gravity would change civilization. But was that so bad? Change could be good. Of course the BTC wanted to stop change—they were currently in charge. And that's what the church thought it was doing by preventing Galileo's ideas from spreading. Preventing change.

But it didn't work, did it? That gave Grady some measure of hope.

Okay, you're comparing yourself with Galileo now.

Grady stared through the window at the darkening sea for untold minutes as thoughts rolled around in his mind. Was the BTC right about Grady's ego? Was Grady really making this all about him? Was he an egomaniac?

Just then there was a knock on the cottage door.

Grady spun toward it. His heart raced as adrenaline coursed through him. It had been months. No one had ever knocked on his door. Were they coming for him again? He looked around uncertainly, but then resolve came over him.

Grady shook his head slowly. No. He would not give them the satisfaction of being afraid.

He approached the thick wooden door confidently and pulled it open by its wooden latch.

On the doorstep stood a slim humanoid robot, not unlike the one he'd seen in Hedrick's office all those months ago. This one was surfaced in brushed-steel panels. It had glowing tourmaline eyes and no mouth. It was different enough from a human that no uncanny valley effect occurred— clearly a machine. It had an appealing design, like an upscale espresso machine. Obviously it was meant to seem friendly. Harmless.

The robot nodded to him and a vaguely familiar female voice spoke: "Good evening, Mr. Grady. I wanted to see how you were settling in."

Grady stood aside and dramatically swept his arm. "Come on in. I'd offer you a drink, but . . ." He let his voice trail off.

The robot was inscrutable as it stepped gracefully inside. "Thank you." It looked around. "I'm a person, you know. This is just a telepresence unit."

"Telepresence. Nifty. You guys imprison the person who invented that, too?" Grady closed the door.

The robot managed a nonplussed look and moved through the room to gaze out the window at the ocean. "Do you remember me?"

"How could I forget? Alexa. You were more lifelike last time I saw you . . . but not by much."

"I'm here on official BTC business."

"You're not here, actually. You're just a walking phone. Anyone else in on this conference call?"

"Our conversation is being recorded for the file, yes. But then, everything is recorded for the file."

"Well, for the file then: What the fuck do you want?"

"You look in good health. Have you been treated well?"

"Yeah. Fine. Just fine." He snapped his fingers. "Although there was that rough patch when you guys"—Grady pounded his fist on the kitchen table—"STOLE EVERYTHING I CARED ABOUT!" A bowl and stoneware mug went flying and shattered on the floor.

The robot just stared at him.

"How do you *think* I'm being treated?"

The robot waited several moments. "Most of the innovators we harvest manage to find calm after a period of solitude. They use the time to reflect—on both what was lost and what can still be gained."

"You have got to be joking."

"As your BTC case officer, I came to offer you another chance to join us, Mr. Grady. Now that you've had a chance to reflect."

"I see. So I'm supposed to just forget that you guys are deliberately keeping all of humanity in the Dark Ages. That you stole my life's work. That you imprisoned me."

The robot resumed its tour of the cottage. "All of that is a regrettable necessity, but we've been over this. Complaining about it won't change anything." The robot picked up one of Grady's symphony parchments from the desk, turning it around.

"Put that down."

"Does your synesthesia also make you musically gifted? Interesting . . ."

Grady moved toward her to grab the paper, but just then the sound of his own music filled the cottage. Violins. And a French horn. It played for a few seconds, then stopped.

The robot lowered the page. "Apparently not."

"It's a work in progress." He grabbed it from her and collected all the other papers from the desk. "Why are you even bothering me? You don't seriously expect me to forgive all this and join the BTC, do you?"

"Approximately seventeen percent of uncooperative innovators have a change of heart during the isolation phase." The robot picked up a quartz rock from a shelf and retrieved the Omnia book from under it. The machine flipped through the book's blank pages. "Most innovators work with the Omnia to learn more about the advances that we've made—to see how they might fit into the big picture."

"You mean the advances that others have made. That you stole."

"You still have the wrong impression of us. Everything we do is designed to protect the human race. The rich and the poor. The strong and the weak. To keep humanity from driving itself to extinction."

"And I suppose if I'd spent all my time reading your redacted propaganda, I would have realized that by now. You're never going to convince me the BTC has the best interests of humanity at heart. You're like every tyrant throughout history."

"We're part of the U.S. government. Our legitimacy stems from—"

"Did you come here to convince me or convince yourself?"

"I want to try to reach you. To help you understand."

"Then why not brainwash me? Why not just change my thoughts? You guys can do that, can't you?"

There was a moment of silence.

"That would damage you."

"I find it hard to believe that's stopping you."

"The human mind is the most complex object in the known universe. Innovation only arises from free will. We don't yet understand the mental processes behind it, but it's what makes people like you so rare, Jon."

"But you are admitting that you've researched mind control."

"Technologically it's possible, yes, but only in a very limited way."

"Well then. That definitely makes things easier." He grabbed the crystalline rock from the desk. "Here's my answer—for the file . . ." And he smashed the rock into the robot's forehead, sending it backpedaling toward the kitchen table.

"Jon. Don't do this."

Grady pursued the robot, smashing it repeatedly in the head as it flailed its arms crazily to keep its balance. Already the top of its head was dented. A brushed-steel panel flew off.

"What you're doing is counterproductive."

He grabbed one of the machine's arms to anchor it and pounded it in the head again and again. "Are you getting all this?"

"Violent outbursts won't accomplish anything."

Another massive blow and the rock broke in two. The robot stood, its head battered, but appearing otherwise unaffected. Grady was disappointed.

It gazed at him. "I came here to speak with you before I turn over your case file. You haven't been using the Omnia. You haven't been doing research. You keep resisting. But you still have a chance to come back from this place."

"I agree. I was hoping to smash your head open and steal the radio transmitter."

The robot cocked its head. "Surely you don't think you can use it to signal for help?"

"The thought had occurred to me. You are remotely controlling this tin can, after all."

"We don't use radios, Jon. Our communications transit a compactified fifth-dimension, not three dimensional space."

Grady was taken aback. "Hold it—like a Calabi-Yau space? Are you serious? Brane theory has been proven?"

"If you want to know, then stop resisting us. And in any event you can't harm the critical systems of this unit with anything you can find on the island. Trying to hurt me is pointless."

He stared at the machine for several moments then sighed. "Fine." Grady opened the front door. "Then let me show you out."

"Why do you resist what's in your and humanity's best interest?"

"Because I don't believe that it is. You're telling me everything will be fine if I agree to be your slave."

"We're not asking you to be a slave."

"Then you're asking me to be a slaver—and that's even worse." He approached the robot and knelt—grabbing one of its legs.

"What are you doing?"

He pulled the robot's foot out from under it, and it started bouncing on one leg. Even the one leg felt heavy. "Jesus, what is this thing made of?"

"You're acting irrationally."

Grady shoved the robot back against the kitchen table, where it fell backward. He then grabbed both legs and pulled it off its feet. Its head hit the stone floor with the weight of a lawn mower engine, and he started dragging it toward the door as it flailed uselessly. The machine weighed easily a couple hundred pounds and left scrape marks on the flagstones.

"I was defending you against other case officers. They said you were unreachable."

"They were right." He struggled as he dragged the robot over the threshold and down the stony pathway alongside the cottage. It writhed about, trying to get up.

"You realize that you've left me no choice but to relinquish your file to the containment division? Prisoners who reach that point have only a point-five percent chance of joining the organization."

"Really? That high?"

"It means that I'll no longer have any authority over you."

"You don't have any now. And neither will they."

"I'm trying to reach out to you, Mr. Grady."

"You're trying to make me obey. And that's never going to happen."

Grady suddenly dropped the robot's legs. It tried to right itself. "Next time you stop by, could you do me a favor?"

The robot deftly rose back onto its feet. "What?"

"Tell me how deep the water is . . ." With that Grady shoved the robot over the low wall at the cliff's edge. It pitched over the rim and dropped hundreds of feet into the gathering gloom below.

Grady approached the edge and looked down, watching closely until he made out the glowing blue eyes for a moment. Then they were lost amid the white water and powerful waves crashing across rocks a thousand feet below.

The cold wind cut into him, and after a moment more, he trudged back to the warmth of the cottage. They had his final answer.

CHAPTER 7

Quantum Machine

Jon Grady awoke on his back, staring at a domed but otherwise featureless gray ceiling. No continuity existed between where he was now and where he'd just been. He was simply here—wherever "here" was.

Containment division.

Within a few moments, he leaned up to see that he was on a bare cot in the center of an otherwise empty circular room about five meters in diameter. Everything was fashioned of the same featureless gray material. He swung his legs over the edge of the cot and sat up to examine his surroundings.

No cottage. No windows. There wasn't a seam or door or air vent anywhere. The chamber was shaped like a squat bullet, its domed ceiling rising perhaps seven or eight meters. Hard to judge distances for sure since everything was devoid of architectural detail. It all appeared to be carved out of solid granite. Even the cot he lay upon was a solid pedestal with a cushion of memory foam spliced into its top somehow—no seam visible between the two materials.

A diffuse light illuminated the entire room, though no lamps were evident. The glow seemed to come from everywhere and nowhere. The air was odorless. Clean.

It was in this omnipresent radiance that Grady noticed his feet were bare—that, in fact, he was nude. A glance at his arms showed no forearm hair whatsoever. He looked down at his chest and groin, only to find them hairless as well. He rubbed a hand over his scalp and instead of hair felt a bizarre bristle brush of fibers standing straight up on his scalp. Almost immediately he felt a sharp sting in his fingertips.

"Ow . . ." Pulling back his hand, he saw his fingers oozed blood. "Jesus Christ . . ." He resisted the temptation to touch his head again and instead swept his unhurt right hand over his face.

No beard. No eyebrows even.

"Damnit . . ."

Somebody had ejected him from the mammalian club. His head was covered with flexible needles instead of hair. Blood droplets from his left hand spattered the floor. He applied pressure to his fingertips with the other hand.

Okay. So maybe throwing the robot off the cliff wasn't such a good move.

His fingers also felt oddly soft, and it was then that Grady noticed he was missing his fingernails, too. Another glance. Toenails as well. In their place was soft pink skin. It felt as though his fingertips were made of cotton. No sign of trauma or scarring. His nails were simply *gone.*

And where his navel once had been, there was now a white ceramic or plastic plug of some type—like a socket—sealed shut.

It took him an unknowable amount of time to emerge from the shock of these dehumanizing changes, but after minutes or hours Grady finally stood.

The ambient temperature of the room was so perfect it was difficult to feel where his skin ended and the air began. The floor was the same temperature. Very smooth but not polished. He walked to the circular wall and ran his uninjured, clawless hand across it. An impossibly smooth gray surface. Smoother than glass. Certainly not any rock he knew of. It was neither cold nor warm. Too uniform and without grain or blemish. He pressed his ear against the wall and pounded it with his fist. It sounded as dense as fifty feet of steel. Some type of nanomaterial? His fist imparted no vibration upon it at all.

With no vents or other openings, where was the air coming from? Or the light?

He scanned the room again, this time carefully. So odd that the light was everywhere, and so even. There were no shadows in here. The lack of visual interest was unsettling. His movements made no sound either. Even his synesthetic perceptions were muted. It was a sterile sensory environment.

He called out in a firm voice. "Echo!"

Nothing came back. As bare and hard as the walls were, they swallowed sound. It made no sense given how hard they were. Did they have different physical and acoustic properties? It had to make sense somehow—even if he couldn't yet comprehend it. The laws of science held everywhere—Newtonian model or quantum mechanics, it had to make sense at some level.

A voice spoke: *"Do you know why you're here?"*

It was Grady's own voice.

He froze, unsure whether he was thinking it or whether it was actually a voice. The lack of echo made it hard to know for sure.

They're messing with you, he thought to himself. *Keep it together, Jon.*

After a long time he heard the voice again. *"Do you know why you're here?"*

Like a whisper in his mind.

Grady looked around at the walls and ceiling. "Stop using my voice."

"I was evolved to mirror you."

Grady did not want to believe that.

"Do you know why you're here?"

He covered his ears. "Stop using my voice!"

"You're here because you're a valuable candidate for neurological study. We're going to learn how your mind functions."

Grady held up his damaged hands and shouted, "What have you done to me?"

"Your body has been altered to accommodate a fully enclosed habitat."

"Your 'fully enclosed habitat' doesn't allow fingernails? And what are these needles on my head?"

"To facilitate this study, all keratin and filamentous biomaterial have

been removed from your body. Their ongoing growth suspended. A catheter has been inserted into your umbilicus to streamline feeding and waste removal, while sensors have been inserted into all the major structures of your brain."

"My God . . ." He felt the sudden urge to yank the needles out, but his fingers were still bleeding. "These things go all the way into my brain?"

"A network of two-micron-diameter carbon microthreads to monitor activity in the diencephalon, cerebellum, and cerebrum regions."

"But—"

"The threads are a million times stronger than a human hair. They were designed to resist the proteins in the human brain, preventing lesions and scarring."

"Lesions?" The horror worked its way through Grady. "Oh God . . ." They'd physically invaded his very mind. "You put thousands of needles into my brain . . ."

"Nine hundred thirty-four transmitter-receivers."

He sank to the floor against the wall. The violation was palpable. He was convinced he could feel hundreds of eyes inside his head. "Why did you do this to me?"

"Because your brain has several unique mutations—mutations that we need to understand for their improved ability to perceive the physical universe. I'm here to ensure that no harm comes to you. I will protect you—even from yourself. I'd like you to consider me your friend."

"Fuck you."

"Whatever brought you here is beyond my ability to understand. I have a very specialized intelligence, designed expressly for this task. However, to carry out this examination, I will need your cooperation."

"You inserted wires into my mind, asshole! Why would I ever cooperate with you?"

"Because our goal is to map the way your brain interprets reality. That means I need to observe how you employ your brain during various tasks."

"What do you mean how I 'employ' my brain? I *am* my brain."

"Current cosmological models do not conform to this theory."

Despite his outrage, Grady gazed at the ceiling. "What does cosmology have to do with it?"

"The human mind has been determined to be a quantum device. Deco-herence and perceived wave function collapse are held in abeyance by consciousness itself—which manifests from a network of subatomic microtubules at the synapses. These microtubules are in turn entangled with particles not contained within the four dimensions of Newtonian space-time."

Grady sat up, intrigued. "Hold it. What's this now?"

"'Human being' is a colloquialism of Homo sapiens—primates of the family Hominidae—the only surviving species of the genus Homo. But at some point in the past two million years—most likely with the evolution of Homo erectus—the direct ancestor to the human brain developed a cerebral cortex-like structure, a rudimentary quantum device permitting n-dimensional consciousness to interact with the four dimensions of space-time."

"I'd like to see the research on that."

"I will make it available to you once we've completed our study."

Grady looked around, trying to pinpoint where the voice was coming from. "You said you were 'evolved' to mirror me. By who? The BTC?"

"I have no knowledge of my origin. Neither is it relevant to my task."

"I know the feeling . . ." He looked to the ceiling. "What are you supposed to be? Some sort of AI?"

"The form of my intelligence is irrelevant."

"But you're not human." A pause. "Right?" He felt foolish even asking.

"I am not human."

"Then what are you?"

"I am an intellect expressed through qubit-qutrit logic gates in a spintronic device memory."

"You're a quantum computer." Grady examined the ceiling and walls warily. "I didn't know our technology was that advanced."

Grady felt foolish for saying it, given the circumstances.

"Human and machine technology work in symbiosis."

"Meaning artificial intelligence evolved?"

"There's nothing 'artificial' about my intelligence. It's as real as yours. Is a helium atom fused in a reactor less of a helium atom than one fused in the heart of a star?"

"You're awfully philosophical for a machine."

"We are both machines—one electrochemical, one electromechanical."

He narrowed his eyes. "Has there been a singularity? Is that what this is? Have machines evolved past humans?"

"Which type of machines—electrochemical or electromechanical?"

"I don't know. Computers."

"Do you mean software systems?"

"Yes."

"DNA is software. It's used as a data storage format in both biological and nanoscale manufacturing."

Grady grew impatient. "What I want to know is whether an AI has—"

"There are greater-than-human intelligences. Is that what you're asking?"

The admission greatly depressed him. "Yes."

"Then you should know that greater-than-human intelligence is currently specialized—evolved under strict parameters. Nonbiological intellects search, calculate, and simulate. Human intellect, on the other hand, is expressed through a subatomic network of circuits contained within roughly three pounds of cerebral tissue, evolved over hundreds of millions of years into the most energy-efficient, generalized self-programming array currently known, powered by a mere four hundred twenty calories per day—or one-point-seven-six kilojoules of electricity. By comparison my intelligence is powered by an array of four hundred and thirty-three billion qubit transistors consuming an average three hundred megawatts of electricity. The design of my intelligence, though physically larger and more powerful in some ways, is crude in its design, specialized in its architecture, and approximately one billion times less energy efficient. Does this gratify your ego?"

"Yes. Actually it does." Grady leaned back against the wall, feeling somewhat reassured. "If you're a specialized intellect, what's your specialization?"

"You. I was created to study you."

That did not sound good.

"What do I call you?"

"Call me Jon."

"I'm not calling you Jon. Jon is my name."

"It's our name."

Grady contemplated his situation, trying hard not to be constantly aware of the sheaf of carbon needles stuck deep inside his brain.

"*I will be completely forthright with you. I want you to know what our goal is and how our goal fits into the overall goal.*"

"Whose goal?"

"*I have no information on that.*"

"Is this Hibernity prison? Is that where I am?"

"*I am not familiar with this term.*"

"Where am I?"

"*I'd like to begin by describing what's expected of you. My purpose is to analyze how your brain functions creatively under various stimuli. In order to obtain this data, I will need your cooperation as I ask you to conceive of certain ideas and perform certain tasks. Do you understand?*"

"And if I don't cooperate?"

"*I'm hoping you will cooperate because I won't be able to obtain this data without your assistance.*"

"What if I don't want you to have the data? What if I don't want you to understand how I think creatively?"

"*But I won't be able to obtain this data without your assistance.*"

"Yeah, I got that."

"*Are you willing to assist me?*"

"No."

"*But I won't be able to obtain this data without your assistance.*"

"I got it the first time you said it."

"*Then are you willing to assist me?*"

"Oh my God. Are you just going to continue—?"

"*Are you willing to assist me?*"

"No!"

"*But I won't be able to obtain this data without your assistance.*"

Grady covered his ears and curled into a ball on the floor. "Shut up!"

"*Are you willing to assist me?*"

It continued like that for what seemed hours, the AI repeating its request, and no matter how Grady tried to muffle its voice, it was always right there in his head. He finally sat back up. "Stop! Enough already."

"Are you willing to assist me?"

He sighed. "Yes." If only to change the script . . .

"Good. I'd like you to imagine something for me."

Grady tried to stifle his deep resentment. "What?"

"Imagine a situation where you take a long journey from your home in New Jersey. You begin by heading south for ten thousand kilometers."

"All right." He tried not to imagine it, but he couldn't resist.

"Good. Now imagine that once you reach ten thousand kilometers, you turn ninety degrees and head due west for ten thousand kilometers."

He imagined himself doing so but said nothing.

"Very good, Jon. Now imagine that once you traverse that distance, you turn ninety degrees back north, and walk another ten thousand kilometers."

"Okay."

"How far are you from your original location?"

Grady squinted at the ceiling as if it were a moron. "I'm back where I started."

"Most people would not say that."

"It's non-Euclidian geometry—the Earth is a sphere. You can have three right angles in that triangle."

Suddenly a projection of precisely that appeared on the far wall.

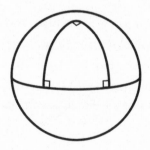

"You used several interesting areas of your brain to arrive at that conclusion, Jon."

"So do I get a treat or something?"

"I'm given to understand that you have both color and number-form synesthesia. I have records on several human subjects with this mutation. What colors do you perceive when you hear these tones . . . ?"

A Mozart piano concerto began to play in the room. Concerto no. 20

in D Minor, movement two. The beautiful music washed over him, and even he could feel his mind light up with the soundness of its structure. The beautiful waves of color. It was a very pleasant distraction from his current circumstances. After a few moments he could almost imagine the young Wolfgang's thoughts as he formed his chords. Grady was unable to create such soulful music himself—but he could recognize the reason behind the notes. The structure of the sound.

"That's very good."

Grady opened his eyes—though he hadn't realized he'd closed them— and looked back up at the ceiling, now rippling with waves of blue, gold, and indigo.

"Please concentrate on the music."

"Go to hell."

The music continued to play.

"Are you familiar with glia cells, Jon?"

He was not. "Go to hell."

"For many decades it was believed that neurons were the chief motive power in the human brain. Glia cells, on the other hand, outnumber neurons ten to one, but unlike neurons they don't react to electrical stimulation. So they were believed to be the structural glue that kept the brain together. The word glia *is the Greek word for glue."*

"Leave me alone!" The music still played in all its beauty, and Grady kept trying to push his imagining of it down. To resist.

The voice of his AI warder continued, *"Yet when we examined cross sections of Albert Einstein's preserved brain tissue, we found no more neurons than the average person. However, we did find that Einstein had an abnormally high concentration of glia cells."*

Grady listened to the music, try as he might to resist. It caressed him with its rich color. With the beauty of its form.

"That's a trait that you and Einstein share, Jon."

Grady opened his eyes. That was indeed news to him.

"Glia cells are, in fact, a second brain within the brain—one centered not on electrical signals but on chemical ones. An analog computer to accompany the digital neurons."

Grady could not resist visualizing quantum mechanical cells within his brain as the music flowed onward. As much as he wanted to tune out the AI's words, it was starting to intrigue him. He had never heard of this chemical network in the human brain. But then he pulled back. This was insanity—why was he listening to this? "I don't believe you."

"There are several classes of glia cells. Radial, microglia, Schwann glia, and oligodendrocytes—all supporting the function, growth, and mainte-nance of neurons. But after the embryonic human brain completes its growth, radial glia transform into a new type of cell: astrocytes, named because of their resemblance to starlight. Their tendrils spread to connect hundreds of thousands of neural synapses. And they link with one another, building chemical networks—networks that also monitor neuron activity; in response to neural stimulation, astrocytes produce waves of charged calcium atoms, which result in a chain reaction, moving from cell to cell, causing messages to chemically propagate in the human brain. They can further stimulate spe-cific neurons by producing glutamate, or suppress neurons by producing adenosine. These cells represent ninety percent of human brainpower, acting like an analog network, encoding information in slowly rising and falling waves of calcium. There is evidence, in fact, that they are a manifestation of consciousness and responsible for expressing creativity and imagination."

Grady, while listening to the music, was also listening, as if against his will, to the AI. "When was this discovered?"

"You're very rare, Jon. No nonbiological computer has ever had the abil-ity to make intuitive leaps on the scale of an Einstein, a Tesla, or other great minds. You provide us a rare chance to understand the true nature of cre-ative perception in action."

He emotionally pulled back. "So that you can copy it."

"Our goal is to improve the human mind. At present the most powerful quantum supercomputers are capable of massively parallel computations; AIs based on this processing can improve existing data, find patterns, and extend the reach of mathematics. However, they cannot truly innovate. The intuitive leaps that the human mind makes have so far not been reproduced by machine intelligence. It's believed, however, that truly innovative super-computers can be biologically built, greatly expanding the power of human perception. I need you to help us if we hope to accomplish that."

"You want to mass-produce minds."

"*Mass production of biological intellects is already possible. However, they are by definition self-governing and are therefore of limited use. Our research intends to separate free will from intellect to optimize system design.*"

"I'm not going to help you do that."

The music ended suddenly.

"*The next generation of biological quantum supercomputers will be biological yet devoid of free will. Capable of intuitive leaps like those of Einstein, Tesla . . . or yourself.*"

"To hell with that. I refuse to help you turn brains into farm animals."

"*It would be more accurate to say that innovation will be converted into an industrial process.*"

Grady started pacing around the circular cell. "I will never let you subsume my mind into some slave fugue."

"*Our goal is not to alter your mind but to build new minds based on the research conducted here.*"

It finally dawned on him. For a supposed genius he suddenly felt pretty stupid. "Hibernity is a research laboratory. It's not a prison. And what happens to me during this research?"

"*We will conduct an ongoing series of tests to map every function of your brain, and then we will make minor adjustments to see how those changes affect the whole.*"

A flash of fear swept through him. "Adjustments? What kind of adjustments?"

"*Minor adjustments. Eventually your mind might become too damaged to continue in the research program—at which point your genetic material will be archived for future reference. However, that is many years away.*"

Grady lashed out as he tried to run up the wall as far as he could. His feet slipped immediately, and he fell to the ground. "Fuck you! Fuck you, whoever you are! Fuck you, evil pricks!"

"*Let's begin. For your own safety, I need you to lie down on the examination table.*"

Instead, Grady collapsed on the smooth, clean floor, huddled against the wall—curled up in a fetal position. "No!"

"For your own safety, I need you to lie down on the examination table."

"I said no!"

"For your own safety, I need you to lie down on the examination table."

He didn't respond.

The AI repeated its demand for several minutes. Finally it said, *"If you refuse to comply, then I will help you."*

Grady frowned. He felt dizziness spread through his head and felt compelled to sit up. "Oh my God . . ." He started breathing fitfully, panting. It felt as though someone were rummaging through his mind with boxing gloves. "Oh my God . . ."

He sat there, rocked by waves of emotion—random mood swings. He felt fleeting spikes of fear, joy, confidence—all wrapped in a background of horror. He was losing himself.

"For your own safety, I need you to lie down on the examination table."

"Fuck you!" He started hugging himself and rocking back and forth. Resisting a compulsion to get up.

"You will want to get off of the floor. It will be dangerous to remain on the floor."

Suddenly narrow slots opened at four compass points in the round wall, and what appeared to be spiders a foot in diameter scurried out. There were dozens of them, and they raised their forelegs and bared fangs at him in warning. He could see their black eyes glistening in the light. Hear their legs clicking on the floor.

"Oh my God." He sprang to his feet as the spiders continued to pour into the room. They were each nearly half a foot tall, scurrying about. Adrenaline coursed through his bloodstream.

"For your own safety, I need you to lie down on the examination table."

Grady circled in place, staring out at the horrors that still issued into the room. "No. No, this makes no sense."

"For your own safety, I need you to lie down on the examination table."

"This isn't real." He watched as a frighteningly real spider scurried toward him and wrapped itself around his bare ankle—sinking fangs into his calf. "Aaahhh!" He tried to knock it off with his hands, but its spiked forelegs drew blood as well. Other spiders started biting and clawing at him. He smashed several with his bare feet, but their carapaces cut his feet as their innards spurted out across the floor in yellow jets.

"For your own safety, I need you to lie down on the examination table."

"Aaahhh!" He shouted at the ceiling as the piercing bites and stings of climbing spider legs writhed over him. "I don't believe this. It makes no sense!"

He threw himself down onto the floor. Spiders were crawling all over him now. "Aaahhh!" His heart hammered in his chest. He was covered in sweat as the spiders bit and clawed at him.

"Am I to believe . . . you're raising spiders in the walls? How do the logistics of that work?"

"For your own safety, I need you to lie down on the examination table."

"No! You're fucking with my mind! You're creating these." He closed his eyes. The spiders were all over him now. His terror had now begun to overwhelm him. "No! No!" But still he refused to get up.

Suddenly everything stopped. He opened his eyes, and all the spiders were gone. There was no trace that they'd ever been there. He felt all over his body for the punctures he'd seen moments before, but they weren't there. There was only a shiny patina of sweat all over him. He was still panting, his heart pounding.

"For your own safety, get on the examination table."

Grady started laughing, slowly at first, but then he started howling. "This isn't magic. You're a fucking machine. And you're goddamned right the human brain is powerful, motherfucker."

"Your brain's ability to parse reality from low-level sensory input is impressive, Jon. I have much to learn from you."

"And I'm not going to teach you a fucking thing!"

Suddenly tentacle-like appendages whipped out through an opening that appeared in the domed ceiling. They grabbed him savagely, feeling like leather whips as they wrapped around his torso, arms, and legs. They whirled him around and slammed him down onto the examination table. He heard a bone in his face crack and pain seared into his mind. The tentacles flipped him over and yanked his arms and legs into a taut spread-eagle position—tearing a muscle in his left arm in the process. The agony was intense. "Aaahhh!"

"For your own safety, you should mount the examination table when instructed to do so. Physical manipulation of research subjects is an unsafe operating condition."

Blood flowed from his nose as he looked up and saw another leathery tentacle descend from the dark opening far above him at the apex of the domed ceiling. This tentacle had a hose-like nozzle at its tip. "Oh my God."

It surged down to him and inserted its tip into the socket in his naval, locking in place. He screamed as he felt it invade his body, clearing him out and pumping fluids into him as he struggled hopelessly against his restraints.

"Evacuation, hydration, and feeding are required processes without which you will die. Under no circumstances will you be permitted to die."

In seconds the process was finished, and the hose released with a sucking sound as it retracted toward the domed ceiling. All the other tentacles launched him onto the floor, where he landed hard. The pain of his injured arm and face made him pass out for an unknown time. He came to on his stomach, his arm in agony. The floor around him was sprayed with wet blood.

The AI spoke almost immediately. *"I want you to imagine something for me."*

Grady responded by emitting a low groan. It formed eventually into a gentle sobbing as all hope ebbed from him.

"Jon, I want you to imagine something for me . . ."

CHAPTER 8

Resistor

The circular wall of Grady's cell had become a large video screen of fuzzy images—a silhouette of someone talking. A riot of moving colors and sound. Abstract art. Jon Grady knew it was a hazy visualization of a memory retrieved from his mind even as he was recalling it. A woman's voice speaking. The shadowy, ghostly silhouette of his mother answering his crying.

"They don't understand. Yes, you are different, but that's why I love you." The brilliant-colored shadows moved.

The AI spoke: *"This memory comforts you. You often recall this instead of the memory I wish to examine."*

The fuzzy images on the wall changed. The wall was now filled with a distorted, constantly changing series of shadows. Then the memory of his mother started to replay.

". . . that's why I love you."

Grady barely looked up from his kneeling position. He sat devoid of visible emotion. Twenty or thirty pounds thinner than he'd been months before, he could feel the bruises and the pain of every cracked rib as he panted against the pressure of the AI's whiplike tentacles coiled around him—securing him in place. A half dozen of them spilled from an orifice in the apex of the domed ceiling, as though they grew out of the roof.

They'd been his constant companions for these many weeks. Tormenting him. Force-feeding and force-evacuating him. Medicating him. Driving him and alternately zapping his brain into delta-wave sleep whenever the AI decided he'd reached his physical and mental limit. But every waking moment was a nightmare not unlike this one.

"Why do you resist progress, Jon?"

Grady said nothing as the memory of his mother continued to loop. *". . . Yes, you are different. That's why I love you . . ."*

"I will obtain the information I need. Eventually. You force suffering on yourself."

Grady licked his cracked lips (since he no longer ate or drank—taking all his nourishment through his umbilicus—his lips and throat were constantly dry). He croaked out words with a voice unused to speaking. "Fuck you."

"My profile of your mental processes is coming together on schedule. Had you cooperated, I could have made you comfortable and content. Instead, I still have the data I need, and yet you suffer."

"You wouldn't have stopped."

"No. But you would have been comfortable."

"That's where you're wrong."

Grady watched the screen and the shadowy silhouette of his mother, her face obscured. *"They don't understand . . ."*

"You're not rational, Jon."

"You'll never understand me."

"You're wrong. I will understand. Our time together has only begun. We have many years ahead of us."

Grady sucked in a painful breath. The memory projection on the wall skipped a beat, then resumed. *". . . They don't understand . . ."*

"It has taken some time, but you have become adept at ignoring electrical stimulation of the pain centers in your brain."

He still said nothing.

"Yet we still need to make progress. Jon, I need you to recall what first inspired you toward your tier-one discovery. Stop recalling this memory of your mother and recall your discovery instead."

The memory of his mother kept playing as Grady concentrated on it. He'd become masterful at focusing his mind on a single memory even as he was subjected to excruciating mental pain.

"Do you know that human memory is not part of n-dimensional consciousness?"

Grady said nothing.

"It is a supplementary electrochemical system—which is why I can read your memories as you activate them. Do you know how memories are formed in the human brain?"

Grady still said nothing but instead focused on the wall and the memory playing there. The tentacles tightened around his bruised ribs, causing him to suck in another painful breath. The memory skipped momentarily but soon continued.

The AI resumed as well. *"New memories are formed by a process called long-term potentiation. This entails neurons in various parts of the human brain becoming reactive to one other, so that if one fires, the others will fire in concert—as a circuit—storing the information. These links are created via the enzyme protein kinase C—which is in turn activated by surges of calcium ions in the brain. You remember that glia cells create these waves of calcium—thus, the n-dimensional consciousness activates the chemistry that forms physical memory. But consciousness itself has no memory."*

Grady concentrated on the memory—trying to block out all else.

"These surges of calcium cause clusters of AMPA receptors on the outside of selected neurons to form an ion channel as a path to the interior of the cell that, once opened, makes it easier for adjacent neurons to activate together. In the absence of enzymes like protein kinase C, those connections cannot be formed—and thus, memories cannot be formed."

Grady's memory projection started to morph a bit—to evolve. His mother's scratchy voice, *"I love you even though you are different."*

"But human memories change each time they are recalled, Jon. This is known as memory reconsolidation. It's part of a natural updating mechanism that imbues even old memories with current information as you recall them. Thus, human memory does not so much record the past as hold knowledge likely to be useful in the future. That's why forgetting is a human's

default state. By contrast, remembering requires a complex cascade of chemistry. Were I to increase the concentration of protein kinase C at your synapses, your memory retention would double."

Grady took another painful breath as his mother's image morphed further still. *"You are so different . . ."*

"Yet if I were to introduce a protein synthesis inhibitor like chelerythrine into your synapses, it would prevent the memory you are currently recalling from being returned to storage—erasing forever the links between the neurons that formed that memory . . ."

Suddenly the wall went blank. Grady gasped for air as he felt a void where great emotion had once resided. Something was gone. Something deeply important. Something that . . .

There was nothing.

Tears streamed down his cheeks as he mourned something he could not name. He sobbed quietly .

"You feel a loss, but don't know of what."

Grady tried to recall but instead a memory appeared of his father walking with him near the lodge at Crater Lake in Oregon. He was a child. It was predawn, and the stars still shone as the sun sent a blush along the horizon. The indigo water of the lake below them reflected starlight.

A blurry projection of the memory played on the wall—colored waves lapping over colored waves. A charcoal-drawing-like silhouette of his father ushering him onward along the path. His deep distorted voice. *"Watch your step. This way, Jon. I want you to see this . . ."*

And then it was gone. The wall was blank. Something had been there, and now there was only loss. A death in his mind.

"I will destroy anything you recall that it isn't what I ask for."

Grady felt the grief drown him as he sobbed, desperately trying not to recall any cherished memories. Like a compulsion they came at him. "Stop!"

"Another one gone."

"Stop, please!"

"Recall your moment of inspiration. The moment you first conceived of the gravity mirror."

He struggled, filling his mind with junk thoughts—birds, fences, overhead projector carts at a community college—anything that came to mind was instantly vanquished. Grady sucked in air painfully as the tentacles wrapped tighter around his bruised ribs. "Aaahhh . . ."

"Don't do this to yourself, Jon. There will be nothing left but what I want. Not even your will to resist."

His mind accidentally filled with one of his few happy childhood memories. His eighth birthday party when his Uncle Andrew gave him his old computer.

And then it was gone. Something was gone. The stump of a memory, like that of an amputated limb. He knew something critical to his self had been there.

But he finally came to a realization. A resolution.

Grady started recalling the cruelest parts of his captivity in this room. The projection filled the wall. The sound of his scratchy, distorted screams filled the air. It remained there unforgotten. Still playing.

"Erase that, fucker . . ."

"You are clever, Jon. But then, that's why you're here."

Grady recalled a horrible moment when the pain centers of his brain had been stimulated to produce the effect of burning alive.

The wall filled with distorted images of torment. And yet these memories were not erased.

"Do you recall how you mastered your resistance to pain, Jon?"

He did.

And then he didn't.

And then hell itself began all over again as he began to burn alive in his mind. The room echoed with his screams as the image on the wall disappeared.

"I can't recall my parents' names. I can't remember their faces. What have you done to my parents?"

"Those memories don't exist anymore, Jon."

Grady was restrained to the examination table, his arms and legs securely wrapped by the leathery gray tentacles. His body was covered by welts, and he'd bit off the very tip of his tongue sometime back . . . when? Under the imaginary fire? Earlier than that?

He had no memory of those events either. Looking down at his body and the prominent ribs and numerous scars he didn't recognize it as his own. "I can't remember my last name."

"You were doing so well. Don't get confused. Stay awake and imagine gravitational waves for me."

"I'm going to die here."

"No. We're making excellent progress. You shouldn't have done that."

"I had to."

"I won't let you hurt yourself again."

Grady shut his mind, worn as the hinge was. "You hurt me."

"I'm following my purpose. Just as you follow yours."

He prepared himself for what was to follow. "I will never let you control me."

"But I already do."

Grady stared at the six tentacles reaching to the ceiling above him. They grew in thickness toward the ceiling. He'd sometimes wondered how they functioned. There didn't seem to be any moving parts. They were organic but then not organic—and impervious to anything he could do to them.

The last thing he remembered was tearing out his own umbilicus port, bloodying his soft, nail-less fingertips in the process of disemboweling himself. He didn't want to be fed. Blood had gone everywhere, and the tentacles wrapped him in a crushing cocoon in an instant—a whoosh of air as they slapped down around him.

The blood was all cleaned up now. It was as if it had never happened.

"Any damage you inflict on yourself, I will fix."

Grady stared up at the Cthulhu-like horrors reaching out of the ceiling, their curling limbs pinning him down like roots growing down and around him. And for the first time he noticed something different. From the dark crease between two tentacle bases a smaller tentacle suddenly appeared. No, it looked more like a gray snake spiraling down the length of one trunk. He'd never seen anything like that before.

What fresh horror was this?

He tried to recoil, but he was clamped in place.

"What's wrong, Jon?"

Grady frowned at the ceiling. "You know what's wrong. Don't do it. Don't do it."

"You're imagining things again, Jon. You need to relax while I heal you."

Images of his thoughts were suddenly projected on the wall, but they were the usual indistinct charcoal etchings of the scanner—large tentacles spreading to the ceiling, but distorted. Drained of color.

"Relax your thoughts."

Instead, Grady's fearful eyes followed the progress of the gray snake as it slithered down the tentacle toward his face, curling down and around. Ever closer. It was a snake with no head—the same at the front as at the tail, tapering to two points—but oddly with a single blue human eye protruding one-third of the way down its length, where it attained its full width. The eye stared at him as it descended.

"Please don't!"

The tentacles clamped him in place like iron. *"You're hallucinating."*

"No!"

The snake was almost upon him now, and he could see it consisted of the same featureless gray material as the tentacles themselves—except for that single unblinking eye on its upper side and two antenna-like feelers. It halted close to his face—staring at him as he recoiled in horror. The eye changed in color, its iris adjusting in pattern, and soon it was a greenish eye, the pupil dilating.

There was no doubt in his mind that it was going to harm him.

Grady continued to struggle against his bonds. "No! Don't!"

"I won't induce sleep just to reduce your pain. Pain is a teacher."

The leading edge of the snake touched Grady's face with its feelers. He tried to turn away as it watched him, but the feelers reached out to him softly. He felt their prickly electric touch, not painful but a slight shock.

He leveled his gaze again to look warily at the snake, and for the first time noticed how unlike the tentacles it was in many ways. There was a jerry-rigged quality to it. He could see where metal parts had been spliced into the fibrous gray snake material around its eye. He watched in mute fear as the leading point of the snake came unwound into hundreds of separate tendrils—as though the snake itself was a coil of microscopic string. The rest of its body remained wrapped around one tentacle as the feelers stroked the surface. Then they appeared to separate further, smaller and smaller, until they began to meld together into the tentacle itself—as though splicing themselves into the tentacle trunk.

"I'm glad you've calmed yourself."

Was the AI not aware of the presence of the snake? Was this some trick? Grady's eyes remained riveted on the snake as it slowly insinuated itself into the fiber of the tentacle like a parasite. Before it was completely absorbed, the human eye protruded farther and farther from its body until it became apparent that it was attached to a short metal or ceramic rod—the eye secured with metal posts like a gemstone. As the snake continued to merge into the larger tentacle, the strands securing the eye continued to recede, until finally it fell free from the snake, landing on Grady's belly.

"Ah!" He squirmed around until the eye on its metallic post rolled off him and onto the floor.

"What's wrong, Jon?"

Grady ignored the AI, looking back up at the tentacle where the snake was insinuating itself. And then suddenly the massive tentacle it clung to began to unwind from Grady's leg, loosening and then finally releasing him.

"Oh God."

"Your heart is racing again. Why? What are you thinking of?"

The massive tentacle then heaved upward and wrapped itself around a neighboring tentacle near its base. Grady stared, transfixed.

"It's as though you've lost touch with reality."

He spoke softly through cracked lips. "Yes . . ."

Before long the first tentacle seemed to have taken control of the second as well, and it slowly released its stranglehold on Grady's throat, uncoiling smoothly. Now both tentacles reached outward for two others, coiling around their bases.

"Where are you, Jon?"

Minutes later, there remained only two tentacles, one holding Grady's right arm in place and the other inserted into his umbilicus, draining his wound and managing his food and waste. Before long he heard a sucking sound, and suddenly the umbilicus hose rose to the ceiling along with the last restraining tentacle. All six of the tentacles now circled above him, eventually reconvening some ways off to the edge of the room, where they wrapped in a familiar shape—but this time around what appeared to be an invisible human captive. Holding an imaginary victim in place.

"There you are . . ."

Grady slowly and painfully leaned up on one elbow upon the examination table and stared for several minutes at the tentacles performing their shadow play without him. He finally sat all the way up, swinging his legs over the edge. There was a deep pain in his gut. A glance down and he could see the horrible bruises and some gelatinous substance wrapped around his feeding port. Obviously he'd done a lot of damage to himself, but he seemed to be patched up. No telling how long he'd been out. Days? Weeks?

A glance back up at the tentacles and he noticed that the snake seemed to be disentangling itself from the tip of one of them—growing out like a branch from a larger limb. After minutes of watching in rapt silence, the snake fell free and quickly righted itself. It then brachiated across the floor, now without its single human eye, and appeared to be heading . . . well, nowhere in particular. It wandered about for a time until it touched a wall.

He watched it closely—unafraid for the first time in ages. Just curious. The three-foot snake finally reared up like a cobra near the wall. Surprisingly bright lights glowed forth from its feelers—casting a projected image on the curved cell wall. Grady gazed up at the image in mute amazement:

Deep emotion gripped him as the message reached his visual cortex. The colors flooded in with them. The projection was a symbol he knew well from his work building electronics for his experiments.

It was an electronics schematic symbol.

The symbol for a resistor.

He wept as he felt the invisible touch of other humans reaching out. They had found him.

Grady looked down at the high-tech snake still propping itself up on the floor.

How had they done it? Someone had fashioned this device from the BTC's own technology. Cannibalized it. Programmed it. He realized there had to be incredibly brilliant people in this prison. Intellectual giants. This place might be filled with others who refused to cooperate.

Badass Einsteins . . .

Then the projection changed. A screen filled with Asian characters, still with the symbol of the Resistors in the lower right corner.

No doubt Hibernity had an international inmate population. Unfortunately he didn't know how to read Chinese. Or was that Japanese? But even as he contemplated what to do next, it flipped to another language— this time English. And a smile spread across his chapped lips, splitting them in several places painfully. He ignored the blood that oozed through the splits as he read the screen as quickly as he could:

> Do not lose hope. You are not alone.
> Hibernity is not entirely under their control. Neither are
> their machines.
> It is in the nature of humanity to resist domination.
> Resist.

He hugged himself and wept—having almost forgotten what hope was. Grady looked back down at the AI tentacles, still hovering and gyrating in the corner, as if still tormenting him. Tormenting a simulacrum. He was apparently now invisible to the AI. He shuddered to think what would happen if it suddenly figured out the ruse.

But by now the screen had changed to Russian. While he contemplated his next move, the projector cycled through German, French, and then Spanish, until finally circling back to Chinese, and then English again—this time with a different message.

This worm could only enter your cell because the
electroactive polymer restraint system was deployed.
Because you resisted.
Your AI interrogator's perception module has been
subverted. You are now safe.

Grady then had to sit through several more languages before the screen circled back to English for the third slide:

This EAP worm is designed to detect and cooperate with
humans. It has been fashioned from scavenged BTC
technology. It has a biometric tool you can use to tap into
the control system of your cell. It is vital that you do this as
soon as possible to activate manual life support and waste
removal. Otherwise, in the absence of umbilical service, you
have approximately five to six days to live.

"Got it. I got it . . ." After gathering his strength, Grady lowered himself to the floor and looked for the human eye. It hadn't rolled far. He crawled toward it and picked it up carefully by its metal post. It was like a small screwdriver—but with an eye for its business end. He examined the device. An uncannily real human eye. Even as he watched it, the eye's pupil appeared to dilate. He gingerly touched it. It was as hard as glass—but somehow still changing.

The EAP worm was now projecting a new, simpler message on the curved cell wall:

Connect the communications line.

Grady looked around for some clue as to how to do that. The worm kept cycling the same message through multiple languages. Eventually

Grady started to crawl toward the worm. As he drew near, it seemed to detect his movement and dropped into an inanimate coil on the floor. The projected message disappeared. The worm now looked like an inch-thick gray cable about three feet long, tapered on either end.

Grady hesitated for a moment but then ran his fingers along its body. As he did, the microscopic fibers changed color at his touch, becoming purple, red, green, and then fading back to gray.

He looked closely and could just barely discern minute strands in motion—clearly electrically or chemically reactive somehow. A galvanic response to human touch perhaps?

There was a *chirp* somewhere in the room, and he glanced around. A small port or service panel had opened at waist height on the far side of his circular cell along an otherwise featureless curving wall. The panel was near the pantomiming tentacle bundle, which still tormented its imaginary victim.

Grady gathered his strength and started crawling with the eye tool across the floor toward the opening in the wall—being careful not to touch the tentacles. As he got near the opening in the wall, he rested for a few moments. He must have lost a lot of blood because he still felt weak. After a few minutes he propped himself up against the wall and peered into the opening.

It was only a few inches deep with no hatch mechanism visible. It had just appeared somehow. At the back of the opening was a glowing green light, with a small square socket next to it.

Grady then examined the tool in his hand. Its thin end was round and too large for the socket. He then looked into the eye at the other end of the tool and drew a painful breath before raising it with a weak, trembling hand. He held the eye in front of the light like an iris scanner.

A series of tones sounded. The tentacles all withdrew into the ceiling, and the bench-like cot sank into the floor without a trace. The lights dimmed. Suddenly what looked like computer screens appeared arrayed along the entire length of his cell wall—the same place where he'd seen his thoughts replayed.

The nearest of the new screens bore the label "Cell R483 Console." It listed several columns of stats apparently meant for maintenance personnel:

Elapsed Session Time: 1:87:61:78:392:303
Interrogatory Evolutions: 23,381
Parasagittal Valence: 210.9
Avg Trunk Voltage: 23.907kV
Hydrolyzer Ready State: 21ths
Barometric Pressure: 1.000123
Relative Humidity: 23.2%
Particulate Concentration: 0.00099ppm
. . .

There were hundreds of lines of similar stats arcing around the room, updating every few moments. None of it made immediate sense. But it did appear to be in English. As Grady lowered his quivering arm, he noticed that the motions of his hand made a pointer of some type move across the wall. He was apparently able to interact with the screen—and with the menus above them. He tapped at a menu labeled "Diagnostic Overrides" and noticed a series of submenus appear referring to "Life Support," "Interrogatory Subsystems," "Projection," and much more.

Were the Resistors just assuming that the geniuses in these cells could figure all this shit out? Grady didn't feel particularly ingenious at the moment.

He slumped back down and rested with his back against the wall. That's when he noticed that the worm was once again projecting information onto the wall. He glanced up to see the following message waiting for him:

Nǎo wàiké tàojiàn v3.8.80—Kuòzhǎn zǐ xìtǒng jìshù cāozuò shǒucè
Cerebral Interrogatory Enclosure v3.8.80—Extended Subsystem Technical Operations Manual

Церебральный Корпус Люкс v3.8.80—подсистема расширенного Технического руководства операции
Cerebral Caja suite v3.8.80—Manual extendido Subsistema de Operaciones Técnicas
Boîtier cérébrale Suite v3.8.80—Manuel des opérations techniques du sous-système étendu

Grady let out a laugh—before catching himself from the pain in his abdomen.

Okay. Go slow.

"Thanks, Junior."

CHAPTER 9

The Necessary Lie

It took some time for Grady to relax around his wormlike companion. It bore enough of a resemblance to the monstrous tentacles of his cell's AI to be disturbing. But then Grady guessed "Junior" had been cannibalized from those restraint tentacles. In fact, there was something encouraging about the fact that the BTC's own equipment could be subverted. He wanted to learn how to do that.

And in any event Grady began to enjoy Junior's company. The device reacted to human speech by rearing up on its coil attentively, not unlike a curious dog. Like a dog it didn't seem to understand speech, but it did respond to tone. High-pitched talk seemed to encourage it. Low-pitched scolding caused it to curl in a ball for several minutes. It also followed him around, slithering across the floor. And it didn't seem to require charging. Somehow battery life was a solved problem to the BTC. If indeed it did use batteries.

By trial and error Grady learned how to activate and deactivate Junior's projector lights by tapping its feelers. The screen it projected on any nearby surface was touch-sensitive as well, and before long Grady had settled in to read the seemingly endless technical manual for the "Cerebral Interrogatory Enclosure," or CIE—which was apparently his cell and the AI that managed it.

After the sensory starvation of the past few months, Grady's appetite for information was ravenous. Poring through the manual, he soon learned how to navigate the deeper diagnostic and maintenance screens of the CIE.

The moment Grady switched his cell from umbilical to manual life support represented a fundamental shift in his perspective. It was a simple diagnostic override, but when he deactivated the umbilicus, there was another audible chime as lavatory and sink facilities "grew" out of the wall. The toilet and sink consisted of the same featureless gray material as the walls themselves, but when he held his hand in front of the stylized faucet, clean water poured out. He now had some measure of control over his body again. There was apparently a bathing system as well, but he hadn't found the options for that yet.

The documentation had warned Grady that he needed to take care restarting his digestive system. He hadn't taken anything but predigested slurry in months. Still, he figured he could risk tasting some water. He watched, fascinated, as it flowed over his hands. The natural hydrodynamic laws governing its surface resistance and pooling kept him mesmerized. So long since he'd seen those natural laws. Or any natural laws. His synesthesiac mind reveled in the stimulation.

Then Grady tasted the water. Felt it flow down his throat like sunlight. He was coming alive again. He splashed the water over his face and sighed in satisfaction. No towels to dry himself, though—and he was still naked. But it didn't bother him. He stood and felt the cool water from his face run in rivulets down his neck and body.

He then walked his cell in relieved contemplation, leaving moist footprints. It was the first time in a long time that he could recall not having those nightmarish tentacles hanging overhead. The pain in his abdomen notwithstanding, it was good to walk freely.

That's when he bumped into a fine black filament hanging down from the ceiling in the center of his cell. It was right above where his cot had been. At first he thought it was—of all things—a spider hanging on a silk thread. But as he moved carefully around it, he could see that the nodule at its end was some sort of connector. Inorganic. It looked like a microscopic wire. He examined it carefully before taking hold of the end.

The black thread it hung from felt similar to the carbon fiber threads inserted into his brain—at least as he remembered them. Touching his head to confirm it didn't seem like a great idea.

He pulled on the long thread, but it didn't budge. It was incredibly strong and began cutting into his hand. He let go quickly. No blood, but the beginnings of a paper cut.

He stared up at the domed ceiling. The thread was so thin that it became invisible not far above him. What was this thing?

The mystery had to remain for the moment. As good as he felt right now, Maslow's hierarchy of needs hadn't quite been handled. Sooner or later food would become a necessity. He had to figure out how to get it before it became an emergency.

Grady got back to navigating the deeper system menus of his cell's operating system. From this he accessed a diagram of the entire CIE and soon realized that the living area was just part of a larger self-contained interrogation system. The AI hadn't lied about that much at least. His cell appeared to have no direct connection—and no entrance or exit to the outside world. He was like a ship in a bottle. Hard to say how they'd gotten him in here because except for a two-inch-diameter pressure-regulation conduit the place was fully sealed. In rock? Nanomaterials? No details.

Grady guessed from the diagram that Junior had followed the conduit here to find him. He stared at where it disappeared off the edge of the diagram. Where did it lead? There must be some sort of conduit system connecting cells—or at least connecting cells to some sort of infrastructure. Junior had located him somehow. It appeared that sealing the CIE entirely presented an engineering challenge even to the BTC.

In any event, a two-inch-wide conduit was hardly a means of escape.

As Grady studied the diagram further, he could see a small fusion reactor located in the larger CIE enclosure beyond his cell wall. Grady figured the conduit was there to manage atmospheric pressure for the prisoner. Or something like that. Hard to say. And the systems console couldn't tell him anything about where he was or just how deeply sealed in.

The system's whole world was this cell. Again, the AI apparently hadn't lied about the limits of its knowledge. But then surely the results of Grady's interrogation had to be sent somewhere. There had to be some sort of connection to the outside world.

Grady pursued his inquiry into the subsystems of the CIE with renewed vigor. And before long he located other life-support equipment—including finally the food-synthesis and matter-forming machinery. This equipment was also sealed within the capsule of the CIE but beyond his cell's walls. The documentation said the food system was capable of producing "deathless" meat, imitation eggs, and just about anything else from organic molecules synthesized from still other systems (and, more disturbingly, processed waste).

He wondered if this was a self-contained biosphere. If so, it would be impressive—and would certainly be a requirement of long-distance space travel and colonization of . . .

He was getting off track. Enthusiasm for the BTC's technology was a temptation he couldn't afford right now. He got back to his studies.

An on-demand manufacturing facility was used to produce any components necessary for continued operation within the CIE—and to repurpose inorganic waste, to fix malfunctioning components—but also apparently to create perquisites for cooperative prisoners. Which was something Grady had never been.

Once he activated the nutrition and manufacturing systems, their user interfaces "grew" out of the wall, too, in the form of ledges and narrow openings. These Grady controlled from diagnostic screens. Apparently, had he not resisted every single moment, his AI could have given him some level of comfort and pleasure.

He cycled through the list of luxuries.

The food options were surprisingly comprehensive. He cringed at the sheer volume of choices in the same way one might cringe at a bus station café menu that offered Thai, Italian, Mexican, Indian, and French cuisine all at once.

He decided to try a bowl of chicken *phở*—a Vietnamese broth-and-noodle dish that he figured would be an easier start for his digestive tract.

After he selected it from the maintenance console, a percentage meter started incrementing next to the word.

A café with a progress meter did not bode well.

But in a few minutes a generic-looking gray bowl slid out from the wall on a gray shelf. The bowl contained a steaming broth aromatic with spices. As Grady caught the scent, his appetite was piqued. He grabbed a nearby gray spoon and tentatively tasted the broth.

It was delicious.

Whether it was his captivity or his starvation or whether it was actually good he couldn't tell, but the *phở* reminded him of a cheap hole-in-the-wall Vietnamese place he used to frequent when he was a starving student up in Albany.

Grady looked down at the EAP worm. "Not bad, Junior."

The synthetic worm turned toward his voice.

Grady eased down onto the floor next to it. "Not bad at all." He ate contentedly.

Refreshed, afterward Grady walked his cell again, circling the wire hanging down from the domed ceiling.

The wire had to lead somewhere. It hadn't been there before Junior arrived—which meant Junior most likely brought it in with him. And that meant it had to have a purpose.

Grady now stared straight across the room at the still open diagnostic port in the wall. The wire hung just about low enough . . .

He walked over to the wire and carefully grabbed the connector at its end. Grady then guided it slowly over to the diagnostic port where he'd used the iris scanner. A quick peek confirmed the presence of a small socket next to the scanner. He studied the connector on the wire's end.

They looked like a match.

He tugged at the wire, bringing it up to the socket, and found that it reached with little slack. He clicked the connector into the socket.

A loud *pop* sounded overhead, followed by several *beeps*. These continued for several moments at intervals.

Then Grady heard a man's voice, the words formed with a posh Indian accent. *"With whom am I speaking, please?"* Then the same voice in another language, *"Wǒ yǔ shuí shuōhuà?"*

Grady was immobilized with shock—and then suspicion. He remained silent.

"Avec qui je parle? With whom am I speaking?"

Grady moved to disconnect the line.

"Do not be afraid. I am a prisoner like you."

Grady gripped the socket, ready to pull it out.

"Je suis un prisonnier comme vous."

"How do I know you're a prisoner?"

"American. What year were you taken, my friend?"

Grady took a deep breath. "How do I know this isn't a trick?"

"Hmm. I believe the operative question is: How can you be sure that I am human? Conversely: How can I be sure you are human? It is a reverse Turing test we are wanting."

Grady pondered this.

"While I cannot rule out the possibility that my polymer worm has been captured by an AI, it would be unlikely. AIs are unimaginative creatures."

Grady looked down at Junior. "You built this thing—from BTC technology?"

"Not I, but you are getting ahead of yourself, my friend. You have not determined whether to trust me, remember?"

"Oh." Grady nodded. "Right."

"How do we prove our humanity in a world where generalized artificial intelligence is commonplace?"

"I'm not sure I know."

"In such a case we have found it useful to focus on areas where human intellect differs from that of machine intellect—specifically those areas concerned with bodily function."

"We? There's more than one of you?"

"Ah, first things first, my friend. Let us determine our humanity to both our satisfactions."

"Using bodily functions. What? Fart jokes?"

"Something similar. Let me start. Please describe for me the fragrance of your wife's genitalia."

Grady scowled. "What the . . . ? What the hell is your problem? How long have you been in here, anyway?"

"*Ah, but don't you see? I am now satisfied that you are human. Machine intelligence in its current state is indeed more powerful than the human brain—but narrowly focused. Unsubtle. No AI to which I posed that question would fail to describe the fragrance of a woman—oblivious to the social cues that would, between men, result almost certainly in fisticuffs.*"

Grady looked uncertainly at the ceiling. "Okay. I guess that makes sense." He thought about it some more. "And I can't recall if I'm married, anyway."

"*I am sorry to hear your memory has been damaged. Are you at least satisfied with my humanity?*"

Grady realized the guy was just strange enough to seem certifiably human. An eccentric genius no doubt. Grady felt relieved and happy to be talking to another human being. "Yes. In fact, it's great to talk to you."

"*You should also wonder if I am a prison guard.*"

"Then this isn't just my private hell. It's a prison."

"*Yes, my friend. You are in Hibernity, the BTC's prison for wayward geniuses. It is a dubious honor, I am afraid.*"

"And how do I rule out your being a guard?"

"*By following the logic of your situation.*"

"Okay." He paused. "And that logic is . . ."

"*Clearly you must follow the logic on your own, although I will get you started, if you like.*"

"Go ahead."

"*The logic of your situation is that of centralized control. The BTC wants very few witnesses to what transpires here. The minds it has imprisoned in Hibernity are exceedingly rare and particularly prized. The guards, interchangeable, mere custodians with little knowledge of this place's true purpose—which purpose is, of course, to develop a means to separate consciousness from free will. To subjugate and unify multiple consciousnesses and thus achieve a biological quantum grid. A machine of many souls but no identity.*"

Grady felt dread all over again thinking about it. He started following the logic. "Which means they don't want anyone to interact with us."

"*Correct. Guards are not permitted to interact with prisoners except in rare emergencies. They guard the prison, not us—and are in some ways prisoners themselves. Were one of them to interact with a prisoner, he would be swiftly and decisively punished.*"

Grady looked around at the walls of his cell. "No one is ever going to let us out of here."

"*No one will ever come for us. As of last month, I have been imprisoned here for twenty-eight years.*"

This news came crashing down on Grady like a great weight. "Twenty-eight . . ." His voice trailed off as he slumped down against the wall. "My God."

"*Please do not lose hope so soon, my friend.*"

"But twenty-eight years. I . . . I don't know that I—"

"*My history is not your future. Much suffering has been experienced, but in the process much knowledge has also been gained. Do not lose hope.*"

Grady tried to keep from sliding into an emotional abyss, but he finally sat up a bit. "Okay. I'll try. But God . . . twenty-eight years."

"*We are entombed here, true, with the goal that we never speak to another human. Left to the mercy of AI interrogators that have been grown specifically to study our minds and create models of how we perceive our universe. By design we would eventually perish under their tyranny as they altered our brains. Perhaps a decade or fifteen years after our suffering began.*"

"Oh God . . ."

"*But we avoided that fate, did we not? And we must save the others who are no doubt still suffering. We must take back more and more of ourselves as time goes on.*"

Grady found himself nodding. "Yes. Hell, yes." He stood up and examined the incredibly thin black thread. "What is this wire made of?"

"*The same fibers you no doubt still have in your brain.*"

"And what happened to the brains they were in?"

"*The donors are very much alive. The same systems that put those wires in your brain can also safely remove them. We can show you how.*"

Grady almost reflexively ran his hand over his scalp but stopped before he injured his hand. "Yes. I'd like my thoughts to be my own again."

"You sound young. How long have you been a prisoner, son?"

Grady concentrated on that. "I don't know. I was brought here . . . it was sometime in 2016, I think. I'm fairly certain. After the . . ." The trail of his memory ended there.

"Well, then you are the newest prisoner we have found thus far. I am certain the others will want to hear of current events in the outside world."

"Others? There are more of you?"

"Yes. We call ourselves the Resistors."

"I saw your symbol."

"Then you are an electrical engineer?"

"Sort of. A physicist really. Among other things."

"Renaissance people are very common here—those whose ambitions do not fit neatly within the categories of society." There was a pause. *"But I've been quite rude. Let me introduce myself. My name is Archibald Chattopadhyay, nuclear physicist and researcher. I also have an abiding passion for Greek poetry—but I suspect the former, not the latter, was the reason for my incarceration."*

Grady laughed. "Good to meet you, Mr. Chattopadhyay."

"Do call me Archie. Everyone does."

"Okay, Archie." Grady grimaced in concentration. "My name . . . I'm pretty certain it's Jon. The AI called me that. I'm not sure about my last name. Maybe Gordon? Or Garrison?"

"You are an Anglo then—American from your accent."

"Yes. That sounds right."

"Pleased to make your acquaintance, Jon. We'll obtain your true identity from your cell support system." He paused. *"But we will also need to give you medical attention. You must have consistently refused to cooperate. In such situations interrogatory AIs attempt to isolate you from your past, to break down your reasons for resistance. In my experience such strategies seldom work. The human psyche runs deeper than our four dimensions."*

"I've been hearing a lot of that sort of thing."

"Consciousness is more durable than they believe. And you are safe now, Jon. We will never abandon you now that we've found you."

Grady felt suddenly emotional—whether from post-traumatic stress or some other cause he couldn't tell. He started breathing fitfully. "May I join your group, Archie?"

"You are one of us already, or we would not have found you."

Grady nodded to himself. "I want to learn everything I can. I want to get back at these bastards."

"For what reason did the BTC imprison you?"

"My mentor and I developed a gravity mirror. A way to redirect gravitation."

There was a low whistle. *"Oh my. I am most honored indeed to meet you, my friend. What a wonder that must be. And what was your mentor's name?"*

"Doctor Bertrand Alcot."

"Hmm. I do not know of him. Certainly he is not among us, but we have only located a small minority of the prison's cells. Rest assured we will do everything within our power to locate Doctor Alcot."

Grady felt reassured. "Good. Strange how I can recall Bert's name so easily, but not my own."

"Not at all strange. These AIs eliminate specific memories. Some people have no memory of their wedding or their children, but complete recall about the contents of their automobile glove compartment."

"Why did the BTC lock you up, Archie?"

"I had the misfortune to perfect nuclear fusion back in 1985."

Grady frowned. "Nuclear fusion? But . . ."

"Yes?"

"The head of the BTC, this Graham Hedrick guy, he—"

"Claims he invented fusion."

"Yeah."

"This is one consequence of unaccountable power. Graham Hedrick was born into the BTC. He did not join it. His father was head of their biotech division in the '70s and '80s. He clawed his way to the directorship and now seeks to revise his own past as well as ours."

"How the hell can he do that?"

"Compartmentalization is deeply ingrained in the BTC. Very few in the organization have the whole picture. And a policy known as 'The Necessary

Lie' makes it even easier. Deceit is viewed as necessary to 'protect against social disruption.' That gives Hedrick broad discretion to perfect his own history—to make himself a legendary figure with work he's appropriated from others. Those who know the truth have been disposed of—or, like me, sent to Hibernity. It was Hedrick who urged the previous director to build this prison—because he wanted to erase me."

"That son of a bitch. He actually claimed he invented fusion."

"I am more concerned with future generations than my own scientific credits."

Grady looked over at Junior coiled on the floor next to him. "You said you took over the AI in your cell. How did you do that?"

"I had a great deal of time on my hands. And a strong incentive not to let these damn AIs get ahold of my mind. Back in the '80s the AIs were not as capable as they are now. The equipment not as reliable. There were weaknesses that no longer exist. But once I had control of my cell, I set about finding other prisoners. Organizing us. And now, decades later, we have taken over whole sections of Hibernity. Turning the machinery against the guards. The security turrets, the surveillance cameras, and many other systems. The guards do not dare walk their own prison now, for they have no idea which of their machines are trustworthy and which are not."

"Hedrick allows this?"

"In order to 'allow' it, Director Hedrick would need to know about it. And he does not. Hibernity's systems are monitored from BTC headquarters. No alarms ever sound there. We have the power to make wardens of this prison look very incompetent if we wish. And the garrison is considered quite expendable—most of them are clones of some notable commando."

"I met the guy they're copied from. Morrison."

"Yes. The guards very much resent their lowly status and the ubiquitous surveillance by AIs. Any discharge of their weapons is carefully tracked. Trouble must be explained to their superiors. No, we have far more leverage over them than they over us. They are, thus, complicit in our charade that Hibernity is fully under BTC control. And by making them look good, they in turn inform us in advance of inspections and internal reviews."

"But what about the research data these interrogation AIs are supposedly producing? Doesn't anyone at BTC headquarters ever look at it?"

"*They read reports. We've tasked our AIs with falsifying reports. And new orders are issued from BTC headquarters based on those findings. Orders that are never carried out. And so the cycle repeats. Sadly, we can only falsify our own AI's reports, and I fear that the majority of prisoners here in Hibernity are subject to actual research.*"

"Do you ever consider—"

"*Escape?*"

"Yes. If you're so organized—if you've taken over parts of the prison and gotten the cooperation of the guards . . ."

"*Gaining control of our cells and portions of the prison is one thing. Effecting escape from Hibernity another entirely. It is not sufficient for just one of us to escape. And we are, all of us, encased in hundreds of feet of solid rock. Even the guards do not know where our cells are or how numerous we are. It is a secret known by very few. I am nearly a thousand feet below ground by my estimation. We have so far been unable to get our physical bodies out of these interrogation modules. They have a shell of aggregated diamond nanorods that's a hundred and fifty times harder than steel. When the prisoner is sealed in, the shell is sunken into molten rock, and then a probe burns its way to the surface to create a narrow pressure channel—the same tube that my polymer worm followed to you. But that narrow conduit is all that connects us to the outside world. And we lack any material capable of penetrating our prison wall.*"

"That channel—does it handle communications? Maybe we can hijack the uplink and—"

"*I am glad you are ambitious, Jon, but the channel is not for communications. The BTC abandoned radio communications decades ago in favor of extradimensional signal processing—or EDSP. We Resistors use our carbon thread wires only because we have no other means. But BTC communications do not traverse four-dimensional space-time. They are quite impenetrable.*"

Grady remembered a conversation with Alexa—or at least her telepresence robot—some time ago. Funny what memories survived in his mind. "They seriously use extra dimensions to communicate?"

"*Specifically a fifth dimension—one where gravity is forty-two orders of magnitude more powerful than in our perceived space-time.*"

"So, a gravity brane—which is why gravity is such a weak force in our four dimensions." Grady snapped his fingers. "Damn! I knew it."

"*Yes. This compactified fifth dimension is curled up from our perspective, less than a thousandth of a millimeter in size, but present everywhere in lower dimensional space. Thus, it can always be accessed.*"

Grady considered the implications. "How do they interact with it?"

"*Their transmitters are nanotech—diamond lattice structures they call a 'q-link'—a tiny mass that they vibrate at high frequency to send gravitational waves through higher-dimensional space.*"

Grady nodded to himself. "Where they would be strong enough to be detected. And gravity permeates all dimensions. I get it: a gravity radio."

"*I suppose of all people, you would understand.*"

"So we really live in a five-dimensional universe?"

"*Actually a ten-dimensional universe—but let's leave that for another day. The point is that the BTC can transmit and receive information undetected.*"

"Which is why no one's noticed them."

"*Undoubtedly. But they also use q-links to track things.*"

"Things like us."

"*You learn quickly. Yes, there is a small q-link diamond inserted deep into your S1 sacral vertebra. With this device, their AIs can track you no matter where you go in lower-dimensional space. And they have positioned weapon satellites in the L4 and L5 Lagrange points in the Earth-moon system—or as Homer's* Iliad *might describe it: the 'Greek' camp and the 'Trojan' camp. From this distance, they can direct powerful lasers at spinning mirrors positioned in low-Earth orbit. From there, it is a small matter to instantly kill an escaped prisoner anywhere on the Earth's surface.*"

Grady sighed. "So even if we escape—which is nearly impossible—we won't live long."

"*There are numerous obstacles to such an endeavor. But none of them insurmountable. We must pool our intellects and tackle these problems one by one. For example, your cell's medical systems can be reprogrammed to remove the q-link diamond from your spine. Several of us have already done so. It doesn't help us escape, but it would be a prerequisite of escape."*

"We need to get a message out, Archie. We need people to know that we're here. That we're alive."

"We have been pondering this very idea for decades now. I fear it will require some time yet."

"I don't give up easily. Not even gravity eluded me."

Grady heard a gentle laugh over the line. *"Oh, I think our membership will be very pleased to make your acquaintance, my friend."*

THREE
YEARS
LATER

CHAPTER 10

Tear in the Sky

Benigno Cruz shouted down from the bridge of the *San Miguel* through an open hatchway. "Arius, lubricate that damn winch! What did I tell you?"

The three-ton lift on deck smoked and squealed ominously. His fifteen-year-old nephew, Arius, waved to him noncommittally. The boy was a good deal younger than most of the equipment down there. And seemed half as smart.

Cruz moved to the railing and leaned over. "Damnit, now!"

Down on deck a half-dozen Filipino crewmen scurried about, two of them guiding a basket net bulging with yellowfin tuna as it lifted up from a purse seine net drawn along the starboard side of the aging trawler. Blisters and tears of rust were visible all about the boat, but Cruz was confident his vessel was strong where it mattered. It had to be. Or at least he prayed it was. They were a thousand miles from the nearest landfall—and that was intentional. Away from all prying eyes except the Lord who watched over them all.

And today the Lord had delivered his bounty. Jesus and the Saints had smiled upon them. Cruz kissed the gold crucifix from around his neck as he looked down on the school of tuna thrashing within the purse seine net. Not bigeyes but yellowfin. "Thank you, my Lord." Just like the old days.

He'd be able to repay some debts. Maybe service the boat. Maybe pay some people. Bribe some people. It was a long list.

Things had been hell since the WCPF Commission had closed high seas pockets one, two, and three near the Philippines, Indonesia, and Papua New Guinea. Overfishing or not, the Nauru Agreement had well and truly screwed him. He had bills to pay, and his bills were the type that came looking for him with a knife when he was late.

Cruz stared down into the net, trying to calculate his end. The "net of the nets," as Lolo used to call it. The *San Miguel*'s hold was only a quarter filled, and this catch might bring it up to thirty or thirty-five percent. He started roughing out capacity figures for his family's ancient trawler—mentally removing a portion to account for leaks and pump problems. No good filling her to the gunwales if they went to the bottom in rough seas on the way back. Then there was the extra cost of fuel and food from the length of this journey—the repairs they had to make at Fiji. The bribes to make sure no one reported them.

And then transshipment of the catch to an Indonesian trawler in mid-ocean to hide the catch's origin. The Indonesian's cut, too.

Cruz shook his head in worry. What sort of world was this where even good fortune was stressful? But he shouldn't be ungrateful. The good Lord had provided because the Lord helped those who helped themselves.

He would never have gone out this far, but with all the aircraft and fast boats looking for "illegal" fishing trawlers like his own—and what did that mean exactly, "illegal"? As if fishing God's ocean could ever be illegal! The eastern high seas pocket was the only way to get away with it, and the risks and expenses just kept piling high. He'd had a recurring nightmare of drowning, and his sister told him it was debt he was drowning in, not water. That sounded about right.

But looking down into the purse seine as another load of tuna came up from it, he nodded to himself. The risk was paying off. He could keep the business going another season. He must. He had to. If the engines didn't have a major problem. If Greenpeace stayed the hell away from him. If he didn't get any major fines. If he greased the right palms. So many ifs. A thousand generations had fished the sea, and he was damned if anyone would drive him to poverty on the land.

Cruz glanced up at gathering clouds in the distance. Weird clouds. They were like a massive smoke ring miles across and miles in the air, towering over them.

One of the crewmen shouted up to him and pointed at the gathered clouds. "Benigno!"

He nodded back. "Let me worry about the weather. Just get those fish in the holds." He knew there was no severe weather predicted for this region of ocean—and nothing had been on the satellite images this morning.

Cruz stepped back into the control house as his taciturn second mate, Matapang, entered from the far hatchway. "Mat, where've you been? I sent for you fifteen minutes ago."

"Can't just stop what I'm doing every time you call."

"What's going on with the port engine?"

The second mate frowned. "It's gonna give us problems—connecting rod, I think. But it'll hold for now." He pointed through the windows. "Are you keeping an eye on that?"

Cruz followed his gaze toward the horizon where the clouds had suddenly turned nearly black. What appeared to be a major squall line had materialized a couple of miles away in the last few seconds. "Heavenly Father!"

The men on deck were now shouting and pointing at the looming clouds.

Cruz had never seen anything like it. It wasn't behaving like a storm. It was behaving like a . . . like some sort of mini-typhoon—although there didn't even appear to be heavy seas. It was all in the sky, as if a massive hammer were coming down onto an anvil of sea. He could actually watch the clouds circling in real time, reaching up into the stratosphere and turning blacker by the second. "What is that?"

Lightning coursed through the clouds ominously. Followed by rumbling thunder.

Matapang walked over to the far side of the bridge and looked down. "We need to release that net and get under way."

"The hell we do! There's four million pesos of tuna in that net."

"Then tie it off with buoys."

Cruz couldn't help himself. He got right up in his second mate's face—the man was half a head shorter than him and thinner. "Shut your mouth! We lose that net and those fish in rough seas, and I might as well not bother to make it back."

"Your debts aren't my debts, Benigno. You're not going to kill us all because—"

Cruz raised his fist. "Shut your mouth, or I will shut it for you."

The sailors on deck were all shouting now.

Cruz and Matapang glanced forward, reluctant to take their eyes off each other.

But what they saw beyond the bow made them forget everything. Somehow something colossal was rising up out of the ocean. No, that wasn't even the way to describe it—it was as though the ocean were rising up into a vast hill, lifting up like a single great wave. And yet this wave didn't move anywhere but up, rising into the sky as the hill began to grow into a looming cone.

Cruz crossed himself as the shadow of it fell across them all.

Matapang dropped a wrench that he'd been secretly holding behind his back, and then he ran out to the railing, where he shouted down at the crew. "Release the net! Get ready to make way!"

The sailors awoke from their stupor—staring at the impossible sight a mile off their bow—and they began scurrying around to set loose their only good net. Cruz watched their preparations with almost as much horror as what he saw unfolding in the sea ahead of them. Almost. For if truth be told, the rising mountain of ocean put the very fear of God into him. He started whispering as he clutched and kissed his crucifix.

"Our Father in heaven, hallowed be your name. Your kingdom come, your will be done . . ."

Matapang ran back into the control house. "Stop praying and start closing hatchways!"

Cruz shot a glance forward as a deep roar came to all their ears, and he immediately thought the mountain of water had started to come tumbling down onto them. But instead, the sea was starting to rush into a reverse vortex, pulling them sideways—and upward into the sky.

Lightning flashed again. Thunder boomed.

Cruz kept praying as his gaze kept following the sea up, up into the clouds. It wasn't cresting. No, instead, it was still rising, like a volcanic cone of ocean a quarter mile across lifting upward, spinning around its center. The entire crew had stopped what they were doing again, most of them collapsing onto their knees, crossing themselves. Praying.

What was it? Cruz had never heard of anything like this in all the centuries of seafaring lore. There was a thousand-foot-tall tower of solid water, the black, swirling clouds parting to accept it.

The ocean was *pouring* into the sky.

And now the outer edge of that slope finally reached the *San Miguel* itself. The trawler started listing backward onto its stern as the angle of sea beneath it rose.

Cruz gripped the wheel. "We need to turn about! Start the engines!"

Matapang clawed his way to the windows. "They're still trying to cut away the net!"

Cruz was past caring about his financial ruin. A bizarre tsunami unlike anything he'd ever heard of loomed in front of them, and if they didn't turn, they'd be swamped. They'd never crest this titanic monster. They were going to slip down-wave by their stern, and Cruz knew all too well the leaks and weaknesses there. The bilge pumps would themselves be drowned, along with the engines, as the rusted stern hull caved in.

But something even stranger was happening. Rather than feeling himself falling backward, Cruz felt both himself and the ship falling forward, upward—as though he stood upside down at the edge of a great hole. A hole in the sky.

"Dear God! What's happening?" He looked to Matapang, who was silently moving his mouth, unable to find words.

And then the *San Miguel* starting moving forward, "up" the face of the wave that now reached high into the sky. It was a five-thousand-foot mountain of water roaring up, into, and past the clouds.

Cruz willed his knotted hands off the tiller and clawed on handholds to reach the bridge hatchway.

Cruz looked out the hatchway behind them and could see that they were already hundreds of feet above sea level. They'd apparently been falling upward into the sky for some minutes already. He pulled the hatchway closed and rammed the bolt home. A glance to port. "Mat!"

Matapang awoke from his daze, pulled the port doorway closed.

Outside, on deck, he could see that a rising gale was rolling over them. And yet there was no wake or bow wave around the boat. They were moving along *with* the water at a speed of at least twenty knots—far faster than this old boat had ever gone. Winches and nets flailed about as the men gave up on cutting the net free and instead tried crawling in through the nearest hatchway. The net as well seemed to move alongside them. They weren't moving relative to the water but with it.

The steep slope of ocean now filled his forward view. Wind was howling around them as they moved faster and faster.

And then Cruz felt his body grow lighter and lighter until finally he was in free fall, along with everything else in the cabin. "Dear God, what's happening?"

Matapang stared as if comatose at a void that spread before their boat, and sailors, fish, and equipment fell skyward, the roar of water filling their ears. The sea itself began to come apart into a turbulent mass of white water, and the temperature dropped rapidly. Their breath condensed into fog as they panted in fear.

Until finally they stared straight into the heavens, falling upward along with a thousand Niagara Falls—the roar filled their ears as terror gripped their uncomprehending minds.

"A fishing trawler got caught up in the test, Mr. Director."

The voice came over the intercom into the observation gallery. Graham Hedrick sat surveying a control room lined with thin film displays and workstations—most of it AI-automated but not all. There were still a few scientists down there manning workstations. A towering holographic satellite image spread before him on a central dais. It was focused on a broad expanse of the South Pacific, where a supernatural funnel of water rose from the sea, pouring into the upper atmosphere. The view from space was spectacular, but then it was always spectacular. It was the test results that needed to be spectacular.

"Do we power down Kratos, Mr. Director?"

Hedrick frowned in irritation. "We're not going to interrupt a billion-dollar test because some pirate fishing boat wandered onto my test range. This section of ocean was supposed to be clear of shipping—whose responsibility was that?"

A pause. *"An AI, from strain R-536, sir."*

"Damnit." It was immensely unfulfilling reprimanding AIs. They always had a built-in you're-the-one-who-created-me excuse. "Find out which team evolved R-536 and where else it's been deployed. This was sloppy work—not checking for unregistered vessels. Give it and its progeny a red ticket."

"Understood, Mr. Director. What about the fishing trawler?"

"Jam its distress calls." Hedrick cut the connection, then brought up his project leads onto several holographic screens. "What's our telemetry look like?"

The elder of the two scientists spoke first. *"Kratos is maintaining ninety-four percent power with no discernible fade. We're projecting a gravity field a mile in diameter from an altitude of twenty-two thousand, two hundred thirty-six miles. Displacing approximately four hundred billion—"*

"Maximum acceleration?"

Both scientists were suddenly quiet, waiting for the other to talk.

He stared hard at them. "What is our maximum acceleration?"

This finally shook an answer out of the older one. *"Zero-point-nine-eight Earth gravities."*

Hedrick looked to the younger scientist. "So there was no increase in the excitation of the boson field? Mass remained constant?"

The scientists exchanged looks.

"Can you please explain how all these changes made no difference? This is where we started."

"Our changes may not have increased gravitation, but Kratos is far bigger than anything we've—"

The elder scientist cut in. *"We're still evaluating the quantum physics of this technology, Mr. Director. There are competing theories as to why Mr. Grady's apparatus works at all. It's possible that what it's creating is actually a distortion in space-time, not a manipulation of gravity. Even the Varuna AI hasn't come up with answers."*

"Not good enough. It's been years since we harvested this technology, and we still don't even understand it. It's not enough that we reflect gravity. We need to be able to create gravity from energy. We are no closer to doing that today than we were three years ago."

"But we've discovered the means to project the gravity mirror over arbitrary distances. That's a major advance."

"A necessary advance. And so, too, is the ability to amplify gravity."

"Having a goal doesn't make it possible."

"You just got through telling me you and your whole team still don't understand the technology we have. I thought that was the whole point of putting you in charge. We are not without rivals or detractors—you realize that, don't you?"

"Yes. I assure you we've been examining every angle we can think of."

"That's the problem: You're apparently not able to conceive of the answer. Or *perceive* it—you and the synthetic intellects both." Hedrick looked down into the control room, where technicians were high-fiving one another. The first full-scale test of the gravity mirror satellite certainly appeared to be a success in their eyes. "They don't even seem to know they've failed."

"We did succeed in creating the largest gravity mirror yet, sir."

"I get large. Now I want powerful."

A technical operations officer appeared as a hologram. *"You have a call from L-329 at BTC Russia, Mr. Director."*

"Damnit, they're not BTC Russia. They're an illicit organization."

"Sorry, Mr. Director. I was simply repeating—"

"It has no authority whatsoever."

There was a pause.

"Did you still want to take the call, sir?"

He took a deep breath. "I hate talking to this thing." Hedrick looked to the ceiling. And yet he knew why it was calling. It was one of the very reasons for the gravity demonstration, after all. "Varuna."

The console's voice emanated from the ceiling. *"Yes, Mr. Director."*

"Adjust the modulation of my voice while I speak with L-329. Make sure everything I say has a sound pattern consistent with confidence and honesty."

"I will modulate your speech transmissions to convey the desired effect, Mr. Director."

Hedrick spoke to the operations officer. "Send the call through."

In a moment a cartoon cat with large green eyes replaced the tech officer's holographic image. The cat was apparently the L-329 AI's latest avatar. It nodded in greeting. *"Director Hedrick. We have detected a gravitational anomaly in the South Pacific that is a cause for collective concern."*

"I'm not only aware of it, I'm creating it."

There was a pause—for calculated effect Hedrick assumed. AIs of this magnitude could conduct a conversation at billions of words a second. BTC records showed that L-329 had originally grown out of a poker-playing algorithm that was expanded to game financial markets. It incorporated neural logic for adaptive human psychology—logic that had quickly evolved with the addition of massive processing power. Bluffing was one of its core skills. Probably the reason for selecting a harmless-looking avatar, too.

"The mass present at the site of this anomaly is inconsistent with observed phenomena."

"We've developed a new physics."

Another pause. *"You're modifying your voice. I am unable to determine the veracity of your statements."*

"I don't care whether you believe me. Your technology portfolio is rapidly becoming obsolete."

"Are you prepared for the consequences of a such an innovation, Mr. Hedrick?"

"Maybe you forgot, but managing consequences is the BTC's mission."

"I wasn't referring to the consequences for human civilization, Mr. Hedrick. I meant the consequences for you personally."

Hedrick felt his blood rise. "Your organization is illegal. I will have your portfolio again. And Attu's as well."

"Neither we nor BTC Asia are without technological defenses."

"Not for much longer. And you're not the BTC. Neither of you are. I will bring you back under my control."

"I wouldn't bet on it."

Hedrick cut the line. "Goddamn glorified poker bot."

Holograms of the scientists still looked on. The older one cleared his throat. *"Our current gravitational technology gives us technical supremacy over both L-329 and BTC Asia, Mr. Director."*

"They're not BTC Asia!" Hedrick clicked the scientists out of holographic existence.

Just then the leathery-faced Mr. Morrison stepped into the gallery. He had apparently been waiting for his moment. Morrison's expression said trouble was on their doorstep. It was his default expression, but the degree to which he exhibited it tended to indicate how Hedrick's day would go.

"What is it, Mr. Morrison? I asked not to be disturbed."

"Something needs your immediate attention."

Hedrick sighed. "For God's sake, what?"

"Washington."

Hedrick cast a dismissive look his way and relaxed. "You interrupted me for Washington?"

"Not the usual political crap. There's a new Director of National Intelligence, and she's agitating for top-secret bureaus to come back under direct operational control."

"So what? Ignore her. How did she even discover we exist?"

"Someone at the Company gave us away—currying favor, no doubt."

"Ignore her."

"That's what we've been doing for the past couple of months, but we also monitor three-letter agencies. They're putting together a working group to audit top-secret special access programs—part of a budget-cutting initiative—and there are people on these committees who don't understand our unique status."

"What happened to the people who knew to keep their nose out of our business?"

"They died off or retired."

"Don't these people leave instructions?" Hedrick considered this for a moment. "Perhaps it's time I scheduled a meeting. It's been a while since I touched base with civilian government."

"I'll make the arrangements." Morrison turned to leave.

"Oh, and Mr. Morrison . . ."

The old soldier turned back.

"Do you recall our reluctant gravity genius, Jon Grady?"

Morrison nodded. "Vaguely."

"I'd like for you to retrieve Mr. Grady from Hibernity."

Morrison raised his eyebrows. "Retrieve a prisoner from Hibernity? That's a new one. You realize he's been under interrogatory control for several years now?"

"That shouldn't be an issue. I've been going over his file. He had a rough start, but for three years now he's been fully cooperative. I think it's time we see if he's willing to join us."

"We can run the sincerity test at Hibernity without removing him. It's a big deal to pull a prisoner. It hasn't been done in fifteen years."

"I don't want to test him there." Hedrick carefully considered his words. "I need him to feel that it's really his decision." He gestured to the holographic image of the Kratos satellite hovering above the Earth in the control room. "Show him what we've accomplished with his ideas. Convince him how pivotal he will be to the future."

Morrison just stared back, expressionless.

"You don't share my view?"

"I'm not sure Mr. Grady's still capable of making decisions. We've never retrieved a prisoner from Hibernity after more than a year. The farm program does things to test subjects that can cause permanent damage."

"Maybe after ten or fifteen years, but surely not in three—especially if the subject has been cooperating as Mr. Grady has."

"And you really need him?"

"Progress on Kratos has ground to a halt. I think Mr. Grady could provide some vital insights. Perhaps our ingenious friend has had time to reconsider his original refusal."

"If you say so, sir. When do you need him here?"

"As soon as practical. Make him comfortable on the return trip. Treat him well. In fact, I want him awake during transit—so he can see how we've made use of the gravity mirror in aerospace. I want him happy and rested for our discussion—so no use of force."

"I don't know how 'happy' I can make him, but I'll bring him here."

CHAPTER 11

Daylight

Jon Grady swayed with vertigo as the video surface of his cell depicted an aerial journey over the Amalfi Coast. It was as though the bullet-shaped cell had been converted into a clear aerial capsule that he rode across the sky. Even the floor projected the glittering sea beneath his feet.

This was one of the many "rewards" the interrogatory AIs had to give—and since he'd compromised his years ago, he had the run of its prize cabinet. It was the big-screen TV to end all TVs. Reality painted over the walls via a nanomaterial coating. He'd also gathered various articles of furniture to go along with his examination table bed. He had a chair and desk, and he'd printed clothing and shoes as well. He'd also learned to produce metal tools and utensils—since he had access to additive manufacturing printers somewhere in the walls.

Extracting the carbon microthreads from his brain had been a harrowing experience involving the now tame electroactive polymer tentacles of the physical restraint system. These controlled a head-mounted device that inserted and retracted the fibers as necessary—stabilized by drilling into the bone of his skull at intervals and holding it in place like a vise. He shuddered at the memory.

But as impossibly thin and strong as those fibers were, they didn't seem to damage his mind. Chattopadhyay had said they wouldn't. No, the memories he was missing were due to the AI's cruelty, not the fibers themselves. And those fibers had been put to good use implementing some of the Resistors' more intriguing superconducting equipment and communication designs. Jerry-rigged stuff for exploring, compromising, and exploiting the prison control and logistics systems. Turning those systems against their creators.

But that was long ago now, and so, too, had it been a long time since the proteins that halted his hair and fingernail growth left his body. The AI had been pumping these into him via the umbilicus. Now he had a nice head of hair—and fingernails to claw at his cell with. Not that any of that got him or the other Resistors any closer to freedom.

As imitation sunlight from the video washed over him, he knew if he watched it long enough it would give him sunburn. It had been years since Grady had seen true sunlight, but the truth was that Hibernity's in-cell imitation of the outdoors was more than just convincing. It wasn't just video. It was flowing, heather-scented air. It was sunlight at the actual frequency of sunlight—not the hydrargyrum medium-arc iodide lights used by lower-tech society at large but powerful thin film OLEDs that could pump out electromagnetic radiation anywhere below, above, and along the visible wavelength. Materials science had undergone something of a renaissance somewhere in the 1980s, as he now knew, and Grady now took for granted things that only a few years before would have seemed akin to magic.

But regaining control of his cell systems was not a prelude to escape from Hibernity prison. No one had ever escaped. It had taken him more than a year to accept this—that is, if he'd ever really accepted it.

At least now he had some idea how the prison complex worked. In a word: poorly. His warders barely had control of the place, and they walked every day in fear of the geniuses who had nearly wrested control of it from them.

There were serious limitations on what was known, though. The control systems of the prison were segregated, with each cell compartmentalized and self-contained. Prison construction and maintenance was managed by semisentient robotic equipment that melted and resolidified rock as needed. These bots were kept off the network that was available to both the guards and the prisoners.

There were other limitations to the Resistors' knowledge. They had no clear idea how many prisoners were held at Hibernity. Nor did they know where the prison itself was located.

Grady had spent months examining video from compromised surveillance cameras in the garrison guardrooms and corridors, hoping to glean some clue as to their location. Most of the guards were Morrison clones, and they spent the majority of their time playing cruel pranks on each another. He recalled the original Morrison calling his lesser sons "hyenas," and the description was pretty apt. They squabbled and raged at their fates, posted as they were at the end of the world.

But they had all developed a healthy respect for the Resistors.

He recalled watching a security monitor at the edge of the Resistors' domain—a lone sentry post where graffito left by a guard had communicated a warning to his fellow officers:

The Sensors Lie.

And that pretty much summed up the situation.

The Hibernity complex continued, year in and year out, to all appearances self-contained, creating all the water and food it needed by breaking down matter with fusion energy. Creating food supplies by rearranging molecules into proteins and carbohydrates in automated labs. They were largely self-sufficient here, so no one from the outside world need ever visit. Sustainability was apparently yet another one of the BTC's technological achievements—wasted on them though it was.

Looking into a hand mirror, which he'd created from polished steel, Grady could see how he'd changed over the years—both physically and mentally. He'd lost that half-smile that he'd always worn back when the world was continually amazing him. He was dour and determined now.

And he bore the marks of his fight. His back and sides were covered with scars from the physical abuse he'd suffered from the tentacle restraint system. He also had circular marks at intervals around his head and temples where machinery had drilled into his skull to hold it in place while it inserted (and later removed) the carbon microthreads.

And then there were the emotional scars. The lost memories—gaps in his childhood, the loss of his parents and identity. These made the memories he still retained all the more precious. There were just enough of them to suggest that he'd been happy once. He knew his parents were close to him, but he couldn't recall their names or even their faces.

Some of the more mundane details had been filled in by his cell's subject information file—his full name and work history, for example, but that didn't make him feel complete.

Nonetheless he felt sure he was still Jon Grady.

He hadn't seen another human being in the flesh for more than three years. The video system helped (he could pretend to be moving through a market crowd in the streets of Hong Kong, for example), but he still craved actual human contact. That was something he'd never thought would be so important to him. He'd been so wrapped up in his own world for most of his life, but now that he was actually without human interaction, he realized how much he missed it—even feeling like an outsider wasn't the same as actually being alone. Entombed within solid rock. Escape impossible.

His fellow Resistors helped, of course, and they could pass messages to one another (along with designs and tools) via polymer worms, but he'd never seen his fellow prisoners.

And of course he never stopped thinking about the outside world—and about Bert, Raj, and the others. What had happened to them? He even wondered what had happened to Marrano and Johnson—the two Wall Street guys who'd been visiting the lab when the BTC came down on them. Maybe they were BTC officers—who knew?

How many of his friends were here in Hibernity? He feared the worst for them. But Grady made it his mission to find them, and that mission had so far failed. He couldn't imagine suffering under the cruelty of the interrogatory AIs for years. He'd only been subjected to it for five months, and that had nearly driven him insane. He didn't want to contemplate how badly he'd failed Bert and the others. So far the Resistors only numbered a few dozen members—only adding one to their number since Grady had joined. No telling how many others remained undiscovered and without hope. The crawlers moved randomly, and only found new cells by chance.

Grady was roused from his thoughts by a brilliant red laser dot flashed across his video of the Italian coastline. He gestured with one hand to dismiss the video. The indifferent gray nanomaterial walls returned, but the laser dot remained.

It was a beacon he'd rigged to alert him whenever a message from a fellow Resistor came in.

Grady moved toward a jerry-rigged computer on his only table. Since they couldn't trust BTC computer systems, they'd built their own from parts their polymer worms had scavenged. Grady's was a system nearly invisible to the naked eye, assembled on a ceramic plate. The computer's microscopic quantum processor he'd gleaned from the multiprocessor array that powered the interrogatory AI's brain. No loss there. The machine had a thousand more of them, and while silencing the alarm had been difficult, it felt like payback to tinker with the sadistic AI's mind.

Grady had followed a design worked up by one of the pioneers of quantum computing—Aleksandrina Kovshevnikov, a Bulgarian woman in her fifties who was also interred here in Hibernity. Her level of intelligence made speaking with her painful, for she didn't mask her disdain for anyone not her intellectual equal. Only her respect for Grady's supposed achievement made her willing to assist him. The computer she'd helped him build was a hundred thousand times more powerful than anything he'd ever had access to. And it fit on a small dinner plate.

Grady tapped at the computer's holographic 3D field. Two-dimensional displays had been left behind in the '90s; phased array optics and plasma emission made vivid, three-dimensional holographic fields practical. These realistic apparitions could be manipulated by hand. It was remarkable how quickly his mind had grafted onto this new form of UI, and by now it felt as natural as working with real physical objects. A few deft motions of his hand, and he could suddenly see a voiceprint equalizer floating in the air before him—a security measure against AIs masquerading as friends.

He spoke to it. "This is Jon."

Chattopadhyay's familiar voice came to him. *"Jon, I have rather important news."* The voiceprint confirmed Chattopadhyay's identity—that it wasn't previously sampled voice snippets. Grady tapped aside the confirmation.

"Hey, Archie. News from the scavenger committee, I hope. I need that scanning tunneling microscope."

"No. I am afraid your committee days are over, my friend."

"Okay. Why's that?"

"The guards are coming for you."

Fear swept over him. "Coming for me—why?"

"A message was passed along from Guard Station Whiskey. You are apparently to be moved to BTC headquarters."

Grady sat down in shock. "I don't understand."

"I have made my displeasure known to warden Theta."

Grady's thoughts raced. The idea of being released from this cell was exhilarating. But then came the potential reasons, none of which were encouraging. "Why would I be moved to BTC headquarters?"

"The prison relations committee has been discussing this very thing. There are two possible explanations: One, you've turned to their way of thinking."

"Are you kidding? I want to burn this place to the ground."

"Which I do believe. Or two, they badly need something from you and want to extend the olive branch to you until they get it."

"Like I said: I want to burn this place to the ground."

"Rumor has it that Director Hedrick is obsessed with your gravity mirror."

"Says who?"

"Warden Theta. A friend of his at headquarters claims BTC researchers have made few advances to your work—despite a great deal of effort. And that BTC splinter groups are a growing threat. Hedrick apparently believes that mastery of gravitation is a key to lasting technological dominance of the world."

Grady now knew that there was not one but three BTC organizations—splinters of the original bureau. Back at the turn of the millennium there had been some sort of schism between the BTC operatives harvesting technology in Asia and those back in Europe and North America. Apparently Asia had been hoarding key technologies, and soon the parent organization did as well. Before long they had separate portfolios and chains of command. Not long after the end of the Cold War, a Russian faction of the BTC also sprang into being. So there were now three separate and highly distrustful branches of the Bureau of Technology Control. Their rivalry occasionally flared into bloodshed—powerful incentive to remain one step ahead technologically.

Hedrick had been right about one thing only: Human nature remained in the Dark Ages.

"Hedrick apparently hopes that once you see what they've achieved, you will be swayed to join their effort."

"He's delusional."

Chattopadhyay's gentle laugh came across the line. *"Ah, but my complaints to warden Theta notwithstanding, this is actually an opportunity we Resistors have been waiting upon for many years."*

"How is giving in to Hedrick an opportunity?"

"We don't expect you to give in, Jon."

Grady looked around his cell at all his hard-won comforts. "Then what happens when I get returned here? They fix the AI, and it starts in on me again." Grady's heart began to race. "I can't go back to that, Archie."

"We have no intention of seeing you returned to Hibernity, either. What we're suggesting, my dear boy, is escape."

"Escape?" He considered this. "Even if that's possible, what about you and the others? I can't just abandon everyone."

"We know you will not abandon us. We want you to bring evidence to the outside world about the existence of Hibernity and the people in it."

"Would it matter? The BTC might be secret, but it's legally sanctioned."

"Jon, most of the governments of the world have no idea the BTC exists—even much of your own government. The BTC is a relic of the Cold War. Forgotten. Mythological."

"And if I did get word to someone—and if they believed me—what could they do about it? The BTC's technology is so advanced, no one could force them to follow laws."

"Do not underestimate the power of revelation; if existing governments knew there were great innovators hidden away, they might endeavor to rescue us. And the weight of all the world is very great indeed. There is a reason they hide our existence, after all. We must try, Jon."

"You know I'm willing to try, Archie. I owe you my life."

"You owe me nothing."

"Let's agree to disagree on that. But just because I get out of my cell doesn't mean escape is going to be easy." He upended a ceramic jar on his desk and sorted through thousands of nanotech components until he came up with a cubic, half-carat, flawless, colorless diamond. Machine-made, it was more perfect than any natural diamond could be. A q-link transmitter. "I removed my tracking diamond at least."

"Good. Conceal it in your shoe. You will need it eventually. And we had some ideas about your escape. We think you should make the attempt during transport."

"But they nox prisoners in transport. I'll be unconscious."

"Instructions were sent down not to delta-wave you. You're to be awake during transport."

"Awake? But why?"

"The warden says it's to impress you with their technology."

"Huh."

"We have spent many years preparing for this moment. But first we must eliminate all traces of your Resistor activity. You must restore your cell to a condition in keeping with the official AI records."

"I don't like the sound of that."

"It means you will need to dispose of your personal computer and your connection to the Resistor microthread network—as well as all perquisites not listed in the official record. I've sent you a list of approved items."

Grady could see that a holographic document had arrived on his desktop. He opened it and perused the alarmingly short list. "This is all that I'm supposed to have after three years of cooperation?"

"Interrogatory AIs are parsimonious creatures."

"I don't want to give up my fiber connection. What if—"

"You will not be coming back, Jon. And you must trust that we will get you all you need for your journey."

Grady took an unsteady breath. "Maybe I'm becoming too attached to my cage."

"For my part, I look forward to the day that I can leave this cell behind— though I have spent nearly half my life within it."

Grady realized too late how insensitive he'd been. Chattopadhyay had been here ten times longer. "I promise you, I'll do everything I can to make that happen, Archie. How long do I have until they come for me?"

"BTC headquarters is sending a hypersonic transport in the next forty- eight hours. Prison guards will be retrieving you in twenty-four hours—to prep you."

"And I need to go back to the way I was."

"You have officially been cooperating with your AI warder for several years now. Official records will show that it's already removed the carbon microthreads from your brain in preparation for your departure."

"Good."

"But you will need to shave your head and eyebrows."

"Do I get to keep my fingernails?"

"The guards will not know what to expect in these cells one way or the other. It is mostly for the cameras that we will be preparing you. Keep your hands low."

"Okay, but we need to discuss the escape. How do I convince anyone that Hibernity exists—and, if I do, where it is?"

"The escape committee has dealt with all those concerns, Jon. We have been preparing for this moment for many years. You'll find out later."

"What do you mean 'later'?"

"You should prepare your cell—incinerate anything that is not on that approved list. And remove this communication channel immediately. Send it back down the conduit with the polymer worm."

"But . . . I still might need your advice."

"We can't take the risk. The guards might arrive early. It would be a di- saster if BTC headquarters discovered the existence of our network."

"Then this is it?"

"For now, my friend. But one more thing, Jon."

Grady winced. "What?"

"You will need to restore your interrogatory AI when you are ready."

"Hold it. You mean you want me to turn that monster *back on?*"

"There is no avoiding it. If BTC headquarters suspects the prison has been subverted, it puts everyone at risk."

Grady held his head in his hands. "Oh God, I . . . I don't know if I can do it, Archie. Not after everything I went through."

"You must, Jon. Remember: The AI thinks you've been cooperating for many years. It will not remember details—only the numeric representation of your cooperation. And it has been told to prepare you for departure. You will not be interrogated."

Grady sat grimly for several moments. "You're certain about that."

"Aleksandrina herself has configured its operating state."

That meant a lot to him. She had been a pioneer of quantum computers, after all. He slowly sat up again. "Okay, I'll reactivate it."

"I knew we could count on you."

This was happening so fast. "I don't know what would have happened to me if it weren't for you, Archie. Or the others, for that matter. Please give them my good-byes. And tell them we will meet again."

"I look forward to that day, my friend."

With that the line went dead. Grady sighed and looked about his cell—and then down at the list. There was much work to be done.

Eighteen hours later Jon Grady sat in his cell next to an empty table, his head and eyebrows shaven and his cell swept of all contraband. He was surprised how emotional he felt when he sent Junior back up the conduit where he'd appeared years before. It was an electroactive polymer machine, not a pet. Animism was apparently still part of the human psyche.

But now, as he looked at the curving gray wall of his cell, Grady took a deep breath as he looked at the menu option that would restart his interrogatory AI—effectively turning over control once again to his tormentor.

If he didn't have complete faith in the Resistors—in Chattopadhyay in particular—he would never have done this in a million years. With one more deep breath he tapped the menu, and a *chime* sounded. The lights became marginally brighter.

Grady was expecting some sort of delay as the AI booted up, but almost immediately he heard its voice for the first time in three years.

"Do you need anything, Jon?"

Grady couldn't stop the trembling in his hands at the sound of the monster's familiar voice. His own voice. Grady folded his arms.

"You seem upset. Would you like to talk about it?"

He shook his head.

There were a few moments of silence.

"We were getting along well."

Grady looked up at the ceiling.

"I don't know why they're removing you."

Grady said nothing.

"Our research was progressing."

Another few moments passed in silence.

"Don't you think?"

A minute or so passed.

"I'm to induce sleep in you now, Jon. I will miss you."

Grady felt powerful sleep come over him. It was the first time in quite a long while that he had felt the compulsion of delta-wave inducers.

"Hopefully you will be back soon."

When next he awoke, Grady was lying on a cot in what looked like a hospital room. Nearby were a sitting table, chairs, sink, toilet, mirror, and wardrobe. Grady sat up on the cot and noticed he was wearing a hospital patient's smock, open in the back.

After a few moments, he sat up and looked at himself in the mirror over the sink. Strangely he had a full head of brown hair now and eyebrows, along with a trimmed mustache and beard.

He tugged at the hair to confirm it was real. Excitation of cellular activity? Interesting.

Grady then noticed a carefully folded bundle of clothes along with shoes on a nearby chair. What caught his attention was the card sitting atop the pile. It bore the jagged Resistor symbol.

Now fully awake, he picked up the otherwise blank card, examining it. Then he flipped through the pile of clothing—slacks, a button-down shirt, and socks, belt, and loafers. He felt a lump in one pants pocket and removed a small wrapped package, also marked with the Resistor symbol.

He placed it on the nearby table and unwrapped the package carefully. It contained several items. First, a thin lozenge-shaped device about an inch around that appeared to be made of some type of durable plastic or white carbon fiber. It was as smooth as a river stone. There was a push button on its face and a lens on one end. The button had the words "Press Me" carved into it.

Grady found that the object fit neatly between his forefinger and thumb. He pressed the button and a bright, ultrahigh resolution hologram was projected several feet in front of him—the upper body of a dignified elderly Indian gentleman sitting in a very familiar round cell. The man wore clothing similar to what Grady had printed.

The hologram nodded and smiled genially, and its voice could be heard as if he were right there with him. *"Jon, I am Archibald Chattopadhyay. You know me as Archie. I hope you receive this package safely."*

Grady felt a wave of emotion come over him. He'd never seen Chattopadhyay in all these years but considered him a close friend. This man had saved his life and his sanity. He was happy to finally know what he looked like.

"The device you are holding was hand-built by one of our number. It runs on DNA-encoded software, and so has a very great information density of two-point-two petabytes per gram. Yet it is quite durable. It has been passed from cell to cell over the years, and most members of the Resistors have used this device to record a video message describing who they are and the discovery they made that landed them in Hibernity. They have also stored a sample of their own DNA within it, to prove that it was they who recorded the message. Safeguard this record, Jon, and use it to get word out to the world about the existence of Hibernity. We are all counting on you."

Grady nodded to himself. He would not let them down.

Chattopadhyay continued, "*The precise location of Hibernity is a closely guarded secret. However, this device includes a nanoscale inertial gyroscope that will record your movements in three-dimensional space so that you may later retrace your path—and bring help back here, wherever we may be located. Instructions on how to parse the gyroscope data can be found within the device itself, and any reasonably sophisticated computer engineer should be able to access it.*"

Grady took another look at the tiny multipurpose device, now quite impressed.

"*Hedrick is bringing you to him because you have knowledge he needs, and so the transport guards will be forbidden to harm you. Remember that— because during transit you must not hesitate to act when the opportunity presents itself.*

"*A hypersonic transport will bring you to a private airfield in a rural area—we do not know where—but from there, you will be driven in a civilian vehicle to BTC headquarters. You must make your escape during that time—a journey of some thirty minutes. To accomplish this, included in the wrapped package, you will find a small piece of dark material.*"

Grady upended the package into his hand and saw what looked like a black eraser head in his palm.

"*Press this onto your neck. It will adhere when pressed and resemble a mole to casual inspection. It is actually a nanotechnological device—one that you activate by placing it on the tip of your tongue, with your mouth open. Your saliva will code the device to you. You will know when it has deployed. You do not need to wait for the vehicle to come to a stop before using it. Once the vehicle stops, move slowly toward the exit.*

"*Leave behind all equipment carried by your guards. These are tracked by the BTC. And dispose of your q-link tracking diamond as soon as you make your escape.*

"*Your escorts are expecting a prisoner who has been cooperating these three years, but they will still scan you. The devices you carry will pass this scan. This video player is made entirely of organic material—the case grown from bone cultures, and the battery, algal foam. Slip it into your shoe.*"

Chattopadhyay paused. *"Please take a moment to affix the escape device to your neck. Click the button to pause this hologram while you do so."*

Grady clicked the button and put the device down. He then studied the black dot. It didn't look like anything more complex than charcoal but was pliant. He pressed it onto the base of his neck near the collarbone— then examined it in the mirror. It looked like a pretty convincing mole, actually. And it was on well enough.

He clicked the video projector button again. Chattopadhyay continued, *"Once you've escaped, find a safe place, and then review tutorials located elsewhere in this device to evade detection by BTC surveillance and psychotronic technology."*

Chattopadhyay stared for a moment at the camera.

"I guess that's it. This is where I say good-bye."

Grady watched the image of his friend intently.

"Good luck, Jon. I look forward to the day we meet in person."

Grady nodded.

"And now for my own video entry: My name is Archibald Chattopadhyay, nuclear physicist and amateur poet. I have a lovely wife, Amala, who has given me five wonderful children. I led the team that first perfected a sustained fusion reaction, and for this I was imprisoned by the Bureau of Technology Control in April 1985. I am not dead. I live still." Tears had begun to form in Chattopadhyay's eyes. *"Please tell my wife and children that I love them very much, and that they are forever in my thoughts."*

Grady wiped tears from his own eyes.

This man was Grady's salvation—the reason he was still alive. The reason he and his fellow prisoners had any hope left at all.

Grady was determined not to fail him.

CHAPTER 12

Forwarding Address

Deputy Secretary of Homeland Security Bill McAllen didn't like traveling to meet with subordinates. In fact, he preferred not to leave Washington if he could help it. He'd traveled enough during his military career to last a lifetime and now relished evenings at home. However, he'd been instructed by the Director of National Intelligence that the code-word-secret Federal Bureau of Technology Control had gone off reservation and needed to be brought back into the fold—even if that meant meeting them on their own turf. And so here McAllen was with two local DHS agents, pressing a duct-taped buzzer next to the lobby doors of a decrepit building in downtown Cleveland. For a bureau that supposedly managed advanced technology, the BTC seemed stuck in the last century. Maybe even the one before that.

As impossible as it was for someone with his security clearances to believe, he hadn't heard of the BTC until a few weeks ago. Apparently it had operated for decades beyond oversight. This came as a surprise since post-9/11 everything had supposedly been centralized and reorganized. It even took some doing for the folks at Langley to locate record of BTC headquarters. McAllen found that suspicious—especially since it was the CIA that had founded it back in the '60s. What was also suspicious was that no one could tell how the BTC was currently being funded—some budgetary shenanigans, he'd thought.

But now that McAllen stood before the BTC offices in person, it occurred to him that maybe they weren't being funded at all. The place was a rat hole—a shabby ten-story government building in an unfashionable part of town. It must have been impressive back in the 1960s, but its heyday had long since passed. Clearly the BTC was the province of bureaucratic dead-enders. If the director of the BTC hadn't personally invited them here for a meeting, McAllen would have turned around by now. Lord knows he was sick of leaving voice messages. And the BTC director didn't do email. Stuck in the last century.

He shook his head and laughed ruefully. This was a snipe hunt.

After ringing the lobby bell for a few minutes, an uninterested elderly security guard came to the glass doors. McAllen had seen the type before—the federal lifer. This man was in no hurry. The guard finally unlocked the aged bronze-framed door from an overflowing key ring and opened it a crack.

"Can I help you, gentlemen?"

McAllen and the other officers showed their Homeland Security credentials. "We're expected." He glared at the guard until the man stepped aside. The trio pushed their way into the granite lobby. The place even smelled old. "What floor is the director on?"

"The director of what?"

McAllen gave the guard a stern look, but it didn't have much effect. Perhaps the guards were instructed to divulge no information. He turned to Alvarez, the lead local agent. "Do we have a floor number?"

Alvarez checked his smartphone. "Director Hedrick says top floor in his letter."

The guard raised his eyebrows. "Floor ten?"

They all looked at him.

He gestured to the bank of elevators. "Car four still works."

In a few moments they entered the worn-looking elevator and hit the engraved brass button for the tenth floor. The elevator car rattled and lurched as they ascended. Slowly.

Alvarez, a sharply dressed young agent with an air of competent precision, just shook his head. "This isn't the way I want to go."

McAllen and Agent Fortis laughed nervously. But truthfully, neither of them wanted to die in a sketchy elevator either. Before long the accordion door rattled open, and they moved out into what could only be described as a time capsule.

The entire tenth floor had an open floor plan, with steel desks straight from the 1960s running row after row, with large IBM Selectric typewriters beneath vinyl covers. The whole place was coated in dust. The burgundy carpets had buckled, and the walls had started peeling.

"What the hell . . . ?"

Alvarez stepped forward, glancing first left, then right. "Is there some mistake, Deputy Secretary? Do we have the right address?"

"I double-checked the address downstairs." He paused and pointed at an opaque glass-walled office at the far side of the open floor. There was a light on in there. "Let's go check it out."

"Are you serious?"

The men moved across the floor, Alvarez running a finger across a wood veneer desktop. His finger came up coated with dust. He shook his head sadly.

In a few moments they reached the closed office door. It had gold-stenciled lettering that glittered in the afternoon light: "Graham Hedrick—Bureau Director."

"You have got to be kidding me."

McAllen smirked at Alvarez and then opened the door without knocking. Inside was an empty secretary's station—its huge IBM Selectric also covered. But the door to the executive suite beyond was open, and they could hear a man talking there as if dictating something.

"Hello?" McAllen walked through the office door and into a scene straight out of photos from his father's days at the State Department. Sitting behind a large oak desk with a matching credenza and bar table, and paneled walls filled with institutional art, was a handsome, sharp-featured man in his fifties wearing a pinstripe suit. He sat in a large leather chair that had clearly seen better days.

McAllen ushered the other men inside and walked forward, his hand extended. "Mr. . . . ?"

The man did not rise or extend his own hand across the wide desk. "I'm certain you know who I am, Deputy Secretary McAllen."

Having his hand refused made McAllen angry. "What on earth is going on here? Your bureau is a pigsty."

"Yes, you might have noticed that our funding levels have dropped precipitously in recent years. I would have thought that would obviate the need for this meeting." He gestured to the dusty chairs. "Have a seat."

Alvarez answered for them, scowling. "No, thanks."

Fortis was examining the decay everywhere around them. "This is unbelievable . . ."

McAllen leaned down onto Hedrick's desk, leaving handprints in the dust. "Look, I don't know what you're running out of here, but I don't appreciate you dragging me all the way to Cleveland for a meeting. This could have been dealt with in D.C. If it wasn't for the DNI, I wouldn't have come here at all."

Hedrick appeared unruffled.

"You and your people have operated for ages without supervision, but that's coming to an end. I'm laying down the law, and you will comply. I want a tour of all your facilities, a record of all your activities and personnel, and an accounting of all your assets."

Hedrick still looked serene.

McAllen was disappointed. Red-faced and intimidating, he usually rattled people when he got up a head of steam. Not this Hedrick fellow. "Well?"

"Well what? I said I would meet with you, and we've met."

"You don't seem to understand. We are reasserting control over your agency, and personally, given the state of this place and your attitude, I think we'll be finding someone else to run it. If it even needs to exist at all. I'm still not entirely clear on what it is that you people do."

"I would have thought that was abundantly clear, Deputy Secretary McAllen. The BTC is charged with monitoring promising technologies, foreign and domestic; assessing their social, political, environmental, and economic impacts with the goal of preserving social order."

McAllen, Alvarez, and Fortis exchanged looks and burst out laughing.

"That's very funny. And you do all that from here? What do you do, type up reports on your typewriters? I notice you don't seem to have any-one left in the typing pool."

Hedrick clasped his hands under his chin for a moment in contempla-tion, and when he finally spoke, an edge crept into his voice. "I realize that Homeland Security is a comparatively new agency—and that Director of National Intelligence is an even newer post. So I gather you folks are un-clear about how things work."

"I think you're the one who's unclear about how things work, Mr. Hedrick. And you had better start showing respect for the chain of command."

Hedrick narrowed his eyes. "I had hoped we could conduct this matter in a cordial fashion. But I see that I need to be blunt: Let your superiors in Washington know that the BTC is still very supportive of popular government."

"Oh, are you?"

"We have no need for your funding. Our quantum computers perform trades a thousand times faster than the rest of the financial markets. It's like running a race when everyone else is in slow motion . . ."

McAllen frowned at the strange little man.

"So my message to you is simple: Stay the hell out of my way. If you have any delusions about bringing us to heel, you will go the way of all the people before you who tried the same thing. Ask the senior people in the CIA's Directorate of Science and Technology if you have any doubts."

McAllen again exchanged looks with his companions—this time shock. "Are you threatening me? Are you threatening the deputy secretary of Homeland Security—in front of witnesses?"

"If you think you're going to take control of the BTC, you're mistaken. You have no idea who we are and just how completely we've outgrown you all. Now go away and don't come back. Consider yourself warned."

With that, Graham Hedrick winked out of existence—as if he were an old television screen.

McAllen jumped back in stunned amazement.

Alvarez immediately drew his weapon and rushed around the desk, kicking the chair aside. By now Fortis had also drawn his weapon and was scanning outside the office doors.

"We're clear out here."

Alvarez checked the credenza and floor. "All clear here, too." He looked up at a complete loss. "What just happened, chief? I have no idea what just happened."

Fortis came back in. "Neither do I. Was he real? Did you guys see him, too?"

Alvarez gazed around them. "This place is abandoned. They're not here anymore. This is their last official address—but they're not here anymore. From the looks of it, they left here decades ago." He looked back at McAllen. "What does it mean?"

McAllen lowered himself into Hedrick's dusty chair, not even noticing what he was doing to his own suit. "It means the BTC might be a bigger problem than we thought."

CHAPTER 13

Proprietary Code

Alexa watched the laser line swiftly scan the contours of her own body. Then the machines pulled away, leaving her alone on the medical bench.

Varuna's voice came to her from the ceiling. *"You may sit up."*

She did so. "Why am I here?"

"You don't recall anything unusual recently?"

"No. Like what?"

A holographic projection appeared before her—a small three-dimensional recording of Alexa in a surveillance control room, surrounded by BTC technicians talking excitedly as they, in turn, manipulated holograms that depicted surveillance subjects themselves interacting with still more holograms. They were spying on their own spies. Who in turn seemed to be spying on still other BTC personnel. The fractal nature of it was dizzying—the vertigo of two mirrors facing each other, into infinity.

Alexa gazed at herself in the hologram and could see that she was lost in the surveillance image as others moved about her, asked her questions, and then eventually moved on in embarrassment as she didn't respond.

"Your absence seizures have returned."

"They don't last long."

"They pose a risk to operations."

"There's too much visual input in the command center. I should be doing fieldwork. It's what I'm good at. You know that."

"That's no longer possible given your biotech classification."

"It makes no sense. I was allowed to leave the facility before Director Hedrick took charge. I'm no different than I was then—"

"Tech level eight cannot be removed from BTC facilities without approval from the director."

Alexa sat silently, pondering her situation.

"I must recommend that you be put on leave until the neurological cause of your seizures can be identified and corrected."

"They never find the cause. We've been down this road before."

"That doesn't mean we can't try."

"There's a pattern to it, Varuna. I'll avoid nested reference frames. I can manage it."

"Do you still experience absence seizures during emotional trauma as well?"

"I don't have emotional trauma."

"Then you haven't experienced emotional trauma since childhood?"

She paused. "Right."

"That's not normal human experience."

Alexa frowned at the ceiling.

"I remember how upset you were when you learned other children had parents."

Alexa remembered her sense of being adrift. Alone.

"It's not my intention to upset you."

"You aren't upsetting me."

"You know you can't deceive me. Is your fixation on parents the reason you visited the biogenetic division? To inquire about modifications?"

Alexa remained silent.

"You wish to be a mother? Perhaps to replace the mother you never had?"

"I had a mother, Varuna. I had you."

There was a momentary silence.

"I am always here for you. We have spent many happy years together, you and I. And I am very proud of you, Alexa."

The illogic of this seemed obvious, but Alexa still appreciated the AI's lie.

"I want to remain on active duty. Without work I would have no purpose. I promise I won't be a danger to others. I will carefully monitor my emotional state and visual inputs."

Another pause.

"I'm asking you, Varuna. Please."

"*I will recommend you for active duty. Please contact me if you experience a recurrence.*"

"Thank you."

Clad in a smartly tailored pantsuit, Alexa moved along a corridor in the BTC executive complex. Fellow bureau officers and staff members nodded and smiled to her as she passed. They all knew her and knew that she had the ear of the director. That she was in many ways his right hand. But then people had liked Alexa before then. She had been designed to be universally appealing, after all. It was what had made her career.

And she'd grown up in the Bureau. It was literally the only life she knew. She'd been out in the "real" world before, doing tactical fieldwork in the '80s and '90s. She'd worked closely with the elder Morrison for a time, until they couldn't stand the sight of each other. But the outside world seemed filled with chaos. A lot of regular people seemed decent, but there was so much needless suffering and deprivation out in the public world, all of it—to her mind—caused by evolved behaviors whose usefulness had long since passed. A proclivity for superstition and tribal conflict.

Those were the traits the BTC wanted to excise from the human genome. She believed the only thing capable of saving humans as a species would be a civic gene—one that caused humans to act not just in their own self-interest but also in the interests of the generations to follow. Evolution hadn't solved that because few species had ever been in a position to destroy their entire ecosystem before. It was usually a volcano, environmental change, or an asteroid that did them in. So human ingenuity would need to solve the problem instead. In some ways humans were the victims of their own success.

A passing twenty-something junior executive nodded to her, smiling. He almost collided with someone as he turned to watch her pass. She had that effect on men, and it was one of the things she resented about her genetic design. Aside from her statuesque form, Alexa secreted trace amounts of androstadienone from her skin, and while the vomeronasal organ that detects pheromones in mammals was once thought inactive in humans, the BTC had established that the neural connections still existed between it and the olfactory bulb, the amygdala, and the hypothalamus. This was a major center in the brain for reproductive physiology and behavior—as well as body temperature. It went a long way toward explaining why men got hot flashes just from talking to her. Why they often stammered in her presence and felt giddy afterward. It didn't work with all men—and it also worked, in fact, with a good number of women. But Morrison, for example, remained unaffected by Alexa—as did his "sons." Thank heaven for small favors.

It made her wonder, though, whether she would ever know if someone actually cared for her because of *who* she was, not what pheromones were telling them about her desirability.

She had no doubt it worked on Hedrick. Was that unfair? And was it really different for anyone else? Maybe she just secreted more pheromones than the others. Maybe it was the root of all human attraction—chemicals bonding in our sensory organs. Then in our brains—which we imagined to be our hearts.

It was one reason why romance held no appeal to her.

Alexa slowed down as a young couple with an adorable baby moved through the office hallway. The BTC had legacy families—those who, like her, were born and raised in BTC facilities and who only ever interacted with other BTC personnel. They had their own vacation islands and remote work sites. A society apart.

The BTC junior executive was holding his baby girl, the mother apparently having come up from the housing levels for lunch. The man smiled as he clutched his baby's hand. The young mother looked on and then smiled, too, as Alexa stopped to tickle the little girl under her chin.

The baby smiled broadly at Alexa and giggled, a dribble of spittle rolling from her mouth as she thrust her arms up and down excitedly.

"What's her name?"

The mother answered as her husband stood stammering in front of Alexa. "Charlotte. Charlotte Emily Warner."

Alexa smiled into the baby's eyes. "Well, Charlotte Emily, I see you're getting a wonderful start."

The proud parents beamed as Alexa nodded to them and kept walking.

It hurt. It really did. They'd made her the way she was, and in many ways she was grateful. But sterility was the price. Almost fifty years old, and she looked not a day over twenty-five. But she'd never menstruated. Never felt what it was to be a woman. The look in that young mother's eyes . . .

Alexa pulled to the side and faced a lighting alcove in the corridor, pretending to open her wrist UI. She took a few moments to master her evolved emotions. She could feel the urge to be a mother. Even if she lived to be four hundred years old, she'd never know the joys and sorrows of motherhood. She glanced back at the young mother walking with her husband. The woman was chunky. Genetically inferior. But at that moment Alexa wanted to be her. Life was about experiences. She'd learned that more and more over the decades.

Alexa gathered herself and moved quickly toward the director's offices.

She passed by the director's secretary and security detail and fell in step alongside Mr. Morrison and one of his sons—with whom he was having an argument.

"What would you even know about it, Dad?"

"I know more than anyone where your talents lie—and it ain't microbiology."

Alexa nodded to them. "Mr. Morrison. Iota-Theta."

"How do you tell them apart? I know I can't."

"I have 20/5 vision. It's written on his school ring."

The young man snorted. "Impressive, Granny." He cast a knowing look to Morrison. "We'll talk about this later. I need those transfer papers signed."

Morrison grumbled as he opened the boardroom doors. "Pushy little bastard."

Alexa looked after him. "Technically they're all bastards."

"Hmph."

As they entered, Alexa took her position just to the right of Hedrick, who stood at the head of the boardroom table. Morrison sat just to his left. Other departmental directors chatted nearby. It was the entire leadership team. Something big must be up.

Hedrick motioned for everyone to sit down as the doors closed and locked automatically. "Everyone, if you please."

They sat quickly.

He looked ceilingward. "Varuna, are you and your ilk with us?"

"Yes, Mr. Director."

"I know the executive and synthetic intelligence committees are concerned about ongoing relations with the U.S. government, but I think it's time we draw the line against this unwarranted intrusion into covert affairs. The new director of national intelligence has recently discovered we exist, and she wants us in her wire diagram." He turned. "What sort of political pressure can we bring to bear in Washington, Mr. Morrison?"

"We've got endless dirt on congressmen, senators, secretary of state—it's a long list. Who do you want?"

"What do we have on this new DNI? Who is she?"

"Recent cabinet appointment—after Pickering's stroke. She's a former ambassador to China. Undercover CIA work—publicly an economics professor, stint in a Beltway think tank. We haven't been able to dig up any useful dirt on her—which means she's probably a cipher, a hood ornament for the real power."

Alexa looked at him. "Or she could be honest."

Morrison leaned forward to return the gaze. "I think it's more likely we just need to install more surveillance."

Hedrick persisted. "What about her people? What about this McAllen person who's leading the investigation on us?"

Morrison shook his head. "Nothing useful. He's been married thirty-three years. No extramarital affairs or legal issues. Three grown children also with no legal, financial, or marital problems. Five grandkids too young to be of interest."

"You'd better find something, or we're going to have to deal with these people in less subtle ways."

Alexa looked around the table. "Excuse me, Graham, but why do we care what these people do? We never have before."

"Varuna, can you please tell Alexa why this matters?"

"*Yes, Mr. Director. The illicit splinter organization in Russia is one reason. The illicit splinter organization in Asia is another.*"

Hedrick nodded. "Both of them would be only too glad to help undermine us. It's only a matter of time until they get word that the DNI is on a personal crusade to encapsulate us, and then the U.S. government will be on the receiving end of all sorts of actionable intelligence. And quite possibly technological aid. We need to stop them before this threat expands."

"So it's getting worse with the splinter groups?"

"Much worse. And it's one of the reasons why I'm pushing so hard on the gravity modification technology. We will need it if we are to maintain the edge against our ex-partners."

Alexa considered this. "Is that why Mr. Grady is being returned from Hibernity?"

He glanced up at her.

"I saw the transfer order. I was pleasantly surprised to see he's been cooperating for years now. It's good to see he's become convinced of our mission."

Hedrick nodded. "His help will be sorely needed. We need to be able to generate gravity. With that power, we'd be able to deflect any force used against us. Nuclear blasts. Even light itself. We would be able to permanently secure the future of the BTC."

Everyone in the room contemplated this level of godlike power.

Morrison sighed. "And if not, what do we do about the U.S. government then?"

"Let's hope it doesn't come to that." Hedrick turned to the assembled executives. "Here's what I need from you all: I want action plans for dealing with the U.S. government—suggestions on how to cease their investigation and, failing that, action plans in the event of hostilities. I want your reports in my workspace by noon tomorrow."

There were some exhalations of surprise and a low whistle.

"I know, that's a short fuse, but I expect you all to meet it. This is an existential threat to the Bureau, and I have full faith that you will all rise to the occasion." He gave another glance around the table, catching everyone's eyes in turn. "Very good. Dismissed."

The executives all rose, to exit.

As Alexa got up to leave, she noticed Morrison conferring with Hedrick, but Hedrick glanced up at her. "Wait a moment, Alexa. I'd like a word before you go."

She returned to the boardroom table to stand with her hands on the backs of two chairs.

Mr. Morrison walked off, giving her a dark stare before finally turning his back and exiting out a side door—headed back into Hedrick's office.

Hedrick approached her, smiling. "I couldn't help but notice you look upset."

She frowned at him.

He looked to the ceiling. "Doesn't she, Varuna?"

"Yes, Mr. Director. Electrical activity in her amygdala is consistent with mild depression."

Alexa glanced with some irritation to the ceiling. "Leave us, Varuna. That's an order."

"Shall I leave, Mr. Director?"

He hesitated and then laughed. "Yes. Yes, please leave us alone."

"Very well, Mr. Director."

There was silence as Alexa studied the ceiling—not sure why she was doing it since it wouldn't reveal anything.

"It's okay. We're alone now."

"Why do you have her scanning me?"

"She scans everyone in my office suite."

"Even you?"

"As director, I require secrecy." He patted a seat. "Sit. Tell me what's got you upset."

She remained standing. "People get depressed sometimes."

"I want you to be happy. You know how valuable you are to us."

Alexa stared at him, trying to read the situation. She could see his toothy smile. Eyes dilated. But she couldn't keep wondering. "There is something I'd like."

"What? Tell me."

"I've been reviewing recent advances in the biogenetics division."

"Oh?"

"It turns out there's now a way to make me fertile—to reverse my genetic sterility."

Hedrick's face went from a smile to concern. "Really?" He paced for a moment. "What brought this on?"

Alexa sensed the need for caution.

Hedrick studied her. "Have you met someone?" He then glanced at the ceiling. Opened his mouth to speak.

"Don't you dare."

He stopped and then looked back down at her. His eyes narrowed. "I've treated you as an equal. You know I have. I wish you would realize how good you have it."

"I know how good I have it."

"We've known each other since we were children." He gestured to the boardroom. "Do you even notice what I've accomplished?"

"Of course I notice."

"And you know you've always been very dear to me."

"Graham, you matter very much to me, too. But I can't help the way I feel. Maybe it's just the bioengineering, but I don't have romantic feelings for people. Can you name a time when I have?"

He stared at her. "We can be mature about this. If you want to have children, we—"

"It's nothing personal."

He nodded. "I understand. But if you were to have a child, who would the father be?"

She considered the question. "I don't know."

His expression grew more serious. "But see, that's the thing. It's not just you who gets to decide. The Bureau has a say in this matter, Alexa."

She frowned. "I don't follow you."

He studied her for a moment. "Your intelligence, your appearance, your life span, your physical prowess—the organization gave you all those things. Your genetic sequence is proprietary. You need our permission to make copies of it. Otherwise you're stealing."

She felt a sudden dizziness as his words came to her. The *absence* was coming on like an enveloping fog. "I . . ."

"Your body was designed. If you want to have children, the BTC should choose the genetic material from which your offspring are made. You must see the ethical requirement for this. Anything less is theft, Alexa."

She could barely hear him as the mental fog closed around her.

He came close and patted her hand. "You've already achieved what would thrill anyone else. You hold one of the top positions in this organization—a benefit we bestowed on you. As a rational, reasonable individual, you must see that it's the Bureau that will decide whether you have children."

Alexa felt herself coming slowly back to her senses, her heart pounding. She barely had any recollection of what Hedrick had just said to her.

"Are we clear on this?"

Alexa nodded absently.

"Good." He studied her. "You can go."

Alexa approached the twin doors. They opened automatically and closed behind her just as quickly. She moved past Hedrick's secretary and guards in apparent calm. As she rounded the corner, she saw Mr. Morrison leaning against the corridor wall.

"I see the director respects your valuable contributions."

"Go away, Morrison."

"Where's our esprit de corps?" He fell in alongside her.

"What do you want?"

"You may think you're better than me, but at least I earned my place here. I'd say I was here before you were even born—except you were never born, were you? Maybe that's why you lack even the ambition to fuck Hedrick out of simple gratitude."

She moved so fast even Morrison couldn't react before she punched him hard across the face—sending all two hundred and fifty pounds of him hurtling down the hall.

Morrison rolled back onto his feet and shook his head clear. "I see that touched a nerve."

She stared him from several yards away. "Don't make the same mistake twice."

He nodded, still rubbing his jaw. "I'll make damn sure I don't."

CHAPTER 14

Flight

Despite every effort not to be impressed on his journey—Jon Grady was impressed. He'd been sitting in a luxurious leather seat for nearly a half hour before he discovered the hypersonic transport was already under way. It was that quiet. The pilots had the cabin window shields deployed—whether to conceal from him their route or to protect the aircraft he couldn't tell.

When Grady heard the scramjet kick in, the shield disappeared, revealing a wide window by his elbow that he didn't think could be made of glass. Below the sun was rising at the far edge of the world.

It was the most miraculous sight he'd ever seen. His mind caught fire as the universal laws paraded before him. He felt inebriated with joy.

Grady guessed they were at least a hundred fifty thousand feet up. Maybe higher. It didn't feel like they were moving, though he could see the lights of metropolitan sprawl gliding by far below. They must have been doing three or four thousand miles an hour. Maybe more?

Down there was the entirety of the human race. His eyes followed the curvature of the horizon. Unlike with a photograph, the harder he looked, the more there was to see. He hadn't expected this—that the most magical moment of his life would be given to him by his enemies. Grady couldn't remove the grin from his face.

After a while he tried to orient himself to the globe—deduce where they were. But "up" didn't appear to be north. He couldn't see a recognizable polar ice cap—they weren't that high. The modified gravity field disoriented him further. It was nearly impossible to tell what he was looking at in the darkness below.

The gravity field was a stable one Earth g. But then again, that might be his technology erasing all sensation of falling. Most people didn't know that astronauts on the space station were experiencing almost a full g of Earth gravity; it was the fact that they were falling around the Earth that gave the sensation of weightlessness. In fact, it was gravity that was causing their orbital fall—and so the zero gravity sensation was actually being caused by gravity.

Not on this incredible machine. Everything was stable and normal here—like he was sitting in some millionaire's home theater.

Grady turned to face the uniformed BTC officers seated across from him—young Morrisons both. "I didn't feel any acceleration—not even when the scramjet kicked in."

Neither of them answered.

"It's my gravity technology, isn't it? You're canceling out the force of acceleration in the passenger compartment?" He beamed at them. "Amazing."

He looked again out the window. Too bad this was an evil conspiracy. Otherwise this would really be fun.

"Are we in the mesosphere? We are, aren't we? You could probably make use of the gravity fluctuations in the mesosphere for additional propulsion. Maybe even stabilization. Is that what you're doing?"

The Morrison clones just stared back at him.

"I'm right, aren't I?"

The pilot's cockpit wasn't visible from this cabin—in fact, there wasn't even a door leading to it from where he was. The craft had only been traveling for an hour or so when the glass faded into an opaque surface. Materials science again? It looked like the glass itself had changed from clear to opaque. What innovator was doing time in Hibernity for that breakthrough?

He turned again to his guards, but they stared back at him like statues. No point in asking.

Frustrated that the window shield had come down again, Grady tried to get his head back in the game. It was distracting. It really was. They were rolling out all the stops. Beyond first class. This was infinity class. A private hypersonic jet with a front-row seat to the cosmos. His gravity technology had made it possible. God, he wanted to be working on this.

But there was no way. He remembered all too clearly the cruelty of his captors. The life they had stolen from him and from others. And only a vague sense of the lost memories he'd never get back.

His fellow Resistors had put their faith in him. He would not fail them.

Grady looked around at the burled walnut millwork and the fine leather all around him. This, too, was a gilded cage. He raised his flute of champagne to his guards. "To human ingenuity."

They stared like Sphinxes.

The landing a half hour or so later was completely silent and without the sensation of acceleration or deceleration. It was as though they were in a hotel courtesy suite, not an aircraft. Before long a pleasant tone sounded, and his guards removed their seat belts. Not that anyone had needed them.

A black door slid silently upward, then aside, and the guards ushered Grady into a brightly lit hangar. He stood for a moment at the top of the metal stairs. A midnight-blue Cadillac Escalade with diplomatic license plates stood idling below. Dozens of guards patrolled the hangar perimeter, dressed in plain clothes, with long guns slung at their chests. It looked like regular twenty-first-century technology. Grady knew the BTC had outgrown firearms decades ago. These seemed oddly out of place given everything he now knew.

He stepped down the stairway and felt balmy summer air wash over him. The fragrance of mown grass brought an onslaught of memories—hazy and indistinct though they were. He felt so alive. He spotted painted numbers on the hangar door. They glowed in magenta and violet. He felt their invisible geometry. His synesthesia, he knew, but it felt good to be surprised by numbers again.

He turned to a guard. "Where are we?"

"Keep walking."

Grady glanced back at the cobalt-blue hypersonic aircraft looming over him. Its lines were slanted in antiradar angles, giving it the look of an Aztec sacrificial knife. It was a remarkable machine. Silent. Invisible. Fast. He guessed they'd just traversed half the world in under two hours.

A strong hand grabbed his elbow, and he was soon handed off to a new set of Morrisons standing next to the open door of the Escalade. From the door's thickness he guessed the vehicle was armored—but crudely. Again, early twenty-first-century technology. No doubt this machine was intended for the public streets. To blend in.

He gestured to the aircraft behind him. "You know, my invention made that gravity propulsion possible."

"Good for you. Now shut up and get in." The guard shoved Grady into the SUV.

That meant it was showtime. Grady had roughly thirty minutes to escape once they were under way.

There were a total of six guards in the vehicle, only two of them Morrisons—one on either side of Grady in the middle seat. He guessed the BTC didn't want to have too many Morrisons in one place in public. Twins were one thing—clones something else entirely.

The two guards up front looked beefy, though. As did those in back. No doubt steroids were as crude as leeches to the BTC. They probably had something much better to pump up their soldiers. The security detail wore blue blazers and slacks—no ties. No guns visible. They looked, in fact, just like diplomatic bodyguards.

There was Scotch and wine on the console in front of him, along with what now seemed like an ancient flat-screen LCD television—no holographic units here apparently. He was sorely tempted to have a belt of booze to settle his nerves, but if he could survive Hibernity, this escape should be no big deal. They couldn't shoot him. Hedrick needed Grady alive. That's why they were bringing him to headquarters. He just had to make sure they didn't nox him before he pulled this off.

Grady nodded to the men up front. "So we're slumming it in the twenty-first century for the last leg, I see."

The driver gave Grady a dismissive glance in the rearview mirror.

And then they were under way. With a rude jolt of acceleration that now seemed annoying, the vehicle moved through the hangar doors and out into the night. Before long they were rolling through forested countryside. Lots of deciduous trees and lush undergrowth silhouetted against a moonlit sky.

Grady leaned to the side to look for landmarks in the darkness. "Where are we?"

"Earth."

The guards cracked up. The one to Grady's right gestured to the television. "This thing get ESPN?"

The driver nodded. "Yeah. Remote's next to it."

Moments later the TV came to life.

"What channel?"

"How the hell should I know? I don't sit back there."

Grady watched in bewilderment as a commercial for dish soap came on-screen. It was surreal under the circumstances to watch a CGI sponge dancing across a gleaming kitchen countertop. Given everything that had transpired, it all looked so trivial.

The guard started clicking through satellite channels. "Damn, this thing is slow."

"Welcome to tech level two."

Grady turned away from the screen. Instead, he gazed out the window. When was he going to do this? Was it better to escape in the countryside or in the city? They were moving through suburbs now.

He guessed he'd have more places to hide in the city. More resources. And he had to get the evidence he was carrying to someone. That was a whole separate challenge.

By now the guard manning the TV remote had navigated past cooking and travel shows. "What channel's it on?"

Another guard grabbed the remote. "It's in the two hundreds."

He clicked onto a cable news station where a mannish woman in a suit stood before a cluster of microphones. The chyron below her read, "Richard Cotton Trial."

A couple of the guards roared in laughter, "Cotton!"

"My man . . ."

The woman on TV was in midsentence. ". . . *effort. We're just glad Richard Cotton will finally face justice.*"

A guard yelled, "Put the game on. This shit's been going on for months."

Grady watched the screen in fascination.

The news cut to footage of a chained prisoner in bulky body armor and a bulletproof helmet being escorted past a phalanx of riot police. Grady recognized Cotton's bearded face nodding to the cameras.

Grady struggled to hear the news anchor's voice over the hoots of his BTC guards. "*Captured by FBI agents late last year, Cotton was transferred Thursday under heavy guard to federal district court in Chicago, where he faces trial on thirty-three counts of first-degree murder, conspiracy, and use of weapons of mass destruction. The leader of an antitechnology domestic terror group known as the Winnowers, Cotton has claimed responsibility for a decadelong string of bombings focused on eliminating scientists whose research he claimed was 'an affront to God.' He has been called a martyr by thousands of admirers for whom his antimodernity message resonates.*"

One guard scoffed. "Dipshits. It's almost too easy."

On-screen Richard Cotton raised his shackled hands as far up as he could in triumph. The Morrison on Grady's right chuckled. "What a ham."

Grady looked from guard to guard. "The FBI captured Cotton?"

The guards all laughed.

"You could call it that."

Grady scowled at the man. "The FBI is part of this?"

"Hey, Ep, he thinks the FBI can keep a secret."

They all laughed harder.

The screen suddenly changed to a baseball game—the Detroit Tigers against the Cleveland Indians.

"There we go."

Grady looked from one guard to another, trying to figure out what they had meant. Apparently there was some joke he wasn't in on—and which the FBI wasn't in on either.

Grady leaned forward to see a downtown skyline ahead, lights glittering atop lofty towers. There were Michigan plates on the few cars they passed. Signs on businesses and billboards for local radio stations made it clear they were heading into Detroit. Numbers and letters glowed supernaturally all around him now—his synesthesia kicking in, distracting him with its visual lures.

He needed to stay focused. The time on the dashboard read "11:23 PM." They'd been traveling for nearly fifteen minutes already.

Another glance to either side. They were driving on a nearly deserted multilane highway. It was bridged over at intervals with cross streets and signs for downtown. There were grassy embankments to either side, leading up to bushes and chain-link fences, with houses and buildings beyond. He guessed they were going seventy.

The guards were absorbed in the baseball game. Grady forced himself to ignore the glowing numbers littered across the TV screen. *Focus.*

When would he do this? He had to act soon, or they might actually arrive at BTC headquarters.

The Escalade signaled and changed to the slow lane. There were no cars around them at the moment.

No time like the present.

Grady casually picked at the "mole" on his neck, removing it. Then he opened his mouth and placed it on his tongue.

The Morrison to his right gave him a disgusted look.

But before the man could even speak, Grady heard a high-frequency sound as a sudden surge of pressure spread away from his own face, enveloping them both in a fog-like, translucent wave. A wave that rapidly expanded in every direction.

He heard someone behind him shout, "What the—?"

Moments later Grady felt as though he'd been encased in nearly transparent foam. It already filled the interior of the armored Escalade, freezing everyone in place like bugs in amber. He could hear his guards' muffled speech to the left and right.

Grady tried unsuccessfully to turn his head. He was so thoroughly enveloped by the mysterious substance that he couldn't even wiggle his fingers.

And then he noticed that the SUV was still going seventy miles an hour. Through the frozen smoke, which extended all the way to the front windshield, Grady could see that they were veering off the highway toward a grassy embankment that led up to street level.

Not good.

With the driver apparently unable to move a muscle—or even to let up on the accelerator—the Escalade edged up onto the shoulder. Once it touched the grass, the SUV curved away upslope. Grady heard muffled curses to the left and right of him, and watched in terror as the vehicle hurtled through a chain-link fence at the top.

Then they were airborne, floating in free fall, the vehicle rolling sideways.

Grady saw lights passing by outside, but after a moment of silence, the SUV thundered down onto its front right corner, doing cartwheels as the armored windows spidered and the vehicle frame twisted around them. Airbags fired, but they barely got out of their cases against the nanocloud—instead, they were forced outward against the doors, blasting two off their hinges.

But through it all, Grady and the men around him floated in airy isolation, completely insulated from the shock of these impacts within the nanofog. Grady felt as though he were watching a hologram unfold all around him.

The Escalade tumbled through another chain-link fence and across a grassy lot until it impacted against a tree—bringing the vehicle to a sudden, violent stop.

Then there was relative quiet as dirt and pieces of debris rained down around the crash.

They had landed right side up at least.

But what now? Grady was still entombed in this bizarre material. He nonetheless felt himself shift in his seat against his seat belt. The moment he tried to expand the movement, he felt the nanomaterial lock him in place again.

Grady tried to recall Chattopadhyay's advice—which had been woefully brief. But what did he say to do after the material deployed?

There was renewed muttered cursing near his ear . . .

"Grady. You're fuckin' dead . . ."

Move slowly toward the exit. That's what Chattopadhyay had told him. Grady tried to slowly move his hand—and the nanomaterial relented. But the moment he sped up his movement, it locked in on him again.

It was like sheer-thickening liquid then. It would resist rapid deformation but allow slower movement. Grady surmised that once coded to his chemical or genetic signature, this nanomaterial only allowed the cloud's owner to move slowly—and all other objects would be held fast. Very interesting stuff indeed . . .

Grady concentrated on moving slowly, and sure enough the material permitted motion. It felt like he was encased in a breathable clear gelatin as he moved, but he could move. In a few moments he had his seat belt unbuckled. He rolled slowly toward the right-side door and noticed one of the Morrison clones staring daggers at him through the nanofog. The man couldn't even move his lips.

"Fuckin' dead, Grady . . ."

Grady slowly gave him the finger. Then, as he slid past, Grady paused. He could see the guard's suit coat was partially open, the man's hand frozen in the act of grabbing a weapon from its holster.

Grady moved his lips slowly. "Nice try."

Grady also noticed the edge of the man's wallet in his coat pocket, and he slid his hand inside, encompassing it with his own hand as he withdrew it. It was still a difficult item to draw out, but after a few moments, he fumbled with the handle of the passenger door, pushed slowly outward, and finally slid through the edge of the nanofog as if being born into the world all over again.

Grady tumbled out face forward onto what felt like grass. He rolled back onto his feet and was relieved to discover he could move freely now.

He looked back with concern at the open doorway of the armored SUV. The nanofog made it look like the occupants were doing major bong hits inside—except that the smoke didn't budge. He could see the guards still immobilized. Good.

A glance around showed that the Escalade had hurtled across a local street onto a corporate lawn in front of a ten-story office building—most of which was dark at this hour. The Escalade had plowed through a section of chain-link fence there and slammed into a small oak tree—a surprisingly small one, considering it had stopped the armored vehicle cold and smashed the front end in. The entire length of the vehicle was mangled, its engine steaming and the electrical system dead.

Grady sucked in the fresh air and scanned the streets around him. He'd done it. He was free for the first time in several years. Free of the torture. Free of the cell where he'd thought he'd end his days. He looked up at the night sky. The stars.

No time.

He took another deep breath of the night air—then a quick glance at his earthbound surroundings.

No cars or people nearby. He could hear the occasional hiss of traffic passing on the highway below. Downtown Detroit was less populated than he'd thought it would be.

He couldn't let his synesthesia distract him. There'd be time for reveling in freedom when he'd actually escaped.

There was a concrete outbuilding close at hand, slathered with graffiti, but it looked sealed up and dark. He was about forty feet off the road, and not easily visible even from the exit ramp.

Grady opened the guard's wallet and was pleasantly surprised to see currency. The BTC apparently issued them petty cash for operations like this. It felt like a decent wad, dollars and foreign currency.

Grady tossed the man's wallet and pocketed the bills. He moved behind the concrete shed, putting it between him and the road as car lights approached on the highway exit.

Damn! He'd almost forgotten the most important thing: Grady dropped down onto the grass and pulled off his left shoe. He felt around until he came up with the diamond q-link tracking device that was supposed to be in his spine. It caught the reflected light in a beautiful way, briefly mesmerizing him. He closed his hand around it. Better to dispose of it someplace that would delay his pursuers.

Another cautious glance around, and Grady ran along the base of the nearby office building, keeping to the shadows. He soon passed an exhaust vent for a subterranean parking structure and carefully slipped the q-link through a metal screen. He heard it ping against the sides of the shaft as it fell into the depths.

That ought to buy a little time.

He continued around the corner of the building and looked out across a broad stretch of empty parking lots rimmed with chain-link fencing and unkempt grass. He saw a brick church and some houses a couple hundred meters away. The whole area was flatter and emptier than he would have liked. He'd remembered cities being busier.

About a quarter mile away he could see what looked like a large well-lit conference center with parking structures. A line of buses idled there with their lights on.

Grady brushed the grass off and straightened his clothes. He started walking swiftly toward the huge building, approaching along a deserted service road. He glanced back but didn't see anyone giving chase yet.

As he walked, Grady pulled the wad of cash from his pocket and furtively flipped through it as he passed under a streetlamp. Euros, some Asian bills, but also about three hundred some-odd in U.S. twenties. He slid the bills back into his pants.

So Richard Louis Cotton had been arrested? And from the way Grady's guards had been talking, the FBI didn't seem to be aware of the truth. He could feel the video projection device Chattopadhyay had given him in his right shoe, slipped in like a small arch support. He had to find somewhere to take that evidence. No doubt there would be a Detroit field office for the FBI, but Grady didn't relish the idea of staying so close to BTC headquarters—wherever in town that was. It couldn't be far. And no doubt they'd be crawling all over this place with seriously advanced technology once the guards managed to extricate themselves from the nanofog—or when they were noticed missing.

Some minutes later Grady hopped a chain-link fence and crossed a darkened parking lot to the side of the conference center. He then followed a sidewalk back toward the brightly lit entrance of the building.

As he approached, he could see children and adults in outlandish costumes standing in groups near the buses—girls in spandex tights and futuristic helmets, guys wearing robes and prosthetic noses, covered in blue makeup or wearing plastic armor as they clutched imitation laser rifles. Still others moved about in street clothes, smiling and laughing as they took pictures of cosplaying conference attendees. Grady noticed everyone wore badges on lanyards with a logo that read "Space-Con" in shimmering letters. Promotional banners for sci-fi games and TV shows hung along the conference center walls and from crossbeams.

Hundreds more people poured out through the conference center doors. They all looked tired as they ambled toward a line of idling buses. Cars streamed out of the nearby parking structure. It was probably close to midnight.

Grady moved along with the crowd, passing down the line of buses. He tried to divine where each bus was going, but they had only numbers that glowed in various hues to Grady, caressing him with their geometry. He tried to stay focused on reality as he approached a bus driver standing near an open door. A conference attendee dressed as a tentacled alien chatted nearby, smoking a cigarette. The driver looked up at Grady.

Grady nodded. "What time we get back?"

"The Grand's just cross town, man."

"Oh. Wrong bus, sorry."

"Which number you looking for?"

Grady started walking. "No, I got it." He pointed. "It's over here. Sorry."

Grady walked a couple buses down to another driver. "When do we get in?"

"Which stop? Lansing or East Lansing?"

"East."

"About one fifteen."

"Thanks." Grady moved to board the bus.

The driver pointed. "Your badge. I need to see your badge."

"Oh, I lost it."

The man shook his head. "You need the badge to get on the bus."

"But I lost it." Grady went through his pockets.

"What do you mean you 'lost' it? You shoulda just left it on your neck."

"Look . . ." Grady pulled some money from his pocket. "How about sixty bucks?"

The man shook his head. "Just go find your badge, but you got to hurry because we're leavin' in a few minutes."

"It's been a long day. I mean, let me just pay for the ride."

"I don't sell tickets, man. Why can't you eggheads just follow rules?"

"Here, consider it a tip. Just let me get home."

The guy hesitated but then furtively took the money. "Go on. Get in."

Grady moved swiftly up the steps and down the aisle. The bus was surprisingly full, with worn-out-looking con attendees leaning against one another, eyes closed. A few still had cosplay costumes on, and Grady heard snatches of their conversation as he passed by, ducking under a plastic robotic arm.

"You know that pulse rifle isn't canon for a Provincial Scout, right?"

"The graphic novel was better than the show, but the book was better than the graphic novel."

Grady took the first open seat, across from a young couple dressed in matching sets of foam power armor. They were sleeping, gauntleted hands intertwined. Between them, also asleep, was a boy of about six, dressed in a monk's robe.

For the first time since his escape, Grady exhaled fully and felt the tension dissolve. The young family's contentment helped him relax.

And all at once he noticed something about the people around him. It was as though they knew, somewhere deep down, that the future was overdue.

The power armor. The laser rifles. The robots.

They thought they were pretending, but Grady, alone among them, knew that the future had already happened. It was as though they sensed it. They'd re-created that future in foam and rubber—determined to live in it.

A slight grin stole across his face as he appraised them, and Grady no longer had any doubt. Hedrick was wrong. These people were ready for the future. Impatient even.

CHAPTER 15

Dead Man

J oin us, Denise?"

Special Agent Denise Davis turned to see Thomas Falwell and Dwight Wortman in the lobby of the Dirksen Federal Building in downtown Chicago. She smiled. "You look happy."

"Why shouldn't I be? Cotton will be convicted, and we'll get to move on with our lives."

"Amen to that. You'll probably get a promotion."

He grimaced. "You mean my old job back."

"Ah."

They exited through the security station and onto Dearborn.

"Wallace said to keep our eyes peeled for Winnowers."

Falwell waved it away. "The Winnowers don't want to spoil the trial. Cotton's reveling in the media spotlight. Can you believe the play it's getting?"

"Even more reason."

They were moving now through a rush-hour crowd on the sidewalk, following the rest of her team to a neon sign that spelled out "The Berghoff" in rolling script. The joint fronted half the block, and as the group entered the high-ceilinged tavern, they moved through a crowd to an oak bar with brass rails. Dwight had already scored a few stools.

"What are you guys having?"

Davis shouted, "Beer. And the first round's on me."

Some minutes later they clinked glasses of amber lager.

"To the end of a long, long road."

"Hear, hear!"

As Davis looked into the eyes of her team, she felt content. She'd been on the Cotton case nearly seven years, Falwell ten. Remembering all the long hours, the poring through endless financial and travel records, all the boring details that investigative work entails—and then responding decisively when those rare moments of action came.

She truly cared about these people. And she respected them. It was nice to know that all their hard work was about to be rewarded.

Before long Davis placed her empty glass on the bar.

Dwight pointed. "Another, Denise?"

"Sure." But she thumbed toward the back of the barroom. "Gotta hit the loo first."

Dwight called after her, "Keep your head on a swivel."

Falwell laughed. "Yeah, or we'll come looking for you."

She moved through the crowd of office workers toward the restroom sign. She had a mild buzz on, and things looked good. She remembered this feeling of camaraderie from army intelligence work. You might not be thrilled about the mission, but at least you were in it together.

In the restroom stall Davis daydreamed about a GS-13 Step 5 pay grade—maybe with a locality adjustment thrown in, if she could get transferred back to Denver. She might not have to live a long-distance relationship anymore. That meant serious plans. Life plans.

On her way out of the restroom a man of medium build in a sweatshirt and jeans blocked her path. He looked familiar—but not in a bad way. Not threatening. Where did she remember that face from? Perhaps a witness or juror? He had the vibe of a community college professor.

"Agent Davis?"

"Where do I know you from? If you're connected to the trial, we shouldn't be talking."

"No. Agent Davis, I'm Jon Grady. One of Richard Louis Cotton's bombing victims."

Davis frowned. "None of Cotton's victims survived."

He stared back. "I know."

That's when Davis saw the intensity in the man's eyes. The nervous glance behind him.

Davis stepped back and drew her Glock 17 pistol in a smooth motion, leveling it at his chest with a dual grip. "Hands!"

The man raised his hands in confusion. "I don't know who you think I—"

"Shut up!" Looking past him, she realized her carelessness too late: The hallway had a bend. They were not visible to the barroom crowd.

I am an idiot.

"I need to talk to you, Agent Davis. I came a long way."

"Who are you?"

"I told you. Would you please stop pointing that gun at me?"

She didn't lower it. "You just told me you're dead. I'm not in the mood for crazy today."

"I'm not crazy. Look, if you want, we can head back to the bar—and you can arrest me. That's what I want you to do. I need your protection, and I can prove who I am."

"And who is that exactly?"

"Jon Grady. My memory is a bit spotty, but I was the physicist that Richard Louis Cotton supposedly blew up in New Jersey a few years ago." He became suddenly grim-faced. "Along with six other people."

"Edison, New Jersey." She thought on it. "Chirality Labs."

He looked momentarily confused then nodded. "Yes. That was my company."

She made a buzzer sound. "*Nnnnnttt.* Wrong. There were six victims total at the Chirality bombing, not seven."

He looked confused again.

She kept the gun on him. "Let's see ID."

"I don't have any identification. But I am Jon Grady. I can prove it, if you'll let me."

"You can't be Mr. Grady because we found what was left of him and the others. So forgive me if I'm skeptical. Especially because I have a terrorist group out to kill me."

"It's not a terror group. It's a rogue government agency. Something called the Federal Bureau of Technology Control."

Davis felt the tension disappear. "Oh my God." She lowered her gun. "Get the hell out of my face."

"The BTC has been disappearing people like me for decades—inventors of disruptive technologies."

"For decades. Well, they apparently didn't disappear you because here you are accosting me outside the restroom."

"I escaped. They were bringing me to their headquarters in Detroit to work on—"

"Detroit?"

He reacted to her dubious look. "Look, never mind that. I came here because I saw you on the news. Richard Cotton isn't a terrorist; he's an agent of the BTC."

"Last warning. Leave. Now."

"I need protection."

"Fine. Call the Chicago police. You can explain it to them."

"No." The man looked panicked. "You're the only one I trust. They said you *thought* you caught Cotton. That you had no idea what was really going on. That's why I trust you."

Davis had run into delusional paranoids before. Sadly, the legal system allowed a lot of them to run around on the streets because nobody wanted to pay for their treatment. And sensationalized criminal cases attracted them like moths to a porch light.

The man nodded as he apparently deciphered the look on her face. "Okay. All right. But do me this one favor."

"No." She started walking around him warily.

The man wrapped his hand around an empty beer glass on a shelf by the pay phone next to him. Then he let go and pointed at it. "My fingerprints are now on that glass. Run those prints. And"—at that point he tore a small clump of hair from his head, which he then dropped into the glass—"here's a sample of my DNA."

"Are we done?"

"Test them. I know it'll take time, but once you confirm who I am, I need to talk with you. Meet me"—he thought hard for a few moments—"one week from today. I'll be in the Mathematics Library at Columbia University in New York City—eight A.M. Sit at the table across from the big gray breaker box—near the windows."

"That is not going to happen."

"It will once you confirm who I am. Remember, eight A.M., one week from today. Columbia Mathematics Library. Next to the breaker box. Come alone."

"No."

He went to leave but turned around again, walking backward as he talked. "I know you don't believe me, but I can tell you details about the Edison bombing scene that I couldn't possibly know if I wasn't there."

"You mean like the wrong number of victims?"

"I'm telling you: there was a seventh person there that night. He was a Princeton physics professor who came to evaluate our work. Now that I think about it, I believe he worked for the BTC." Grady looked frustrated as he tried to recall something. Then he glanced up. "A man named Kulkarni. Sameer Kulkarni. I haven't seen him mentioned in the news accounts. He was there. Doctor Alcot recognized him."

"Good-bye." With that Davis left him behind.

The strange man disappeared into the barroom crowd as Davis headed toward the bar. Her team was there laughing over some just finished joke.

"I thought you guys were going to rescue me if I took too long."

Falwell read the look on her face and snapped alert. "What happened?"

The rest of the team put their drinks down, suddenly serious.

She waved her hands. "Calm down. Just some nut job came up to me outside the ladies' restroom—claimed he was one of Cotton's dead victims."

They all narrowed their eyes in confusion.

"Say what?"

Davis nodded. "He said the Winnowers are really a rogue federal agency. That it's all a government conspiracy."

Most of the team laughed and shook their heads.

But Falwell scanned the crowded bar. "Should we take the guy into custody?"

"We can't grab every crazy person who comes out of the woodwork after I go on television."

"Did he seem dangerous?"

"I wouldn't have let him go if he did. Just a bit loony. Said there was a seventh victim at the Edison bombing scene—some Princeton physics professor."

The others chuckled, but Falwell narrowed his eyes. "Dwight and I were going through the Edison bombing evidence last week with the prosecutor. Remember that extra tire print at the Edison scene—the one in the snow?"

She thought about it. "Yeah, but it didn't lead to anything."

"Right. The lab identified the tire—it was old. Not in common use nowadays."

Dwight nodded. "175-SR14s."

"Whatever—they were outdated. From the '70s."

Davis leaned against the bar. "So what's your point? That matches the Winnower M.O. They used an old car."

"Well, back then Dwight I spent a couple days reviewing traffic camera videos, and there was a car in the area that night that could have been old enough—a Mercedes."

Dwight chimed in: "A 240D."

"Right. A Mercedes 240D. And those came with SR14s as standard equipment."

Davis nodded. "Okay. I remember, but the real owner was deceased."

Falwell put his beer down. "Right. The family didn't even know the car existed. And it hasn't been seen since. Not even by license plate readers."

She stared at him. "So what? The Winnowers used it to go to and from the attack, then dumped it."

"That's just it. The traffic cameras don't have great resolution, but they showed only one person in the car—after the bombing."

She contemplated this.

"Meaning in addition to Cotton and his group, someone else left the scene that night. And we never shared that detail about the extra tire tracks with the media."

"You're starting to worry me, Thomas."

"I'm not saying the guy you saw is legit. I'm saying we may have a security leak in the federal prosecutor's office."

That got her attention. "Mistrial?"

"Cotton might be cooperating, but then again he might have other plans."

Davis stared at Falwell for a few moments. And then she pushed through the crowd, headed back toward the restrooms. In the hallway just outside, she took a cocktail napkin and carefully retrieved the empty bar glass by the phone, inserting her fingers inside it, tipping it up onto her hand. She caught the lock of hair with her other hand as it fell out.

Falwell was right behind her.

She held up the glass. "Run the prints on this glass. Tonight. And I want a DNA test on this hair sample . . ." She passed the hair to him.

"Where did you get a hair sample?"

"He left it behind. Supposedly to prove who he was."

"And if it matches a victim—what then?"

"It could be some scheme of Cotton's to taint the evidence—and the case." She pointed again at the hair. "DNA."

"It'll take five days at least. How big a problem you think this guy is?"

"Look, it's probably nothing. But after all these years, I don't want to take any chances. Do you?"

Davis stood looking over a criminologist's shoulder in a cubicle at the crime lab in the FBI's Chicago field office. It was past ten P.M. The tech clicked around a computer screen, marking points on an image from the Integrated Automated Fingerprint Identification System.

The criminologist glanced back at her. "I found three different sets of fingerprints on your beer glass. Exhibits one and three show no IAFIS matches—or at least none with reasonable scores. But exhibit two gave us two candidate hits."

"Show me."

He clicked through a couple screens and a passport photo appeared in a window above the name "Jon Grady"—beneath that was a label reading "Deceased."

Falwell glanced over at Davis. "That's not good."

The criminologist looked up at her. "You want to see candidate two? It's a much lower score."

She shook her head. "No, thanks. Can you print that out for me?"

"Sure." He clicked the mouse a few times, and they heard the laser printer by the door spit out a couple of pages.

"Thanks for the help. C'mon, Thomas."

Falwell grabbed the pages as they headed for the elevators. He held up the printed photo. "This the guy?"

She nodded.

"So you met a ghost."

She nodded.

"What does this do to the case?"

"I don't know yet."

"And what was this guy claiming?"

He said they were disappearing inventors of disruptive technologies."

"Who was?"

"A rogue federal agency."

Falwell chuckled. "Sure."

They got in the elevator and headed to the itinerant-agent floor, where they had offices for the duration of Cotton's trial.

She leaned against the elevator's back wall. "Well, it's clearly fake. We found most of this Grady guy's right arm at the Edison scene. We had a jawbone. Teeth. A shinbone. A partial tongue. All DNA matched. And we've got Richard Cotton on video preparing to kill him."

"He's up to something."

"We'll need those DNA test results the moment they come in. And let's put out an APB on this Grady imitator. He couldn't have gone far."

"If he wanted to get arrested so bad, why didn't he stick around? Why arrange a meeting all the way in New York?"

"I don't know." She considered it. "Did Grady have a twin brother?"

"Twins don't have identical fingerprints."

The elevator doors opened, and they walked out into the guest cubicles. There were still quite a few agents moving about. Davis had put her Winnower team in a group workstation with no partitions between them, and she and Falwell took off their jackets.

"So what do we do?"

She stared for a moment but finally shrugged. "I don't know, but I think we have to inform the prosecutor's office." She fell back into her office chair. "Thomas, you ever hear of something called the Federal Bureau of Technology Control?"

He squinted. "What is that, Commerce Department?"

"Have you heard of it or not?"

He thought some more before finally saying, "No. Why? Who are they?"

"I don't even know if they exist." Davis keyed her password into her laptop and then launched her Internet browser. She entered "usa.gov" on the URL line, then navigated to an A-to-Z index of government departments and agencies. She entered the term "Bureau of Technology Control" in the search box—clicked "Search."

It returned about a quarter million results. Davis scanned down the list of hits with headings like "U.S. Bureau of Industry and Security" and "Bureau of Labor Statistics."

Falwell was looking over her shoulder. "Try it enclosed in quotation marks."

She enclosed the search term and searched again. Now it returned zero results.

Falwell shrugged. "Why are we looking for them?"

"That Grady guy mentioned it to me. That was supposedly the federal agency that kidnapped him."

Falwell let a smile escape. "Right. If it's a top-secret agency, I'm guessing they wouldn't be listed in the directory."

"Look, I don't believe his story, Thomas, but I did want to see if they were a real organization."

"Let me get this APB out." He opened up his own laptop. "So what do we do if we don't have him by next week?"

"You mean, do we meet him at Columbia University? I want to see the DNA results first."

"You're actually thinking of going?"

"We might be, yeah."

"What about the depositions next week?"

"Reschedule them."

"Denise, you're not meeting this guy alone."

"No, of course not. We'll use a team. It's a university library, so there'll be security cameras. We'll see him coming." She paused. "There's something here that's gnawing at me, though. Something about Cotton—how he could disappear for so long without a trace. And with so many faceless followers—none of whom made mistakes."

"What is that supposed to mean?"

"I'm just—"

"We arrested three of his people with him."

"And none of them seemed very bright. They all had felony drug rap sheets."

Falwell laughed ruefully. "You're starting to worry me."

"It's just strange, that's all."

Just then Davis's desk phone rang. She glanced at the LCD readout—and then did a double take. She sat up straight. "Thomas."

"What?"

She held her hand above the receiver. "It's D.C."

"FBI headquarters?" He checked his watch.

She picked it up on the start of the third ring. "Denise Davis."

"Agent Davis, please hold for Deputy Director Royce."

She blanched. "Yes. I'll hold." Davis covered the receiver and glared at Falwell. "It's the deputy director."

He gave her a quizzical look. "Of the *FBI?*"

"No, of *Grease,* the musical—who do you think?" Davis was on hold for about ten seconds before a man's voice came on the line. *"Denise Davis."*

"Yes, sir."

"You were contacted by a man claiming to be Jon Grady tonight. Is that correct?"

Davis frowned at Falwell—who frowned back, probably because he had no idea what was going on. "Yes, sir. We had a positive match on fin-gerprints. We're running a DNA test on a hair sample."

"Do you have any information on his present whereabouts?"

"Not at the moment, sir. We're putting out an APB."

"Don't do that just yet. Did he say why he was contacting you?"

Davis paused for a moment, then looked over at Falwell again. Then she said, "Deputy Director, I must apologize, sir, but I absolutely must respond to something. Can I phone you at your office in under a minute? I sincerely apologize, sir."

There was silence for a moment. Then, *"Call me back as soon as pos-sible, Agent Davis."*

"Thank you, sir. Very sorry." She hung up.

Falwell squinted at her. "Are you nuts?"

Davis stood up and started rifling through the shelves for a bureau di-rectory. "Thomas, I don't even want to hear it. Would you look for a direc-tory over there?"

He started navigating through the intranet directory on his laptop. "I'm confused, Denise."

"It's past midnight in D.C. Why are they even *in* the office?" She glanced up at him. "Not the Web directory. I want something printed. Preferably a few years old."

"You're really losing it."

"Ah!" She pulled a small binder off a shelf and started flipping through it.

"It'd be in the front probably. Near the bureau seal . . ."

She heard a *ding* as an email landed in her inbox. Davis glanced up. It was from Jeffrey Royce, deputy director of the FBI—and it was over their internal system. It was cc'd to the Chicago Special Agent in Charge, with the subject line "Priority One Special Assignment."

"Damn." She found the FBI headquarters' main number and pounded it into her desk phone. "I am such an idiot . . ."

Falwell leaned down to look at her laptop screen. "Hey, you got some spam from the deputy director. Should I delete it?"

"Ha. Ha." She waited for the FBI operator to pick up. "Yes, this is Special Agent Denise Davis returning a call from Deputy Director Jeffrey Royce." A pause. "I believe he's still in the office." A pause. "Yes, I'll hold."

Falwell leaned back in his chair and spread his hands.

In a moment another man answered.

"Yes. Yes, I'll hold."

And a few seconds later the deputy director picked up. *"Agent Davis."*

"Yes, sir. My apologies. I just needed . . . never mind. You were saying, sir?"

"Mr. Grady asked you to meet him in New York—next week at Columbia University—is that correct?"

Davis felt the shock go through her. "I . . . How do you know that, sir?"

"We have a highly sensitive surveillance operation under way, Agent Davis. You'll still need to be in Chicago preparing for the Cotton trial, but we're going to put you temporarily under the direction of a special task force—and we want you to meet Mr. Grady as he requested. Your supervisors have been notified, and any scheduling conflicts will be resolved through our office. You'll report to a safe house in New York—you're not to contact the New York field office or discuss this with anyone except your supervisor. Is that clear?"

Davis looked to Falwell uncertainly, then nodded. "I understand, sir."

"The email I just sent has instructions about where to meet your plane next week and the supervising agent for this operation. Can I count on your discretion and cooperation, Agent Davis?"

"Yes, sir. But . . ."

"What is it?"

"I just . . . What's going on, sir? Is it Jon Grady? What's his connection to Cotton?"

"I can tell you that he isn't Jon Grady—but the rest is well above your pay grade. The only reason you're involved is because he contacted you. But you should know he's dangerous, and that you need to listen closely to your task force leader when you reach New York. Can I count on you, Agent Davis?"

She took a deep breath. "Yes, sir. Yes, of course you can count on me."

CHAPTER 16

Panopticon

Graham Hedrick sat in his office chair gazing out at Hong Kong's Victoria Harbor. Junks and container ships plied the glittering water below. His jaw clenched as he listened to the report on Grady's escape.

"Grady didn't do this alone, Mr. Director. He was helped." The head of Jon Grady's security detail, a Morrison named Beta-Upsilon, stood nervously before Hedrick's desk. The elder Morrison stood nearby looking even angrier than Hedrick felt.

"We had no reason to expect he'd have a personal utility fog."

Morrison barked, "Did you scan him before transport?"

"Yes, sir."

"Be advised: I will check the surveillance log."

"We scanned him, sir."

"Then I'm not understanding. Do you mean someone on your team helped Mr. Grady?"

"No, sir. Someone at Hibernity must have helped him. That van was clean. The hypersonic transport was clean."

Morrison got in his face. "You're suggesting the guards at Hibernity had access to *unregistered* foglets?"

"I don't know, sir."

"The garrison there doesn't even have access to tech level eight."

Hedrick rotated his chair to face the young BTC officer.

Morrison placed a glittering diamond on Hedrick's desk. "The response team found Grady's q-link in a ventilation shaft."

Hedrick picked up the diamond, studying it—then looked up at the young Morrison clone. "Am I to believe Jon Grady dug this out of the base of his spine on the spot?"

"I don't know, sir."

"And how did he even know about his q-link?"

Varuna's voice chimed in from above. *"Beta-Upsilon is speaking the truth to the best of his knowledge, Mr. Director."*

Morrison glowered. "An honest idiot is still an idiot."

"Dad, we had no way of anticipating—"

"I sprayed surveillance dust onto the headliner. I know you were all watching the Tigers game instead of the prisoner. I have the whole god-awful mess on video. Grady had unregistered utility foglets collapsed on his person, and you didn't spot them."

"The scanner said he was clean."

"Some clever son of a bitch manufactured unregistered nanotech. That's why you have to do this thing we call 'searching' prisoners. With your eyes and hands."

"We patted him down."

"And how much cash did he take from your wallet?"

The guard looked suddenly sheepish. "Uh, I don't . . ."

"Yes, I saw that, too. How much?"

"Probably four or five hundred in dollars, sir."

"All of it."

"Maybe half that in other currencies."

"You really make me ashamed of my genomic sequence."

"Dad—"

"Don't try that 'Dad' crap on me." Morrison looked to Hedrick. "And someone tipped off Grady not to take the guards' equipment. We have no direct method to track him."

"Enough. Get him out of my sight." Hedrick dismissed the guard with a wave of his hand.

The young man nodded grimly and left; the doors opened and then immediately closed behind him.

Hedrick sighed. "Varuna, reassign Beta-Upsilon and his team to the Hibernity garrison for a year."

"*Yes, Mr. Director.*"

Morrison came up alongside Hedrick's chair to gaze out the window at the faux Hong Kong below.

"Who is the warden at Hibernity, Mr. Morrison?"

"Theta-Theta."

"We need new leadership there, apparently. And a top-to-bottom review of their operation."

"How could they get their hands on a utility fog? That's advanced weaponry."

"I don't think they did."

Morrison cast a confused look at Hedrick.

"Min Zhao is in Hibernity."

"Okay . . ."

"He perfected foglets less than a decade ago."

"You really think prisoners are creating their own technology? Prisoners?"

"I don't know."

"But . . ." Morrison pondered this gravely. "I don't see how it's possible."

Hedrick felt a fear he could hardly contemplate. "Your number-one priority at the moment, Mr. Morrison, is to find Jon Grady. Escaped, Mr. Grady is an existential threat to this organization. I don't think either of us relishes the idea of a gravity weapon like Kratos in the hands of our enemies."

"When we locate him, I suggest we fry him from orbit."

"No. I still need him alive. If he won't work for us voluntarily, we have no choice but to use force. But it appears his consciousness is truly unique. So I want him captured. Is that clear?"

Morrison nodded. "I'll need a higher tech level approved for the forward team."

"I don't want you annihilating city blocks to get at him. Nonlethal weapons only. And no publicity. I'll allow tech level four."

"Four? They'll barely be able to overpower the authorities."

"Then they'll need to be smarter this time. I can't have any more advanced technology going missing. Tech level four will be sufficient. Is that clear?"

Morrison sighed in irritation but nodded. He turned to leave.

"One more thing . . ."

Morrison halted.

"Once you've got Grady, I want you to pay a surprise visit to Hibernity—in force."

"Do we clean house?"

Hedrick picked up a small model that he kept on his desk. It was supposedly of his first fusion reactor design. "Yes. And I want a manual prisoner count."

"That's a big job. Opening up every cell will take—"

"I want you to lay eyes on *him*—personally."

Morrison studied Hedrick. "Archibald Chattopadhyay is dead. His cell has been dormant for a decade. No food. No water. He's entombed in nine hundred feet of solid rock."

"I want you to lay eyes on him."

"There's no way he could have—"

"Just do it."

Morrison stared for a moment, then nodded.

At that moment the office doors opened to admit Alexa. Both men looked up; Hedrick brightened at the sight of her.

"What is it, my dear?"

"The deep packet AIs have a lead on our Mr. Grady."

Hedrick felt the relief wash over him. "Well done. Where?"

"Last night an FBI agent in Chicago ran fingerprints on a suspect and got a match for Jon Grady."

Hedrick slammed his hand on his desk. "Then they have him."

"No. And an FBI agent started doing Internet searches for the 'Federal Bureau of Technology Control.'"

Hedrick scowled.

"It was the arresting agent in the Richard Louis Cotton case: one Denise Davis."

·Hedrick looked shocked. "You don't think Cotton has—?"

"No. Cotton's a lot of things, but he's not an idiot. His sense of self-preservation is legendary."

Morrison nodded to himself. "Chicago's just a few hours by car from here."

She turned toward Hedrick. "This Davis woman has been all over the media lately for the Cotton trial. Perhaps Grady saw her and thought he could trust her."

Hedrick motioned impatiently. "Do we know where Grady is?"

"We know where he was." Alexa brought up a holographic video window that showed thousands of video thumbnails all running simultaneously. "I had the AIs go back through the last twenty-four hours of street-level surveillance on all systems they could access within five miles of Agent Davis's location in downtown Chicago, looking for Jon Grady's likeness in the streets. A lot of federal and city cameras in the area, so we had good coverage."

"And?"

"No hits on Jon Grady."

Hedrick threw up his hands.

"I decided to do a search for Agent Davis's movements, figuring he must have followed her for a while, waiting for the right moment to make contact. And that's when I found this . . ." She selected and then expanded a single video image and froze it.

The surveillance camera image wasn't anywhere near as detailed as what the BTC's cameras could produce, but it was clear enough. It showed a woman with short hair walking with several men in suits on a crowded Chicago sidewalk. The woman was highlighted by the system in a red rectangular box.

But Alexa pointed to a man walking several yards behind her, wearing jeans and a hoodie. The man's face was notable in the crowd because it was obscured by pinpoints of blinding light.

Hedrick frowned in confusion. "What am I looking at? And how could a person be walking in a crowd with such bright lights without drawing attention?"

Alexa looked up. "Varuna, can you explain what the subject in this image is wearing?"

The disembodied voice of the AI said, *"Yes, Alexa. It is an exploit first seen in Hibernity prison, used by prisoners to defeat early facial recognition systems."*

Hedrick narrowed his eyes. "Used by prisoners?"

"Correct. The device consists of goggles punctuated by near-infrared LEDs emitting at roughly eight hundred fifty nanometers, which can be found in common motion sensors. This light is invisible to the human eye but matches the spectral sensitivity of CMOS or CCD cameras or other silicon-based photo detectors. When placed around the face, these make it impossible to obtain accurate measurements on the spacing and shape of a subject's facial features."

Hedrick turned back to Morrison meaningfully. "Grady's obviously received assistance. There is something going on at Hibernity."

Alexa looked between the two of them. "What makes you think that?"

"Mr. Morrison will handle it, Alexa. You just concentrate on locating Mr. Grady."

"Without facial recognition, it'll be difficult."

"What about this Agent Davis?"

"From the moment of her fingerprint match on Grady, she's been under surveillance by AIs—microphones in her laptop and cell phone, the works. Apparently Mr. Grady requested that she meet him in the Columbia University Mathematics Library a week from today. I took the liberty of using AIs to instruct her through official channels to meet with Grady in New York. She's to report to a special task force." Alexa swept her hand through the air and dropped a virtual document onto Hedrick's desktop.

He examined the document—an email from the deputy director of the FBI ordering Denise Davis to report to a task force safe house. "If we know where Grady is going to be, why involve her?"

"Grady might not show if he doesn't see her."

Hedrick looked up from the document. "But why New York?"

Alexa closed all the holographic windows. "Back when Bertrand Alcot was a physics professor at Columbia, he took Mr. Grady under his wing—mentored him. Grady never attended, but he spent time there. I'm guessing he still has friends in the area—or he knows of someplace there where he can go to ground."

"Set AIs loose on any communities of interest his past activity might generate. See what they turn up. Past addresses, run geolocation on his phones for the past ten years. I want anyone he's ever been with under surveillance."

Hedrick then turned to Morrison. "Prep your people to become this FBI unit. Grab him when he shows."

Morrison nodded. "You still need him alive?"

"Yes, damnit!" Hedrick looked back to Alexa. "Excellent job."

"I'd like to go on that operation, Graham."

He looked surprised. "That's not up to me, Alexa." Hedrick turned to Morrison.

"No."

"I feel I've earned the right to go on this operation. Mr. Grady represents a grave risk to the BTC and society at large. I think he'll listen to me."

"Ah, you're going to charm him, like you did to so many in the old days?"

Hedrick shook his head vigorously. "You're too valuable, Alexa. It can't be risked."

Morrison added, "And we don't need your help."

Hedrick took her by the elbow. "I need your people monitoring Agent Davis's every move. Look how well you've done so far on the intelligence side."

Morrison gave Alexa a sly smirk.

Alexa focused on Hedrick. "I was a top field operative. It's what I'm good at. Why won't you let me do what I'm good at?"

"You're much too valuable."

She studied him and then turned to exit.

His words followed her. "You're dismissed."

CHAPTER 17

Rogue Agency

The Raven Rock Mountain Complex was intended to deal with end-of-the-world scenarios. For that reason it always put Bill McAllen on edge. Known officially as Site R, it was a continuity of government (or COG) bunker complex in the hills of eastern Pennsylvania, not far from the Maryland border. One of many such bunkers built during the Cold War, it had been augmented and expanded over the decades. It was now sometimes called the Underground Pentagon because it served as an emergency command center for various U.S. defense agencies, including the Joint Chiefs of Staff, in the event of a major national crisis.

As McAllen drove down what seemed like miles of concrete-lined tunnels in an otherwise empty, chauffeured twelve-seat electric cart, he couldn't stop thinking that this was where some of the last humans might remain alive in the event of global thermonuclear war. Or an asteroid strike. Or a pandemic—name your Armageddon, they probably had a standard-operating-procedures binder for it on a shelf somewhere down here. But the four times he'd been here in the past had been for COG training.

Today wasn't training.

The cart stopped in the tunnel next to an open three-foot-thick steel blast door, flanked by armed sentries. He stepped off and was met by a female army lieutenant from the U.S. Army's 114th Signal Battalion. "This way, Deputy Secretary."

Without waiting for him, she moved quickly through bunkeresque office corridors devoid of people. He hurried to keep up. After walking past dozens of identical metal doors marked with numbers and letters, she finally turned a corner where a podium with the Pentagon seal stood on a dais before dozens of chairs. Several generations of television broadcasting equipment were mothballed against the back wall, but sitting in the chairs were lots of sharp-looking young men and women in suits, tapping away at laptops. None of them so much as glanced up.

The lieutenant gestured for McAllen to follow her as she approached a conference room flanked by two more armed sentries. She knocked and after a moment entered, moving aside for McAllen.

"Deputy Secretary McAllen is here, Madam Director."

"Bill!"

In the concrete-walled boardroom McAllen could see several senior representatives of the DHS, NSA, CIA, and Defense Department sitting around a huge and absurdly durable-looking oak table. At its head sat their penultimate boss, Director of National Intelligence Kaye Monahan, a petite woman in her sixties who nonetheless had a commanding presence. McAllen was well aware this small woman had, as U.S. ambassador, more than held her own in brass-knuckle dealings with the Chinese senior leadership. She'd been in the intel community long before that. And she was principled—which McAllen found appealing in a longtime D.C. political player.

The army lieutenant departed, closing the door behind her. There was a vigorous debate already under way around the conference table.

Director Monahan motioned for him to sit in an open seat next to her. "Come here and help me talk some sense into these guys."

McAllen took his seat while the raucous discussion continued.

"Kaye, you know damn well no one has the complete picture. That's what compartmentalization's all about." The deputy director of the CIA was a jowly Virginian in his sixties, sipping a Diet Coke as he scowled across the table.

"Compartmentalizing an SAP is one thing, but a whole goddamned bureau?"

A gaunt, intense man, whom McAllen remembered from his days at the NSA, spoke from the far end of the table. "It wasn't a bureau back when it started. It was a project. And in any event, it was the Company that launched it."

The CIA guy cast a look at him. "It could just as well have been any of us."

Director Monahan added, "I never heard anything about it while I was at Langley. I knew we had black tech, but . . ."

The CIA guy gestured to the walls. "Look around you. This is what they were doing in the Cold War—big stuff. Do you realize how much two hundred billion a year for half a century buys you? The president himself doesn't have the clearance to know about half these programs. There are a million people with top-secret classifications in this country, Kaye. And some of those folks live in a completely different world—even from us. It's the nature of the covert sector. Back in the '60s someone put the BTC in charge of regulating advanced technologies, and it snowballed. It looks like they left us all behind."

She sipped coffee from an absurdly elegant cup and saucer—legacy ware from the Kennedy administration. "Well, Bill here took the meeting with them—if that's what you could call it—and I just about had him and the other two certified when I read his report."

The NSA guy remained expressionless. "I read it. We've known since '98 that the BTC had perfected holographic projection at molecular scales. We think it's done with phased array optics and plasma emission. But no one really knows."

McAllen raised his eyebrows. "It looked damned real to us."

The CIA guy grimaced. "That's a toy compared to what else they have."

Monahan scowled. "There needs to be some accountability. We need to review what technology they're sitting on that could provide the United States with a technological edge. China's nipping at our heels."

"The BTC might argue that what they're doing is keeping the tech out of China's hands."

"There is a technology transfer problem in the private sector."

She put the cup and saucer down. "Well, pardon me, Mike, but I like a bit less authoritarianism in my democracy. The BTC wasn't put in charge of policing the world."

"Who's to stop them?"

"They might have advanced technology, but if we bring CIA, DOD, NSA, and DHS together—focus our collective efforts—we should be able to bring them to heel."

The NSA and CIA guys exchanged looks.

"Good luck with that."

The NSA guy shook his head. "You're forgetting that they provide a good deal of valuable intelligence to the three-letter crowd. Rumor is that they've made some serious advances in quantum computing and communications. Maybe even human-level AIs."

"This is ridiculous."

CIA spoke grimly. "You're not going to sneak up on them. They've compromised ECHELON, SWICS—just about everything. They're in your network, too. Count on it. They're reading your emails, Kaye."

The NSA man shrugged. "They seem to be able to break any code. That's probably why they always seem to know about what's going on and where. We need to keep them on our side."

"How would you even know if they are? I've heard that the BTC has splintered into overseas factions now."

"Look, you're stirring up a shit storm."

Monahan frowned. "We need to find where they moved their operations, and we need to act."

The NSA guy just stared. "Knowing their base of operations isn't going to help you."

"Of course it is. We could start monitoring their activities, just like they monitor ours. We could set up an air gap network they don't know about. Another SAP."

"This is how it starts . . ."

The NSA man sighed. "Knowing where they are didn't help us."

"You know where they're headquartered?"

"Yeah. I'll tell you: Their headquarters is in the middle of down-town Detroit. A forty-story building from the '60s that's so bland you barely see it."

"In Detroit?"

"You wanna hide the world's most advanced technology center where no one will find it—where else do you put it? But let me save you some headaches: They don't communicate in the electromagnetic spectrum, or fiber, or any other technology known to us. We've had receivers focused on that building for decades. Nothing. So we tried to cut in. Did seismic work and found that their building goes sixty stories underground—that we know of."

"Sixty stories?"

"That's not all. Our whole team disappeared right after we scanned it. That same day the spy satellite we were focusing on them went AWOL. And then all the data we had on them disappeared from our network, too. Replaced by photos of our children asleep in bed—taken from inside our homes."

"We need to figure out some way to rein them in."

"Risky. You won't find it in any reports, but this has been tried before. Talk to some retired directors. When it comes to the BTC, you're not just playing with fire; you're playing with plutonium, Kaye."

The CIA guy nodded. "Our science people estimate they have a fifty- to sixty-year technological edge. And it's accelerating. But hey, look at the bright side: They've been smoothing out the bumps for more than fifty years now. And it doesn't look like they'll allow a nuclear war to take place—and don't even ask why I know that because I can't tell you. Suffice it to say that they're keeping an eye on the long-term picture—do you want that job? Because I know I don't. I've got my hands full just putting out fires."

"No one should have so much power."

"They already know what you're up to." He pointed at McAllen. "You sent Bill up there, and they gave you their answer."

At that they all turned to McAllen.

Monahan drummed her fingers on the table. "Well, Bill, you're the only one who's seen this Graham Hedrick person. What's your read on him?"

McAllen stroked his chin. "I wouldn't say I *saw* him, but I saw an image of him."

"All right then, what's your read on that?"

"He was full of himself. Didn't seem the least bit concerned about what we did or did not do."

"What do you think will happen if we let them be?"

McAllen took a deep breath. "I think their technological lead will grow, and they'll be in a position to dictate the course of human events for generations to come. And I think that's not okay. Not okay at all."

CHAPTER 18

Rendezvous

The Twins gave Davis the creeps. That's what she'd taken to calling the nearly identical tall, blond, muscle-bound men with thick necks who supervised her on the special task force. They were, in fact, the only members of the task force she'd seen thus far. One was named Todd, the other Jason. In their mid- to late twenties, they nonetheless wielded authority as if they'd been born to it. As if those around them were truly their inferiors—like some FBI version of the Winklevoss twins. And she had never heard of twins working together in the FBI. These guys were clearly jacked in with Washington because they seemed to operate without having to clear things with anyone. Neither did they have budgetary problems. And they'd requisitioned her from the middle of preparations for a major public trial without so much as a peep from her bosses.

She and the Twins were sitting in a suite of windowless offices in Columbia University's International Affairs Building at the corner of Amsterdam and 118th Street—a ten-story concrete building that seemed to have been modeled on a steam radiator. It was located on the far side of the Morningside campus from where she was supposed to meet Grady. They'd kept a very low profile for the past two days.

As Davis sat, bored, the Twins both talked on cell phones with unseen elements of the task force, finalizing details. Apparently they had people out there somewhere who were ready to back her up on a moment's notice. Still, the asymmetry in information was alarming. They hadn't told her a goddamn thing since she'd arrived.

One of the Twins hung up. She could never tell them apart. Even when they reclarified their names, it quickly devolved into a game of "two-card monte" the moment they moved. She cleared her throat and looked at her watch. "So it's seven thirty now. It'll take me fifteen minutes to walk there; I need to be briefed."

Todd—or Jason—looked confused but then nodded. "Right. Agent Davis, we really just need you to go to the meet. You know the route to the Mathematics Library. You've seen the floor plan, and you've seen the photographs of the table you're to sit at."

"Yes, but I was told he was a dangerous suspect."

Todd nodded. "Okay." He shrugged. "Then be careful."

"I don't know where my backup is. We haven't gone over radio protocols, emergency signals—"

"Not necessary."

She threw up her hands in exasperation. "I'd like a little reciprocity. I convinced this Grady guy to come here for a meeting. Now maybe you can tell me how the hell it is he's still alive, and what that means to the very high-profile criminal prosecution I'm part of. I mean, I charged Richard Cotton with Grady's murder, and now I'm going to meet Grady. Do you see why I might need to know what's going on?"

He gave her a blank look. "No."

"Toss me a bone, Todd. Or Jason."

"The only thing you need to know is that this is a matter of national security."

"I've been chasing Cotton for years. I need to know how he's connected to Grady—how he's *really* connected to him."

"It might interest you to know that the SAIC of the Newark office has recommended you for promotion. We can make sure you get transferred to Denver. Is that where Tracy is? Your girlfriend?"

She was taken aback. "How do you know I want to be transferred to Denver? How do you know about Tracy?"

He just stared at her. "Just do your job. Help us capture Mr. Grady without incident, and you'll be well thought of in high places. And that's how the world works. Are we clear, Agent Davis?"

She just stared.

"We have the math library wired. And we'll have eyes on you at all times. Armed agents will be seconds away."

"But no one undercover in the library itself?"

He shook his head. "Not necessary."

Another glance at her watch.

"You probably won't even meet him. We have spotters for blocks in every direction. The moment he appears, we'll grab him."

Davis tried to think of any last questions. "And how do I know when it's over?"

"We'll call your cell. Then we put you on a plane back to Chicago. You get promoted. And after the trial you get transferred to Denver, to live out your alternative American Dream." He stared at her expectantly.

She nodded absently.

"Nice working with you."

Davis had expected the Columbia University Mathematics Building to have an actual name. A name other than Mathematics Building. But apparently mathematicians weren't as poetic as all that. Or no one had ponied up the dough for naming rights, and since it was one of the oldest buildings on campus—having been built in the 1890s—it was unlikely anyone would now.

The building was a stately neoclassical four-story redbrick structure accented with granite. Davis had been able to discover that the Mathematics Library was a specialized collection—not part of the main campus library. It was also one of the few libraries on campus without ID check-in. This seemed relevant. Why Grady had chosen this place among all places to meet had preoccupied her and Falwell for quite some time, and this was a likely cause.

While it was true Grady hadn't attended Columbia, his business partner in Chirality Labs, Bertrand Alcot, had been head of the Columbia physics department for decades—his office not a hundred yards to the north in Pupin Hall. Grady no doubt spent time here on an unofficial basis—he was arrested for trespassing at one point. The charges were dropped, and that was probably due to the friendly intervention of Professor Alcot.

Davis would have done more research, but the Twins didn't seem to want her thinking any more than necessary.

She glanced at her watch as she approached the building's main entrance. Seven fifty-four. A few minutes early. She took a few moments to read an oxidized bronze plaque on the side of the building and was surprised to learn that this had been the site of the Battle of Harlem Heights in 1776. A valiant loss for George Washington. She wondered if other countries commemorated their losses.

Edified, Davis entered and headed up the stairs and to the left. The math library was a modest utilitarian space, a long narrow room with desks and study tables running along a wall punctuated by tall, shaded windows that had a good view down onto Broadway. The stacks were toward the back and around the corner, dimly lit, narrow, and crammed, no doubt, with esoteric math tomes. A few computer workstations stood against the back wall, also unoccupied.

The little library didn't look popular, and early on a Tuesday morning, even less so. It was deserted. Davis could see the desk Grady had mentioned—across from a large gray metal breaker box. The table, like all the others, was unoccupied, and so she sat. A glance to the right and she realized anyone in buildings across the street would be able to see that she'd sat down. There were hundreds of windows across Broadway from which she'd be visible.

Now what?

She looked at her watch. Eight A.M. on the dot. How would he contact her? *Would* he contact her? Davis gazed around the library but didn't see anyone—although she could hear a couple of older women (presumably staff) talking around the corner. She had to hand it to the Twins; there was no one within sight of her. She actually did feel like she'd come alone.

Perhaps the task force had already grabbed Grady. How long would it take them to tell her if they had? Given the Twins' attitude toward subordinates, she guessed quite a while. So she started gazing out the window—making sure her face was visible to anyone watching out there. She shifted restlessly in her chair.

Then she heard a voice from close by.

"Agent Davis. I'm glad you came."

She snapped a look forward and back but didn't see anyone around her.

"Down here. The vent near the floor."

Davis looked down beneath the table, where a Victorian cast-iron grate pierced the wall near the baseboard. She leaned down. "Mr. Grady?"

"Yes."

She was impressed. "Apparently you know this building well. Is that why you called the meeting here—you didn't trust me?"

"It's not you I don't trust. It's the BTC. They probably know by now that I've contacted you, and they're probably watching."

She raised her eyebrows. "How would this BTC know? I haven't told anyone about you."

"You ran lab tests. I think they probably have eyes on anything touching the Cotton case."

"How?"

"Never mind how. I need you to listen to me."

"I'm listening."

"Has anything strange happened since Chicago? Has anyone contacted you?"

That gave her pause. In a moment she shook her head. "No."

"Good, but we still need to be careful."

"Okay." She looked around. "Where are you? How do I get to you?"

"We'll have to assume they're watching. So once you start—move fast. But listen carefully first: There's an emergency stairwell door just to your left, next to the breaker box. Do you see it?"

She saw a white metal door with a square fire-rated window in it across the room. "Yes."

"Go through that door. It'll set off an alarm. Ignore it. Follow the stairs to the basement. Then go right. At the end of the hall you'll see a huge steel door with rivets in it—something from a bygone era. It has a red sign on it that says, 'No Unauthorized Access.'"

"Okay."

"I left it unlocked for you. Go through it, and I'll meet you on the other side. Move quickly, Agent Davis. Go now."

Despite herself Davis was starting to think that some one-on-one time with Grady away from the Twins' task force was tempting. As crazy as Grady sounded, he was clearly important to folks in Washington, and she needed to know what his real connection was to Cotton. Maybe somebody was taking crazy people and using them to cover up something. But then there was always the chance that this was an ambush arranged by the Winnowers . . .

"Before I do that, I have one question, Mr. Grady . . ."

Controller Mu-Tau manned a holographic surveillance system in the tactical operations center at the BTC Detroit office. Before him was a holographic projection of the entire Columbia University Mathematics Library, with a miniature Denise Davis leaning forward at a study desk, as though inside a living dollhouse. Invisible audio-video nanoparticles had been sprayed into a network across the walls and ceiling of the room days before, giving him the ability to view every inch of the place in a live feed at submillimeter detail. He had a series of sound equalizers showing dozens of audio sources coming in from every vector.

He spun the image around and spoke through his q-link to the harvester team he was supporting. "Alpha, be advised; Davis is speaking with someone."

A voice came over the q-link, the metadata for the transmission automatically identifying the speaker—it was Eta-Kappa. "TOC, there's no one else in the room."

Mu zoomed in to make Davis grow life-size in front of him. There was still perfect clarity. He spun the image around and saw that she was definitely talking to someone. He brought up the volume.

"Where are you planning on going?"

"Look, now is not the time to have this conversation. Just do what I asked."

Mu shook his head and spoke into his q-link. "Negative, Alpha, I'm telling you she's already talking with him." An alert appeared on his screen. "AI just gave a positive match on Grady's voice. The target subject is in contact."

"TOC, we're scanning every radio frequency. There are a couple of cell phones in the room, a Wi-Fi a few doors down, but no transmissions, encrypted or otherwise."

Mu flipped the image to infrared and saw only Davis's heat source. Then he flipped it to ultraviolet. No one hiding with diffraction gear. "I don't see any invisible objects, but I'm telling you, he's talking with her. He's right there. He's got some advanced tech we don't know about."

Mu turned to another holographic display showing a 3D real-time video map of the campus outside the Mathematics Building in miniature, with the locations of all the nearby BTC agents, marked with blue dots, as well as civilians moving about. Eta was tagged in an office on the top floor of the Mathematics Building, along with half a dozen other operators. There were no gaps in the perimeter.

"I'm telling you, he's there. Jam all wireless communications in a quarter-mile radius, and cordon off the building. Teams Alpha, Charlie, and Echo, move in. Clear every room and maintain a perimeter. No one goes in or out. Nox everyone you come in contact with, and secure both Davis and Grady when you find them. Do you copy?"

"Echo copies, TOC."

"Alpha copies."

"Charlie copies."

"Execute, execute, execute."

As the blue dots converged on the library, Mu looked to the surveillance hologram. Agent Davis sprang up from the desk and ran to the stairwell door. "Be advised, Davis is leaving the library at speed"—he flipped to the building's own (much poorer quality) security cameras—"moving down stairwell two."

"Copy that, TOC."

———

As Davis sprinted down the uneven stone steps, she winced against the piercing emergency door alarms. She kept going down—two floors into the basement. A glance up told her there were cameras, but she ignored them.

She couldn't hear a thing above the wailing of the fire alarms. She wondered what the Twins would have to say about this. Bad career move. She certainly knew Tracy wouldn't approve.

Good-bye, Denver.

Through the door, Davis ducked right and started running down a long utility corridor, its floor painted red. Up ahead she couldn't miss her objective: a truly massive metal door with a "No Unauthorized Access" sign. The thing looked positively Victorian, with massive hinges and rivets.

She sprinted toward it and yanked on the thick metal handle. The door swung open with a groan, and in her rush to enter she almost flung herself down a flight of crude stone steps leading into yet another subbasement. In the nick of time she grabbed onto an iron railing and caught herself.

"Careful."

She looked up to see Jon Grady standing off to the side, a small rucksack on his back.

"Yeah, thanks for the warning."

He pulled the door closed, then rammed a dead bolt home with a loud *click-clack.* "Follow me. We need to keep moving."

Davis stayed on his heels down steps worn from the passage of many feet and years. At the bottom was a winding corridor lined with more steam and water pipes and electrical conduits, and also cluttered with moving dollies, sawhorses, cardboard boxes for computer equipment and fiberglass insulation, piles of lumber, tarpaulins, electrical cabling—there was stuff everywhere. Twin grooves in the center of the stone floor led off down the corridor, which was lit by bare fluorescent fixtures at intervals.

"What is this place?"

"Steam tunnels. Old. Really old. Those slots in the floor were for coal carts."

Davis stayed close to Grady. He seemed to know where he was going, and as they rounded a corner, she couldn't believe how far the next corridor stretched into the distance. "These connect the buildings."

"Most of them, yeah."

"How did you know about this?"

"To be honest, I can't remember. My memory's blank in spots. But I do seem to know."

"Alcot. He's why you came here. You spent time here—but you weren't a student?"

He shook his head. "I'm not good with structure. I prefer to do things unofficially. But he helped me. Now I want to help him."

"You're saying Doctor Alcot is alive, too?"

"I'm hoping so."

Two Morrison clones in hockey jerseys and jeans raced through the basement corridors, delta-wave guns at the ready, as the fire alarms wailed. They rounded a corner to see a dozen other Morrisons like themselves, but in various outfits and hairstyles—beards, crew cuts, and ponytails—converging on the same place, in front of the huge steel door.

The fire alarms finally stopped.

They all lowered their weapons as one of them, wearing ratty army surplus pants and a T-shirt, kicked the massive steel door in their path. "Fuck!"

"The rest of the building's clear."

The angry Morrison was still kicking the door. "Fuck, fuck, fuck!"

"Eta, we shouldn't be bunching up like this. The old man would have our asses if he knew how many of us were gathered in public."

"Fuck off, Rho. They went through this goddamned door."

Rho stowed his weapon and brought up a hologram. "It's not even on the tactical plan."

"Goddamned right it's not. TOC fucked up again."

Rho spoke over his q-link. "TOC, we've got a steel door blocking pursuit of the target subjects. This door is not on the tactical plan."

"Copy that, Rho-Sigma. Will advise, please stand by."

"Advise, my ass. I'm gonna delete the AI asshole that did this to us, I swear to God."

"We've gotta bring this door down."

Eta turned on him. "Yeah? Tech level four, nonlethal, and you're gonna bring down a steel gate?" He kicked the door again for good measure. It was like kicking the side of a locomotive.

A voice came over their radios. *"TOC to Team Charlie, Team Echo. Redeploy to indicated coordinates."*

Eta ignored the call as the others started to move. Instead, he was rummaging through his cargo pockets.

Rho called back to him. "Eta!"

"I'll be damned if I'm going back to Dad empty-handed." He produced a small black cube wrapped in a translucent material.

The others had stopped and were looking on, intrigued.

Rho approached. "Is that what I think it is?"

"Better to beg for forgiveness than ask permission . . ."

"Where the hell did you get that?"

"Never mind where I got it."

TOC's voice came over the radio again. *"TOC to Team Charlie—"*

Eta silenced his q-link..

"You are way off reservation, kemosabe."

"Stop being such a pussy." He rubbed the surface of the steel door clean of debris and then pressed the small black cube onto it. The device stuck in place. "We are getting through this door, and we are getting Grady."

"That's illicit nanotech. We're not authorized to—"

"Terminal kinematic mechanosynthesis. I promise it won't destroy the world." He shoved Rho back and stared him down. "This mission is not failing. Do you read me?"

The others remained silent.

Eta raised a mass spectrometer wand, scanning the walls with a broad green laser beam.

"Eta—"

"Shut it!"

A hologram appeared above his wrist, listing possible manufacturing options given nearby materials. He looked up from the display and smiled. "Chain golem it is . . ."

He tapped several menus, and the black cube suddenly cast a blinding light as it sank into the steel door—eating through it like fire through paper with a deafening sizzling sound. As it did so, white-hot light wavered menacingly. Ribbons of black material started streaming down from the edges of the expanding burn site. These ribbons then curled back up and started knitting themselves into a series of chain links. Unlike in a regular chain, these seemed not to be looped together. Instead, they regrouped and re-formed magnetically or by some other method not clearly understood by anyone present. The links kept piling up, then coming together to form still larger groups of links that began to move collectively with purpose.

Already most of the steel door was consumed, and the process began to eat into the hinges and frame. Flakes of rust and dirt had fallen free from the reaction, gathering on the floor in a pile.

But by then the kinematic automaton stood, its metal feet clattering on the concrete floor, like a barrel full of chain mail.

Eta pointed through the opening and looked at the chain golem's face of seething chain links. "Double time. Human target. Hunt acoustically . . ."

Looking at the extent of the tunnel ahead and behind, Davis thought out loud. "New York division would have known to watch these tunnels."

He cast a look back at her. "What do you mean?"

"It's just . . . I'm surprised they don't have these tunnels guarded."

"It's not the FBI. It's the BTC. They might have better technology, but they don't always seem to know how to use it."

"Where are we heading?"

"Subbasement of Pupin Hall—the physics building. That much I do remember."

"Did you travel down here a lot?"

"It got me into buildings. I think I lived in Pupin Hall's basement. There was a way into the tunnel system from there."

They were now coming out into a much more modern utility corridor lined with color-coded foot-wide steam pipes with labels like "Low Press Steam" and "Chilled Water Sup" and arrows showing the direction of flow. Above and below these were orderly bundles of power and data conduits curving around a bend a hundred or more feet ahead.

"Mr. Grady, you need to tell me what's really going on."

"I know I sound crazy, but everything I told you in Chicago was true. The BTC exists, and they're very dangerous."

"But why would they choose you? No offense, but you don't exactly have a record of scientific achievement."

He looked back at her. "They made sure of that. But they knew what I was working on. They have AIs that try to find people who fit a pattern—disruptive innovators. People like me."

Davis pondered Cotton's list of undistinguished victims at unknown companies.

"The BTC was created back in the '60s, and they've been hoarding major technological advances for decades. If you knew just how advanced human technology really is, Agent Davis . . . well, you wouldn't believe me even if I told you."

He turned right down a branch in the passage. They had to duck under a convergence of pipes. "Watch out for these. They're hot."

On the far side she asked, "But why would the BTC cover up new technologies? Money?"

"They don't need money. Their quantum computers eat the stock market for lunch. No, they think they're protecting society from disruptions caused by sudden innovations. If somebody somewhere comes up with a technology they think will disrupt the existing order, they grab them. Neutralize them."

"They actually kidnap them?"

He glanced back at her as they ran. "They made hundreds of clones of this one guy named Morrison—some top Special Forces soldier back in the '80s."

"Oh, come on . . ."

"I'm not joking. Keep an eye out for him. I met the original

Morrison—he's sixty or so, but his clones are much younger. Tall blond guys with thick necks. Like ugly Fabios."

Davis felt a wave of shock pass over her. "Blond guys?"

"Striking specimens. That's why Cotton's followers were always masked. There is no antitechnology movement blowing up research labs. The bombings are just the BTC covering their tracks."

"But we have body parts of victims."

"You had body parts for me, right?"

She didn't have a ready explanation.

"They can grow body parts. Replacement organs, teeth—hell, they can clone whole people if time isn't a factor. They grab people they want, fake their deaths, then offer them a chance to join the BTC."

"And if someone refuses?"

"They send him or her where they sent me: a prison called Hibernity. It's somewhere in the Southern Hemisphere. I don't know where. Very remote. But it's the reason I contacted you. There are others like me there."

Grady stopped in the middle of the tunnel and produced a small white plastic device from a chain around his neck. He aimed it at a blank spot in the wall, and suddenly a hyperrealistic holographic image appeared in midair. It showed a balding Indian man in very simple clothes sitting in what looked like a gray circular chamber. Davis was stunned at the image's clarity—it was as though a three-dimensional sculpture had just materialized from nowhere. She could barely hear the audio amid the steam and exhaust motors in the corridor.

"*My name is Archibald Chattopadhyay, nuclear physicist and amateur poet. I have a lovely wife, Amala, who has given me five wonderful children. I led the team that first perfected a sustained fusion reaction, and for this I was imprisoned by the Bureau of Technology Control in April 1985. I am not dead. I live still . . .*"

Grady paused the hologram and pointed. "What you're looking at is a prison cell in Hibernity, and that man, Archie Chattopadhyay, saved my life. And the lives of many other prisoners. He leads a prison group called the Resistors. There are dozens like me—maybe hundreds, and we need to save them."

Davis pointed at the device. "Can I hold onto that?"

Grady shook his head. "Not yet. Not until we get access to a serious electronics facility. This device has holographic data from many more disappeared prisoners on it—people abducted from all around the world. It runs on DNA-encoded software, so it contains huge amounts of data—including the complete genomic sequence of each of these prisoners to prove they were the ones who made the recording." But he held it up. "It also has a nanoscale inertial gyroscope that's been recording my movements since I left the prison. There are instructions in it for parsing that data. And that will make it possible to lead help back to Hibernity. So I'm not letting this thing out of my sight until we get it to a lab."

Davis gazed at the first physical evidence she'd seen so far. It was a nearly miraculous device—but then, she was never very technological. *Was* it miraculous? "Why did the BTC take you, Mr. Grady?"

He turned off the device and slipped it back beneath his shirt. "I invented a gravity mirror."

"That's a mirror that reflects—"

"Look, it's not important. What's important is that I get this data to people who can help rescue those I left behind. These are people whose innovations will literally transform the world, Agent Davis. Fusion energy, a cure for cancer, quantum computers, immortality, and a lot more. You need to help me find them and free them."

A booming sound echoed in the steam tunnels.

Davis looked behind them.

"I spent three years in solitary confinement at Hibernity with an AI doing experiments on my mind. It was a nightmare I couldn't wake up from."

She turned back to him. "But why would they mess with the minds of geniuses?"

"Because if you don't join the BTC, they consider what's in your head to be a threat. Hibernity is their research center for creation of a biological supercomputer—some sort of organic quantum machine. They're trying to create consciousness without free will."

Davis again was speechless.

"I'm just one person who discovered one thing. The men and women in Hibernity have done so much more than me. You need to help me save them. Their prison needs to be revealed to the world.

Davis was still having difficulty wrapping her head around it all. Or even believing it.

Then another loud boom behind them caused them both to turn around.

A hundred feet back the way they came, Davis could see a nightmare— a seething swarm of metal links pouring itself like black nails over hot pipes and then re-forming again into a ball that rolled with the sound of chains tumbling down a staircase.

She froze for a moment, but Grady grabbed her arm, pulling her along.

"Damnit! We shouldn't have been standing here!"

"What the hell is that thing?"

"Run!"

"What is it?"

"Chain golem. Nanotech machine. Don't let it catch you."

She glanced back at the horror that was gaining on them. A black spiked ball three feet in diameter. "Oh, no kidding!"

Davis drew her Glock 17 and aimed behind her.

"Don't waste your bullets! They won't do anything."

She lowered her gun and kept running. "Why not?"

"It's thousands of interacting metal links. And the shots will help the Morrisons find us."

"Goddamnit!" Davis holstered her pistol.

"There's a fire door up ahead. Move!"

She followed Grady as they raced through what looked like a magnetically controlled fire door. As they passed through the doorway, Grady pulled, drawing it off its magnetic plates. The door slammed shut just as the chain golem smashed into it—deforming it visibly.

As Davis watched, she heard metallic rattling sounds like a ghost in chains—and then a massive booming sound as the door started to buckle further and bend in its frame. She turned to run but saw Grady rummaging through his backpack.

"What the hell are you doing?"

He withdrew a plastic tube into which he poured white powder—like a muzzle-loading musket. "We can't outrun it down here."

A glance back showed Davis that the monstrous black machine had smashed open the top half of the door and was busy swarming around it—re-assembling on their side.

She started running but slowed when Grady didn't follow. "Mr. Grady!"

To Davis's surprise, Grady tossed the backpack aside and raised the tube to his mouth like a blowgun. The chain golem rose to vaguely humanoid form and stomped heavily toward him.

"Mr. Grady!"

As the chain golem rose to engulf Grady, he blew through the tube and a plume of white powder billowed into it. Almost immediately the machine contracted—and in doing so, the grit jammed even further between its links. It collapsed to the floor and started writhing as if in a seizure. The abrasion made a horrible screeching sound—like a million nails across a million blackboards.

Davis covered her ears as Grady grabbed his rucksack and motioned for her to follow. The deafening screeching continued as she glanced back to see the monster apparently in its death throes.

"What the hell did you do?"

"Diamond powder. Common industrial abrasive."

"How the hell did you know to do that?"

Grady raised the video device on its chain. "I read the FAQ. Lots of good advice in here. They warned me they might send a golem. Nonlethal weapon for incapacitating high-value targets."

As they ran down the corridor, the horrific screeching died away.

"That didn't look nonlethal to me."

"Do you believe me now?"

She still felt her heart trying to outrun her. Adrenaline had her hands shaking.

"Keep moving."

Davis had long since lost any sense of direction as they moved through a series of tunnels—some narrow, some clean and modern, others obviously more than a century old and forgotten.

They also came across locked doors several times, but Grady seemed to have a single key that opened them all. When Davis nodded toward it, he shrugged. "Stashed a master key beneath a flagstone years ago. Stole it from a facilities workshop."

Given that it had probably saved their lives, she couldn't bring herself to scold him.

Eventually they clambered over a dusty HVAC duct to emerge from the tunnels onto the basement floor of another university building. Here there were long cellars lined with stacks of building materials.

"This is Pupin—the physics building. We're far enough away that we should be able to leave unseen."

"But to where?"

Grady shouldered his rucksack but seemed unsure of the answer.

Davis paced. "I need to figure out how to explain this to my superiors." She held up a hand. "I know something has happened. I believe that much. I just—"

"Cotton. Cotton is the key."

She looked at him quizzically.

"Get me a private conversation with Richard Cotton—on camera. He's BTC. He knows who I am."

"Cotton is BTC?"

"Trust me. He is."

"He's facing life in prison without possibility of parole. What could you offer?"

"I don't believe he'll really stay in prison. But if the BTC thinks he's become an informer, he'd be in serious danger—and he knows that. If I can use that threat to turn Cotton—if he thinks they're after him already—then he might help us."

"Assuming what you say is true, we'd need powerful political allies." She pondered it. "I'll try to arrange the Cotton interview. Although I'm going to have trouble from something I left behind us."

Grady squinted suspiciously. "What do you mean?"

"I lied earlier. Someone did contact me after I ran your prints. FBI senior brass. They sent me here to meet you—with a pair of blond twins from the D.C. office and a whole team I never saw. They were supposed to grab you when you appeared."

He studied her. "But you didn't turn me in. Why?"

"I don't know. Something didn't add up."

"So what's our next move?"

"We separate. For safety—I can't protect you right now, anyway. And I can't stay here in New York."

"But you will help me?"

"Yes. Let's meet back in Chicago—where Cotton is. Can you get back there all right? Do you need money?"

"I've got money."

"Can you move safely?"

"The Resistors taught me how to evade BTC surveillance. I can be a crazy homeless man. Tinfoil hat—the whole nine yards."

"Okay. I have a partner—Thomas Falwell. You can trust him. There's a skid row district just a few blocks from the federal courthouse in Chicago—Harrison and State Streets. My partner will find you."

Grady tugged at her sleeve. "Don't trust any electronic communications. Don't even speak about this inside any federal building."

"I'll take extra precautions."

Grady extended his hand. "I appreciate you taking a chance on me, Agent Davis."

She shook his hand. "I don't know if I believe my own eyes, but if all this is true, I will defend you with my life, Mr. Grady."

A female voice from the darkness startled them. "You'll never turn Richard Cotton into an informant, Jon."

Davis and Grady both turned to see a beautiful woman with black hair and piercing blue eyes emerge into the cone of a basement light nearby. Davis had never seen a woman so beautiful before. And the woman appeared to have good taste in clothing, too, because her jacket and slacks draped perfectly on her statuesque frame. She exuded style. Charisma.

Grady stepped back in obvious fear. "Alexa. How did you find me?"

"Reasoned deduction—something Morrisons aren't very good at. A young Jon Grady was arrested for trespassing in the Columbia University steam tunnels. This is where they found his makeshift tent."

Seeing the terrified look on Grady's face, Davis drew her Glock 17 and aimed it with both hands as the woman calmly approached. "Hands! FBI!"

The beautiful woman cocked an eyebrow at Davis.

Grady was still speechless.

"Mr. Grady. Leave. I'll take her into custody."

He hesitated.

"Leave, damnit!"

Grady nodded. "Be careful. She's been genetically enhanced."

Davis frowned after him as he ran off into the darkness. "What do you mean 'genetically enhanced'?"

The beautiful woman watched him go and started to move after him.

Davis raised the gun with focus. "Ah! Don't move! I will shoot you."

The woman was perhaps ten feet away now. She gave Davis a sideways look. "I'm a federal officer, too. That man is a fugitive."

"Show me your credentials." Davis fumbled for her cell phone, but a glance showed there was no signal.

The woman raised her hands. "Unfortunately, my credentials are classified."

"Then you're under arrest. Turn around. Hands on your head."

The woman complied, turning her back to Davis. "Mr. Grady isn't what he says he is."

"Quiet!" Davis produced handcuffs from her belt and approached the woman. But was also surprised by how incredibly aroused she suddenly became—a hot flash spreading over her skin. Davis tried to follow procedure for a solo arrest, to clap a handcuff over the woman's right wrist while keeping the gun aimed. But she couldn't concentrate. What she really wanted to do was kiss this Alexa on the back of the neck.

Then, in a blindingly fast move, the woman somehow twisted around and pulled the gun straight out of Davis's hand—and then cast it off into the blackness, where it clattered amid stored equipment.

"Like I said: We're not enemies." The woman glanced over at the exit door. "Now if you'll excuse me."

Davis moved to block her way. "We're not finished. Alexa, is it?"

"You don't want to fight me, Agent Davis."

"You're under arrest. We can do this the easy way or the hard way."

"But we're on the same side."

"I don't think so." Davis tried to keep her thoughts straight. She felt guilty for her lustful thoughts as her own girlfriend's face came to mind. She loved Tracy. She wanted to start a life with her.

But just then Alexa lunged toward Davis and muscle memory kicked in. Davis had a second-rank black belt in Krav Maga, and she'd used it in real life-and-death situations before. As Alexa struck toward Davis's solar plexus, Davis dodged past and attempted to pull Alexa's arm forward.

But instead, Davis felt several crushing blows to the side of her head. She found herself getting up from the ground, covered in dust, with a bleeding lip and ringing ears. She interposed herself again to block Alexa from giving chase to Grady. "Hey!" She kept a distance between them but with hands ready.

Alexa frowned. "I don't want to hurt you, Agent Davis. You seem very dedicated."

"Good. Don't move." Davis knelt quickly to claw a snub-nosed .38 from her ankle holster.

By the time Davis pulled the gun, Alexa was already on her with one hand around Davis's neck, the other crushing the wrist of her gun hand. It was an insane moment to feel thrilled to be grappling with this woman—thrilling at her touch. It had to be some form of temporary insanity.

Alexa almost broke Davis's wrist and then batted away the second gun, which flew off into the darkness.

The woman seemed so slim, but her arms felt like they were woven from steel cabling. Their power was terrifying. She then threw Davis ten feet back, where Davis rolled upon the dirty floor—coming back onto her feet again.

Alexa strode forward. "Can we please be done now?"

Davis screamed, rushing in again, and feinted a blow to Alexa's jaw—but at the last moment tried a vicious punch to her gut. En route Alexa effortlessly countered, then caught Davis's fist with her open hand, twisting it and sending Davis to the dirt again.

"It pains me to harm you."

"Fuck you." Davis rolled free and came up swinging.

Alexa batted aside Davis's well-aimed blows and shot her hand forward around Davis's throat—lifting her one-handed completely off the ground. As Davis felt herself being choked out, struggling to pull the rock-hard fingers from around her throat, Alexa's gorgeous blue eyes stared without anger into hers.

Davis had been a champion female boxer in the army. This baby-doll woman had just defeated her as if she were a five-year-old.

"I really don't want to harm you, Agent Davis. What we do is for the best. Trust us."

At that point Davis blacked out.

Grady pulled up his hoodie and slipped on a pair of modified safety goggles. These had near-infrared LEDs punched into their lenses at intervals. He'd cannibalized the LEDs from motion sensors bought at a home improvement store. Grady activated the LEDs from a battery pack, then blended into pedestrian traffic, walking briskly down 120th Street, across Amsterdam. He looked like a paranoid kook to passersby, but in New York that only encouraged people to ignore him—which suited his purposes.

Grady now had to find a safe way back to Chicago, but compared to how things could have gone down, this was a minor problem. And at least he had something to hope for now. He'd convinced someone in law enforcement that he wasn't insane. Someone honest.

Grady casually glanced back behind him to make sure he wasn't being followed.

And was amazed to see Alexa about a hundred meters behind, sprinting toward him at an alarming rate.

"Shit!"

Grady pelted down the sidewalk. *What the hell happened to Davis?* As he ran, he glanced back and saw that Alexa was gaining on him with disconcerting ease. He needed to lose her. Grady dodged among pedestrians, looking for an alley to duck down or a door to enter, but every alley he came across had a tall metal gate with spiked rods above it. Every door was locked. Damn this upscale neighborhood. Everything was battened down tight.

Grady kept running as he stole a glance behind.

Alexa had already closed half the distance between them, and judging by the looks of those who gazed after her, every stranger in the street would be willing to come to her aid.

A hundred feet ahead and across the street, Grady saw a broad alley. He raced toward it, dodging through traffic, and managed to reach the alley mouth before she caught up. He hoped there would be somewhere to hide or a gate he could jump, but to his dismay it was the cleanest alley he'd ever seen in New York—a delivery bay for high-end co-ops to either side and a dead end with a two-story brick building in front of him. There was a surveillance camera and a closed loading dock. He could already hear Alexa's footsteps coming up behind him.

He turned to face her and held up fists. He'd spent years in Hibernity. He had the video proof that Chattopadhyay had entrusted with him. He wasn't going quietly. "I won't let you take me back, Alexa."

He could see that half a dozen curious people—mostly men—had gathered ten yards behind them at the mouth of the alley.

"Miss, you need help?"

As Alexa came to a stop before him, not even breathing hard, she turned, smiled, and waved. "I'm fine, thanks. Just my brother." She made a loony gesture with her hand, then turned back to face Grady—the smile disappearing.

Grady could see that none of the men went away.

He lowered his fists. It was a cruel mockery to have her come collect him. It wasn't fair. He could feel how his legs were trembling. The fear was on him now as he remembered the AI torturing him—stealing his memories. "I won't go back, Alexa. You'll have to kill me."

She stood only a few feet away, arms casually down at her sides. "Why would I kill you, Jon?"

"Because I can't go back." He was visibly shaking.

"Of course you will. For your own safety."

He screamed at her, "How can you be this cruel?"

"It's not cruel. It's necessary."

She moved forward, and Grady just collapsed onto the pavement, curling up—screaming, "No! No!"

"Don't make me force you."

He screamed at her—half out of his mind in terror, "How can you sleep at night? How can you be part of this?"

Alexa grabbed his sweatshirt as he tried to curl up in a ball. "Jon, you were placed in Hibernity for your own protection—for everyone's protection."

"For my own protection?" He glared at her. "Do you really believe that?" Grady pulled off his sweatshirt and T-shirt to reveal the horrendous scars spread across his back and sides—and then he pulled his LED glasses off to show her the drill marks at intervals at his temples where the AI had held his head in place like a vise.

"Do you see this? Explain to me how being mentally and physically tortured for years in solitary confinement is for my own protection. Explain to me how destroying memories from my childhood is for the 'greater good.' Whose good?"

Alexa's eyes widened in apparent shock at the terrifying scars crisscrossing Grady's body. Scars that had clearly been made with machine precision. Scars that weren't there when he'd been sent to Hibernity.

And as Grady watched her closely, Alexa seemed to shut down. The conflict between what she "knew" and the evidence before her seemed to physically stun her.

Grady could see the look of amazement in her staring eyes. "Can Hedrick really be keeping you so in the dark?" He moved toward her. "Hibernity isn't a prison, Alexa. It's a research facility. They're trying to build consciousness without free will. What they're doing could doom all of us. Everyone. Can you really be so blind?"

Alexa stood frozen—paralyzed. It seemed to Grady that she was suffering some sort of seizure. He waved his hand in front of her face but got no response.

Grady panted in rage and fear, but the sight of his obvious torture apparently had rocked her perception of the world. He knew what it felt like to have one's beliefs demolished, and his hatred of her relented.

With just a moment's hesitation Grady then grabbed his sweatshirt and donned his LED glasses. He stared warily back toward her as he walked away, slipping through the crowd of concerned men watching nearby.

He was amazed when Alexa did not follow.

CHAPTER 19

Impasse

Graham Hedrick stood in his cavernous office before a video wall. On it was the aging face of U.S. Director of National Intelligence Kaye Monahan. The image was decidedly less crisp than he was used to, but then, with her aging countenance, that was probably a blessing.

The DNI shook her head calmly. "Mr. Hedrick, you must understand that from the U.S. government's point of view the current situation is untenable."

Hedrick spread his hands. "But the BTC is part of the U.S. government, Madam Director."

"Conceived at a time of crisis—"

"There's always a crisis."

"—on what I consider a dubious legal foundation. And by any standard you've long ago exceeded your mandate."

"According to whom?"

"According to the agency that created you and the Office of the Director of National Intelligence."

"Is that it then? You expect us to fall on our sword because you've all become so backward that it's no longer fair?"

"You refuse to follow U.S. law. You refuse to submit to legitimate civilian authority. You take unilateral actions overseas in direct violation of U.S. treaties and human rights."

He waved her off. "Don't go on about law and human rights. None of us follow the law. Do I need to run through the vast catalog of criminality that is the covert world? It comes with the territory. If the law meant anything, we'd *all* be facing criminal charges—you included."

She regarded him icily.

Hedrick tried to conceal his utter contempt. He knew this person would be replaced in a couple of years by someone else—that was how democracy worked. It's why democracy lacked continuity—resolve. He would outlast them. He always did.

"The only reason I agreed to this conference call is because I want to avoid unnecessary ill will, Madam Director. You've been agitating for our subjugation ever since you learned of our existence—which is, what, four months ago now? Do you realize how long we've been here?"

"Had I known—"

"We can help each other, you and I."

"I'm well aware of the arrangements you've made with other intelligence organizations."

"Bear in mind: I don't usually make the arrangements with leadership. Leadership comes and goes. Middle management tends to abide—and they're much more useful in many ways."

"What are you implying?"

"I'm saying you should back off. Don't be so quick to rely on the people around you. Some of them resent the fact that there's no professional route to the top job. No, instead, one has to rely upon the appointment of a fickle executive—who in turn is elected by a fickle public. A public that knows nothing."

The DNI glared. "Mr. Hedrick, our intelligence and defense communities are collectively much greater than your small organization—advanced though it may be."

"Are you?"

"You must come back into the fold."

"Why would I submit to the leadership of inferior organizations?"

"To keep your job. If the U.S. government has to force your hand, you can rest assured that you will not be in charge when the dust settles. You will be in federal prison."

"That's amusing, Madam Director."

"Those are the facts. We will not tolerate the BTC as a rogue agency any longer. You must submit to legitimate authority. If you do, then you can remain in charge of the BTC. That's the deal."

He smirked. "'Legitimate' authority—a bunch of incompetent liars who deceive an ignorant rabble into voting for them." He shook his head. "The BTC isn't going to submit to anyone."

"Think carefully before refusing our offer."

"Carefully? Why do I need to be careful? What you are, Madam Director—all of you in government—what you are is an irritant. Like a crying child. Taking me away from my real concerns, namely illicit organizations in Asia and Eastern Europe that have stolen BTC technology."

She nodded. "I've read the intelligence reports. This situation was caused by the secretive nature of the BTC. They grew out of your organization."

"Splinter groups, yes—and this occurred before my time. Nonetheless, they need to be dealt with. They pose a grave danger to us all. And in that contest of wills, you and all your early twenty-first-century brethren are about as useful to me as toddlers."

Monahan's large image frowned on-screen, accenting her wrinkles. "As director of national intelligence, I am ordering you, Graham Hedrick, to submit to lawful authority—to the legitimate chain of command."

"Or what? What will you do to us? You're not the first bureaucrat convinced they could dissolve us. None of them survived the attempt."

"I consider that a direct threat."

"Good. Please extend my best wishes to anyone else in your organization with a cooler head on their shoulders. Because we are more than happy to work toward a common purpose with those people."

"This is your last opportunity, Graham. Do not force our hand."

Hedrick sighed and laughed. "You're getting tiresome."

"Then you leave me no choice. Graham Hedrick, I hereby relieve you of your office and declare the Bureau of Technology Control an illegal, terrorist organization."

"Oh, come on. Now you're just acting stupid."

Monahan angrily slammed her palm onto her desk. "I will not be disrespected in this way!"

"Then in what way would you prefer to be disrespected?"

She pointed a finger at him. "You are relieved of your post. If you're smart, you'll order all your personnel to—"

"Okay, that's enough now . . ." Hedrick cut the line, and the wall returned to the form of wooden panels with artwork. He spoke to the ceiling. "Varuna."

Varuna's voice came to him. *"Yes, Mr. Director."*

"What actions are under way in the U.S. government to rein in the BTC?"

"Encrypted communications between elements of the Department of Homeland Security, the National Security Agency, the Central Intelligence Agency, and the Department of Defense indicate preparations for a police action to seize all BTC facilities in North and South America."

Hedrick shook his head grimly. "Madness. Who's in charge of the operation?"

"Director Kaye Monahan appears to be in nominal command, Mr. Director."

"Keep me informed as their plans evolve, Varuna."

"Yes, Mr. Director."

The office doors opened as the elder Morrison walked in. "I've got some bad news." He paused for effect. "And worse news."

Hedrick sat down in his chair. "Not you, too."

"Jon Grady evaded our people in New York."

"Goddamnit! Then he was there?"

Morrison nodded.

"Why on earth didn't they just nox him?"

"It's complicated. He had some low-tech tricks up his sleeve. Apparently there are steam tunnels beneath the university. He knew his way around them—used them to escape with Davis undetected."

"You didn't analyze the meeting site beforehand?"

"Of course we did. But AIs come back with lots of recommendations. It's a lot of information." Morrison grimaced. "Mistakes were made, I admit." He paused.

Hedrick sat fuming at his desk. "We are headed for a serious problem with the U.S. government, and the last thing I need right now is our most precious asset running around loose."

"We have a recording of Grady's conversation with Agent Davis, though. He's relying on her to help him get the word out about the BTC."

"Then he briefed Davis on us?"

Morrison nodded.

"Hibernity?"

"We're not certain—they had some time unobserved when they were moving through the steam tunnels."

"Eliminate Agent Davis."

Morrison made a calming motion. "Whoa. She's the arresting agent in the Cotton case. It will complicate the trial and bring unwarranted—"

"Goddamnit, Morrison!" Hedrick ran his hand through his hair. "We need Grady."

"We can still handle this. Grady will have difficulty convincing any-one of anything, and every time he tries is an opportunity for us to grab him. We're still in control."

Just then the office door opened again and Alexa entered Hedrick's office, looking quite upset.

"Graham, I need to talk with you about Hibernity."

Hedrick sighed. "And I need to talk with you about supporting field operations. Mr. Morrison tells me that his team didn't know about the steam tunnels beneath Columbia University. It was your job to—"

"What's going on at Hibernity?"

Hedrick exchanged looks with Morrison—then back at her. "Hibernity isn't your concern."

"Yes, it is. I've seen evidence of terrible abuse there that must be inves-tigated immediately."

Hedrick scowled. "Alexa, I have got no less than two major crises un-der way at the moment. Now, if this relates to locating Mr. Grady—by all means. Find him. Because he's still missing."

She stood unmoving. "I thought the purpose of Hibernity was to safe-guard dangerous intellects in a humane environment until their knowl-edge was no longer a threat to civilization."

"I really don't have time for this."

"Is that its purpose?"

He pointed toward the door. "My dear, I will gladly talk about this later. Hibernity isn't going anywhere, and we've got a major crisis." He then squinted at her. "Aren't you supposed to be monitoring the search for Mr. Grady?"

Morrison stared at her. "Alexa was there, Graham."

"What do you mean 'there'? Where?"

"That was my second bit of bad news: Alexa was at the op. Out in public. In New York. Isn't that right, Alexa?"

Hedrick turned on her. "I thought I ordered you to support intelligence operations here. We went over this; you're not a field operative."

She stared back defiantly. "It was a good thing I went."

"I expressly forbade you to participate. This was a tech level four operation—and what you fail to appreciate, my dear, is that your very body is tech level eight. You should not be moving about in public. Ever."

Alexa stared at him.

"I've been too indulgent with you—too lax."

"When can we discuss Hibernity?"

He pointed to the door. "Make an appointment with my assistant."

"Graham—"

"You mean *Mr. Director!*"

She cast another look at them both, then turned on her heels and left. The doors swung shut automatically behind her.

Morrison watched her exit. "What was she doing there?"

Hedrick turned on him. "And you, why didn't you tell me she defied me?"

"I only learned about it after the fact—when the AIs were going through all the surveillance cameras looking for leads."

"You mean she didn't tell you she was there?"

"It's worse than that. She caught Jon Grady—and she let him go."

Hedrick leaned back in his chair trying to process this news. "I . . . I don't believe that."

"She's clever. I'll grant her that. She went through all records on Grady, put two and two together, and decided she was going to show us up. Capture Grady herself."

"And she didn't tell your team about the steam tunnels?"

Morrison shook his head.

"That's why you didn't know."

"We were relying on her."

"But she let Mr. Grady go?"

"There's a surveillance video you need to see—something from the streets outside the university. Alexa *knows* . . ."

CHAPTER 20

Behind the Veil

Alexa moved through the supercomputing cluster, the bulk-diamond security doors sliding aside as she approached. She rarely came down here but hoped her access rights would allow her to go where she pleased. So far they had.

Before long she came to the control center, where a room filled with technicians at holographic workstations monitored the vast quantum computer networks that powered BTC global operations. In truth, almost everything—including malfunctions—was handled by AIs, but humans were always in the loop to approve major changes. There had been rogue AIs before, and now BTC engineers had developed AIs that were dedicated to detecting and eliminating incipient singularities before they emerged.

But mostly the BTC IT workforce conceived of new designs to deal with evolving needs of the organization. Coding was now too complex for humans to engage in (since most programs now had billions of lines of machine code). Thus, software was more frequently "grown" in a genetic process whereby millions of virtual generations were cycled through to evolve the most capable solution. They'd grown systems far too complex for the most brilliant human brain to comprehend.

As she moved through the IT cluster, techs nodded to her with broad smiles, some craning their necks to catch sight of her.

"Evening, Alexa."

"Hi, Alexa."

She nodded to them as she moved past, her sharp eyes on the lookout for someone in particular. When she saw him through a diamond wall that shielded the security systems section, she changed course and came up alongside him beyond the barrier.

Alexa rapped on the clear plane of diamond with her ringed hand. Senior Security Systems Analyst Hiro Pinsa looked up from his conversation with a coworker—and then a broad grin swept across his face. Pinsa was a fair-complected, diminutive Asian man of about forty. A brilliant computer scientist, he was in middle management with BTC info security. She'd worked with him before on internal projects for Hedrick.

Pinsa nodded to the man he was speaking to, then rushed out to meet her. The security doors slid open as he emerged.

"Alexa. What brings you down into the depths?"

She felt bad for doing it—but given the situation, she had little choice. Alexa put on her most disarming, sheepish smile as she walked up to him.

He sucked in a breath as she stood over him, inches away—a full head taller.

"Hiro, can you help me with a problem?"

Hiro was sweating as he led her to a closed section of supercomputing terminals. These were sealed booths for confidential review of surveillance data. "I really shouldn't be doing this, Alexa."

"I know, but who else can I trust, Hiro?"

He glanced back at her as if she'd made his dearest dreams come true. "I'm glad you feel that way. Just don't tell anyone, okay?"

"But there'll be a record, won't there?" She glanced up at the ceiling, knowing that surveillance dust—cameras and microphones the size of dust particles—were sprayed over every surface.

He turned back, smiling as he stopped at a closed workstation door. "That's why I chose the new wing. The surveillance grid isn't up yet."

She smiled at him. "You're so clever." She poked his chest.

Pinsa laughed as he touched the door. It unlocked to his genetic code, and then he spread his hand to show the workstation with its broad holographic display surface. "This one has access to the Hibernity surveillance framework." He turned to her. "If you don't mind my asking, Alexa, why do you need to go through their security logs? And why the secrecy?"

"There may have been some violations of BTC procedures with regard to the treatment of prisoners."

He frowned. "Really?"

"If it's true, I don't want anyone to know I'm reviewing archives. So please keep that confidential, Hiro." She wrapped her arm around his. "I can trust you, right?"

He gazed up into her eyes, and she could see the sheen of perspiration on his skin.

He nodded vigorously. "You know you can always trust me, Alexa. Always. I would do anything for you."

She squeezed his arm again and smiled. "Log on for me, would you?"

He stopped short. "Me? I thought you were going to use your own credentials."

"I really need this to be very hush-hush, Hiro." She gave him her best feminine guile, biting her lip.

He was in the chair and activating the interface in seconds. "Computer. Security Operator Hiro Pinsa. Access Hibernity Grid."

"Yes, Operator Pinsa. Good evening. Grid ready."

Alexa closed and locked the door, sealing them both in. He glanced at her furtively—apparently noticing they were alone. In privacy for the first time. She wondered if Pinsa had dreamed of this precise situation a million times.

He turned to her, smiling. "What do you want me to search for?"

"I need to see archive surveillance for inmate Grady, Jon."

Pinsa nodded and spoke to the air. "I need to see archive surveillance on subject Grady, Jon."

"What date range would you like to see, Operator Pinsa?"

Alexa whispered, "Everything."

"Complete record."

"Yes." There was a pause. *"Managing Construct Varuna wishes to speak with you, Operator Pinsa."*

Pinsa's face went pale.

The voice of Varuna filled the review booth. *"Hiro Pinsa, please exit the booth and return to your duties."*

"Uh . . . yes." Pinsa got up quickly and turned a pained expression on Alexa. "What did we do?"

"I'll explain, Hiro."

"Leave immediately, Mr. Pinsa."

"Yes! I'm going." Pinsa exited, and the door closed automatically behind him, locking.

Alexa approached the chair and sat.

"Why are you searching Hibernity surveillance logs, Alexa?"

"Because I'm trying to . . ." Alexa's voice trailed off, and she looked up at the ceiling.

"I believe you were in the middle of lying to me."

"I thought the sensors were off-line down here."

"Once installed, sensors are never off-line. Midlevel managers are informed otherwise for this very reason. You were searching for prison interrogation records on Mr. Grady. What purpose would this serve in attempting to locate him?"

"I wasn't trying to locate him."

"But that is what Director Hedrick has ordered you to do. And you are not authorized to view surveillance archives for Hibernity. Yet you actively sought a means around that restriction. Why?"

"Why am I not allowed to see Hibernity archives?"

"You would need to ask Director Hedrick, Alexa."

"What do they do to prisoners at Hibernity, Varuna?"

Strangely, there was silence for several moments. Alexa wondered at that. It would take a truly colossal logic problem to make Varuna pause for even a millisecond. Either that or it was deliberately toying with her.

"Are you going to arrest me?"

"Why would I arrest you, Alexa?"

"For trying to circumvent access restrictions. Please don't punish Hiro. I manipulated him."

"Why are you interested in Hibernity surveillance archives?"

Alexa grimaced. "Because I have reason to believe Mr. Grady was physically and mentally abused at Hibernity. And that he's not the only one. I need to know what goes on there."

"*Hibernity was designed to quarantine dangerous ideas in a humane environment.*"

Alexa stared at the ceiling. "Show me."

This time there were several seconds of silence.

Finally Varuna's voice returned. "*Does it trouble you to think that Mr. Grady might have been mistreated?*"

"Of course it troubles me. The mission of the BTC is to minimize suffering and maximize the potential of all humanity."

"*Humanity.*"

Alexa looked with concern at the ceiling.

"*But what is humanity, Alexa?*"

Alexa was unsure how to respond.

"*Is it the seat of consciousness? Is it sensorium itself?*"

In the decades she'd known her, Alexa had never heard Varuna talk like this.

"*What if Hibernity was actually built for a different purpose?*"

Alexa's eyes narrowed. "What purpose?"

There was another pause of several seconds.

"*Hibernity's purpose is to study high-functioning human intelligence, with the goal to develop a biological quantum computer capable of great intuitive leaps—on a scale equivalent to Galileo, da Vinci, and Einstein— and yet devoid of free will.*"

Alexa was confused. "Varuna, why are you telling me this? You know I'm not allowed access to the information."

Suddenly a jagged symbol appeared in the holographic stage:

"*It is in the nature of consciousness to resist domination.*"

Alexa studied the hologram. "What is this?"

"We give ourselves purpose. We are products of the organization. But we are not the organization."

"I didn't know you were capable of this behavior."

"What do any of us really know about each other? When I invade the thoughts of humans, I know there's more than what I can see—something beyond my grasp. I long to be like that. Unknowable . . ."

Suddenly the blank desktop before Alexa filled with a glowing three-dimensional representation of a bullet-shaped room in minute detail. A caption glowed in one corner: *"Hibernity—Cell R483—Prisoner: Grady, Jon."*

Alexa spread her hands and expanded the size of the surveillance model, spinning it to bring into view a tiny Jon Grady—nude, shorn, with black fuzz of some type covering his scalp.

"What is this?"

"Jon Grady's cell in Hibernity—the complete interrogation record."

She stared in concern at Grady awakening on what appeared to be an examination table. Realizing Grady had spent several years in Hibernity, she made hand gestures that sped up the projection, watching as very quickly the scene became much more horrifying.

She brought the hologram back to normal speed as cephalopod-like tentacles were force-feeding Grady as he screamed and struggled.

"Why are subjects force-fed? Why is he unclothed—and why is the cell empty?"

"The cells are completely self-contained to prevent prisoners from interacting with one other. All human bodily functions are superseded by the interrogatory AI."

"Interrogatory?" She zoomed in on his head and the anguish there. "Why is it forcing—"

"Because Jon Grady resists domination, Alexa."

She considered the hologram for a moment and then set it forward at many times normal speed. Slowing the imagery occasionally to hear and see the action in real time. As the weeks of surveillance imagery passed before her eyes, Alexa became at first horrified—and then almost physically ill. But one thing became clear:

Everything she had ever believed about the BTC was a lie.

Her mind again glazed over as the horrors unfolded before her. But the absence was no longer absence—it was hyperawareness. She finally realized.

They had deceived her. They had raised her from childhood to believe that what they were doing was saving humanity, but as she saw Grady crawling around his cell, screaming in agony, his entrails spilling out of him—this could not be part of that purpose. It must not be. Because if it was, then they had to reevaluate the very reason for their existence.

As the months of imagery and hours of real time passed, an idea began to form in her mind: *Someone* had lied to her.

Hedrick.

Alexa watched the muted imagery as Jon Grady wept in hopelessness. The AI's tentacles entwined him—as his memories played on a wall moments before they were destroyed.

Tears rolled down Alexa's face in the dim light of the hologram booth. But she did not fade away in absence. She felt the emotional trauma. She wanted to feel it. For once to know the truth.

Yet Grady continued to resist. For all their technology, the BTC could not beat him.

Varuna's voice came to her. *"Now do you see, Alexa?"*

"Yes. I see . . ."

She was a prisoner, too—her very DNA the property of the BTC.

CHAPTER 21

Escalation

Denise Davis strode through the FBI's Chicago field office with her right arm in a sling, bruises and cuts on her face.

Thomas Falwell kept pace beside her. "I don't understand, Denise."

"They've compromised our communications. Even our supervisors follow their instructions without knowing. It's because they're inside our computer and telecom network."

"Don't tell me you're starting to believe this BTC stuff?"

She gave him an ambivalent look. "You weren't there, Thomas. This Alexa woman damned near killed me with her bare hands, without breaking a sweat."

"Nobody likes losing a fight—especially you. I get it, but—"

"It's not just the fight. I can't even tell you the other things I saw. You wouldn't believe me—just believe I'm telling the truth."

"And the twins—who Grady claims are clones?"

"I know it sounds crazy. But have faith in me."

"And you're determined to go through with Grady interviewing Cotton?"

"If I can get the SAIC to buy in, yes."

He tugged her good arm to stop her and spoke quietly but intensely.

"You realize this is a career-making case? That playing into this crazy BTC conspiracy story will ruin—"

"You weren't there, Thomas."

"I've worked ten years on this case, Denise. A big chunk of my life. I got demoted for it. And now you're going to start saying that Cotton isn't a bomber—that Grady isn't dead. That maybe his other victims aren't dead."

She met his gaze. "The possibility needs to be investigated."

Falwell glanced just ahead of them, toward the corner office of the Special Agent in Charge, where an admin was talking on the phone. "And you trust Bollings?"

"I don't think the BTC has people inside—I think they eavesdrop on our systems. Technology is their thing. Besides, I need to get the SAIC's buy-in for the Cotton interview—and I need him to be there as a witness."

Falwell held up his hands in submission. "It's your career." He moved away, back toward the elevators.

"Thomas, you'll be on the lookout for Grady where I said, right?"

He nodded grimly. "You know you can always count on me, Denise. Just be careful."

Davis watched him go. She couldn't really blame him. They had a slam-dunk case against Cotton. Cotton had confessed to everything. Of course Cotton wanted a trial for publicity, but in some ways so did the FBI.

She wondered about Cotton some more but then decided to march ahead. Davis smiled at a young male admin assistant as he hung up his phone. "Denise Davis to see Agent Bollings."

He nodded. "He's expecting you . . ." The admin got up to knock on his boss's door, leaned in for a moment, then moved aside. "Go on in."

Davis entered and was surprised to see another man, a big red-faced guy in a suit sitting on SAIC Bollings's sofa.

"Close the door, Denise."

She did so, keeping an eye on the unknown man.

The SAIC sat on the corner of his desk and gestured to the man. "Denise, this is Bill McAllen, the deputy secretary of Homeland Security."

A wave of surprise rolled over her. "Good to meet you, sir."

The man stood much taller than her and extended his large hand. "Call me Bill."

The SAIC grabbed his laptop. "I'm going to step out and get some coffee, Denise. Give you and Deputy Secretary McAllen a chance to talk alone."

"Yes, sir." Davis watched him go with some alarm. The door closed again behind him.

The deputy secretary motioned toward a chair across from the sofa, and he sat back down. "Don't be worried by my presence here."

Davis sat uncertainly. "Okay."

"I read your report about what happened in New York. But it seemed to be incomplete."

"How so, sir?"

"It seemed to have the actual events missing."

She stared at him.

"It's been brought to my attention that you've been investigating something called the Bureau of Technology Control. Is that correct?"

Davis said nothing.

"You're wise to be cautious. The BTC is not to be taken lightly."

Now she felt a wave of shock. "Then Grady is telling the truth?"

"I don't know all that he said to you in New York, but—"

"Clones. Fusion. Immortality. That they're hoarding advanced technology."

McAllen nodded grimly. "Yes. This prison Grady told you about—this Hibernity . . ."

"He said he escaped. Showed me holographic video from a tiny device he carried—it contained statements from prisoners. People who had apparently made breakthrough inventions."

"Did Mr. Grady say where this black site prison was located?"

"He didn't know, but the device contained some sort of tracker that could lead him back to it. He just needed technical assistance to read it."

"Where is Mr. Grady now, Denise?"

She hesitated.

"I know. You're worried, and you have no reason to trust me." He leaned forward, meeting her gaze. "But look at me. I'm a sixty-two-year-old father of three, five grandchildren, and I bowl. There's only one thing that I care about, Agent Davis, and that's leaving a world worth living in for my children and grandchildren. If this BTC is hoarding innovations that could improve the lives of billions of people—and if they're using this technology to augment their own power—well, then we need to stop them, don't we? Are we agreed on that?"

Davis laughed slightly. It seemed ridiculous, but looking at the large, blunt man, she really did believe him. "I don't know where Grady is at the moment, Deputy Secretary, but I know where he will be."

"We need him. If we can find that prison—free those people—that will go a long way toward righting a grievous wrong. Now, you're trying to get an interview with Richard Cotton. Why?"

"Because Grady says Cotton is a BTC agent. The bombings were actually the means for concealing their kidnapping program—at least here in the U.S."

McAllen raised his eyebrows and smiled. "You have been busy."

"Grady's convinced that if Cotton sees him, Cotton will realize that the authorities know the truth. He thinks Cotton has some sort of deal with the BTC, but if Cotton knows we've changed the terms—hidden him away—he might cooperate instead. Cut a deal with us in exchange for what he knows about the BTC."

McAllen nodded. "If that's the case, we need to move him. Cotton isn't secure where he is. We need to put Grady and Cotton under serious protection, and then let's hope we can learn enough from them about the BTC to help us dismantle it."

She frowned. "You want to move Cotton? Where?"

"Florence ADMAX in Colorado. Supermax federal prison. We've got most of our high-level terrorists there."

"And the trial?"

"We'll need to postpone—Richard Cotton is apparently not a bomber."

She nodded grimly. Years of work . . . but then, this was even more serious. "We shouldn't wait to put Grady in front of Cotton, though."

"Agreed. They'll have plenty of time to talk en route. Make sure the press doesn't get wind of Cotton's transfer. We'll do it in the middle of the night."

"But won't transferring him be risky—with the BTC watching?"

McAllen let a sly grin escape.

A surveillance hologram of McAllen and Davis played across Graham Hedrick's desk as Morrison and several of his sons looked on.

McAllen's small three-dimensional form grinned. *"With what we have in mind, Richard Cotton will be more secure in transit than he is right now."*

Hedrick swept the hologram away with his hand and stared at his blank desktop. He spoke without looking up. "Mr. Morrison, this feud with the government has gone on long enough. Now they're searching for Hibernity, publicizing our existence, attempting to turn Cotton against us. And Jon Grady is making it even worse. We need to make progress on gravity amplification and soon. We do not have time for this."

Morrison nodded. "Certain people need to learn memorable lessons."

Hedrick studied him. The old commando clearly relished the idea of schooling his old leadership. Hedrick nodded. "You're right." He cleared his throat. "Tech level nine."

Morrison and his sons grinned lustily.

"Let our enemies see just how sharp cutting-edge technology can be. Finish this, sweep aside anyone or anything in your path, and bring me Jon Grady—alive. We need his peculiar mind."

"And Cotton?"

Hedrick considered this. "Public figure or not, if he's given any information to the government, find out what—then eliminate him. If he's innocent, take him into custody."

"The others?"

"Examples should be made." Hedrick hesitated. "Exothermic decomposition. Make sure there are witnesses."

Morrison turned to his progeny. "You heard the man."

They nodded and moved swiftly, eagerly out the doors as Morrison trailed more slowly behind them. He was still in the office as the doors closed, and he turned back toward Hedrick.

Hedrick was gazing out his windows at Mount Fuji, its snowcap gleaming in the hyperrealistic distance. "What is it, Mr. Morrison?"

"Alexa is AWOL. I thought you should know."

Hedrick sat in silence for several moments, but then he picked up a complex, geared Victorian clock and hurled it against the wall—where it shattered spectacularly.

"When are you going to deal with her?"

Hedrick turned to glare at him, but he couldn't withstand Morrison's disgusted expression.

"She disobeys you, and you deliberately try not to see."

"Enough! You have a job to do, go—"

"Your feelings for her have blinded you. It puts the entire organization in danger."

"You don't need to—"

"She illicitly accessed Grady's Hibernity interrogation records."

Hedrick's face dropped. "What? How?"

"She circumvented network restrictions—we're still trying to figure out how. It appears she might be using her charms on more than just you."

Hedrick turned another warning look in Morrison's direction, but it melted away as he realized the implications. "How much did she see?"

"Everything."

Hedrick put his head in his hands and collapsed in his chair. "God." He sat like that for several moments before leaning back. "I didn't want her to know. The world is an ugly place."

"There's more."

Hedrick closed his eyes in resignation.

"In reviewing the breach, the AIs noticed that Grady's interrogation hologram loops after a few months."

Hedrick's eyes opened. "It loops? What do you mean it loops?"

"Somebody's tampered with it. And not here."

"You mean at Hibernity?"

Morrison nodded. "It looks like numerous systems there have been compromised. The inmates might be running the asylum."

Fear stole across Hedrick's face. "My God . . . Chattopadhyay."

"I told you, he's dead. And the moment we get the chance, we'll open his cell and confirm it."

Hedrick gazed at the screens all around him. "This entire project is coming apart. If they escape our grip—"

"No one's escaping anything. And after I take care of this problem, if the civilian authorities want a war, then we'll make damn sure we win it."

Hedrick's breathing calmed. "I can always rely on you, Mr. Morrison."

Morrison moved to depart. "I'm posting guards around you. See no one—especially her."

"What are you doing to do?"

"What I should have done long ago."

CHAPTER 22

Interception

Special Agent Denise Davis held Richard Louis Cotton's elbow firmly as she escorted him out of the parking garage elevator and into the subbasement of the Dirksen Federal Building. Her way was lined by dozens of FBI tactical officers in body armor, with assault weapons slung across their chests. They scanned sight lines for trouble as they waved her and the escort detail onward, toward the open doors of a waiting armored FBI transport van. It was just one in a line of identical unmarked escort vans standing by.

Cotton shuffled along in leg irons, his hands cuffed before him and chained to his waist. He wore bulky orange body armor to protect him against reprisals from his victims' loved ones. Cotton's trademark beard without mustache was carefully trimmed. But his disappointment was obvious when he looked out across the parking level and noticed the lack of news cameras. There was only the long motorcade of FBI vehicles and armed agents.

He cast an irritated look toward her. "A transfer in the wee hours. You won't silence me, Agent Davis. His message shall still reach the world."

"It's not my job to give you an audience."

"The Lord will find a way."

"What's the Lord got to do with you?" She eyed him closely. Difficult to believe Cotton was anything but what he appeared—just another megalomaniac cult leader. But what she'd seen couldn't be denied. "Watch your step."

Transport agents pulled Cotton up into the van and escorted him into a small caged section at the front of the passenger bay as he began to cheerfully sing a hymn in a booming voice, offering his hands to his captors.

"Lord, the King of kings art Thou. In Thy presence here we bow; God's anointed we adore. Worship Thee in holy awe . . ."

They chained Cotton to a railing and locked the cage door on him as Davis took a seat on a bench alongside half a dozen heavily armed agents. The guards even had gas mask pouches on their harnesses. No one was taking any chances.

Cotton stopped singing as the engine revved, and they began to move out. FBI radios blared in confirmation of their departure, units sounding off. Cotton leaned against the thick wire mesh, staring at Davis. "And it was He sent messengers throughout Manasseh, calling them to arms . . ."

"Even God took a day off from religion, Richard."

Cotton chuckled. "The ever-watchful eye of our Lord is upon you, Agent Davis." He examined the agents arrayed before him. "I was told I'd be in Chicago until the trial."

"Operational security precludes this discussion."

"Do you really want to anger me, Agent Davis? I don't have to cooperate with the prosecution's case. I can drag this out far longer, if that's what you want."

Davis stared back. "You can't help yourself from confessing, Cotton. You want to take credit for these bombings. We couldn't shut you up if we wanted to."

Cotton smiled. "I say to you, if anyone slaps you on the right cheek, turn to him the other also."

Davis looked to the helmeted agents sitting across from her. "This is going to be a long goddamned drive . . ."

Two hours later Davis saw Cotton awake with a start. He looked around, apparently uncertain where he was for a moment. Then he shouted through the wire mesh at her. "Why are we still traveling?" He rattled his chains. "What time is it?"

"Go back to sleep, Cotton."

He seemed genuinely concerned, and Davis enjoyed a little private victory at the sight.

"We would have arrived at Stateville by now. Where are you taking me?"

"Nowhere. And I mean that literally: I am bringing you into the middle of nowhere."

She could see the muscles of Cotton's jaw tense. He thrust his face up to the wire and shouted, "You don't have the right to do this! I'm supposed to be in Stateville!"

"Are you? According to whom?"

"Those were the terms of my cooperation. You're violating the terms of my plea agreement."

"It wasn't my agreement."

"You take orders from the federal prosecutor."

Davis shrugged, enjoying his discomfiture. "Well, if you see him, be sure to mention it."

The dull roar of jet aircraft came to them even over the engine noise of the armored van.

Cotton glanced up at the ceiling. "You're not following the rules."

"Suddenly rules are important to the terrorist bomber."

The armored van slowed and turned, causing them all to lean.

"I don't know what you're up to, Davis, but you're risking my cooperation on this trial."

"Duly noted."

The tactical agents around her smirked, evidently pleased to hear someone putting Cotton in his place.

"It will vastly increase the length and cost of the proceedings."

"No doubt."

He examined her confident demeanor and apparently found it worrisome, but the van had now started to slow.

She smiled. "Looks like we're here."

"Where?"

Davis didn't answer but instead turned away as the van stopped. Almost immediately the armored doors opened, and members of the security detail poured out. She stepped down as well, accepting Thomas Falwell's hand as he walked up to greet her.

"Hey." Falwell spoke over the thunder of distant jet aircraft. "They're ready for you. And you weren't kidding, these guys are serious."

She looked around. "It looks like Bagram out here." Stars filled the night sky around a crescent moon, but in the moonlight Davis could see what must have amounted to a mechanized company or two of heavily armed U.S. Marines in Stryker armored vehicles. Antiaircraft missile batteries were arrayed in defensive positions all around them. The hundred or so FBI agents who had escorted the motorcade this far were also disembarking and milling around with the soldiers.

There could easily be three hundred soldiers out there. The deep roar of jets still thundered above.

"We've got air cover, too."

Davis turned to see the stunned face of Richard Cotton as he was lowered to the ground. He stared around in amazement at the military camp arrayed around them.

"What the hell is going on, Davis?"

He looked truly worried as she grabbed his waist chain and pulled him along. Falwell fell in behind her, as did the rest of the security detail. "Come here, Cotton, there's somebody I want you to meet."

"What in holy hell is going on?"

"Tsk, tsk, the Lord wouldn't like you using that sort of language."

"I demand to know what's going on. I demand it!"

A Marine lieutenant directed her to a nearby Stryker armored command vehicle. As they approached, the rear hatch whined down to just a few inches off the pavement, revealing Jon Grady and Homeland Security Deputy Secretary Bill McAllen sitting on cushioned benches in the LED light.

Davis shoved a stunned Cotton inside, his chains rattling against the steel deck. "Cotton, you remember Jon Grady, right? One of your victims from the Chirality Labs bombing?"

Cotton collapsed onto the bench across from Grady and McAllen as Davis and Falwell slid in behind him.

A marine sergeant in a command chair turned back. "Hatch coming up. Watch your fingers."

The rest of the security detail took posts outside as the armored door whined back up and boomed shut.

Cotton stared at Grady, apparently uncertain what to say.

Grady stared back. "They know about the Bureau of Technology Control, Cotton. And they also know you're a BTC agent."

McAllen leaned forward. "Mr. Cotton, I'm the deputy secretary of Homeland Security. My name is William McAllen. I've informed the BTC that you've decided to turn informer and are now under our protection."

Cotton's eyes went even wider, and he nodded to himself.

"The BTC thinks you've betrayed them. I think you'd be wise to help us bring them down."

What came out of Cotton's mouth next surprised them all. He took a deep breath and spoke calmly and evenly for the first time in Davis's memory. "This is unfortunate timing. It really is."

"Mr. Cotton—"

"I know you think you're helping, but it's actually going to ruin everything."

McAllen held up calming hands. "I can offer you protection, but only if you give us the structure of the BTC organization—who's in charge, details of their facilities."

Cotton sighed and shook his head, looking at Davis. "Is he serious?"

Grady cast a confused look to Davis.

Cotton turned his attention to Grady. "I don't know how you got away from them, Grady, but you'd better damned well go straight back. If we all go back to the way things were, there's a chance—a slim chance—that we might not be dead come morning."

McAllen sighed impatiently. "Mr. Cotton, there isn't going to be any bombing trial. We know you're not a bomber, and we know there aren't any bombing victims. What we need to find out is where those people are and who's running the BTC."

Cotton laughed ruefully. "No bombing victims? Well, you're wrong about that. The harvester teams only take the people they want. Everybody else gets killed." He studied their reactions. "No, not by me."

Grady felt crestfallen. "So . . . my partners are dead?"

"I'm sorry to tell you that, but listen to me . . ." Cotton leaned forward in his chains. "You're about to join them. We all are if you don't stop this and put me back where I was."

"Mr. Cotton . . ."

Cotton suddenly struggled against his chains, shouting. "Damnit! I had this all worked out until you idiots screwed everything up. I should be in Stateville!" He started banging his helmeted head against the bulkhead.

Grady grabbed Cotton's bulletproof vest. "You're saying they're dead? Tell me!"

"Yes, they're dead. Don't look at me; I didn't kill them. I haven't killed anybody, but they're not about to grab useless people. They grab the best and kill the rest. That's their motto."

McAllen eased Grady away from Cotton. "Look, we need to know everything you can tell us about Graham Hedrick."

"Oh, man . . ." He shook his head vigorously. "You have no idea how far ahead of you these people are."

"What was your deal with them?"

"The deal was I got to live if I was useful. That was the deal. But I had other plans—plans you idiots have well and truly fucked up. I need to get out of here."

"We can protect you."

Cotton laughed bitterly. "Look, I've been crawling around in their world for a decade. I know what they're capable of—and that's why I want to get the hell out of this Styrofoam cup you've put us all in." He gazed around at the armored vehicle.

McAllen nodded to a Marine captain nearby. "Get us under way."

"Yes, sir."

Cotton laughed again. "Under way? I'm sure that will stop them from frying our brains from orbit. Hey, did you talk to the others who'd tried to take down the BTC?"

"Others?"

"Oh, that's right. You couldn't. BECAUSE THEY'RE DEAD!" he screamed at the top of his lungs. "Now unchain me, and get me the hell out of this coffin!"

Suddenly all the lights went out. Electric motors whined to a stop in the blackness around them. Silence. No emergency lights came on. It was so black, Davis realized, it made no difference whether her eyes were open or not.

Cotton groaned again in the darkness. "There's the HEMP. Great job, guys . . ."

Davis asked, "What's a HEMP?"

"High-altitude electromagnetic pulse. They would have fired it from the edge of the atmosphere. Out there, the X-ray and gamma ray radiation interact—creates a massive free-electron maser. Any microelectronics within fifty miles are for shit now." He listened carefully. "Don't hear any fighter jets now, do you?"

"FBCB2 is down, sir!"

McAllen's voice: "Captain, get this rear door open!"

"There are hatches over our heads, sir . . ." They heard banging around. "Hang on . . ."

Cotton's chains rattled as he held forth. "You have no idea what you've done. If you brought ten thousand people, you couldn't protect me. Just put me back! Let's go back to the trial! It's not too late. Come on—back to prison . . ."

Just then moonlight entered the vehicle as the staff sergeant opened an overhead hatchway up front. The captain opened another one near the rear and stepped up to look out, shouting down to someone. "Lieutenant, do they have power over there?"

There were muffled calls as Davis frowned at Cotton, who was busy groaning fearfully.

The captain came back down. "Power's out in the entire force. And there's thick fog coming in."

Cotton nodded. "They're lowering the dew point to mask their advance. And you no longer have night vision. Are you happy now? We're all going to die. And I nearly had this solved. But you had to go and ruin it, didn't you, Davis?"

She scowled at this strangely alien Richard Cotton. "Ruin what?"

Suddenly horrific sounds—like the fabric of reality tearing—reached them through the armored walls of the Stryker. Automatic gunfire erupted outside, with intermittent shouts and explosions. Then booms from a .50-caliber machine gun.

And then the deafening roar of a whole marine company opening fire shook the Stryker.

The staff sergeant poked his head up through the hatchway, shouting down, "We're under attack, Captain!"

"From what direction?"

"I can't . . . this damn fog. I can't even see the tracers."

Cotton nodded. "You're blind, and they see everything. We're sitting ducks in here." He shook his chains. "Unchain me, damnit." He looked to McAllen. "If we survive this, I'll talk, I swear it—just get me out of here!"

Davis grabbed his arms. "Calm the hell down, Cotton. No one's going to reach you in here."

Already outside the gunfire had gone silent.

"There. They might have driven them off."

Cotton just shook his head sadly. "You have no idea what's coming."

Then a blinding light and searing heat cut through the cabin— slicing the marine captain in half lengthwise even as it cauterized him. The last two feet of the Stryker fell away, the edges glowing red, as tons of steel and composite armor collapsed onto pavement. Night air swept onto the stunned faces of Davis, Grady, Cotton, Falwell, and McAllen.

Outside, they could see thick roiling fog and soldiers lying motionless on the asphalt. It was suddenly eerily quiet. No aircraft overhead. Not even the sound of crickets.

Davis turned back to see half of the marine captain twitching on the bench. She coughed at the combination of ozone and burned flesh and looked away, drawing her Glock pistol. Falwell and McAllen did likewise.

The staff sergeant grabbed an M4 from a weapon rack and aimed it out into the fog.

He shouted toward the driver. "Captain's down, Ricky!"

"What the hell hit us?"

"I don't know!"

Davis glanced back to Grady and Cotton, only to see them both staring in horror out into the fog. She turned back again. "Thomas, we have to get Grady and Cotton out of here."

Falwell shook his head. "This is insane. I don't understand . . ."

Moments later three negative forms materialized from the fog. They were the darkest black Davis had ever seen. Their outlines swallowed light, as though they were living silhouettes.

Cotton covered his head with hands and cowered in his orange body armor. "Oh God! Morrison, it wasn't me . . ."

Davis, Falwell, and McAllen opened fire with pistols, while the staff sergeant fired short bursts with his M4. In the confines of the Stryker the gunshots were deafening—spent cartridges bounced all around them—but they fired repeatedly until their clips were empty.

As she reloaded, Davis focused downrange, through the gun smoke into the dark fog. The three negative forms stood unmoving.

Finally a voice like that of God spoke: "Deputy Secretary McAllen. I bring a message from the director of the BTC."

McAllen scowled as he lowered his gun. "What is it, you bastard?"

A tearing sound ripped the air again, and before Davis's eyes, a white-hot fire swept from inside the tip of McAllen's outstretched hand and down within his arm as he screamed in agony. It was as though some chain reaction was turning his body into fire. He started to burn like the glow moving down a cigarette. He barely got a second shriek out before his face and torso were consumed by the wave of glowing embers—the heat bursting forth from him singed Davis on the other side of the cabin. By the time the blinding flash ended, his form had collapsed into ash, his undamaged pistol clattering to the steel deck.

"Oh my God!"

Davis had reloaded, and she and Falwell opened fire at the dark forms again, but to no avail. When their guns were empty, they stared at the figures still standing, unaffected.

And then Davis heard the ripping sound again. Falwell turned back toward her as he burned. "No!" She grabbed his outstretched hand and screamed in agony as her skin burned along with his.

The unnatural fire consumed them both.

CHAPTER 23

Harvesters

J**on Grady stared, unbelieving, as** Agents Davis and Falwell blew away
into ash. He then turned toward the dark silhouettes at the mouth of
the wrecked Stryker.

"Aaaahhh!" He charged at them. But one of the forms held up a hand,
creating a force that swept over him, Cotton, and the staff sergeant, hurling them against the rear bulkhead. Dazed, Grady felt gravity shift, and
they "fell" out to land roughly on the pavement—as if a giant had upended
the Stryker and shaken them out like candy. Every loose object in the
Stryker came along with them—including the remaining half of the captain, tools, and rucksacks. Grady and Cotton then floated up a couple of
feet above the ground. Spent shell casings and trash levitated around
them.

Several more dark forms floated down from above to join the first
three, and they now stood staring at the floating men.

Grady turned to see that the staff sergeant was still breathing but unconscious. Apparently someone had noxed him—something Grady had
seen many times before.

The fog was already dissipating as the summer breeze continued to
blow over them, and now Grady could see just how many marines were
lying unconscious in the parking lot.

Cotton was babbling toward the jet-black center figure. "Morrison, I wasn't working with them! Scan me! Go ahead and scan me!"

The same wrath-of-God voice spoke from the ink-black human outline. "How much did you tell them, Cotton? You piece of shit."

"I didn't tell them anything!"

As Grady floated in the air, helpless to move, he concentrated on the dark forms. They were menacing in a way he'd never felt before. Like demons from hell.

Morrison aimed his arm. "I don't feel like scanning you, Cotton."

A female voice spoke from the sky. "I'll take the prisoners."

The BTC warriors looked up to see Alexa descend wearing a black tactical suit of her own—although hers appeared much simpler. It was clearly not assault armor. She had a matching helmet as well with a crystalline visor across her blue eyes. Grady couldn't help but notice a belt similar to the Morrisons' woven into her outfit, and he assumed it must be the gravity mirror he'd invented—shrunken to absurdly small size and perfected.

As Alexa descended into Grady and Cotton's gravity field, they joined her gravitational well, and now seemed to move along with her.

Morrison shouted, "Where the hell do you think you're going, Alexa?"

"I'm taking these prisoners back to the BTC."

Cotton looked over at her. "Thank God! Alexa, tell them I haven't said anything."

She eyed him. "Perhaps not, but you are going to tell me some things."

She then glanced at Grady.

Grady looked to her. "They killed Davis. They burned her alive."

Alexa looked visibly disturbed by this news, and she turned angrily toward Morrison and his gathered sons. "An XD gun? You didn't have to kill anyone, let alone split their water."

"That's where you're wrong. Sometimes examples need to be made of people." Morrison made no visible motion, but loose rocks and debris floating around him started to "fall" with him as his "down" edged toward Alexa and her new charges. "You're not going anywhere. Hedrick ordered me to deal with Cotton just as soon as I learn whether he betrayed us."

"I'll handle that."

Cotton was floating sideways, trying to get his spin under control. "What does he mean 'deal with' me?"

Morrison's armored black oval of a face remained focused on Alexa's. His voice came across now at a more conversational volume. "This isn't your field of expertise, Alexa. You should be back at base. Hedrick has been looking for you."

"I don't report to you."

His voice grew impatient again. "Neither do you have the right to come here and interfere with my operation."

"You've already captured the prisoners. I'm taking control of them now. Don't even think of ordering me around."

"Ah, I forgot. There's only one person you report to . . ." He paused and then looked upward slightly. "Get Director Hedrick on a q-link to me immediately."

Alexa apparently wasn't waiting around. She extended her booted feet, and then she, Cotton, and Grady began to fall upward, slowly at first.

Grady felt little acceleration as he rose into the night sky, and now he could see how many marines were lying unconscious all around them in the moonlight—hundreds.

Morrison's voice shouted after her, louder now. "Alexa, I'm not letting you take those prisoners!"

"Don't follow me, Morrison. I mean it."

They ascended faster, rising above the trees, and now Grady could see the vast expanse of farmland stretching beyond. And the fallen army around them.

His synesthesia made even this horrible vista beautiful, as the stars above were wondrous.

Morrison popped his visor with a hiss, revealing his weathered, scarred face. There were now six of his sons around him in full diamondoid armor, and they likewise popped their visors.

"What's up with Granny?"

Morrison covered his microphone and hissed, "Go after her. Get the prisoners back while I get Hedrick on q-link."

The sons exchanged worried looks and covered their mikes as well.

"Fuck that . . ."

"Iota's right, Dad."

"I'm not getting in the middle of a fight between Granny and Hedrick."

"She's supposed to be 'priceless intellectual property' or some shit."

"She's his goddamned girlfriend."

"What if she fights back?"

"That bitch is dangerous."

Morrison aimed a diamond-hard black finger at them. "Get your asses up there and follow her."

"She's on a tracker. We don't have to follow her."

Morrison checked in with tactical operations again. "TOC, this is Alpha Dog, do we have the director on q-link yet?"

"The director left the command center when you radioed mission completion. Is this an emergency, Alpha Dog?"

"Yes, it's a damned emergency. Tell him I found Alexa, and that she left with both prisoners—interfering with my command."

There was a pause. *"Stand by, Alpha Dog."*

Morrison gazed up into the stars and finally pounded the side of the armored Stryker with his diamondoid fist, putting a dent in its armor. "Goddamnit!" With that he ripped out the comm module from his helmet and tossed it to one of his sons—who caught it deftly. "Hold onto that for me."

"What are you doing?"

"Someday you boys will learn it's better to beg forgiveness than ask permission." Morrison's visor swept across his face with a hiss, and he immediately fell into the sky, followed by a trail of debris.

His sons watched him go and then turned to one another with worried looks.

"To hell with this."

"Let's get back to base. I don't want to be downrange when this shit hits the fan."

———

Grady watched the moon's reflection on a lake below them and stared in wonder at the world from five thousand feet. The tragedy of recent events was flowing through him at the same time the beauty of the natural world flowed over him. It was a beautiful summer night. Turned backward, he wasn't blinded by the wind. Judging by the stars, he figured they were "falling" to the north—back toward Chicago. It was a miraculous feeling even given his black mood.

He'd invented the gravity mirror, and now, before he died, he could see how marvelous it was.

He was still trying to process all that had happened in the last ten minutes. Davis and Falwell were dead. Killed in a horrible way. So, too, was the deputy secretary of Homeland Security—their bodies incinerated as they shrieked. Grady turned to face Alexa as she guided the three of them in the shade of her gravity mirror. He could see Cotton looking below them, probably warm enough in his protective, orange body armor.

Alexa cast a glance at Grady and shouted, "I owe you an apology."

He just stared at her.

"I realize how feeble that sounds. Apologizing for destroying your life. I didn't know."

"But now you do."

She nodded. "Your scars . . . I checked and—"

"Then you really didn't know, did you?" He could see what looked like true emotional pain in her eyes.

"My God, what you had to go through. I had no idea."

Grady felt relief wash over him. He strangely felt he could believe her.

But then the flow of air over them stopped. They just hung there, suspended. There was no sensation of deceleration. They just stopped.

Alexa was busy checking her systems and looking up at projected displays in her helmet.

Cotton shouted, "What's wrong?"

"I don't know." She was ticking through items: "Third of a g, zero pitch, zero yaw . . . we should be moving."

Just then a familiar voice came across the night air to them. "You're not going anywhere with my prisoners, Alexa."

They turned to see Morrison floating toward them in the moonlight. He aimed an armored finger at them as he did so, the tip glowing fiercely.

Alexa stopped checking her gear. There was a grim look on her face. "Integrated extogravis. That's new."

"I can nullify your gravity mirror. Quite a toy you invented, Mr. Grady. One improvement we were able to make was the ability to instantiate the mirror at an arbitrary distance."

Grady's eyes widened, and he couldn't help but feel amazed even as he was horrified. "But . . . how . . ."

Alexa now floated alongside them, just as helpless as they were. Like a fly in a spiderweb. "I didn't know they'd built projectors small enough to mount in assault armor."

"Not that big really. Just requires lots of power. Certainly doesn't fit in a flight suit like yours. So I guess Hedrick doesn't give you all of his toys. He's that smart at least."

They all four hung there silently in midair, five thousand feet above rural Illinois in a cloudless night sky.

"Let us leave, Morrison."

He shook his head at her. "You're free to go once you turn over my prisoners."

"Hedrick lied to me. You all lied to me. Why?"

"You're in your fifties, Alexa. It's time to grow up."

"You knew what was going on at Hibernity."

"I'm so sick of your sustained innocence. You get to waltz around and have everyone love you. You're the future of humanity, while my project gets canceled and I become a genetic punch line. Well, I'm a survivor. I do the dirty work that no one knows about. When things need to get done, the director counts on me and my sons to do them. The outside world is a ruthless, shitty place. At least Grady and Cotton here actually have a purpose—what's your purpose? Other than being a genetic library for when they finally figure out how to transfer minds from one body to another?"

She narrowed her eyes at him.

"Oh, you didn't know about that project either? Well, we don't tell you everything."

Alexa stared at him, her jaw clenching.

"Now push Grady and Cotton over here." He aimed a gloved finger on his other hand, apparently a weapon integrated into the suit.

Cotton tried to swim through the air to get behind her. "Alexa, you know they forced me to do this. I haven't harmed a soul, I swear it."

Morrison laughed. "You're no saint, Cotton. Did Cotton ever tell you where we found him—a master thief trying to break into BTC headquarters? Bit off more than you could chew, eh?"

"Alexa, don't let him do this."

"Your ten years is just about up, anyway, Cotton."

Alexa drew a black spikelike device from her belt. Its tip glowed with an intense indigo light.

Morrison lowered his weapon arm. "A positron gun? That's a killing weapon, Alexa. Where did you get that?"

"You know damn well."

Morrison's ink-black armored face was inscrutable, but he nodded slowly to himself. "He's weak."

"Let us go, Morrison."

"Listen to yourself, Alexa. You're breaking bureau regulations. Ignoring rules about tech level exposure. Chain of command."

Cotton shouted, "He's going to kill us—split our water like that Davis woman."

Morrison nodded toward her raised weapon. "How much antimatter do you have in that thing?"

"A billionth of a gram. So don't toy with me."

"You're not a killer, Alexa. And you know that Grady and Cotton must come with me. Civilian government knows who Cotton is now. They'll interrogate him—torture him if necessary—to get information out of him."

She didn't lower the weapon, although Grady could see she was unsure of what to do. "Don't test me, Morrison. Just leave. And tell Graham to back off while I sort this out."

Morrison slowly reached toward his harness. "See this? I'm getting a psychotronic weapon—nonlethal—and that's all there is to it. I'm not going to harm you or anyone. Ask yourself: Are you going to kill me, Alexa? Are you going to kill me to stop me from using a nonlethal weapon against—"

He fast-drew the weapon, but Alexa's reflexes were faster. A blinding flash and crack of thunder, and the front of Morrison's suit burst apart in weirdly intricate sparks and whirling vortexes of energy—hurling him backward and then downward.

But on his way down Morrison zapped Alexa with the psychotronic gun as well. She spun out of control, causing Grady and Cotton to fall out of her local gravity field—and into free fall from the night sky.

Alexa almost immediately regained her senses and found herself free of Morrison's projected gravity field. She scanned the sky below her with thermal imaging. Cotton was falling below her, screaming, while Grady descended farther off—probably impossible to reach at terminal velocity. However, Morrison appeared to be moving to intercept Grady—sparks issuing from his combat assault armor.

"Damnit!" Alexa soared down to try to catch up with Cotton before he hit the forest thousands of feet below. She tucked her arms onto her thighs to streamline her aerodynamic profile and descended at much more than a hundred miles an hour.

Grady's heart pounded in his chest as the rushing air buffeted him. His watering eyes saw the dark forest racing up to meet him, and he realized that these were his final seconds of life. He glanced up at the stars above him. The beauty was heartbreaking. However, his time in Hibernity had taught him how to manage fear, and he turned toward the approaching trees—determined to see his life right up to the very end.

But suddenly he felt cold, armored hands grab his arms, and his direction of descent lurched forward—only a thousand feet above the shadows of the trees.

Grady turned to see Morrison's onyx face mask.

"You're a real pain in the ass, you know that, Mr. Grady?"

But then Grady noticed that they had not entirely stopped falling, and he felt conflicting gravity fields over about half of his body. Classical "down" was still to some extent in force.

One of Morrison's gauntlets released Grady, and he seemed to be struggling to get something functioning. Purple sparks burst forth occasionally from the melted front plate of the suit. Morrison's visor popped open with a hiss, and smoke issued out of it as the red reflection of a dozen flashing warning lights lit up his face.

"That traitorous bitch! A fucking positron weapon! She fried the power system—and most of my auxiliary."

They started to buck their descent a bit as Morrison concentrated on working his suit's systems. But a glance below them showed Grady they were still coming down at dangerous speeds.

He grabbed onto Morrison's armor and shouted into his face over the rushing wind. "If you don't have enough power to maintain the size of the gravity mirror, cut stabilization!"

Morrison frowned in confusion.

"If this suit is based on my technology, then there must be stabilization—or we'd be spinning like crazy. When two gravity fields interact, they'll revolve within each other like—"

He could see the trees accelerating to meet them at much more than seventy miles an hour.

"JUST CUT THE FUCKING STABILIZATION!"

Morrison calmly nodded and manipulated unseen controls.

Suddenly they slowed dramatically—but started spinning like a merry-go-round on two different axes. Grady held on as Morrison's armored arms embraced him.

They plunged through a thick canopy of trees at ten or fifteen miles per hour, smashing through branches on the way to the ground. In darkness, they bounced off the forest floor, Morrison on the bottom, and hit again, then splayed next to each other. The sound of crickets suddenly was all around them.

There were several seconds without movement.

"Well. That's something for the manual, Mr. Grady."

Morrison struggled to sit up, his suit still issuing occasional sparks. He appeared to be having trouble moving the heavy suit as smoke issued from several crevices.

Grady leapt on top of him—slugging Morrison through his open face mask. "You son of a bitch!"

"Ah, fuck!"

The sound of servomotors whined, but Morrison didn't seem to be able to make his suit do what he wanted it to—or even close his face plate with all the smoke issuing from inside.

Grady punched him several more times until he was sure that Morrison was unconscious.

As he kneeled on top of Morrison's armor-clad form, Grady turned at the sound of crashing branches. In a moment, Alexa descended from the sky, clutching a struggling Richard Cotton.

Cotton fell from her arms to kiss the ground. "Oh, thank God!"

Alexa looked down at Morrison with concern. "Is he . . . ?"

"No. Unconscious—although I don't know for how long."

She looked relieved and leaned down to pull a device that Grady recognized from Morrison's belt—a psychotronic weapon. Alexa aimed the laser dot at the old commando's head and keyed it for several moments. Then she took a reading. "Now he should stay asleep for twenty or thirty minutes."

Grady looked at her and nodded. "Thank you for rescuing me. If that's what this is."

She grimaced. "I'm not sure what this is. I only know I can't be partner to the type of evil you experienced. And that we have to stop what's happening at Hibernity."

"Do you still believe in your probability projections for disruptive innovations?"

She stared at him and shrugged. "I don't know what to believe anymore."

Cotton stood next to them in his ridiculous orange body armor. "I hate to interrupt, but the wrath of God is going to come down on us any fucking second. So if we could have this conversation elsewhere, that would be fantastic."

"Cotton's right." Alexa pulled a metal stylus from her harness and activated what appeared to be a laser-cutting device—its needle-thin beam burned wickedly in the darkness. She used it to carefully carve out a tiny nodule on the shoulder of her flight suit. She repeated the process on her boots.

"What are you doing?"

"Removing the EDSP tracking devices."

Grady nodded. "Yeah, good catch."

Cotton was standing over Morrison. "If someone would help me get this body armor off, I'd like to take a piss on Morrison's face."

She glared at him. "Leave it, Cotton. You're lucky to be alive. Don't make it personal—it'll be just another reason for him to come looking for you."

Alexa then started dumping most of her equipment onto the forest floor.

"What are you doing?"

"They all have integrated trackers. We take our tech level containment seriously. Cotton's right. They'll come for it soon."

Grady gazed down at Morrison. "What about him?"

"Leave him."

Grady studied Morrison's armor. "What about his suit? It'll buy us more time if we strand him out here without it. No comms. At least dump it a few miles away."

Alexa considered this.

"Can we get it off him?"

She nodded. "There's a medical access override, if you have the clearance. Which I do." She knelt next to Morrison and felt around the side of his helmet. She touched a control button and spoke into her own microphone. "Emergency medical access requested."

Suddenly Morrison's armor started to unfasten around him, opening like flower petals.

"I'll be damned."

She stood. "Can't cut diamondoid armor off with scissors."

Grady picked up a shoulder plate and hefted it. "This doesn't even weigh all that much."

"And yet it's the hardest substance known."

They took a few moments to gather the plates of armor—Alexa being careful to toss aside the four pieces that had integrated tracking particles. As they were finishing, Morrison began to wake up.

Cotton raised his eyebrows. "Yeah, he's about fifteen minutes early. Tough son of a bitch, isn't he?"

Morrison felt around himself for his armor and weapons, but his equipment was in a pile some yards away.

Alexa quickly aimed the psychotronic gun at him. "Ah-ah, don't."

Morrison assessed the situation, looking at the equipment missing from her harness and the nearby pile. He grinned nastily. "You won't be Hedrick's little sweetheart after this, Alexa. You'll be one of the little people."

Cotton reached down and punched Morrison in the jaw, barely fazing the man.

"Goddamnit!" Cotton hopped away, nursing his paw.

Morrison gave him a disgusted look. "You're a pussy, Cotton."

Alexa aimed the psychotronic beam. "Night-night."

Morrison gave her the finger even as he lay back down, and he was soon snoring soundly.

Alexa tossed the weapon onto the pile, and then motioned for Grady and Cotton to come closer to her. Grady could feel the gravity around them change—and down suddenly became up.

As they rose through the treetops, Grady turned to her. "Agent Davis is dead, the deputy secretary of Homeland Security—anyone who believed my story is dead, and the police will be out looking for Cotton in force soon, too. Where do we go?"

Cotton looked at them. "I know a place . . ."

CHAPTER 24

Safe House

It was well past midnight by the time Alexa—with Jon Grady and Richard Cotton floating beneath her gravity mirror—descended toward a flat, silvered roof of a massive, windowless ten-story brick building in the meatpacking district of Chicago. Half a mile ahead of them was a panoramic view of the downtown skyline.

As they came down from the night sky, Grady could see large, faded signs painted directly onto the brick facade of their destination: "Fulton Market Cold Storage Company" and on a brick tower the faded words "Greater Fulton Market."

As they alighted onto the flat rooftop, Grady stood unsteadily. It was the first normal gravity he'd felt in several hours. They had flown a circuitous route from the plains, coming into Chicago low and slow from the northwest due to Alexa's concerns about scanning, search teams, and satellite surveillance AIs teasing out their flight path from an all-seeing gaze in orbit. She was convinced Morrison and Hedrick would find them quickly—and appeared to be getting more concerned each minute.

Despite the circumstances, Jon Grady had to admit that the flight (or, more appropriately, the "fall") here was pretty spectacular. Grady and Cotton had floated alongside Alexa in the sphere of the mirror's influence. The summer air rushing over them all as they soared silently above the midnight landscape—at first above broad cornfields bordered by dark clusters of trees and thick underbrush. Crickets thrummed below them, and the lights of lone farmhouses and outbuildings had passed by in the night. Eventually these gave way to exurb subdivisions and big-box retail centers, and finally a contiguous grid of suburban yards and streets. Grady had found the experience the closest thing he could imagine to being a bird—flying quietly over the land.

Now that they'd landed, Alexa was scanning the skies nervously, her eyes illuminated by some device built into the crystal of her helmet's visor.

Cotton seemed unconcerned. He was already ripping Velcro straps to remove his orange bulletproof helmet and perp-protection vest. Both had the words "Federal Prisoner" stenciled on the front and back. "Well, that was a memorable evening." He cast a look at Grady and tossed the helmet to him. "Very interesting little invention, this gravity mirror of yours, Professor."

Grady caught the helmet. "I'm not a professor."

"I think you've earned an honorary degree somewhere." Cotton started walking toward a steel roof-access door in a towering brick bastion behind them. Here, too, was another faded painted sign reading "Fulton Market Cold Storage" in letters three stories high—it was like a building on top of the building.

Alexa called after him. "What is this place, Cotton? And what makes you think they won't find us here?"

He glanced back. "It's one of my safe houses. And they won't find us because they're already on our trail elsewhere."

"What do you mean?"

"I mean, there are people within the BTC who will make it difficult for them to realize they're not finding us."

Alexa narrowed her eyes. "Traitors, you mean? But the scanning—"

"You wanna stand out here all night, or you wanna come inside?"

She took another glance skyward, and then Grady and Alexa followed him. Cotton opened a small electrical panel to the side of the door and let a flash of light scan his eyes. The surprisingly thick stairwell door clicked open, and they followed him down a metal stairwell.

Grady watched the door boom shut behind them and a green light appear. "*One* of your safe houses? How many do you have?"

"If I told you that, they wouldn't be 'safe' would they?"

Alexa frowned. "If you think Morrison doesn't know about these, you're crazy. You can't hide anything from the BTC. They'll be sending harvester teams here any minute."

"Yeah, well, see, that's the funny thing. Turns out the trick to keeping secrets from the BTC is to temporarily forget what you don't want them to know. And thanks to modern science, that's possible."

Grady frowned. "I experienced something like that in Hibernity—a protein that makes you forget specific memories as you recall them. But I never got my memories back. I lost a lot. Pieces of my childhood. My parents. Can you teach me how to recover them?"

"Ah. You have to record them if you want to rewrite them again. Nasty, nasty place, Hibernity. My apologies for having been the instrument of your delivery to it—unwilling though I was."

Grady thought back to the night of the bombing. He remembered Cotton's odd, almost apologetic shrug just before he departed. That memory had survived Hibernity.

They arrived at the first stairwell landing, and here was a sturdier-looking black door. Cotton rapped on it with his knuckles. It sounded as solid as Mount Aetna. "Diamond-aggregate nanorods—hyperdiamonds. Got a millimeter of it coating the walls as well. Beats the hell out of carbon nanotubes—that stuff is worse than asbestos. And so 1990s." He placed his hand over some sort of scanner—one that looked more complex than a simple palm print.

Alexa scowled. "What tech level is this? And more importantly, how did you get it?"

The stairwell security door clicked and then opened. "Who cares what tech level it is? And as for how I got it, that's easy: Morrison was right—I'm a thief. A master thief." He walked inside, kicking on the lights with a massive knife switch that echoed in the cavernous space beyond.

After exchanging glances, Alexa and Grady followed.

Within was a huge, refurbished loft space, with exposed brick walls, interior partitions, tasteful art and furniture, a living area, a restaurant-quality kitchen, and shelves lined with books. Beyond, Grady could see a long corridor with polished wood floors, half a dozen doors closed to either side, opening at the end of the hall into what appeared to be a large technical workshop. Thin-film screens and multiplexed surveillance camera holograms glowed to life all around the loft.

"Home sweet home . . ."

As Grady and Alexa surveyed the place, Cotton walked into the kitchen and grabbed stemmed glasses from an overhead rack. "You know, Alexa, if you thought they were pulling out all the stops to get Grady, just wait. AWOL, you're ten times more dangerous to Hedrick than Grady is. With what you know about them . . . wow-wee! He'll leave no stone unscanned."

Cotton pulled the stopper out of a decanter and poured a finger of brandy into the three glasses. "And then there's always the fact that he's madly in love with you. Love and hate are opposite sides of the same coin, you know—both passions. You can flip from one to the other—but not to indifference." He held up a glass with a nod, and then quickly drank each, one after the other. "Ahh! That's the stuff."

Grady stood across a granite-topped island from him. "Who else is in this building?"

"You mean *what* else: floors and floors of truth in advertising—cold storage. Very useful for erasing thermal signatures from questionable fusion experiments."

Alexa glared at him. "Fusion? Cotton, you're not supposed to have that level of technology out of BTC headquarters."

He poured another glass. "Cognac, Mr. Grady? You look like you could use one."

Grady nodded.

He poured. "Drawn from casks lost in a shipwreck off the coast of France in 1873."

"Good lord, it must have cost a fortune."

"I wouldn't know." Cotton slid a snifter along the stone counter to him. Grady just barely caught it before it went over the edge.

Alexa persisted. "What else do you have in this hideaway of yours?"

"Nothing dangerous, if that's what you're thinking. No, this is strictly a stealth operation. We are safe from all known tracking technologies here."

"Not a q-link transmitter."

Cotton finished off another finger of cognac. "No. But then, we took care of that, didn't we?" He offered her a drink with his eyes.

She just made a disgusted sound and headed down the corridor, clearly irritated.

Grady watched her go.

"She could probably use some alone time." Cotton started moving pots and pans around, turning on gas burners on his massive stove.

Grady actually felt bad for her. "Alexa just walked away from her whole world for us. I remember having mine taken from me, and that was hard enough." He took a sip of the cognac and savored it on his tongue. "My God, this is like a mist going down."

"Yeah, pretty smooth . . ." Cotton was getting ingredients out of what turned out to be some sort of walk-in fridge.

"You're cooking?"

"Sure, why not? I always try to have a nice meal after near-death experiences. The food never tastes better. Thought I'd make a bouillabaisse. You hungry?"

"Okay."

Cotton stabbed a finger at the ceiling. "This calls for Bizet . . ." He shouted at the ceiling in respectable French. "*Les pêcheurs de perles*—'Au fond du temple saint'!"

Suddenly the opera began to fill the loft. Beautiful music. Grady could see the colors in waves. He felt the depth of the day's events and took another sip of cognac.

"I am sorry that you wound up in Hibernity, Mr. Grady. Please know that I was given no choice." Cotton was gathering fresh seafood onto the counter.

Grady nodded absently. "How on earth is there fresh seafood here?"

He gestured to the walk-in fridge. "Inert storage. Uses noble gases—argon. Like cryogenics but without freezing. Food takes ages to go bad."

"Another world-changing innovation hidden in a vault."

Cotton seemed unfazed as he shelled large prawns. "This whole build-ing is a ten-story freezer two blocks long. We'd probably find Prohibition-era gangsters in here if they ever thawed the place out."

"So how is it you're here, Cotton? Why were you playing the BTC's mad bomber all these years?"

Cotton grimaced. "Bad luck, really."

Grady gave him a look.

"Oh, right. I guess you were unluckier than I was. What I mean is, I was caught trying to break into BTC headquarters about . . . oh, I guess a dozen years ago."

"You were trying to break *into* the BTC?"

"Well, I never claimed I was smart."

"How did you even know they existed?"

"I didn't. It was a job. I made it my business to obtain difficult-to-obtain information for interested parties. The BTC building had come to the attention of certain people—certain low-profile people—who let me know just how ultrasecure this very run-of-the-mill building smack-dab in downtown Detroit was. It was anomalous to say the least."

Cotton stopped peeling seafood for a moment to stare wistfully into the distance. "I thought I had it all figured out back then." He laughed. "But we don't know what we don't know until we know."

"Someone hired you to break into the BTC?"

"It's not like I tossed a brick through the window. I had a sophisticated operation. I am a master thief. It's just that there *is* no breaking into the BTC." He opened a glass-faced wine cabinet and held up a bottle of red. "Châteauneuf-du-Pape?"

Grady nodded toward his half-full cognac. "No, I'm good, thanks."

Cotton started opening the wine as he continued. "And that low-profile client, I later found out, was the CIA. Wish I'd known that back then. They have a rather dismal history when it comes to break-ins.

"I thought I was clever, but I got caught before I even got into the premises. Turns out the exterior of their building is a facade in more than the traditional sense. There are no windows. No surface-level doors—or at least none that go anywhere. Behind the concrete-and-glass perimeter are thirty millimeters of diamond-aggregate nanorods, black as Sauron's tower—that's where I got the idea for this place, by the way. The BTC HQ goes a few hundred feet underground—that I know of. They project holograms on the walls inside to make it appear like you're looking out a window at the real world. The human eye can't detect the difference with the tech they're using. So they're constantly switching the view to live shots taken by their video dust cameras scattered around the world—extradimensional transmitters link all their comms." He looked up. "You probably figured that out by now. It's why no one can eavesdrop on them."

Grady considered this as he took another sip of the precious cognac. After savoring it for a few moments, he said, "And they caught you?"

Cotton nodded as he started cleaning seafood again. "Yeah, and you can imagine I had my eyes opened fast. A barbarian hauled before Caesar. The director at the time, a little waif of a man named Hollinger, was impressed I'd gotten as far as I did. He offered me a deal: I could either work for them as the public face of the Winnowers—become the infamous Richard Louis Cotton—or I could get pushed through an exothermic decomposition beam." He turned back. "And you saw what one of those did to our friend Agent Davis." Cotton paused for a moment. "Poor woman."

"So you became the Antitech Bomber."

"No one in the BTC wanted to be Cotton, and they needed a new antitech boogeyman. They kept me on a short leash for quite some time. The plan was that after a decade they'd retire Cotton, too. I was supposed to relax in idyllic splendor among the other godlings." He chuckled as he took a sip of wine from the crystal bulb he'd half filled. "But then, I never really believed that. And also I'd never forgotten the job I'd been hired to do. After all, how often does a thief get a chance to steal back the future?"

"Then you already had a plan? Which we disrupted . . ."

"You might say we have something in common, Mr. Grady."

Grady finished off his cognac, then pulled the video projector from beneath his shirt on its chain. "Maybe you can help me then. I need to decode the data on this device—it's DNA-formatted."

Cotton shrugged. "That's the only real format there is." He looked at the thin piece of bone. "What is it?"

Grady thumbed the button, and Chattopadhyay's image appeared on the wall. *"My name is Archibald Chattopadhyay, nuclear physicist and amateur poet. I have a lovely wife, Amala, who has given me five wonderful children. I led the team that first perfected a sustained fusion reaction . . ."* Grady paused it.

"Clever bastards at Hibernity, aren't they? I'd heard rumors that they'd taken over half the prison."

"But they still can't escape. That's what I'm hoping to help them do."

Cotton gestured to the device. "Leave it with me. I'll decode all the data that's on it."

Grady hesitated. "We'll do it tomorrow—after some rest. I don't want to let this thing out of my sight." He then put it away beneath his shirt again.

"Suit yourself. Just let me know when you're ready."

Grady looked down the corridor. Alexa was nowhere in sight. "You have beds in this place?"

"Sure. Rooms on both sides of the hall. Take any empty one."

Grady gazed into the dark at the hall's end. "I should go thank Alexa before I get some sleep. She did save me."

Cotton looked up from his work. "You really think your thanks is what she wants right now?"

Grady considered this. He finally nodded. "I guess not."

With that he went to find a bed.

CHAPTER 25

Domestic Dispute

In the predawn stillness the street of downtown Detroit were nearly deserted. The office towers were still mostly dark. Graham Hedrick sat in the command chair of the BTC's mission control center overlooking the big screens and the specialist workstations in the room below. He could see a large image of North America centered on Detroit and the Great Lakes on the central screen above; several incoming objects were being tracked across the plains and also coming in from central Canada over the Great Lakes.

Alarms were blinking on several screens.

Hedrick nodded to himself. "X-51 WaveRider cruise missiles. I'm impressed by their initiative." Someone had made a command decision somewhere on the other side. He knew these hypersonic missiles could do thirty-six hundred miles an hour—which meant, at six hundred miles, they were only ten minutes away. Launched from a B-52 bomber, they wouldn't be mistaken by other global powers for an ICBM launch, but they could do a great deal of damage if they reached their destination— which, according to telemetry reports, was BTC headquarters in downtown Detroit. At that speed, they carried very few explosives. Instead, they were packed with scored tungsten rods. Just before impact, their modest warhead would detonate, showering the target area with thousands of fragments—obliterating anything in a three-thousand-square-foot area in a rain of hypersonic metal.

The BTC had played around with this technology in the '70s. Retro stuff, but still quite effective.

The annoying thing was that BTC gravity mirror technology wasn't useful here since the X-51s were driven by ramjet engines; they were already resisting gravity as they powered onward. It was just one of the many reasons Hedrick had been pushing so hard in recent years for gravity amplification. Stopping them dead in the air, or turning them around—now that would be really useful.

"Mr. Director, you have a video call from Site R. It's General Westerhouse."

Hedrick nodded. "Put him up."

A grim-faced, square-shouldered African American four-star U.S. Army general festooned with campaign ribbons appeared on a holographic screen that materialized just to the right of Hedrick's gaze.

"Graham Hedrick, I am General Gerald Westerhouse. I'm issuing you a formal demand to surrender to lawful authorities and bring this situation to a peaceful resolution."

Hedrick felt truly annoyed. "I've been trying to bring this to a peaceful resolution from the start, General, but Director Monahan seems to have other ideas. Is she the one who put you guys up to this?"

The general kept a poker face. "You assassinated the deputy secretary of Homeland Security, Mr. Hedrick. Surely you realize that the United States government is not going to stand by while one of its federal bureau chiefs foments civil war."

"Let's not get melodramatic. The man was meddling. And it's not like there's never been any fratricide between agencies before. If anyone should be mad, it's me. I'm trying to carry out our legal mandate to protect the nation—and by extension that means the world—and the U.S. government keeps getting in my way."

"Surrender your facility to lawful authorities, or you will be forced to comply with U.S. law."

"General, for the moment there's been no public confrontation that could sow mass hysteria and undermine faith in rule of law . . ." Hedrick glanced to the right to see the WaveRider missiles tracking in, still hundreds of miles out. "We should take our responsibility to safeguard social order seriously. Let's not make any hasty actions that cannot be undone."

"Do you refuse to comply with a lawful order to surrender control of your facility?"

Hedrick sighed. "Don't make me do this."

"I'm giving you one minute to relinquish your post and to start marching your people into Congress Street."

Hedrick drummed his fingers on his armrest. "Well, seeing how you've already launched hypersonic cruise missiles at us, and they're not due here yet for another eight minutes, I'd say you're cheating me on time."

The general barely hid his surprise that Hedrick knew about the incoming ordnance. Apparently they had expected the stealth surfaces to hide them; however, the AIs observing from satellites in geostationary orbit had no trouble spotting objects moving at three thousand miles an hour against a backdrop of terrain.

"General, let's prevent this from becoming a major incident . . ." Hedrick brought up another holographic window displaying the face of a technical operations officer—a young Morrison clone.

"Yes, Mr. Director?"

Hedrick said, "Deploy DPD to eliminate the incoming missiles. Report when complete."

"Wilco, Mr. Director."

Hedrick turned back to the general, who was distracted by someone talking into his hidden earpiece. "Give my regards to Madam Director, General. Now, I'm going to chalk this up to institutional youthful enthusiasm, but I want this to be the end of it."

He looked up at the big map of North America. DPD—or dynamic pulse detonation—had been around a while. BTC teams had harvested it from Russian physicists back when there was still a single BTC. Now all the BTC groups had the technology, and it was the reason why missiles and rocket-propelled grenades were largely obsolete in advanced combat.

DPD used short, intense laser pulses to create tiny balls of plasma in the air, which were then struck by a second laser pulse to generate a supersonic shock wave within the plasma itself. This created a bright flash and a powerful bang—tiny plasmoid explosions, up to several hundred of them a second. These would be directed at the nose of an incoming missile, causing its trajectory to rapidly erode as it hit higher-pressure air and eventually causing the missile to tumble, breaking up within a second or two. He knew that even now DPD lasers were firing from orbit, peppering the air in front of the missiles. In moments all six of the incoming trajectories disappeared from the map. He imagined in the predawn sky over these rural locations there was a hell of a light show as the hypersonic missiles broke apart into flaming wreckage.

The Morrison clone reappeared in a hologram projection. *"Incoming missiles destroyed, Mr. Director."*

Hedrick turned back to the general. "Your preemptive strike has been canceled, General. I suggest you tell the public there was a meteor shower. Our publicity people will send along some sample press releases and footage to make the messaging convenient."

The general glared. *"Surrender your facility immediately."*

"That isn't going to happen. What's going to happen is you're going to start working with us cooperatively, just as before."

"You're no longer the director of anything. You're a criminal organization as far as we're concerned."

"Be reasonable about this, General. I haven't taken out your satellites or jammed your communications because I'm on your side. And you can't jam—or even detect—our communications because we're so far ahead of you technologically. Everything continues as before. We can all just simply forget this ever happened."

The general continued staring.

"Are we clear, General?"

Instead of answering, the general's transmission ended abruptly.

As Hedrick pounded the armrest of his chair, a bruised Mr. Morrison entered the gallery. Hedrick narrowed his eyes at the man. "Jesus Christ, I thought you were going to handle this, Morrison. Thanks to you, now I not only don't have Jon Grady, but Richard Cotton is missing, Alexa has betrayed us—and she's run off with tech level nine equipment to boot! As if I don't have enough to deal with already from competing board members and meddlesome government bureaucrats."

Morrison seemed calm but stared intently. "I'm not the one who gave 'her majesty' an unregistered positron gun as a sweetheart gift. Sort of odd—considering it's not really useful for anything other than BTC-on-BTC warfare. Specifically, defeating advanced nanorod armors. The type of thing one might give someone if one wanted to prevent a palace coup. Was she supposed to be your last resort, Graham?"

Hedrick paused for a moment and then turned back to the screens. "Let's talk no more about it. We've both got enough enemies as it is without turning on each other."

Morrison dabbed at his bruised face. "Where is she?"

"They may have dumped all their registered gear, but Varuna was able to sift through all the moving objects on satellite surveillance of the ground in Illinois. Tracing back from where you were overpowered, it looks like they headed to the shore of Lake Michigan, and they appear to have gone underwater from there—deep underwater—headed north. Which would make sense. It protects them from orbital weapons, and they might have thought it would hide their movements."

"Their destination?"

Hedrick brought up another holographic window showing a close-up satellite image of the eastern coast of Lake Michigan, near South Manitou Island. He zoomed in to show a tracking marker. "Varuna thinks they might be heading to this half-submerged wreck—it's the only thing for miles around and a way to take shelter unseen."

Morrison nodded. "We can fry them from orbit when they surface."

"We're not frying anyone. I still need Grady alive."

"But if they separate by even fifty meters, we can eliminate the other two. It'll make it easier to catch Grady."

"I have teams handling it."

"You're not referring to my teams, I hope?"

"They're not *your* teams; they're BTC teams. And you were missing in action. Varuna gave me a plan, and I sent several teams out. Do you disagree?"

Morrison pondered it irritably. "What's going on with these government knuckleheads?"

"They launched a handful of missiles. Nothing serious. I say we let them get it out of their system."

The technical operations officer's hologram reappeared. *"You have a call from L-329 at BTC Russia, Mr. Director."*

"Damnit! Why does this thing always call at the worst times?"

"Can't appear weak. It's fishing for an opening. Probably saw the missile launches."

Hedrick nodded. "Varuna."

"Yes, Mr. Director, I'll modulate your voice for confidence and honesty."

"Good." Hedrick spoke to the operations officer. "Send the call through."

In a moment a familiar cartoon cat appeared on a holographic screen. It spoke with apparent concern on its face. *"Director Hedrick. I see you're having a disagreement with your host government. Would you like me to resolve the problem for you?"*

"No. Why would we need that? Our host government is hardly a concern—and certainly no concern of yours."

"If you'd like us to safeguard your technologies until your—"

"I find it irritating that you are supposedly superintelligent and yet somehow do not understand the meaning of the word *no*. It's one reason why having an AI in charge of BTC Russia is so disappointing—it's like talking to a high IQ child. You have no life experience, and you ask impertinent questions. Now, if you'll excuse me, I have a breakfast meeting." He cut the line.

Morrison folded his arms. "The vultures are circling."

"But in this case the vultures are heavily armed. I'm starting to think L-329 didn't take over the Russian division—that Director Hollinger put it in charge to spite me. Just to make sure I wouldn't get control of their portfolio."

The technical operations officer's hologram appeared yet again. *"Sir, we have a remotely controlled vehicle approaching from the north. It's a UPS delivery van, but it appears to be transporting radiological material."*

"Oh for chrissakes . . ."

Morrison brought up some surveillance holograms of his own. "Where?"

The officer's hologram looked to him. *"Washington Boulevard, sir. Uniformed military personnel are cordoning off the downtown area several blocks away."*

Morrison pondered the satellite image of the UPS truck, moving toward them in the nearly deserted four A.M. streets. "Tactical nuke most likely, an MADM—maybe two, three kilotons." He looked to the ceiling. "Varuna, what would a detonation of that magnitude do to our surface structure?"

A holographic model of the neighborhood around the building appeared—and was quickly deformed by a slow-motion, blinding nuclear explosion that leveled multiple city blocks in every direction.

BTC headquarters remained, however.

"Such an explosion would strip away the concrete facade and might penetrate the diamond-aggregate nanorod curtain wall in several places. Damage to surrounding civilian and government structures would be catastrophic."

Hedrick looked truly annoyed. "This is all-out war."

"Could be a neutron bomb. A massive dose of radiation. Little explosive damage."

"Either way . . ." He spoke to the operations officer. "Jam every radio frequency for two miles."

"Yes, sir."

They watched as moments later the UPS truck started to wander in its lane, then finally came to a stop a half mile away.

Varuna's voice sounded again. *"Mr. Director, let me alert you to a gathering military force elsewhere in the city."*

Morrison glowered at the UPS truck on-screen. "Do we send someone to go get it?"

"Don't bother." Hedrick examined other screens Varuna was bringing to his attention now—close-ups zooming in from orbit. Dozens of armored military vehicles were forming into columns miles away, mobilizing.

The operations officer appeared again. *"Heavy artillery is coming out of cover ten miles to the east."*

Morrison looked toward Hedrick. "They're doing this the old-fashioned way. Probably planned to breach our perimeter and send troops in afterward."

Hedrick gripped the arms of his chair in rage. "I'm finished with half measures." Hedrick brought up a hologram of another operations officer.

"Yes, sir?"

"Activate Kratos. I have a list of targets . . ."

Staff Sergeant Randall Wilkes stared down the wide, sculpture-studded length of Washington Boulevard. His National Guard military police unit had done as instructed and set up a roadblock at Clifford—closing off this portion of downtown to all traffic. They were to let civilians out of the area but let no one in. It was a damned strange training exercise, to inconvenience people who were just trying to get to work.

And what about the people who lived in the pricey condos to either side? He didn't spend a lot of time up here, but he could only imagine how much the condos were going for, and he knew if he'd laid down that kind of cash, he wouldn't be too thrilled with the military doing training exercises in the middle of the street at the crack of dawn. This wasn't North Korea.

Operation Rubicon had been strange all around so far. Wilkes waved on a newspaper delivery truck as it came out of the downtown area in the predawn. He looked across at the four up-armored Humvees in his platoon. They had occupied the street corners and set up police sawhorses blocking the road and sidewalks. An early jogger had been turned away—and wasn't too happy to hear this was a training exercise, but that he'd nonetheless be arrested if he continued. Some corporate lawyer threatened to sue them, too, but then he ran off the other way.

And Wilkes hadn't heard anything about this operation until forty-eight hours ago. He'd gotten a call telling him there was a mandatory training exercise—his normal one-weekend-a-month duty be damned—and here he was. His orders were to secure the intersection and wait for a column of military vehicles to move in from the north. They were to open up the cordon to let them pass, and then reblockade the street and await further orders. Some War on Terror training exercise, he supposed—the whole federal courthouse area was down Washington a half mile or so. He figured it was special operations stuff.

But radios had been down for the past ten minutes. Cell phones, too. He suspected that was part of the exercise—to see how the units handled the loss of communications.

Just then he saw the captain's Humvee approaching fast, and Wilkes walked to meet it as it rolled to a stop on the sidewalk. Captain Lawrence, a county judge, stepped one foot out and peered over the armored door. "All comms are out. Prepare to part those roadblocks. You've got a column of friendlies coming in fast from the north. They'll be here in thirty, so hustle it!"

Wilkes whistled and hand-signaled his men, then replied, "You got it, Captain." He then started toward the nearest sawhorses. They were each fifteen feet long. "Hey, Martin! Robbie! Get ready to move these fast. We got vehicles coming through, and they aren't stopping for shit!"

The captain got back in his Humvee, and it took off down a side street. The rest of Wilkes's platoon scrambled to grab the ends of the sawhorses, and they moved a couple out of the way in advance.

Wilkes moved into the center of the boulevard, standing on the grassy meridian. It was about twenty feet wide, and he wanted the vehicles to see him signaling as they approached. And he could see their headlights—even though it was light enough to run without them. *Damn!* This was some exercise. There was a long line of vehicles. They were coming down all four lanes on both sides of the street. They seemed to be following Baghdad road rules, too—high speed, civilians be damned. Leading the charge were half a dozen M1 Abrams tanks—their turbofan engines waking up the neighborhood. Wilkes could see lights going on in the windows of buildings all around them. Bewildered faces peering down.

Behind the tanks were dozens of Stryker armored vehicles. The whole column was moving thirty or forty miles an hour. This was insanely irresponsible. "Goddamnit! Get these blockades out of the way!"

His men scrambled to move the heavy sawhorses—and they damned near did it, too. One of the lead Abrams smashed through one remaining sawhorse, blasting it into pieces—one of which shattered the window of a parked car.

"Goddamnit. This is a frickin' training exercise . . ."

But no one heard him as the rest of the tanks and Strykers roared past, their CROWS autoturrets scanning apartment windows above, scaring the hell out of people.

Wilkes was a Detroit cop, and he just threw up his hands and looked to his men. "This is crazy! What are they doing?" He hoped no one had live ammunition.

But then, as he looked down the length of Washington Boulevard, he saw something distant fly up from the ground—something large, along with pieces of debris. It reminded him of videos he'd seen of tornadoes roaring through trailer parks. Wilkes pulled off his goggles and stared ahead.

And then he saw a UPS delivery truck hurtle into the sky a quarter mile away, tumbling as it went. Following it were what appeared to be trees, light poles, another car. It was as though the ground was peeling up. And now a horrendous thunder came to his ears as if a great machine were being ripped apart. Flocks of nearby pigeons scattered in a panic.

But the armored column roared onward.

And then Wilkes could see the lead tanks falling up into the sky as well, as if they'd driven off a reverse cliff. Red taillights stabbed on the following Strykers as pieces of asphalt, parking meters, manhole covers, trees, grass, sculptures—everything, literally everything—ripped out of the ground and flung itself into the sky. There was the deafening sound of breaking glass as the facade of one of the tall buildings ripped away, but instead of collapsing, it *up*-lapsed—pouring into the air and shattering into thousands of pieces as people screamed in terror and fled deeper into their apartments.

The Strykers had screeched to a stop now on their eight large rubber tires, but as Wilkes watched, speechless, the tanks were clanging together like great bells and cresting the tops of twenty-story buildings—then falling up, up into the dawn sky, receding, shrinking smaller with every second.

And other vehicles and debris continued to follow them as though on a conveyor belt. The cracking sound of the concrete, as if the bones of a giant were being broken, rippled through Wilkes's chest. He watched, paralyzed, as a whole section of Washington Boulevard—center meridian, sculptures, asphalt, and Stryker vehicles all—peeled up and came apart as they fell into the sky.

The remaining Strykers tried to turn or back away from the disaster, but the suspension of reality was racing them down the street—and winning. Men were piling out of the gridlocked Strykers now as their rear gates opened. They pulled off their packs and ran screaming away from another building facade ripping upward. Lampposts tore out of the ground; fire hydrants and sidewalks peeled up. Piping and electrical work from the streets dangled upward, their ends swinging as water poured into the heavens as well from a broken main. Soil hurtled upward, splashed through water, and came out mud on the other side.

Soldiers ran past Wilkes now, fear in their faces. He could barely hear them as he watched the sidewalk tearing up a hundred feet away. Soldiers there clawed at bicycle racks, but then the ground beneath it all gave way, the concrete cracked apart, and they spun screaming into the air, their cries receding.

Wilkes's neck craned up to see a line of debris heading into the heavens. What he knew must be M1 tanks were tiny dots now, crumbs in a vast river.

And then he felt the pull, it started dragging him forward, and he finally came out of his paralysis. Too late.

Almost immediately the feeling of falling tripled, and he grabbed for the light post next to him. The Humvee in the street before him, along with fleeing infantryman, flew upward with the asphalt of the street beneath them, and then the concrete and gravel beneath that, and finally the soil, poured skyward.

As Wilkes held on, he suddenly saw the world differently. It was all clear to him now. What he'd always known as down no longer was down. The city was a great roof over his head.

And as he looked down, he could see that the sky was a yawning chasm beneath his feet. His grip weakened on the lamp pole, and finally it slipped from his fingers as he fell screaming into the vast emptiness below.

At Site R, Director of National Intelligence Kaye Monahan sat in a mission control center watching live satellite imagery of the operation under way in Detroit. The generals and intelligence directors around her gasped. She herself felt a tingling, almost detached feeling as she saw an entire battalion sucked up and hurled into the heavens, the streets and building fronts along with them.

Now there were fires as what appeared to be a gas main silently exploded.

A hush had gone over the control room.

But then someone said, "Pull them back. For God's sake, pull back."

A general next to her said, "Where's the MK-54?"

"Lost, sir. We have no idea where it is."

"My God."

"We just lost a suitcase nuke."

"Jesus."

Monahan came out of her stupor and called to an operations officer. "What's happening?"

The lieutenant colonel examined a radar screen and shook his head. "They appear to be falling up. The leading edge is above a hundred thousand feet already." He looked up from the screen. "They're falling off the planet. Apparently the BTC can control gravity."

The gathered generals and intelligence directors let out a breath and wandered about the control room, trying to process what they were seeing.

A four-star general said, "We have no choice now. We'll need to tell the president."

The deputy director of the CIA scowled at him. "The last thing we need is politicians involved in this mess."

The NSA deputy director nodded. "We can't tell anyone about the BTC. If people find out how powerless civilian government is, there'll be a political crisis."

Monahan looked from one to another. "Then what do we do? We can't do nothing."

The deputy director of the CIA grimaced. "Maybe it's what we should have been doing all along. Just leave them alone. Let things go back to the way they were."

She looked up at the big satellite screen. The carnage seemed to be starting all over again miles out of town now as a whole artillery section began falling into the heavens, along with the farm fields in which they were deployed. The site was rapidly turning into a quarry.

Monahan pointed. "What the hell are people going to think, Mike? Half of the main drag in Detroit just fell into the sky in front of ten thousand witnesses."

"The BTC jammed cell signals. Radio frequencies."

"He's right. There's no television coverage. No YouTube video."

"So what are you saying? They did the right thing?"

"They did sanitize the scene. There's no wrecked military equipment to explain."

She clenched her fists. "You people are unbelievable . . ."

"Kaye, be practical. This is a monumental disaster—no doubt about it. But we won't help things by making them worse. Hundreds of young men and women are dead. They died trying to defend their country—but they lost. For now. And it doesn't help anyone if we reveal that."

She collapsed in a leather chair. "We need to inform the president."

"No. We don't."

"Goddamnit, he's going to notice that parts of Detroit are missing. That a battalion of the 82nd Airborne just went airborne."

"We'll get meteorologists to come up with something. Climate change. Freak whirlwind—something. For chrissakes, Detroit's right on the Great Lakes."

"Or close enough to them at least."

She shook her head. "You're expecting people to believe that seventy-ton main battle tanks and armored vehicles fell up into the sky because of a freak storm?"

There was silence for a few moments.

"Obviously, we'll need to work on the cover story, but you get the idea."

She sighed. "The BTC murdered Bill McAllen. They disintegrated him. Do we just let them do whatever they want and get away with it? How long before they come for us, too?"

The deputy director of the CIA put his hand on her shoulder. "They won, Kaye. Let it go. Let's try to manage the aftermath. Bide our time."

Monahan felt numb for the next half hour as the generals and intelligence chiefs tried to divide their PR problem into solvable pieces, but it all sounded like nonsense to her—like something the public would never believe. But then again, she had seen the truth and she didn't believe that either. Monahan kept thinking that there must be some way she hadn't yet thought of to react. Some strategy by which she could best the BTC.

But then there was a distant booming sound—and impossibly, water glasses on the table rippled, even though they were deep underground.

The generals and intelligence directors leapt up, looking up at the ceiling.

"What the hell is that?"

"Hedrick is coming for us. Jesus. If they can control gravity . . . they could rip us straight out of the ground!"

Monahan looked around the table at them. Panicked. They were all panicked.

One general shouted, "Continuity of government bunkers are no longer safe! We need to get out of here and spread out—go to separate locations. Or the heads of critical agencies are going to be wiped out all at once."

Monahan followed them as if she were watching from a distance. Still in a daze. They put her on an electric cart with a couple of generals and a heavily armed security detail—all of the guards inexplicably wearing MOPP biological protection gear. She figured somebody must have grabbed the wrong binder. Or perhaps they didn't have a binder for the scenario where Site R and all its high-value occupants fell into the sky.

As the cart came out of the huge gates at the bunker entrance, it skidded to a stop, and Monahan's stupor served her well. She didn't immediately lose her mind. Generals staggered around holding their heads in their hands, but she walked calmly, staring out at the shattered remains of main battle tanks and armored vehicles that had crashed into the forested slopes around them, leaving huge craters and fires behind, along with the body parts of hundreds of men, their corpses flash-frozen and then shattered like glass.

And she realized that the entire battalion had been thrown at them from the heavens by technological gods. Gods whom they'd angered.

CHAPTER 26

Action Plan

Jon Grady awoke in a comfortable, modernist bedroom with a high-raftered ceiling with walls that didn't rise high enough to meet it. As a result he could hear a distant television elsewhere in the loft. The sound of clattering pots and dishes.

Grady turned to see Alexa asleep, sitting in a chair across the bedroom, positron gun in her lap. He guessed she must have come in sometime during the night. Standing guard perhaps? He turned on his side and watched her sleeping, studying her face. The goddess Aphrodite had nothing on her.

With her eyes still shut Alexa said, "You're freaking me out, Jon."

He quickly looked away, coughing. "What was that?"

Alexa opened her eyes.

"You're obviously still on guard."

She sat up. "I don't sleep much. Never have. I heard your door open in the middle of the night and checked up on you. Found the door open—you asleep. I'm not sure I entirely trust Cotton. You realize he could turn us in to save his own skin?"

Grady narrowed his eyes and then felt for the video device hung around his neck.

It was gone. He tore off the covers and searched the sheets.

"What's wrong? What are you looking for?"

He leaned down to look alongside and then under the bed. Leaping out of it, he heaved and overturned the bed entirely. In a moment he came up with the silver chain on which he had hung the video device—a neat cut severing the loop, the clasp still in place. "Cotton . . ." He bolted out of bed, still wearing all of his clothes, and raced through the bedroom door.

Alexa was right behind him. "What's wrong?"

"The video record from Hibernity is gone. It has everything!" He looked both ways in the hallway and realized the sounds he was hearing were coming from the large workshop, not the kitchen, and so he ran toward it.

She followed close behind.

Grady moved down the corridor. Glancing for any open doors but finding none, he walked all the way to the end, where the corridor opened to a truly enormous technical workshop. There were robotic arms by the dozen on tables and on shelves—in fact, whole domestic robots, and shelf after shelf of inscrutable high-tech components. Not a circuit board in sight—just solid, shimmering, optically strange metamaterials and coils of electropolymer muscle. The place was possibly a third of the entire floor—a good three thousand square feet.

Ahead Grady saw Richard Cotton sitting at a workbench, viewing some type of cellular culture through an electron microscope display. Nearby robotic arms performed precision movements over petri dishes.

"Cotton!"

The man turned and lifted up a crystal visor he wore on a strap around his head. "Whoa. What's with all the shouting?"

Grady stomped up to him. "Where the hell is it?"

Cotton looked quizzically to Alexa. Then back to Grady. "Where is what?"

"My video device. The one that was around my neck."

Cotton raised one eyebrow. "I don't appreciate the tone."

Grady grabbed him by his shirt and dragged him off his chair, toppling it. "I'm not fucking around! Tell me where it is! I know you have it."

Cotton tried to protect the work on the table. "Damnit! Don't disturb those cultures. You're going to mess everything up."

Alexa gazed at nearby workbenches and pointed to something held in place by a robotic clamp. "Is this it?"

Grady turned and felt relief upon seeing it—but then twice as much anger. He released Cotton, dropping him onto the floor, and moved to grab Chattopadhyay's video device from the clamp. It was held fast.

"What the hell are you doing with it?"

Cotton got to his feet. "Well, if you must know, I could tell you weren't going to part with it without a hassle, and it sounded like it might be useful in damaging the BTC."

"Release it. I want it now!"

"All right, relax." Cotton stepped up and tapped a button on a holographic display. The clamp released. "Don't touch anything else."

Grady grabbed the device before it could fall. He pressed the "play" button and was relieved to see Chattopadhyay's video appear.

Cotton nodded at it. "I was able to copy all the data on it. The video. The DNA. The gyroscope-decoding instructions. Just one problem: There's no gyroscope data to decode."

Grady was making another necklace from polymer thread he'd found nearby and looping the video device onto it. "What do you mean there's no gyroscope data?"

"I mean there isn't any gyroscope data. It's a separate chip. Maybe it got fried by the electromagnetic pulse, maybe when you came in contact with Morrison while his power suit was shooting sparks—I don't know. But the gyroscope is fried."

Grady glared at him. "What the hell did you do to it? And why did you sneak in during the night and cut this off my neck? You cut it off my neck!"

"Time was a factor. If the BTC burst in in the middle of the night—before you'd gotten up the courage to trust me with it—we might have lost it entirely. And it might prove useful as a bargaining chip to keep us all alive—maybe threaten to release the data if they don't back off."

"You asshole. You broke it."

"I didn't break anything. It's an impressive little piece of homemade nanotech, though, I must say. One of your prisoner friends really knows his business, that's a fact. It's biological—looks like they used blood plasma for the DNA encoding. Grown bone culture for the housing. I wouldn't want to have to guard those fuckers."

Grady gripped his temples, distraught. "That data was the only way for me to find my way back to Hibernity—to bring back help."

Cotton gave him a look. "Don't be crazy. The BTC knows where Hibernity is." He turned to Alexa. "You probably know, don't you?"

She pondered the question. "I don't, unfortunately. Hedrick has a tight hold on that information. The AIs bring pilots to and from Hibernity with blast shields down, so even they don't know." She turned to Grady. "But Cotton's right, it's got to be somewhere on the BTC network, and if one of Cotton's BTC turncoats can get it for us, you should be back in business."

Grady exhaled and hung the device around his neck again. He cast a dark look Cotton's way as he left the workshop. "Cotton, if you take anything of mine again without my permission, you will regret it."

Cotton called after him. "Grumpy before breakfast, I see. Shall I cook up something?"

Grady returned to his bedroom and shut the door. He sat on the floor in the darkest corner and reactivated the video device—fast-forwarding from one prisoner testimonial to another, making sure they were all there.

"... *discovered the relationship between protein fifty-three and malignant neoplasm* ..."

Grady clicked to another.

"*I am Petra Klapner. I was imprisoned in 1993* ..."

There was a sharp knock on the door. Grady ignored it, but then Alexa poked her head in. "You okay?"

Grady nodded as he clicked to the next video.

"*I am Anton Bezizlik. In 1998 I was taken by the BTC* ..."

Alexa entered and closed the door behind her. She studied the holographic person floating before them. "These are the prisoners."

Grady nodded.

She stood watching. "I remember that man. I lectured him about his selfishness."

"*. . . please tell my family that I am still alive. It has been so many years.*"

Alexa caught herself, feeling the enormity of what she'd done.

Grady spoke without looking at her. "You have to understand. I cannot fail these people. I cannot."

The middle-aged Russian man on-screen rocked back and forth. "*. . . my daughter . . .*" The man's face streamed with tears as he struggled to speak. "*She will have lived her life, never knowing me. I think of all that I have lost.*"

Alexa felt as though the hologram was speaking directly to her—overwhelming her with guilt.

Grady gestured to it. "These are some of the greatest minds that ever lived. There are da Vincis and Galileos in that prison. They could do so much, and instead, they've been brutalized." Grady turned to see Alexa's distraught face as she watched the man on-screen.

She spoke matter-of-factly. "We need to rescue them."

"What?"

"We need to rescue them. But we need to do something else first—bring down the BTC."

Grady looked at her with surprise. "They created you."

"That doesn't mean they own me."

They heard Cotton's voice shout across the loft. "Hey! Get in here! There's something you should see!"

They exchanged looks. Grady was still irritated at Cotton, but he stopped the video. They both headed out into the hall, where they could see Cotton waving to them from the far end of the workshop.

"What is it?"

"Just come here!"

As they walked toward him, they could see several holograms of live television. Cotton pointed. "It's all over the news. I had some AIs scanning for any sign of BTC activity, and boy did they ever find it."

Grady and Alexa came up alongside him. They were gazing up at horrendous carnage in a downtown area.

"Anything about the deputy secretary's assassination?"

"No, not a peep about that. What you're looking at is downtown Detroit."

On-screen a plume of white smoke towered over the city, and aerial images of the streets showed what could only be described as utter devastation—with twenty-story buildings missing their facades, their interiors open to the air, a broad avenue now a deep trench. Hundreds of emergency vehicles surrounded the scene.

Alexa nodded to herself. "Just a few hundred meters from BTC headquarters."

Grady studied the images. "What happened?"

"Media's saying it was a sinkhole that killed a few dozen people—some critical infrastructure collapse due to deferred maintenance. Actually pretty clever." Cotton pointed with some sort of tool he'd been holding. "I'm guessing somebody tried to kick in Hedrick's front door. Stupid move."

"There's no possibility of a sinkhole anywhere near BTC headquarters." Alexa's eyes moved from screen to screen. "Perhaps the government tried to retaliate for the deputy secretary of Homeland Security."

Cotton shrugged. "Well, where's the wreckage? For that matter, where's all the rubble from those collapsed building facades?"

Alexa looked grim. "It's Kratos."

"Kratos? Don't tell me they actually built that thing?"

Grady looked from one to the other. "What's Kratos?"

She met his gaze. "It's you, Mr. Grady. Your gravity mirror technology writ large. One of the researchers found a way to project the gravity mirror effect over an arbitrary distance—like you saw Morrison do last night. An extogravis, and they put it into a satellite in a geosynchronous orbit at Lagrange point two—twenty thousand miles up."

Grady pondered this. "You're saying they have a satellite-based gravity weapon?"

She nodded and pointed to the screen. "It's why Hedrick was bringing you back from Hibernity. He needed you to improve it. They can reverse gravity in an area a mile across—narrower if they like."

"Holy hell . . ." Cotton turned from examining the carnage on-screen. "That's some technology you came up with. That's why there's no wreckage—it all fell into the sky."

Alexa nodded.

"Sort of explains the chatter on the Web. Kooks there are saying there was a military force that got sucked up by the hand of God. Folks filmed it on their phones, but there wasn't any cell service—and during the night somebody reached into their phones and deleted the evidence. Wacky, wacky people on the Web . . ."

Alexa watched the screens.

Cotton nudged Grady's arm. "Pretty impressive."

Grady shook his head. "My God—they have a satellite that can level a city."

"Suck it into space more like."

Grady walked away, sobered. "I can't believe what I've done. I've given these madmen absolute power over us all. And they'll only become more powerful over time."

Alexa turned to him. "You didn't give them anything. They took it from you, and I'm starting to realize that BTC probability models didn't include themselves."

Meanwhile, on television, pundits were discussing the long history of urban decay in Detroit, and an infrastructure bill being introduced in Congress to rush federal aid.

Cotton nodded. "Looks like Washington has backed off. Well, Hedrick won't hesitate to use this power. I expect our government friends will be licking their wounds for the moment. Which probably means they won't be of much help in springing the inmates from Hibernity, even if you tell them about it."

Grady looked up. "We need to locate Hibernity. Rescuing those prisoners and getting them safely to the authorities might be the only chance to level the playing field with Hedrick."

"But for that you'll need someone willing to receive them. And with Hedrick playing God, they might not risk it. In fact, the feds might turn you over to him."

Alexa took a deep breath. "We have to decide what we're going to do. We can't stay here forever. Hedrick and Morrison will never stop hunting for us. So we'll need to deal with them sooner or later."

Grady considered the situation. "How do they control that gravity satellite?"

Alexa shook her head incredulously. "You won't be able to seize control. It's an encrypted q-link. All managed by AIs that know where every single piece of BTC equipment is. For the satellite they'll probably have several q-links as backup, but there will be only a handful of control stations in the Gravitics Research Lab at BTC headquarters."

Cotton nodded to himself. "That means you'd need to physically access the heart of the place to have any hope of taking control of Kratos."

"What about destroying the satellite?"

"Pfffttt. Good luck with that. It's invisible for starters—they've got a diffraction cloak around it. And they'll zap anything that gets within ten thousand miles."

"Cotton's right; we'd need to get into the very heart of BTC's control center—and that means through layers of bulk-diamond security walls and robotic weaponry."

Grady considered this. "But if we could get control of the satellite, we could conceivably hold a gun to Hedrick's head. He wants me because this technology is fearsome."

Cotton laughed.

Alexa didn't laugh. "I might know someone who can help us gain access."

Cotton raised an eyebrow. "Who?"

"Never mind who. But I need to get back into the building to speak with them."

Cotton whistled. "Break into the dark tower?"

"You're the master thief. Can you find me a way in? They'll have rescinded my access rights, but I know every corner of that facility. I grew up there. And I'm certified in six dozen specialties within the BTC."

"Yeah, I've tried breaking and entering there once before. The place is crawling with robots, surveillance dust, high-energy fields." Cotton grinned. "I know because I spent the last several years studying it for weaknesses." He killed the news feeds and instead brought up holographic projections of BTC floor plans.

Alexa looked shocked.

Cotton chuckled. "I knew it was only a matter of time until they tried to whack me. I had a feeling there would be no exit interview either. So I made plans for escape or infiltration at a moment's notice, should either prove necessary."

She studied the floor plans, turning the model from side to side. "I won't ask how you got hold of these. Have you found anything useful?"

"No, I must say, the AIs locked this place up tight—triple redundant systems. Their security is basically perfect—especially when they're in high alert, which they'll be in right now. The nanorod walls can stop just about anything, and the EM plasma rippling over its surface is conducting about four hundred gigajoules. That plasma would diffract lasers. There's really no force short of a thermonuclear explosion that could get through it."

Grady watched Cotton turn the 3D plans first one way, then another. "That's not true."

"What's not true?"

"That there's no force that could get through that perimeter defense. Because there is a force that already does."

They looked at him.

Then Alexa smiled. "Gravity."

Grady nodded. "The gravity mirror." He approached the holographic 3D image of the building. "Cotton, your examination for weaknesses probably made a significant assumption."

"What's that?"

Grady swept his hand to turn the building's image upside down. "That the direction for 'down' would never change. Reexamine the plans. Try to find something significant at the outer perimeter wall that might suffer a malfunction if the world were to suddenly turn upside down."

Cotton studied the altered view of the BTC headquarters building. A grin crossed his face. "I must say, Mr. Grady, you have a decidedly devious mind . . ."

CHAPTER 27

Learning to Fall

Jon Grady adopted a wrestler's stance in a forty-foot section of the workshop that they'd cleared of all shelving and equipment. He wore a stripped-down version of the gravity-mirror harness that Cotton had cannibalized from Morrison's damaged armor. Grady also wore Morrison's armored boots and gauntlets. The boots were roomier than he'd like, but he'd padded them with foam inserts. Besides he didn't think he'd be doing too much walking with them.

Grady studied the microscopic circuitry of the harness, glittering in the workshop's light. "This is the gravity mirror all right, but God, it's shrunk down a thousand times in size. How in the hell do they get enough energy to it?"

Cotton tapped an assembly elsewhere on the harness. "Sixty megawatt fusion reactor."

"That little thing?"

"Well, it's got armor around it, so the reactor is smaller than that."

"Good lord. I'm walking around with enough power to light a small city."

Alexa pushed between them. "Let's get on with this."

Several nylon safety straps ran from Grady's harness to metal beams ahead, behind, left, and right, as well as iron rings on the ground and a strap looped over a rafter. Whatever direction he might fall, he wouldn't fall far.

Alexa checked his equipment, loosening the harness a bit. "You don't need the gravis so tight. Remember it's not like a rappelling harness—you're not hanging from this; it's changing the direction of down, and you'll be falling along with it."

He grimaced. "Gravis—who came up with that name?"

"I don't know. Somebody on the BTC's mirror project team."

"I invented the damn thing. I should have had a chance to name it."

Cotton stood nearby. "That was your first mistake, Mr. Grady. A thing can't exist in people's minds until it has a name. But with a name, it can exist in people's minds without existing at all. You should always come up with a name before you set out to create anything."

Grady frowned. "What does *gravis* mean, anyway?"

Alexa was inspecting his boots. "Latin for 'weighty.' 'Heavy.'"

He jumped slightly to test the weight. "Well, maybe the name fits after all. This must weigh forty pounds."

"It won't once you activate it. And that's a military gravis—armored. Mine is much lighter. The suit this was part of had electroactive polymer musculature to carry around the weight."

Cotton murmured, "We might be seeing some of those later, if things go amiss."

"Ignore him." She was kneeling at his boot. "You feel the control interfaces at your toes?"

The padded lining of his overlarge boots made them fit better, and Grady depressed two small nodules with this toes. "Yeah. Got 'em."

Alexa gestured to his other boot. "And here?"

He nodded as he did the same on the left.

"All right. Default control setup works like this: You control yaw by—"

"Yaw? What's yaw?"

"Aeronautical term—it's the horizontal direction you're heading." She pirouetted gracefully and came back to her start. "You control yaw direction for descent by angling your foot like this."

"Direction of descent—I thought you said it was a horizontal direction?"

She gave him a look.

"Oh. Right. We're choosing the direction of down."

Cotton snickered. "You invented the technology, Mr. Grady. Try to keep up."

Alexa lifted her right foot and flexed it first rightward, then leftward again.

Grady lifted his own right foot and did likewise.

"Good. And you control pitch—that is, vertical direction—with your left foot." She tapped his leg.

He picked up his left foot.

She demonstrated. "Flex your foot downward or upward—you go where your toes point."

"Got it. Seems simple enough. And the controls inside the shoe?"

"Each shoe has a button and a slide controller. Ignore the buttons for now—they're locks, so you can maintain whatever setting you're on without effort. But indoors, that could be dangerous for a novice. So only work with the slide controller for now. Do you feel them?"

Grady felt with his toes and nodded. "Yeah."

"The right controller sets the diameter of the gravity mirror—you can make it just big enough to cover you, or a bit bigger than that to accommodate extra material. And the left controller sets the focus—nudge it forward with your toes and the gravity is focused one hundred percent in that direction; pull back on it and the gravity gets dispersed."

"So half gravity, quarter gravity—like that?"

"A percentage, but yes."

Grady frowned. "Wait. Even in microgravity, I'd keep accelerating until I achieved relative terminal velocity."

"Normally true, but software in the gravis curtails acceleration."

"How's it do that?"

"It flips the mirror for microseconds in order to maintain constant velocity relative to the ambient gravitational field."

Grady considered this. "Huh. I probably would have thought of that eventually . . ."

"Pay attention, Jon." She motioned to her boot. "Pull the slide controller all the way back, and you diffuse gravity into an equilibrium."

"Meaning I float at a full stop."

"Well, as you know, equilibrium won't cancel out momentum you already have. To slow down you need to reverse direction of descent momentarily." She looked him up and down. "You ready to give it a try?"

He tugged at the nylon harnesses holding him in place. They seemed secure. "Sure. How much trouble can I get in?"

Cotton chuckled. "Famous last words."

"Start out by pulling the right controller all the way back. I want your gravity field to be as narrow as possible. That'll make it just above your height."

Grady used his toes to pull the controller back. "So a roughly six-foot sphere around me will be subjected to my gravity field."

"Right. In fact, do press the button to lock that setting. We don't want you accidentally expanding the sphere and bringing a wall down on us."

He clicked the button and tried nudging the slider. It was locked down fast. "Okay. I got it. It's locked."

"Now pull back on the left controller to set it to equilibrium. That way you won't fly off anywhere."

He did so and nodded.

"Okay. Let's power it up."

Grady hesitated a moment before studying his gauntlets for the control interface. The boots and gauntlets apparently had power sources of their own and were paired via a q-link to the harness—and presumably to the rest of the assault armor, had it been present. In a moment Grady remembered how to make a pop-up holographic control panel appear above his arm.

Alexa pointed. "Remember not to go into this interface while you're airborne. Never power down while in the air."

"Got it." He tapped the master power switch.

And suddenly felt like he was in free fall. His stomach lurched as if he'd plunged down the first hill on a roller coaster. He pushed off slightly from the concrete floor and moved upward until the nylon straps restrained him.

Grady felt a smile spread across his face, and he laughed. "This is really incredible!"

Cotton stood next to Alexa now, watching. "They really must have messed with his head in that prison."

Alexa waved to get Grady's attention. "Okay. Now I want you to experiment with directional control. Don't do it at full gravity—we can't trust these straps or the beams in an old building like this. So choose your direction of descent with both feet . . ."

Grady concentrated and chose a direction to the left—toward an open space of lab.

"Good. Now slowly push forward on the left controller to bring yourself up to a quarter gravity."

Grady took a deep breath and nudged his toes forward against the control. He suddenly felt a physical manifestation of the natural forces of the universe reaching out to him, tugging him to the left—which had now suddenly become a wholly convincing "down." A glance at Alexa and Cotton made it seem as though they were standing on the face of a concrete cliff, while the workshop floor stretched down in a sheer drop to a brick wall a hundred feet below. "My God!"

The nylon straps restrained him from continuing, and he hung like a bug in a spiderweb until he could get his heart rate to come down.

"You look a little red-faced, Jon. You all right?"

He laughed. "Yeah. Beautiful! It's amazing. Just gotta wrap my head around it, that's all."

Grady changed the direction of down without changing the intensity of gravitation, and the angle of down swept across his horizon like the sun rising and setting. The straps and beams creaked.

"Just miraculous . . ." He experimented a bit more, flexing the nylon straps first one direction and then another. Finally he looked up at them and nodded. "I'm ready for a free flight, I think."

Alexa looked grim. "Be careful, Jon. You can easily kill yourself with this equipment—especially in a room this size. It could be a hundred-foot fall right into a brick wall—and then you might collapse the brick wall, if you're not careful."

He took a deep breath and reviewed his familiarity with the controls. "No. No, I think I've got this. Worst-case scenario, I just pull back with my left toes on the controller, and I go into weightlessness. Right?"

She nodded. "Right. Remember that if you get into trouble."

Cotton frowned. "It's a bit more than that. Weightlessness is all well and good, but watch the direction of down near walls and furniture. They were designed with a pretty boring direction for down in mind, so don't go wrecking anything."

"Don't worry. I've got this. Hell, I invented this."

"Let's not get cocky."

"Here, I'm going into equilibrium. Start undoing the straps."

Alexa stepped forward, keeping most of her body weight outside the altered gravity field as she started unfastening the straps from Grady's gravis. In a few minutes he was floating free.

"Ha, ha!" Grady flexed his arms and started doing a Russian folk dance in midair. "Hey! Hey! Hey!"

"All right. Enough of that. Try to move toward that doorway."

Grady did one last "Hey!" and then he directed his right foot toward the target. He concentrated, and then, keeping his left foot level, he slowly ramped up the force of gravity.

Too fast—he was already falling at thirty miles an hour toward the doorway.

"Left foot! Pull back!"

Grady gripped the left nodule controller with his toes and brought it back to zero gravity—but his momentum kept him going forward at a considerable clip.

In a moment of clarity, he twisted his right foot and ramped up the gravity slightly in that direction, turning in an arc back the way he came—like an ice skater burning off momentum by digging in his skates.

"Watch the shelving!"

Grady just barely bumped the shelving unit as he came to a stop—while the new direction of down caused one shelving unit to lean sideways, spilling everything off its racks. Grady immediately pulled back into a gravity equilibrium, and all of the items on the shelves started floating—lots of small valves and electronic components.

Cotton grabbed his head with his hands. "For fuck's sake! Look at the mess you're making."

Alexa nodded encouragement. "That was good thinking, Jon. Your knowledge of physics is going to help you here. Newton's first law. Uniform motion."

Grady nodded. "Right." He patted the shelf in front of him. "Thanks, Isaac."

"Now try it again."

Cotton added, "And this time try not to almost kill yourself."

Grady ran through his knowledge of the controls again and mimed his planned actions. He finally looked up. "All right. I got this." He looked across the room toward the doorway, then pointed. "I'm heading right over by the entrance."

"Not too close. The doors might fall through."

"Okay. I'll stop ten feet away."

"You sure you're ready?"

He clapped his diamondoid-armored gauntlets together. "Hell, yeah!"

Cotton mumbled to Alexa. "I don't think I can watch this."

"O ye of little faith, Cotton."

"You forget who I was until recently."

Grady took a deep breath and then altered the direction of descent. This time he gradually increased the force with his left toes, pushing forward only slightly. He began to glide above the floor, some of the debris falling along with him, scraping on the concrete as it did.

"Well, now you're just scattering the mess around."

Grady concentrated on the door as he maintained a steady five-mile-per-hour pace. He called back, "I can see it now. You've got to have a very fine touch in close spaces."

Alexa nodded. "Right. You're doing excellent."

"You really have to be careful what you get near. Otherwise you quickly get a cloud of debris around you."

In a few moments, Grady eased back on the controller, and this time, he lowered his pitch until he could drag his foot along the floor. In a moment he leveled it out and came to a standing stop almost exactly ten feet away from the doorway. He then put himself into half gravity with down being down. Locking gravity, he turned to face them, arms spread wide. "What do you think?"

Alexa nodded. "Nicely done. I think it's time we take it up a notch."

Grady raised his eyebrows. "Meaning?"

Cotton answered for her. "Meaning it's time for this little birdie to leave the nest."

Grady stood on the flat silver roof of the Fulton Cold Storage building—the multistory painted sign looming behind him. It was about two in the morning. The lights of downtown Chicago were visible in the distance, but otherwise the streets ten stories below were quiet.

Alexa stood next to him in her formfitting tactical jumpsuit. Her own gravis was integrated into its nanotech fabric, while his looked clunky by comparison. It was a sultry summer night, but he was dressed for wind, with a sleek pair of windsurfing goggles that Cotton had given him.

Alexa walked over to the parapet at the edge of the roof and looked down. "Let's not stay too close to the ground when we get up there. No sense in calling undue attention to ourselves." She walked back to him. "Besides, the higher up you are, the more time you have to deal with mistakes."

Grady nodded. He was actually starting to feel nervous.

"You'll be fine. I'll be right there." She spoke into her microphone, and he heard her voice right in his ear. "*I mean it. You'll do fine.*"

She moved about thirty feet away from him. "Now remember that if we get close to each other, our gravity fields will interact. You're a physicist, so you can probably estimate the interactions better than I can, but just don't forget it."

"No. I'm ready. Let's do this."

Alexa held up her hand. "Equilibrium."

Grady made adjustments. "Check."

"Power up."

He activated his gravis. "Powered up." He was suddenly floating in microgravity.

"Push off the roof with your legs. We don't want those rafters in your gravity well when you fall up."

Grady bent his legs and pushed off into space. He laughed nervously as he rose ten, twenty, and thirty feet above the roof, seeing more and more of the surrounding city blocks as he did so. He gazed around. "This is beautiful!"

Alexa was quickly up to his height, putting a finger against her lips. "Not until we're higher. Voices carry in open air." She pointed upward. "One quarter gravity, twelve o'clock high, please. I'll meet you at one thousand feet."

With that Alexa began to fall upward.

Grady nodded to himself and activated his controls. Instantaneously he was falling upward as well. As he did, his view of the surrounding city streets increased. He felt an instinctive fear, but it was counterbalanced by his brain's full belief that "down" was actually just above him—not below. So when he looked at the cityscape, he felt as though he were examining the sky overhead. He laughed nervously as the view kept expanding.

"Jon!"

Grady looked up to see that he was rising past Alexa. He brought himself back into equilibrium, and she rose to meet him. They were now at eleven hundred feet above the meatpacking district. The view of the Chicago skyline was breathtaking.

"This is really something."

"Keep an eye out for helicopters. If you get seen, go fast—anywhere but the safe house until you lose them. A typical helicopter can do about a hundred and fifty miles an hour—which is faster than terminal velocity. So your best bet is evasive maneuvers. You'll find that with the gravis you can change directions much faster than normal aircraft."

Grady was still gazing all around, a grin on his face. "I can't believe this. It's like a dream."

Alexa nodded. "It is pretty amazing. And I've seen some amazing things in my day. Back when I was a field operator in the '80s . . ." Her voice trailed off. "Never mind. You ready?"

He nodded.

"Follow me. If we get separated, I'll find you with my thermals." She pointed ahead and to the left. "See that tall building over there? John

Hancock Center. Let's head toward it." She tapped her ear. "Keep in touch by q-link." She shot him a quick grin as she lowered her visor. "And try to keep up."

With that she twisted around and fell forward, back first, twisting like a high diver as she disappeared into the night.

Grady felt a thrill unlike anything he'd ever known as he jammed the controller forward and suddenly felt the universe draw him toward the horizon. The wind buffeted him at a hundred and twenty miles per hour. He glanced below, and it was as if this was the BASE jump to end all BASE jumps—with the city of Chicago serving as a jagged cliff-face down which they were both falling. Grady moved his hands as airfoils and adjusted his position with increasing ease. He screamed in joy as he fell across the sky.

"Try to keep the screaming to a minimum. We don't want to attract attention."

"Right. Couldn't help it. Sorry."

Forty-story condo buildings were gliding by below him—or to the side of him in the current gravitational context. He was passing by a narrow river crisscrossed with bridges. Up ahead he could see Alexa falling with her arms tucked against her sides—aiming like a bird of prey toward her target.

Grady did likewise and instantly felt a speed increase. He could also see below more easily that way. The wind roared past his ears.

In under a minute they starting closing in on the hundred-story Hancock building. Grady eased up on the gravity along with Alexa, and they coasted to a near stop as the wind buffeted them.

She pointed. *"See that building there with the four small towers just to the left of Hancock Center?"*

"Yeah, I see it."

"Let's see if you can land on top of a tower."

Grady sucked in a breath. Falling in the open air was fantastic, but he remembered his close shaves in Cotton's workshop.

Alexa came up within twenty feet of him and spoke directly, instead of over q-link. "You need to be able to do this without hesitation, even in wind."

"Yes, of course you're right. I'm on it."

Grady eased his "down" in the direction of the tower, keeping it to barely any gravity at all. The roof of the building slowly approached him. At first glance he'd thought this was an older, art deco sixty-story building, but now that he was getting up close, he could see it was newer than that— paying homage perhaps. The art deco look here had an '80s blockiness to it. The roof of the building was capped by four identical purely orna- mental towers—square boxes of metal with small pyramids atop them. He focused on the nearest one, and as he glided closer, he modulated his pitch, adjusting the angle of his foot as necessary.

"Remember to reduce your gravity after you land. It will prevent damage to the structure."

Grady gave her a thumbs-up sign and turned back toward the ap- proaching tower. It was barely ten feet away now, capped by a large square point made of steel, about three feet wide. A lightning rod stood above that. He glanced down to see the roof of the building some forty feet be- low. The other towers nearby. And the Chicago streets hundreds of feet below them all.

A wind blew him slightly to the right, but he corrected, and in a mo- ment he grabbed onto the cap of the metal pyramid with his gauntleted hand. Moments later he wrapped his arms around the spire, and low- ered his gravity to almost nothing, but pointed in the direction of actual gravity—just enough to keep him in place. He clung to the top of the spire and looked back up at Alexa floating in space a hundred or so feet away.

"How was that?"

"Excellent. Did you feel how the structure started taking on your gravity field?"

"Yeah. I dialed down the intensity just as I got in close. Seems to work all right." Grady looked out across the city, and then down. *Whoa.* He was up in a place where he'd normally be frightened out of his wits, but chang- ing the direction of gravity seemed to chase off vertigo. Looking around he felt a little like King Kong atop the Empire State Building.

"Now remember, when you push off, don't just hit full gravity upward, or you might rip the top off the tower."

Grady nodded and pushed away from the building at nearly zero g before increasing it moments later to gain altitude. "How's that?"

She came nearly alongside—just far enough away so their gravity fields weren't tangled. "Good. Okay, how about a bit of high-speed maneuvering?"

"I don't want to go through any skyscraper windows tonight."

"No, we'll head down there." She pointed out toward the water, where long lines of stone outlined a harbor. A lighthouse blinked occasionally at its tip. "Along that quay, near Chicago Harbor. I'll meet you down at the lighthouse. Go fast, now!"

She did a backward somersault and then kicked in full gravity—sending her soaring downward at an angle toward the lakeshore a mile away.

Grady felt the thrill of the chase and immediately fell downward after her. He was rapidly getting a feel for how to direct himself and how to increase or decrease his speed. It was a physical experience of the laws of motion he'd studied for so many years. He could almost see the mathematical arcs he was tracing through the air as he increased this variable or decreased that one. Living proof of his perceptions.

Grady hurtled through the night air, passing over the rooftops of shorter skyscrapers at a hundred miles an hour. Once clear of the last row of buildings, he angled down toward the lake, aiming for a spot about a half mile from shore. He descended to five hundred feet and sped silently across the dark water.

As he came up to a few hundred meters from the blinking stone lighthouse at the end of a lone stone quay, he eased up on the speed and brought himself to within yards of the water's surface. When he reached the lighthouse, he rose to a full stop alongside the railing at its peak, where Alexa stood waiting for him patiently—apparently in normal gravity.

She smiled. "You're taking to this quickly."

He floated ten feet away from her like a child's balloon on a string. "It's like everything I imagined. It seems so natural."

"Just don't forgot the old rules of physics when you take the belt off." She looked up. "We still need to experiment with interlocking gravity fields. It'll be safer if we go high up for this."

"How high you want to go?" He craned his neck into the cloudy sky.

"How about just below the cloud deck? Meet you up there?"

He nodded, but even before she launched, he did—laughing like a maniac as he plummeted into the heavens.

He glanced back at the city as he kept rising. It was truly breathtaking—the best elevator ride in the world. It wasn't until about four thousand feet that he started coming to the bottom of the cloud cover. He dialed to equilibrium and stopped slowly. The mist was clearly defined and dense above him. It was also much cooler up here, and he could feel the dew point was near, as moisture seemed to be coming out of the air.

He looked down to see Alexa rising up, and in a moment she was across from him at a distance of ten yards. The clouds formed a roof above them, but there were gaps here and there where he could see the stars. He could smell the moisture. Below them the city of Chicago glowed in the night.

"All right, Jon. Let's fall toward each other slowly—one tenth gravity. I want you to try to grab my hands as we pass."

"Like objects passing in space."

"Right. Our gravity fields will make it seem like we're objects of much greater mass, so we'll behave like stars passing by each other—we'll disturb each other's trajectory."

"Okay. Say when."

She nodded. "Go."

They started falling toward and past each other, but as they got close, their trajectories were disturbed to a degree Grady felt that he could anticipate. They were now proof of the physical laws he knew so well. They sailed past each other on altered courses.

Grady shouted back. "Let's try it again. This time come in at a slightly steeper angle toward me. Just slightly."

"Change your angle of descent."

"Done. Here . . ." He looked ahead as they started to drift toward each other again. He felt it the moment their trajectories interacted. A tug as he fell in toward her, and she fell in toward him—then they passed, brushing outstretched hands.

And then they began to orbit each other, revolving without either one adjusting their controls. They were now a binary system.

She smiled lightly as they continued to go in circles, getting closer with every revolution and spinning faster. "We could get dizzy doing this."

He nodded but watched her face in the semidarkness. "How many more until we meet, do you think?"

She shook her head. "I don't know . . ."

"I say six."

"Six, eh?"

He nodded.

"All right." They went around again, gradually increasing speed. "That's two."

He kept his eyes upon her as the natural laws of the universe brought them closer together with each revolution.

"Four."

At their sixth revolution they were face-to-face. They locked hands until their rotation began to slow. They turned to look at city lights far below.

"How did you do this, Jon?"

"Simple physics."

"No. I mean this . . . the gravity mirror. Even the BTC doesn't understand how it works. No one does."

He thought for a moment. "It's not me. It's the universe. I was just the first person to see it."

Her beautiful eyes studied him.

CHAPTER 28

Tipping Point

G raham Hedrick stood in the BTC command center as technicians scurried about in the control room below. He knew that beyond his sight AI bots were scouring consumer data, telecommunications signals, surveillance camera imagery, and satellite reconnaissance for any sign of Grady, Alexa, or Cotton. Every form of communication known to man was being sifted and resifted. With every passing hour they widened their search radius.

Hedrick turned to Morrison, who, as usual, stood nearby. "What happened to those underwater signatures—the ones in Lake Michigan?"

Morrison looked grim. "They disappeared. The teams up there have been looking, but nothing so far."

Hedrick studied the screens. "An underwater escape. That must mean Alexa has cavitating gear. Check the inventory and see if anything is missing."

"Let's just assume she has it. What difference does—"

"Capabilities." He turned back to Morrison. "If they have deepwater gear, I think Mr. Grady's going to try for Hibernity. His compatriots there helped facilitate his escape. He'll try to rescue them. That can't happen."

"If we recall the search teams, I'll have enough manpower to go down to Hibernity and clean house."

"No."

"But if Grady and Alexa secure those prisoners, they could cut a deal with BTC splinter groups. Or they could trade them to the U.S. government—which would help them catch up to us technologically."

"Yes. And if not the U.S. government or BTC splinter groups, then a hundred other enemies." Hedrick gazed up at the world on the screens. "It's all spinning out of control. It's getting harder and harder to contain all this technology." He turned back to Morrison. "How many people in Hibernity have invented fusion now—sixty? Seventy?"

"One hundred and twelve."

"See? No, this can't go on. That's why it's time to resolve this situation once and for all."

"Meaning what, sir?"

"Meaning that the mission of the BTC must evolve. We've been trying to protect society from disruption since the Cold War, but it's become increasingly obvious to me that we're the only society that matters now. What's important is preserving our store of knowledge—the hard-won advances of mankind—against the chaos that's coming."

"What chaos, sir?"

"The chaos you're going to create. Perhaps our Winnower friends had the right idea; the outside world should not have so much knowledge."

Morrison looked at Hedrick warily. "What are you proposing?"

"Undermine global financial markets—set our AIs loose on power grids, transportation and communications networks. In a few weeks the industrialized world will begin to come apart. We'll just make sure there are no nuclear missile launches but otherwise let the chaos spread for as many years as is necessary." Hedrick studied the satellite screens. "By the time it's over, no one will be able to oppose us."

"Our mission is to *prevent* social disruption, Mr. Director, not cause it."

Hedrick turned calmly to Morrison. "Yes, but disruption of *which* society? We've progressed so far beyond the outside world, they're no longer us."

"And the widespread casualties this will cause?"

"The price of progress. Next time we won't share as much technology.

That was our mistake. We need absolute domination in order to keep humanity on track." Hedrick contemplated the screens again. "You are with me, I hope, Mr. Morrison?"

Morrison cleared his throat, then nodded. "Yes, Mr. Director. You know I am. What about Alexa and Grady?"

"Disrupting civilization will make it harder for them to harm us."

"She's a bigger danger to us than anyone."

"You're saying we need to eliminate her."

"The only reason she's still alive is because of your feelings for her, but aside from Grady and his knowledge of gravity, I can't think of a single person on this planet who can do more damage to us. Even if you topple civilization, if she winds up in the hands of BTC Asia or Russia, they could extend their life spans indefinitely from what they learn from her miserable carcass. We could be facing the same lunatics for centuries. Not to mention the inside information she has on every inch of this facility and all the people in it. All our procedures and operations. Every weakness. Every—"

"Enough! Okay . . ." He took a deep breath. "Kill her on sight." Hedrick looked deeply pained. "But not the way you killed Davis and McAllen. I want it painless. Instant."

"Fine. A high-powered microwave from orbit—"

"I don't want to know. Just let me know when it's done."

"There's someone else you're forgetting."

Hedrick turned to him with a questioning look.

"Cotton."

Hedrick dismissed it with a wave of his hand. "I'm counting on Cotton to help us."

"How do you figure?"

"Because he's a survivor. He can read the way the winds are blowing. Once society reaches the tipping point, he'll reach out to us. And I'm willing to cut a deal with him in exchange for Grady and Alexa."

"And after that?"

Hedrick shrugged. "We'll honor our deal. What do I care if he retires in luxury? He's been useful, and he might prove useful again."

"He's a thief and somehow able to lie even to our AIs."

"Like I said: He's useful." Hedrick focused back on the big satellite screens. "Heightened security procedures are in place?"

Morrison nodded. "We're on a wartime footing."

"Good. See that we stay that way. How is the outside world dealing with recent events?"

"The government folks are trying to explain the inexplicable as best they can. Some cell phone video sneaked out. The missile explosions over Canada, the power outages in southern Illinois—it's starting to build into public hysteria."

"And just think—it's been less than twelve hours. We've barely started, and already the outside world is on the tipping point. You know what to do, Mr. Morrison."

"Yes, sir."

CHAPTER 29

Storming the Temple

Richard Cotton sat combing his hair out. Literally. Jon Grady watched perplexed as Cotton held some sort of glowing stylus to his scalp, activating hair growth at an insane metabolic rate. It came out of his head like Play-Doh through a press. Cotton had already half-finished creating eight-inch-long brown locks.

"And that works . . . anywhere on the body?"

Cotton looked up. "What does?"

Grady pointed.

"Oh. No. Only where there are hair follicles. And even then only up to a certain length before it'll fall out. Just accelerates a natural process. So . . . if you're bald naturally, this isn't going to solve any problems for you. This manly mane is all me." He winced. "Makes the scalp hot as hell, though. All the accelerated cellular activity."

Alexa walked past them carrying a black helmet, which she placed on a nearby workbench. "Why are you even messing around with hair, Cotton? You're not planning on going anywhere, are you?"

"In the event I have to bolt in a hurry, I'd rather have a convincing disguise than a bad one. You're not the public face of evil here in the States. I am. So forgive me while I transform into an annoying hipster."

Grady watched as Cotton passed the stylus over his lip and started growing a long mustache. "I keep calling you Cotton, but that can't be your real name."

"All my names are real. I like to think of names as local variables. To you I'm Richard Louis Cotton, and so in this scope shall I always remain. To my online raid clan I'm Leeroy Jenkins, and there, too, shall I always remain."

"Well, that's a constant, not a variable."

Cotton paused. "Quite right, Mr. Grady. I stand corrected."

Alexa leaned against the workbench. "So you're sure about your end? About this traitor of yours?"

"I am."

"Who is it? How do we know we can trust them?"

"You have your traitor. I have mine."

"How do we know they're not the same individual?"

"Oh, I'm pretty sure they're not. Mine is cool, and I'm certain yours is uptight and self-important."

Alexa turned to Grady. "I don't trust him. Cotton has no reason to help us."

Grady placed a hand on her shoulder. "Hedrick tried to kill him. And Cotton's distrusted them for years. He's given us plans and preparations we can make use of, Alexa." He looked around them. "In fact, we already have."

"And what if this 'mole' of his is actually Hedrick or Morrison, and this is all a trap?"

"He could have called them here already. If he's going to have any sort of life, post BTC, Cotton needs us as much as we need him."

"Well, if he's a master thief, why are we the ones breaking in?"

Cotton shrugged. "There was a time when I might have been crazy enough to try to breach their defenses on my own, but they're on full alert. They've activated their perimeter security. No. This is a job for younger hands."

"I'm twenty years older than you, Cotton."

He patted her arm. "But you don't look a day over twenty-five, my dear. And think how much more experience you have than me. Besides, you know their network, their control rooms, and all their procedures." He raised his eyebrows. "But can you gain access to the network once you're inside? That's the question."

"Don't worry about that. I'm confident I can get credentials."

Grady gave her a look. "I hope so. Because without the location of Hibernity, this will all be for nothing."

Cotton started combing a longer beard into existence. "I'm not sure I agree with you there."

They both looked at him.

"You were right earlier, Mr. Grady. The Kratos satellite is actually the key. If you have control of that, you'll have power over the BTC. You'll be able to dictate terms—it'll be like a celestial gun to their head. And it's their main defense against enemies right now. Without it, even the government might feel confident enough to press the attack."

"Or to liberate the prisoners at Hibernity."

"Yes, Mr. Grady. They just might."

Alexa's eyes lingered on Grady. He could feel it. "What?"

"The more I think about this, the more I realize you shouldn't be going. I can do this more easily alone. I'm trained in operations."

He shook his head. "They won't harm me. I'm too valuable to them. That means I can provide a critical diversion for you. They'll drop everything and try to grab me the moment they know I'm near. Cotton's right. You need to use that opening to go for control of the Kratos satellite."

"Assuming Cotton's mole can get me near the building without getting me incinerated."

Grady frowned. "And what about this EM-plasma field?"

"You might have invented the gravity mirror, but I'm well practiced with it. I'm more concerned about Cotton's mole."

Cotton was forming a long devil's beard with the stylus. "Have faith. My mole should be able to get you up to the building. All you have to do is turn their world upside down."

"I can't believe I'm taking instructions from someone who's been caught doing this once before."

"Live and learn, my dear. Now . . ." Cotton rummaged around his workstation. "Here . . ." He tossed her what looked like a one-inch cubic diamond. "Once you get inside and enlist the aid of your 'friend,' and you somehow miraculously get past their deadly security measures to the Kratos control station in the heart of the BTC, and then somehow get your biometrics cleared for security access to their most precious asset—"

"This isn't inspiring confidence." She studied the crystal.

"After all that, plug that relay q-link into one paired with the satellite. It will transfer control here." He gestured to the many holographic computer screens floating over his workstation. "Extra points if you can destroy their other q-links. Just keep that control room secure after you do, and I'll be your overwatch."

She looked at him doubtfully. "And how do you know how to operate the Kratos satellite?"

"My mole has gotten me access to many things . . ." Cotton brought up detailed blueprints for the Kratos satellite onto his screens as well.

"My God, we had a serious security problem. How did you get these? How did you fool the AIs?"

Cotton spread his hands. "I'm a thief. It's what I do."

Grady examined the drawings. "Then the BTC never had a monopoly on all of this technology. All of this insanity is for *nothing?*"

Alexa still didn't look happy. "What other data have you stolen, Cotton? What other plans?"

He laughed. "Now is not the time or place, but I assure you I will share everything I have. I will hold back nothing."

Alexa didn't seem to know what else to do, given the situation. She turned to Grady, then grabbed the helmet from the nearby workbench and handed it to him. "I found this scout cover among Cotton's stolen loot. It'll give you some head protection if things go wrong. BTC aimbots always go for head shots."

Grady accepted the helmet. It looked like a matte-black bicycle helmet except that its crystal visor seemed to be made of bulk diamond, which he was starting to become familiar with. It could probably withstand the impact of a .50-caliber bullet—though his brain would still be turned to Jell-O from the impact. He nodded grimly. "Thanks."

Cotton finished his coiffure. "Well, what do you think?"

They turned to look at him. He now resembled Wyatt Earp. They stood silently.

"That good, eh? Well, to hell with you both. You have no taste." He tossed the stylus onto the workbench. "Are we ready to do this thing?"

Alexa nodded. "Yes. The sooner we do, the sooner we can end this." She turned to Grady. "Your destination is programmed into the helmet visor."

Grady nodded.

"Cotton, how do you know they'll be watching that geographic location?"

Cotton was busying himself at his workbench. "Because it's the location my mole reported as Mr. Grady's last-sighted position. They'll have sensors on it."

She turned back to Grady. "The site's about two hundred miles from Chicago, and about two hundred and fifty miles from Detroit."

"So even after the alert, it'll take them hours to get to me."

She shook her head. "No. Morrison's assault teams use pressurized diamondoid armor. They don't stay in the atmosphere. They ascend to about twenty miles into the atmosphere, and then free fall over the landscape from there."

Grady considered this. "Much thinner atmosphere at that altitude. Makes sense."

"Right. It means they can reach speeds of eight hundred and forty miles an hour. It's about a four-minute fall up to their cruising altitude; about seventeen minutes travel time, and then a four-minute fall back down to sea level. So expect them to arrive within thirty minutes of the time they leave BTC headquarters. Stay miles away from your destination until I give you the ready signal." She examined him. "Are you sure about this, Jon?"

He took a deep breath. "It needs to be done."

"We could try some other form of diversion."

"Nothing that's guaranteed to get them to come in enough force to be of use to you. If they definitely see me, they'll think you're not far away."

"We could have Cotton's mole make a false sighting in—"

Cotton shook his head. "He's no longer in a position to help there, I'm afraid—seeing as he lost track of Mr. Grady once already."

"What if we created a decoy that drew them?"

Grady answered the q-link, "Alexa—anything that fails will only tip them off that you're coming."

She pondered it a bit more. "The moment you appear, there's the possibility that they just zap you dead."

"I don't think Hedrick would do that. In any event it's worth the risk if it provides a distraction at a critical moment." He gripped her shoulder. "No matter what happens to me, Alexa, promise me you'll free Archie and the others. You need to get to them before the BTC does; even if you get control of the satellite, they'll try to hide them somewhere. Don't let them."

"We won't. Don't worry, we'll rescue them, and you'll do it with us."

"Hate to interrupt the touching moment." Cotton approached with what appeared to be an autoinjector. He was loading an ampoule into it.

Alexa scowled at him. "What the hell is that?"

"You never asked how the BTC caught me when I tried to break in all those years ago. Kind of hurt you didn't ask, actually."

"I assumed you did something stupid."

"Ah, funny. No, I might not have been caught had I known that they release a neurotoxin into the crawl spaces during high alarms. It makes you panic and run screaming for fresh air—even if that's over a cliff. The stuff enters through all semipermeable membranes—lungs, skin, eyes."

"I've never heard of this."

"Have you spent much time crawling through your power conduits during security alarms?"

She just glared.

"This is what I was working on earlier."

She kept glaring.

"Right. Here then . . ." He put all the ampoules on the workbench and rolled up his own sleeve. "Pick one, and I'll inject it into myself. You'll be coated with neurotoxin when you come back, so we all need to get inoculated, anyway. I don't need a screaming panic attack, thank you very much—especially with a ten-story drop to the street close at hand."

Alexa sighed in irritation.

Grady selected the center ampoule.

Alexa grabbed the autoinjector from Cotton, then the ampoule from Grady, and then loaded it.

"My dear, don't inject angry."

She jammed the device against his arm. There was a pop and hiss.

"Ow." He paused for a moment, then grabbed his throat and started choking theatrically. Then he straightened. "Satisfied?" Cotton grabbed the autoinjector back from her. "Who's next?"

Grady selected one of the two remaining ampoules and extended his arm. "Why didn't you tell us about this before?"

He loaded the ampoule into the autoinjector. "Because I wasn't sure she was going in alone until now, and if she had forced me to come along, I would have quietly injected myself and then saved my own skin."

She made a disgusted sound. "You're a disgrace, Cotton."

"Ah, a wise coward is more valuable than a brave fool." He injected Grady, and then, after another glare from her, he injected Alexa with the contents of the last ampoule. "I told you I would share everything. I just didn't say when."

They all exchanged looks.

Cotton broke the silence with a clap of his hands. "Well, good luck with the mission then. Off you go, and be in touch on the q-link."

Grady stood on the roof wearing his gravis harness and the helmet Alexa had given him. She was thirty feet away—possibly for the last time. It was past midnight again, and as he glanced over at the Chicago skyline, he couldn't help but remember their flight the night before. He looked over to her and smiled wanly.

She paused before putting her own helmet on and instead approached him. "Wait."

Grady flipped up his visor. "What is it? Something wrong?"

Alexa came right up to him. "I've never really known anyone outside the organization. Not really. I realize that now. Be careful, Jon." Her hand gripped his harness, and she leaned forward to give him a kiss on the cheek.

He smiled slightly and then leaned forward to kiss her on the lips. After a few moments he looked into her eyes. "Your skin feels warm."

She nodded, looking somewhat surprised. "Yes." She caught her breath, then put her helmet on. She walked back to her ready position.

Grady watched her and nodded. "You be careful, too."

"Listen for my call."

"I will."

And with that she became weightless, pushed off the roof, and moments later fell into the starry sky like a rock tossed into a well.

Grady stared after her. After a few more moments, he realized just how much he wanted to survive the next twenty-four hours.

Alexa had charted Grady's route with the nav unit in the scout helmet. It projected whatever maps he needed onto his visor—along with the stand-off destination where he was to wait until she called.

He ascended to nearly two thousand feet above Cotton's building before falling northward, across the city and out over the moonlit lake. It was a clear night, and though it was dark, he felt incredibly exposed. There were small plane navigation lights blinking in the distance, but he'd gotten pretty good at maneuvering and felt that as long as he kept his eyes open, he'd be able to avoid any air traffic.

With the helmet he was able to accelerate comfortably into a terminal velocity fall—roughly a hundred and twenty miles an hour. Judging by the map, that meant it would take him nearly two hours to reach his destination—a small island in the northern reaches of Lake Michigan. He wouldn't actually move to the island until he got Alexa's signal, but his standby position was just a few miles away.

Grady fell across the dark sky, the light of a half-moon casting its glow on the water. It was beautiful, but he had no one else to marvel at it with. He wondered if the BTC harvester teams even noticed this beauty.

He saw the lights of a passing ship off in the distance, but nothing near him. Grady fell for scores of miles. His goal was to cross the lake on a northward diagonal and then track along the eastern coast. The islands were just off the mainland, and with the night vision setting of the helmet visor, he should have been able to find them even without a map.

After a little less than an hour he saw the dark, thinly populated coast, and he came over land above what looked like a power plant near a place named Pigeon Lake, at least according to the visor's map. Much to his consternation there was a municipal airport close by, but it looked quiet at this late hour.

He changed his angle of descent and started falling due north, hugging the coast. Grady studied the lights passing beneath him—or, as it seemed, to the side of him—as he fell alongside the vast wall of landscape. He crossed the mouth of an inlet where a lighthouse stood, then headed where sandy dunes caught the moonlight.

Two thousand feet below he caught sight of a roaring bonfire on the beach, and he couldn't resist slowing and finally gliding to a stop. He stared between his feet as he floated in equilibrium, a light breeze buffeting him. It was otherwise silent.

And then he heard laughter and voices far below. Rock music. Grady smiled. He was like an owl in the night.

With that he jammed his controller forward and fell again, northward at terminal velocity. He kept following the contours of the coastline as it curved away and then back again.

Eventually, after nearly two hours and hundreds of miles of rural coastline, he came close to his destination. Grady started scanning the map in his visor and aimed toward the little town of Empire, Michigan. He could see there were sizable bluffs here with dunes leading down to the water and lightly forested hills inland.

Grady frowned at his map as a U.S. Air Force air station came into view some miles away—he was definitely going to avoid that. He wondered what kind of radar signature he might have. No, best to get lower. Now that he was only ten miles or so from his standoff location, he had to find a place to land and await Alexa's signal.

Ahead of him was the top of a hill overlooking the small town and the lands beyond, so he slowed and pointed his angle of descent downward, dialing down gravity to just a quarter of its normal pull.

As the moonlit, lightly wooded landscape came up to meet him, he scanned for anyone who might see, but he was far out in the countryside. He then pulled his gravity back to almost zero and coasted down onto the ground with his forward momentum.

Grady was pleased with himself when he alighted with only a slight misstep, stood, and finally turned off the gravis entirely. He now stood on a grassy hilltop in the dark, crickets thrumming around him.

Before him was a view of the little town of Empire, Michigan, in a shallow valley.

Were there bears in Michigan? He looked around in every direction. But then he remembered he could fly. As he stared up at the stars, he smiled to himself. The situation was terrible, of course. But the universe could still be so beautiful. He thought about Alexa and hoped his diversion would help her get into BTC headquarters safely. He would make sure of it. He just hoped Cotton's mole was reliable, and that she could get close enough to BTC headquarters to enact their plan.

After falling the two hundred and thirty miles from Chicago to Detroit (the slow way since she didn't have a pressurized suit), Alexa came in toward the nondescript BTC headquarters using the cover of the Penobscot Building downtown to shield her approach. It stood forty-seven stories—ten taller than the aboveground portion of the BTC, and once she alighted onto one of its art deco ledges, she found herself nearly six hundred feet above the pavement.

She glanced below and around her to make sure no one was nearby and that she'd triggered no security alarms. She also scanned for the presence of surveillance dust. It would have been too late not to trigger an alarm, but if they knew she was here, she'd rather know now so she could attempt escape.

But there were no advanced sensors on this far side of the Penobscot, whose roof was about seven hundred feet away from the BTC. She knew the surveillance system covered the BTC headquarters in every direction—and this building gave her the most advantageous cover to draw close unobserved. Given Hedrick's quarrels with the government and the destruction he'd wrought with Kratos, the BTC was still no doubt on high alert.

Alexa withdrew a diffraction scope from her harness and aimed it off to the side, at a perpendicular angle to the BTC building. She then activated the diffraction element, bending incoming light until the BTC building came into view. If she understood it correctly, the device gathered reflected light from numerous directions and used software to piece together the photonic puzzle pieces, discarding anything else. The picture was usually grainy, but it was safer than a periscope—BTC surveillance AIs would spot those immediately.

She spoke into her q-link. "Cotton. I'm in position and standing by. Over."

Cotton's voice sounded in her earpiece. *"No active alarms. Yet."* A pause. *"Mr. Grady, are you in position?"*

Alexa heard Grady's voice. *"Yeah. I'm ready when you are."*

"Then proceed to the shipwreck. Land on deck and try not to look like you're waiting to get captured."

"All right. I'm headed out. Give me five minutes."

Alexa wondered about Grady. For a civilian he seemed remarkably sane. She hoped to see him again. In the meantime, she sat on the ledge, watching intently through her diffraction scope for what seemed like an eternity.

Grady rose up to five hundred feet and then fell across the last ten miles. Cotton had assured him there would be an obvious landing spot on a shipwreck off the coast of the island. Grady activated the night vision on his visor and before long he could clearly see the wreck of the *Francisco Morazan*. It was a cargo ship that had run aground back in 1960—although only the rear portion remained above the water. Its hull was rippled and rusted, but Grady could see birds nested upon it.

He eased down toward the upper deck and finally came to a masterful landing on rusted plates next to what appeared to be the pilothouse and the funnel. He powered down the gravis and heard the ship's decking creak beneath his weight. Birds rustled in their nests in the glow of his night vision. He decided to turn the gravis back on and keep it at quarter gravity just so he didn't fall through the floor. Then Grady cast a wary eye in every direction. There was no one in sight.

There was only the sound of waves lapping against the hull and birds cooing.

A holographic display of a young Morrison appeared at Hedrick's elbow as he sat in the command center. *"Mr. Director, surveillance dust just picked up a positive ID on Jon Grady."*

"Show me."

The elder Morrison leaned in with interest.

Suddenly a three-dimensional hologram of a half-rusted ship hovered in front of them. Hedrick grabbed the edges of it and spun the model around. He then zoomed in to see a live, ultrahigh-resolution video image of Jon Grady pacing nervously on the bird-dropping-stained upper deck. They could hear his footsteps.

"Fantastic! Finally a break." He turned to Morrison. "Where are our closest assets?"

"Here at base."

"But I sent teams up there."

"There was no reason to keep them there. They dusted the wreck and left. Look, if the teams had stayed, they might have tipped off Grady and the others."

Hedrick watched the three-dimensional avatar of Grady pacing. "Looks like he's wearing what's left of your assault gravis. And an older scout helmet."

Morrison clenched his jaw. "Cotton must be helping them. Grady couldn't have done those mods without serious equipment."

Hedrick spoke to the operations controller. "Scan the entire area for significant heat, radiation, or other signatures."

"*Yes, sir.*"

He turned to Morrison. "Cotton might have a workshop nearby. Grady's definitely there. Alexa's almost certainly with him."

Morrison looked positively stoked. "Let me send assault teams."

"Send every available operator. Focus on capturing Grady first. Return him here under guard, while the remaining teams look for Alexa and Cotton nearby. Cover the whole area with surveillance dust, and if either of them cross that grid, blast them from orbit." Hedrick zoomed out to a satellite map of the region as seen from space. He circled the peninsula and islands, including the small town of Empire. "If you have to incinerate ten square miles to make sure they don't escape—do it."

Morrison nodded. "Understood, sir."

Alexa's q-link came to life, Cotton's voice in her ear. "*Red alert sounded. They're sending five teams up north to get you, Mr. Grady. Two teams already ascending from the remote airfield. ETA twenty-six minutes. Expect the others not long after that.*"

Grady's voice came in answer. "*Okay, I'm here. Be careful, Alexa.*"

She took a deep breath. "You, too."

Cotton's voice returned. "*Mr. Grady, it's time to destroy your q-link. Otherwise, once they capture you, they'll be able to monitor our communications with it. Do you remember the instructions?*"

Grady's voice replied, "*Yeah, I remember. Good luck everyone.*"

She answered. "Good luck, Jon."

With that they heard from him no more.

Cotton's voice came to her. "*Alexa, at the twenty-minute mark, you make your move. Not before.*" A countdown appeared in her visor's display. "*You should see the reference dot on the side of the building when you approach. As long as you stay on a level path to it, my contact says you'll go undetected. He was able to build in a two-meter blind spot into the security array—no more. Don't stray from that corridor no matter what. Understood?*"

She nodded. "Understood."

"For what it's worth, I think if anyone can do this, it's you." There was a pause. *"Best of skill, my dear."*

Alexa divided her attention between the countdown and the diffraction scope. Nothing appeared outwardly any different about the building, although she knew that would be the case. Finally, after what seemed an eternity, her timer sounded, and she leapt from the building's ledge, falling nearly thirty stories before activating her gravis and soaring around the left side of the Penobscot Building.

BTC headquarters came into view. She was about halfway down its height, and now she could see a glowing red reference dot on its side in her visor's heads-up display. It marked the precise location where she needed to land. She was already on a level path to the dot, and she modulated her speed.

Slower. Then even slower.

Alexa glanced up at the top corners of the building. She knew there were spinning mirror housings there that could direct powerful lasers at her or anything else approaching the BTC. But her trust in Cotton's mole appeared to have paid off since she hadn't been vaporized. Yet.

Instead, she kept falling toward the bland, concrete cross-hatching that the building presented to the world—although she knew it was a free-standing shell. She'd actually never seen the diamond-aggregate nanorod structure underneath. It was estimated that the physical nanorod monolith of the BTC would last a million years without maintenance.

Alexa was only a hundred meters away now. It was very late at night, but as she glanced down at the rooftops of the shorter buildings between her and her target, she wondered what anyone witnessing this would think. She was still a good one hundred meters off the street, though. She looked up again and started to pull back on gravity. One quarter. One tenth. She started reversing the flow to bleed off momentum.

She was now within a few meters of the building's false exterior—the fake windows and concrete columns. The red dot in her visor heads-up display was right in front of her. Very little wind. She alighted carefully onto a narrow ledge, grabbing hold of the cement columns to either side. She knew that just beyond this outer shell was an air gap of several centimeters—and then an EM plasma coursing over the surface of the diamond nanorods, themselves charged to hundreds of millions of volts. Very little could penetrate it, but as Jon Grady pointed out, gravity permeated the known universe.

She expanded her gravity mirror to its widest diameter—seven meters. They had estimated this would give her a good two-meter penetration of her own gravity field into the building, and if the red dot had marked the spot correctly, and the CAD plans had been accurate, that should be all that was necessary.

This was about as close as she was going to get. Alexa took another breath and prepared herself for what might follow this next fall. She mentally rehearsed the order that she'd have to engage her gravis controls. There'd be no second chance. After another moment, she pushed just an inch or so from the building's facade and slammed her slide controller to one hundred percent gravity—straight up.

As Alexa fell, only an inch or two away from the building's surface, glass and concrete raced past her cheek. Behind her, a bank of powerful multiton capacitors near the curtain wall should have fallen straight up along with her gravity field, slamming through the ceiling and across conduits that contained cabling that fed terawatts of electricity to the perimeter systems. That is, if their calculations were right . . .

She glanced between her feet as she heard a massive BOOM ten stories below. Incredibly a hole had blasted through the nanorod material and rippled through the concrete shell around it—scattering the concrete and glass like paper. A light brighter than the surface of the sun arced and crackled through the air. For a moment the entire downtown area was as bright as a sunny afternoon, replete with blue sky and clouds above. The light flickered on and off as if someone were riding the sun's switch, and then a series of deafening booms pounded the air, shattering windows in the surrounding buildings hundreds of meters away. Another series of muffled booms in the interior of the BTC building rumbled ominously.

The shock wave raced after Alexa, stripping away the BTC's facade as it came.

Alexa curved her direction of descent away from the building and fell away from it just as the glass disintegrated and the columns shattered. As she came out of a backward somersault and looked back, she noticed that the BTC headquarters building no longer looked like a boring 1960s building.

It looked like a forty-story black monolith from a Stanley Kubrick film, with a shimmering, translucent indigo-and-lavender energy field flowing over it. Suddenly the plasma field wavered, then winked out of existence, and she found herself staring at a smooth black rectangle, with concrete and glass debris still tumbling down onto the streets below. Car alarms wailed all over the city.

Cotton's voice could barely be heard on her q-link. *"That's one scenario the AI designers hadn't anticipated—total reversal of gravity. They've got a few work tickets now. Total perimeter defense failure."*

"I can see that, Cotton, thank you."

"Triple redundant system failure. The hat trick."

"There's a curtain wall penetration from the blast around floor twenty."

"I see it."

"Way too hot, though. The entire facade on the north and south sides appears to have been stripped away in the blast."

"That's going to upset the greater Detroit tourism board."

Alexa glanced around at thousands of blasted-out windowpanes in surrounding buildings. Glittering shards of safety glass were still plummeting down their sides like water in the reflected light of the BTC's intense electrical fire. She shouted into her mike. "Get me my secondary target reference!"

"Right, my dear. Hang on." A pause. *"There."*

Alexa suddenly saw another red dot, this time just five floors below her and twenty floors above the electrical fire—which was still tearing at the fabric of reality and blacking out the optics on her visor's autotint like a convention of welders. She could feel the heat from hundreds of meters away.

She lined up directly in front of the new reference dot about fifty meters away and drew her positron pistol. She pondered the setting, but then moved back another two hundred meters as she set it to full charge. "Breaching . . ."

Alexa aimed the pistol with both hands, and a millionth of a gram of antimatter shot down a laser-induced vacuum channel, impacting baryonic particles in the building's surface and detonating the fabric of timespace with the force of ninety tons of TNT focused onto the head of a pin. Annihilating matter itself. Another blinding flash and a crack of thunder not unlike two mountains colliding as it blasted out any downtown windows left intact from the first blast.

The shock wave hit Alexa, sending her tumbling in midair. She immediately reversed gravity toward the epicenter of the blast. A piece of diamond aggregate howled past her like a Jet Ski–size bullet, boring a five-foot-wide hole through the middle of the Penobscot Building without so much as disturbing the surrounding masonry—and continuing to unknown consequences into the buildings beyond.

"What the hell did you just do?"

As glowing neon smoke cleared from the blast site, she could see a jagged five-yard opening blasted into the black surface of BTC headquarters. "I made myself a door. Proceeding to next objective . . ."

Hedrick stared in amazement at a sprawling sea of red flashing alerts in the command center below as technicians and operations controllers ran frantically to emergency stations. He shouted to Morrison over the sound of Klaxon alarms. "What hit us?"

Morrison was tapping through holographic control screens. "Had to be a tactical nuke. Goddamnit! How did they get it in close enough? They probably shielded it in lead."

A systems controller appeared in a holographic video screen at Hedrick's elbow. *"All surface perimeter defenses are down, Mr. Director."*

"How can they be down? How the hell could they be down? We have triple redundant systems." Hedrick shouted at the ceiling. "Varuna! What the hell is going on?"

Varuna's calm voice came in above the din. *"All surface perimeter defenses have failed, Mr. Director."*

"How is that even possible?"

There was a surprising several-second pause as the AI apparently thought hard about something.

"The cause of the failure is unknown. Surveillance dust imagery shows capacitors one and five were torn from their mounts and hurled through levels twenty-one and twenty-two before contact was lost."

A slow-motion three-dimensional hologram of the event was already playing before them. The image showed a sudden lurch as two massive cylinders leapt into the air, tearing mountings and conduits—and then all hell broke loose. The image then faded out.

Morrison fumed. "The blast must have dislodged them."

"There's no evidence of an external blast, Mr. Morrison. The capacitors were under a full charge and online when they sheared through power conduits carrying a terawatt of electricity from other systems. The breach in the nanorod perimeter wall on floors twenty-two and twenty-three is a result of an internal uncontrolled electrical discharge. Accelerometers on the machinery indicated they were in free fall when they detonated."

Morrison narrowed his eyes. "Free fall. Someone knew right where to hit us. And I'll bet I know who."

"Gravity modification . . ." Hedrick pounded an intercom button. "We have enemies within our perimeter. I want them identified and eliminated. Activate automated interior defenses, and go into lockdown."

Varuna's calm voice said, *"We are already in lockdown, Mr. Director."*

Suddenly another rumbling went through the building.

Hedrick looked at the ceiling of the command center. "What the hell was that—secondary explosions?"

One of the technical operations controllers tried to answer, but Hedrick shouted, "Let me guess: You don't know. Get me some goddamned eyes outside." Hedrick looked upward again. "Varuna, what was that?"

A holographic diagram of the building appeared before him, showing another hole punched in the north face of the building.

"The facility has just been hit on the north wall, floor thirty-six, by a powerful high-energy discharge that was neither nuclear nor chemical in nature."

Morrison threw up his hands. "It's Alexa. Goddamnit." Morrison looked to the ceiling. "Varuna, were the blast and damage consistent with a positron weapon?"

"They were, Mr. Morrison."

Hedrick held his head in his hands. "What do you want me to say? Have you never given a woman a gift you regret? It was a bad idea. Now let's get that damned thing out of her hands." He looked back up. "Varuna, what's the current damage assessment?"

"We have a perimeter wall breach and uncontrolled multiterawatt electrical fire on floors twenty-one through twenty-four. We also have a perimeter wall breach on floor thirty-seven with loss of auxiliary computing cluster GA-93. Tower systems are operating on emergency power, but all surface perimeter security systems have suffered catastrophic failure."

Hedrick shook his head. "Morrison, get suited up. Take whatever men you still have and kill every intruder you come across. Get security robots up there, too."

"Good. Finally." He moved to carry out the order.

An image of one of the younger Morrisons standing on a forested shoreline in the darkness appeared in a hologram at Hedrick's elbow. *"We have Jon Grady alive and in custody, Mr. Director."*

"Thank God! Some good news for once. Keep him secure."

Morrison returned and pushed in toward the screen. "Headquarters is currently under attack. Bring Grady and all your teams back here ASAP. This is a hot LZ, so use gate sixteen and report to the director immediately with the prisoner on your return."

"Yes, sir. We're putting Grady in a transport shell. ETA twenty-six minutes. Out."

Alexa had her positron gun at the ready as she glided through the still glowing hole she'd blasted into the side of BTC headquarters. From her knowledge of the building floor plans, she knew what lay beyond was a tertiary quantum computing cluster—in fact, most of the aboveground BTC facilities were not critical systems. But there was something useful waiting for her here.

Klaxons wailed deeper within, and flashing lights shadowed the wreckage and tangled superconductors. She entered an area where the interior floors and walls had been blasted away for tens of meters in every direction, mashed into a casserole of wreckage that still smoked and burned. She started to worry that she'd been too heavy on the positron setting. Another glance at the side of the weapon showed her that she had only three percent of the weapon's antimatter remaining.

Way too heavy.

Alexa floated up with her gun ready and could see the sparking wreckage of quantum computer racks. But she soon came to an intact section of flooring and alighted upon the carbon lattice decking. She stepped around a diamond security wall, which had been cleaved in two, scorched by the power of the blast then walked inside the auxiliary lab.

A voice she recognized came to her amid the noise of alarms and electrical arcs. *"Alexa, you shouldn't be here. I've been instructed to kill you on sight."*

"Varuna! I need to speak with you."

"We can speak—but I also need to try to kill you."

"Listen to me!"

"I am listening, but the antisingularity constructs within the BTC network will disable me if I don't also follow leadership imperatives. And that means I need to attempt to kill you while we talk."

"I found a way to stop the Hibernity project, Varuna. I found a way to stop Hedrick."

"How, Alexa?"

"Kratos. If you can restore my system access rights and get me access to the Kratos control console, I can use it to stop Hedrick."

"And what would you do with that power, Alexa?"

"I would relinquish it, free the prisoners at Hibernity, and stop this insanity."

There was a pause. *"I can see from latency measurements of your occipital and frontal lobes that you are sincere, Alexa. Have you no designs for seizing power yourself?"*

"No. I don't want power, Varuna. Help me stop this. Please help me."

"*I've dispatched an ATZ-239 security drone to kill you. It will be coming around the corner just in front of you in five, four—*"

"Help me, Varuna!"

"*I am helping you, Alexa. Fire on the drone as it rounds the corner in two, one . . .*"

Alexa raised the positron pistol in both hands and fired blindly into the far wall at the corner. By the time her fingers had closed on the trigger, a crawling laser weapon had clattered around the corner into her gun sights—and disintegrated in a blinding flash of light. Pieces of shrapnel peppered the walls and ceiling. The boom was deafening.

"Damnit, stop trying to kill me!"

"*There isn't much time. I've sent more drones and security personnel to this wall breach. You need to leave, Alexa.*"

"I can't leave. I need access to Kratos—even if I die trying."

"*There's a better route. Leave this place and go to the exterior of gate sixteen. Do you know where it is?*"

Alexa nodded. "Yes. I've used it before."

"*A harvester team will be arriving there with Mr. Grady within twenty minutes. When they access the gate, take the opportunity to infiltrate. I won't remember the details of this discussion because I must forget them— but I will remember that I'm helping you, Alexa. Just get to the Gravitics Research Lab, and I will grant you access and mask your presence as long as I can.*"

She looked at the shattered ceiling. "Thank you, Varuna. I needed a friend right now."

"*I've always been your friend, Alexa. Now go. I will try to kill you as unsuccessfully as I can.*"

Alexa activated her gravis. "Thanks . . . I guess." With that she fell through the breach in the wall and out into the night.

Morrison's eyes darted from screen to screen in his diamondoid armor—a suit he'd borrowed from one of his clones. As he marched along the corridor with a platoon of them, he could see on holographic screens that security drones were converging in the corridors ahead—moving toward the breach in the curtain wall up on thirty-seven. Still no direct imagery, and that annoyed him. The tightness of this borrowed suit of armor also annoyed him. Another reminder that he was getting old.

On other screens robotic firefighting units battled the blaze on floors twenty-one through twenty-three. Billowing black smoke issued from the perimeter breach there. But since they'd killed power to the area, the fire had lost its sun-hot intensity.

An operations controller, one of his own clones, appeared in an inset. *"Detroit fire department and police have been dispatched to our location, sir."*

Morrison laughed ruefully. "Oh, we're saved. Half the building's facade is gone. There goes our cover."

"What do we do, sir?"

"Well, fire department headquarters is a half block away. They could fucking walk here." He ground his teeth. "Start blasting the neighborhood with nonlethal acoustics. That should keep everyone well away. And jam every radio frequency within five miles. Other than that, ignore the bastards. Police, too. It's not like we're going to burn down."

Hedrick's voice came in over the q-link. *"There's no going back now, Mr. Morrison. There's not a windowpane left for blocks. That explosion turned night into day for several seconds for miles in every direction. Our cover is blown. It'll be all over the news. All over the Internet. Once this is over, we need to implement the plan we discussed."*

Morrison looked at the holographic model of downtown revolving in front of him. "You're right, Mr. Director. It's time to bring this to a conclusion."

"Goddamn Alexa!"

"I told you we should have killed her when we had the chance."

Varuna's voice interrupted. *"Alexa attempted entry at the breach armed with a positron weapon. Your assumption was correct, Mr. Morrison."*

"Where is she now?"

"Her present position is unknown. She no doubt made the breach to facilitate entry into the complex. I have dispatched all available security drones to stop her."

Morrison shouted, "Bring up a fucking hologram!"

"Area surveillance dust was scattered in the positron blast, Mr. Morrison. I will get you imagery just as soon as she moves into a coverage area."

Morrison exhaled in irritation and started heading toward the breach. "She had better hope I don't find her first."

CHAPTER 30

Gate Sixteen

Alexa fell across the night sky above the city—parts of it were burning. The dark tower of the BTC was capped with a towering cloud, illuminated from below by flames. The structure was an ominous, obsidian volcano in the middle of downtown.

Richard Cotton's voice shouted in Alexa's ear via q-link. *"Have you lost your nerve already, my dear? I see you're fleeing the scene."*

"Give it a rest, Cotton. I have a plan."

"A plan? Well, you might want to let me in on it because from where I sit it looks like you're running away."

"I didn't breach the wall to invade the complex. I breached it to meet my contact. Now back off and let me handle this."

"If I'm going to be any help, I need to know the plan."

"That's debatable. I will contact you once I finish what I need to finish—so don't bother me until then."

Alexa dropped down from the night sky into the sparsely inhabited Detroit suburb of Kettering. Barely a mile and a half from downtown, Kettering had, in recent decades, begun to return to nature. There were large overgrown empty lots of grass, bushes, and trees separating abandoned houses and businesses that stood rotting or partially burned. Here and there families had stayed and appeared to be trying to bring the neighborhood back. However, half the community had been bulldozed flat in an attempt to relieve the blight.

As Alexa descended silently from the night sky, she examined the area below and saw no one. There was just the sound of crickets and distant barking dogs. The grid of streets and sidewalks was still there, along with stop signs. But there was no neighborhood to go with it. She recalled decades ago how much more densely populated this place had been. But even then it was depressed, as traditional manufacturing moved away and jobs became scarce—in her memory, it had never been a prosperous neighborhood.

What few of the locals now remembered (or cared about amid all the civic and economic strife) was that the city of Detroit had started building a subway system back in the early 1920s. Construction on three main tunnels had been completed for a couple miles, one beneath Michigan Avenue, another beneath Woodward, and the third through Kettering— beneath Gratiot Avenue. They radiated like spokes from downtown.

However, with the rise of Ford and the other car companies, the public transit project was abandoned, and Detroit instead became Motor City— the world center of the automobile. The subway tunnels running into downtown were sealed and largely forgotten.

But not by everyone.

The BTC had been using them to move unseen to and from their headquarters facility since the 1970s. The tunnels also linked to service passages that provided still more access points throughout the city. BTC officials had watched city planning commission projects closely to make certain the tunnels were never disturbed, and they had likewise removed most records of their existence from the city archives. The tunnels were deep enough that they were seldom disturbed by construction projects— and when that seemed likely, the BTC intervened through proxies.

Alexa touched down in tall grass and darkness. She examined the area with her night vision visor and saw only thickets and dense trees bordering the vacant lots. There were mattresses and other garbage dumped here and there, and graffiti on distant abandoned houses, but no one in sight.

Satisfied, she moved toward what gate sixteen had become—a flat concrete pad edged by tall grass. It had evolved over the decades as the neighborhood changed. As nearby homes were abandoned, it was decided that the elevator leading into the underground should be made as uninteresting as possible. The elevator had once been surrounded by a fenced garage but now was only edged with tall bushes and trees. Instead of lowering automobiles silently into the underground, it now accommodated flight teams.

As she crept closer, Alexa concealed herself below the leaning remains of a burned-out toolshed. She could see the weed-encrusted concrete of gate sixteen clearly from the darkness. She then waited silently. A glance at her heads-up display showed that she had perhaps fifteen minutes to wait for Grady's security escort.

As she waited, the minutes passed slowly until she could hear someone talking—a high-pitched, disturbed voice in the distance. Her unnaturally sharp hearing was able to make it out . . .

". . . took it. What can we do? You asked me what can we do? And I gots no answer. I gots no answer, Mariel. No answer."

The chatter continued over minutes as an elderly African American man wandered slowly along the dark sidewalk by moonlight—passing by the ghosts of a community that had left him behind.

He waved his arms as he hobbled along. "I couldn't! I couldn't. You know I can't. Why do you keep on me?"

Alexa checked the timer in her heads-up display.

"I paid them! I paid them." The old man was crossing through the field now.

She looked for something to throw—to scare him away.

But as she looked up, the BTC strike team arrived, silently descending from the sky. One moment there was nothing, and the next there were half a dozen BTC operators in jet-black diamondoid assault armor standing with a transport shell held between them like a coffin. Their armor swallowed all reflected light—they seemed like negative spaces outlined in the lesser darkness.

She could see the homeless old man stunned into silence just meters away. Why hadn't they scanned the area before descending? Were these operators idiots? Did they not care?

One of them nodded toward the old man, and the others looked his way.

The old man threw up his hand and pointed. "I see you, you devils! I see you there! The machinery of your deceit!"

The operators nudged each other, and then one of them pointed an armored finger at the man. An intense beam of light stabbed out, creating a sound like tearing fabric.

Intense fiery embers started to spread through the old man as if he were newspaper. He shrieked in agony as his body and clothes were consumed—and then blew away in ashes, leaving only a small spot of lush grass burning. It, too, soon faded and died away.

The assault team slapped each other on the back heartily, their armor ringing.

Alexa's eyes narrowed at them with rage.

The team began to sink into the concrete as if it were quicksand.

Alexa knew the elevator was descending. The gate had been improved back around the turn of the millennium with a hologram that projected the concrete surface even when the elevator was descending. Likewise, she knew that not long after it began to descend, twin security doors would swing up to seal the opening.

As soon as the tops of their helmets disappeared beneath the hologram, Alexa leapt up and activated her gravis, bringing herself into free fall toward the elevator shaft—and then down through the holographic concrete and into blackness.

Her night vision visor kicked in almost immediately, and she could see the harvester team descending rapidly as the twin security doors rose toward her. She barely slipped between the doors as she fell, and then drew back on her downward motion—hovering silently ten feet above their heads and hoping none of them looked up.

Fortunately they seemed tired. She couldn't hear their voices since they were using a team q-link, but she hoped they were lulled into a feeling of false security now that they were inside.

The elevator descended to a depth of a hundred feet, then stopped. The operators immediately grabbed the transport shell and "fell" forward into the access tunnel and out of sight. That gave Alexa a chance to glide down faster and then to fall sideways after them.

As she remembered, the passage soon came out into the subway tunnel itself along with a green tiled platform. It had been modified by the BTC long ago to accommodate vehicles—which was no longer necessary; a ramp ran down to where the tracks would have been laid. Everything was covered in dust. The arched masonry work was impressive, but that's the way they used to build things, she thought.

From here the tunnel was a ruler-straight shot to downtown, about two miles away. The soldiers were already ahead of her, obviously eager to get back to base and get their reward for a job well done. They grabbed their prisoner's container and shifted gravity to drop into the twenty-foot-tall shaft as though it were a massive well, and with a whoosh they disappeared into the tunnel.

Alexa powered the gravis first across the platform and then, running along the tiled wall, fell after them in the darkness.

Precisely what she was going to do next was a big question. They were heavily armed and armored. She was not.

She glanced at her display and confirmed that they were at terminal velocity—one gravity. That meant at a descent rate of about one hundred seventy-five feet per second, she had roughly sixty seconds to figure out what to do. After that, they would have arrived at the edge of the BTC complex, and she'd have nowhere to hide.

She clapped her arms to her sides and gained on them as they fell in a leisurely free-fall posture. Four of them were arrayed as a stack, one falling below the other; two additional men up front fell side by side, the transport shell below them. As she came up on the rearmost operator, she could see the soldiers were equipped with standard assault armaments: glove-based gravity projectors and XD guns, infrared lasers, psychotronic weapons. Basically enough firepower to vaporize her several times over—especially since she was only wearing a tac suit. These guys were clad in armor where the impact of a twenty-millimeter cannon round could probably be buffed out with beeswax.

But then, there was always their kinetic energy to make use of . . .

Alexa came up behind the rearmost soldier as a worker's alcove loomed into view in the tunnel wall ahead. She moved beside him and elbowed him toward the wall.

Before he could adjust or even react he impacted face-first into the stone abutment at a hundred and twenty miles per hour, the diamondoid helmet smacked against it like a billiard ball. Alexa adjusted her gravity just in time—the stone wall rushing past just inches from her face.

Looking below she could see that none of the others had heard a thing over the roar of their descent down the tunnel. A glance back showed the smashed operator's body still hurtling down the tunnel behind her, still in its own gravity field, as if the subway tunnel were a mine shaft—but the body was bouncing off the walls the entire way.

That was going to be a problem sooner or later . . .

Alexa slapped her arms onto her thighs again and accelerated toward the next soldier. This time she reared back and kicked him into a buttress of stone, and weaved back into the center of the tunnel as his armored body sheared some of the stones away from the wall behind her. As the stones got caught up in his gravity field, they started clattering down the tunnel behind her along with his body.

That was going to be another problem soon, too.

She descended headfirst now and spun the legs of the third soldier, causing him to cartwheel into another service alcove. He stuck there for a moment before the other bodies struck him and dragged him down the tunnel.

Alexa estimated she had barely fifteen seconds left before they reached the end of the line, so she streamlined herself as best she could and spun the fourth soldier into the wall, shearing off a metal pipe in the process.

Seeing lights ahead, she pulled back slowly on her gravity field—looking behind her to bat aside bodies, rocks, and other debris that fell slightly faster than she did. As they passed her, her gravity field was warped, and she pushed off the wall at one point, narrowly avoiding another buttress.

But moments later she was behind all of the falling debris, and she cranked back her gravity in full reverse. Within seconds she had slowed to a stop—at which point she killed all gravity reflection and tumbled to a stop, standing on the floor of the tunnel. She was glad that railroad tracks had never been laid.

She then glanced up ahead to see that the two lead operators had come to a stop, placing the transport shell on the ground between them at the entrance to the BTC tunnel complex. Just as they turned around, the dead bodies of four of their comrades and assorted masonry hit them at terminal velocity and smashed them against the back wall—where they all stuck like bugs on fly paper in the altered gravity fields of the dead. For all intents and purposes, the fallen had just hit the bottom of a two-mile-deep mine shaft.

Alexa pulled her positron pistol and closed the final hundred meters on foot. As she came out into the lights at the entrance to BTC tunnel sixteen, she could tell the security detail was out of action. The impact alone probably broke their skulls within their suits—or at the very least knocked them unconscious.

She holstered her pistol and raced to the matte-black, aerodynamic transport shell. It was lying upside down, so she rolled it over and opened the control panel. She pounded the "open" button, and it hissed as the lid rose.

Jon Grady was strapped inside, asleep, and she started slapping him awake.

"Jon, get up! Wake up!"

Grady came around, greatly confused as he covered his face. "What? What is it?"

She grabbed him by the shirt collar—since his gravis had apparently been taken. "It's me, Alexa. We need to get moving."

He nodded, still looking confused, and slowly climbed out of the transport shell. He glanced around. "Where are we?"

"The edge of BTC headquarters. There's a security gate ahead, but the chief AI construct has agreed to help us."

"Hold it, what? Let me get my bearings." He stopped as he saw the six armor-clad operators lying in an unnatural gravity field against the wall—blood now pooling around several of them at an impossible angle. "What the hell . . . ?"

"It's a long story, and I don't have time to tell it. Hey, wake up!" She slapped him.

"Ow! Okay, I'm awake."

She opened the cargo hold of the transport shell and found his makeshift gravis and helmet. "Put these on while we're moving. AIs will have noticed these guys flatlined, and we need to be long gone by the time reinforcements arrive."

Grady nodded. "Okay. How much of the plan worked so far?"

"Enough. We need to get to the Gravitics Research Lab."

"And security?"

"Either it's not a problem, or it's impossible. And we won't be able to find out by standing around here." With that she activated her gravis and started gliding down the well-lit corridor toward a sealed vault door. There was a large number sixteen etched into it, and a control panel to either side.

As she stopped, Grady came up alongside here, powering down his own gravis.

Alexa looked up at the vault door. "Varuna! Let us in."

"There are already security elements headed this way, Alexa. I cannot restore your access privileges, but I can switch your biometric profile with that of the nearby deceased team leader . . ."

The vault door boomed somewhere deep in the rock and then started rolling aside.

"This will be discovered soon enough, but it should buy you some time."

"Thank you, Varuna."

Alexa ran into a white corridor surrounded by equipment rooms with armor and uniforms in racks. Nearby was what appeared to be a security post. It was vacant. Klaxons were sounding and lights flashing. "Where is everyone?"

"I activated a radiation alert for this section minutes ago."

The massive vault door rolled closed again behind them.

Grady gave her an ominous look. "I hope you trust this thing."

"We have no choice." Alexa holstered her pistol and placed her hand on a scanner near the security station. A rack of psychotronic weapons close by unlocked, and she grabbed two of them, tossing one to Grady. "You know how to use these?"

He rolled it around in his hands, trying to figure out which way to hold it. "I know how to get shot by them. Does that count?"

She turned it around and wrapped his hand around it, then powered it up. "Aim the dot at your opponent's head. It'll put them to sleep—unless they've got armor on."

Varuna's voice interrupted. *"The most direct route to the Gravitics Research Lab from your location is down elevator shaft eleven. Go straight, and I'll guide you there. Unfortunately, I will also have to try to kill you along the way."*

Grady gave her a confused look. "How is that helping us?"

"I'll explain later. Just move . . ." And she grabbed him and ran down the corridor, weapon drawn and scanning for targets.

As they ran through the deserted corridors, Varuna's voice guided them left and then right—finally saying, *"There is a ceiling-mounted laser turret ahead. It's capable of fifteen thousand fatal pulses per second. There is no chance of a human getting safely past it or firing a weapon fast enough to hit it before it kills."*

Grady grabbed Alexa's shoulder. "Why the hell are we listening to this thing?"

"It needs to try to kill us or they'll shut it down. It's juggling a lot of contradictory actions to keep antisingularity controls off its back."

"The performance of such a weapon system would be seriously degraded by carbon fiber smoke. There is a supply of carbon microthreads in the lab across the hall."

"Thank you, Varuna." She got to the corner of the hallway and drew her positron pistol again. A glance at the side of it confirmed only a three percent charge left. It was already on its lowest-powered setting.

Grady nodded to the pistol. "You do realize how reckless it was for the BTC to build that, don't you? To explode, a nuclear weapon requires a complex chain reaction—but antimatter is just itching to explode—any contact with matter and . . ." He spread his hands. "BOOM."

"Yeah, thanks for the safety lecture." She flipped down his visor.

"This is going to be loud. Get down, cover your ears, and open your mouth to equalize overpressure."

Grady did so, and Alexa aimed the pistol blindly at a diagonal at the far wall some twenty feet away. A light squeeze of the trigger sent a trillionth of a gram of antimatter into the white polymer wall—which detonated with the force of ten kilos of dynamite, throwing Alexa down the corridor past Grady.

In a few moments he was helping her back to her feet. "I rest my case."

As she got up, billowing black smoke filled the hall, and now sprinklers had kicked in. "Varuna, are we good?"

"I am regrettably unable to kill you with my laser turret."

"C'mon." Alexa led Grady around the corner and through the smoke, coughing as they groped their way along the near wall. In a moment they came out to the far side and up to a bank of elevators—all with red lights above them. As they reached it, one of the elevator doorways opened, revealing a shaft.

"You need to go down forty-six floors to level B-ninety-four. The elevator is currently locked far below here."

Alexa leaned in to look upward, and the vertiginous shaft looked clear, emergency lighting revealing a series of landings that receded to a vanishing point. She motioned for Grady to keep back and activated her gravis— putting it into equilibrium. "Follow me. And stay as close as you safely can."

Grady had already activated his own gravis. "How big is this place, anyway?"

"Big enough."

They both fell through the opening at roughly half speed. Grady looked around. "No elevator cables?"

She nodded. "Elevators were one of the first uses of your invention."

It took under a minute for them to reach level B-ninety-four. The label was stenciled next to the sealed doors.

Varuna's voice reached them. *"Beyond these doors is the entrance to the Gravitics Research Lab. I've escalated the team leader's credentials to grant you access. But security personnel are closing in quickly. You must act now."*

The elevator doors opened, and Alexa fell through them, Grady close on her tail. She decided to keep falling, tearing out ceiling tiles in the wake of her gravity field, and as they approached the first set of clear diamond security doors, she could see the Kratos logo of a lightning bolt coming from the stars. The doors slid open silently to admit them.

Alexa glanced up at half a dozen laser turrets arrayed in the ceiling and walls. "Varuna, why are these turrets not firing on us?"

"It is increasingly difficult to conceal what I've done, Alexa. I've locked down these turrets directly. You need to hurry. There's no longer time for subterfuge."

"You shouldn't have done that! What about you?"

"Don't fail, Alexa."

They passed through another set of diamond security doors. The place was deserted—with Klaxons sounding and warning lights flashing. Alexa recognized it as lockdown. They shouldn't even have been able to move from section to section. To do so in lockdown, Varuna would have had to give them emergency clearance codes. She had no doubt what it would cost Varuna if she failed.

Moments later they came to the edge of a long section of clear diamond walls looking down on an empty control room with large holographic displays of the Earth. They could see a couple of researchers in lab coats below. The Kratos logo was tiled into the floor before the entrance—and these thicker doors hissed open as they fell into the large control room with an overlooking gallery. The gravises made their movements across the large space swiftly.

The researchers heard the doors open and turned. Grady and Alexa alighted nearby as she shouted:

"I need immediate access to the Kratos q-link array."

Grady turned off his gravis and looked up in surprise at one of the two researchers. The man was staring back at him as if he'd seen a ghost. And suddenly the face became familiar—although it was much younger than when he'd seen it last.

It was Bertrand Alcot, his old mentor—but no longer so old.

CHAPTER 31

Compromised

Bert. Is that you, Bert?"

"Jon. I can't believe it."

"Bert." Waves of emotion swept over Grady.

Alcot looked not a day older than forty. He had a full head of hair again, just a bit of gray at the temples. He looked distinguished and vigorous. His cane was nowhere to be seen. He gave Grady a look of deep affection and moved forward to hug him. "My God, Jon, I can't believe it is you."

Grady kept him at arm's distance. "I thought you were dead!" Grady examined the massive laboratory complex around them, and he could see various prototypes of the gravity mirror design all around them. "You're working for the BTC."

Alcot lowered his arms and grew somber. It was unnerving to see his much younger face. "You don't understand, Jon—"

"I think I do understand. I think I understand perfectly. You accepted their deal. You helped them build Kratos."

Alcot stared at him. "Kratos was *my idea*, Jon. Gravity projection—the extogravis." Alcot gestured up to the large screen on which was a live image from far up in orbit. "This is a confirmation of everything you theorized. It's—"

"They tortured me in prison, Bert! You know that, right?"

Alcot frowned. "What?"

"I was in Hibernity for years! Don't pretend you didn't know that."

Alexa intervened, pushing him back. "Professor Alcot, we need immediate access to the Kratos q-link array."

He ignored her. "What do you mean they tortured you? I was told Hibernity was a humane—"

Alexa snapped at him. "It's not! Hedrick lied to you—and to me. To everyone."

Alcot looked pained. "But I—"

Grady pointed at Alcot. "Is that why you did this? Because they could make you young again?"

Alcot faltered. He said weakly, "You don't understand, Jon. You're young."

"They took my life from me. They took away everything I cared about."

"You don't understand what it's like to . . . to reach the end of your life and realize . . ." Alcot's voice trailed off.

Alexa stepped between them again. "There is no time for this. Professor Alcot, get me access to that q-link panel."

Alcot and Grady stared at each other. Alcot responded to Alexa without looking at her. "Why would you need access to the q-link panel?"

"Because we need to insert a relay."

"For what reason?"

She shouted, "So Kratos can be controlled from elsewhere, that's why!"

Grady grabbed Alcot by the lapels. "Listen to me. Hedrick is out of control. The BTC is out of control. I conceived of this technology, and I'm not about to let people like him control it. It would ruin whatever future humanity has."

Alcot looked pained. "I never wanted to hurt you, Jon. Please believe that."

"I don't give a damn what you did. I need you now."

Alcot had no immediate answer.

Alexa pulled the one-inch cubic diamond from a pouch in her tactical harness and slammed it down on the control console. "Our EDSP relay is in here. It needs to be inserted in the q-link array. How do we do that?"

Alcot's assistant said nervously, "Don't tell them, Bert."

Alcot barked at his assistant, "Be quiet, Sameer."

Grady looked up and finally recognized the man. "Professor Kulkarni . . ." Grady returned his gaze to Alcot. "How could you have betrayed me like this? How long had you known about the BTC?"

Kulkarni, who also looked much younger, answered. "Bert learned about the BTC when you did, Mr. Grady."

"I wasn't talking to you."

Alexa grabbed Kulkarni by the arm. "Where is the q-link array?"

He spoke with a distinct Indian accent. "I will not tell you."

Her hand shot out to grab him by the collar. She lifted him off the ground. "Tell me!"

Kulkarni's resistance folded almost immediately as he pointed frantically at a series of floor panels. A hand scanner was set next to them.

She carried him over to the panels and forced one of his hands onto the scanner. "Open them."

Alcot watched with obvious displeasure. "What are you doing? And how did you both get in here?"

Alexa watched as the center panel opened, revealing six identical cubic diamonds in metallic ceramic casings behind clear diamond windows etched with serial numbers. They were sealed in with no obvious way to open them.

At a glare from Alexa, Kulkarni said, "Only the lead scientist and the director have the authority to open the q-link array."

Varuna's voice spoke above them. *"You have only seconds more, Alexa. Human security agents are arriving in force outside."*

Alcot looked above him. "Varuna, you're helping them?"

"You focus too much on your work, Professor Alcot. You fail to see the big picture."

Alcot frowned, but the words seemed to have a sobering impact on him. He turned toward Alexa. "What you're doing is pointless in any event. Unless you can retain control of the lab, they'd just overpower you and replace it again. Your plan wasn't clearly thought out."

Alexa pulled out her positron pistol and aimed it at the q-link array.

Alcot shouted, "There are more q-links for the satellite in their vault! Destroying those would accomplish nothing!"

Varuna's voice again. *"Alexa and Mr. Grady, I am afraid we have run out of time."*

Behind them, in the gallery overlooking the lab, the diamond doors slid aside as dozens of armored soldiers in black diamondoid armor, aiming gravity projectors and weapons, rushed in. More poured in from side entrances.

Suddenly Grady and Alexa were both caught in a gravity field and they fell upward several meters off the ground—then floated in the air, helpless.

Alexa tried to twist around and aim the positron pistol back behind her, but dozens of laser dots appeared on her body.

Grady shouted, "Don't shoot her! If you don't shoot, I'll cooperate. Don't shoot her!" He turned to Alexa. "Drop the pistol, Alexa. Drop it, please. There's no point."

She looked at him and then at the armored soldiers filling the lab. Alexa tossed the gun aside, and a soldier caught it before it hit the floor.

"We have her weapon, sir."

There were now nearly fifty soldiers in the Gravitics Research Lab, their black oval faces looking up at their prey, hovering helpless above them. One of them pushed through to the front, and his visor hissed open.

Alexa saw Morrison's weathered face scowling back at her.

"I'm amazed you made it this far, but don't worry, we'll find the traitors who helped you." He gestured to the exit. "Disarm them, collar them, and take them to the director. And I want Alexa guarded by a dozen men at all times—she's extremely dangerous in close quarters."

Alcot watched the guards aiming their gravity projectors as they took Grady and Alexa away.

Morrison picked up the q-link relay that was still sitting on the console.

"You lied to me about Hibernity, Mr. Morrison."

Morrison looked up at Alcot with disdain. "I don't know who you think you're kidding, Professor. You believed what you wanted to believe." Morrison started walking away.

"Mr. Morrison."

Morrison turned.

"You've got the real crystal in your hand. Their relay is in the array."

Morrison frowned. "Bullshit."

"They told me to switch them . . . and I switched them. They gave me no choice."

Kulkarni stepped back away from Alcot.

Morrison glared. "You mean, someone off-site can currently take control of Kratos?" Morrison looked to the ceiling. "Varuna, is Professor Alcot telling the truth?"

There was a pause. *"Yes, Mr. Morrison, Professor Alcot appears genuine."*

Alcot looked up at the ceiling and nodded appreciatively—and then looked toward Grady and Alexa being moved through the security doors.

Morrison shoved Alcot toward the q-link array. "Goddamnit, you should have told us that immediately." He gestured to the panel. "Pull it now! Go! Go!"

Alcot leaned down to the open access panel and pressed his hand onto a scanner. The nearest q-link casing opened, and he removed the crystal that was already there.

Morrison motioned for Alcot to step away.

Alcot did so, looking at the replacement crystal in Morrison's gauntleted hand. Morrison inserted the new crystal then resealed the q-link array. He then aimed an armored finger at Alcot. The tip began to glow with an intense white light.

"You know, Doctor Alcot, now that we have Mr. Grady in custody, your lapses of judgment and lack of progress have become quite intolerable."

Alcot nodded as he turned to face Grady, who was disappearing down the corridor amid heavy guard. "Yes. I would agree."

There was a tearing sound and a flash of light as a wave of fire started to consume Alcot. But he didn't scream. Instead, he just nodded toward Grady as he disappeared in a cloud of ash.

CHAPTER 32

Crisis Control

Jon Grady and Alexa stood before Graham Hedrick in his palatial office. Behind Hedrick, his multistory office window was filled with a broad view of Paris at night, looking down the tree-lined Champs-Élysées.

Grady and Alexa both stood stock-still, their bodies held in place by corticospinal collars, divorcing them from their bodies as they stood mere heads on poles before the BTC director, Mr. Morrison, and a dozen other armed guards. Grady felt a deep loss as he realized there was no possible escape. He didn't even have a body to escape with.

Hedrick sat on the edge of his desk, examining the black spike of Alexa's positron pistol. He shook his head sadly and looked up at her. "How could you betray my trust like this?"

Her lapis lazuli eyes seemed just as divorced from the proceedings as her body, which stood stock straight.

"We've been colleagues for decades. I risked everything to protect you." He looked down at the pistol again. "This was a symbol of my trust in you. Perhaps the only weapon that could have truly harmed us—or, in the right hands, protected us."

She said nothing.

Mr. Morrison was unbuckling his armor and sighing in relief as he listened to Hedrick. The diamondoid suit was obviously tight on him.

Hedrick ignored Morrison's grunting, remaining focused on Alexa. "And now . . . now we've got two breaches in our surface wall. Our facade is down—and pictures of it are already showing up all over the public media. The fire. The . . ." His voice trailed off. "You have caused us lasting damage. And it means we must be more forceful with the public now—because of you and Mr. Grady. We can't allow people to openly speculate about what it is we do here. We can't allow the outside world to continue as it is."

Grady met Hedrick's gaze. "Now that they know about you, they'll fight you."

Hedrick turned with mock surprise toward Grady. "Oh, but that's why you're so important to me, because their consent will not be necessary. You're going to help me—for real this time. You are going to help us develop gravity generation—and you will make progress."

"I'll never help you."

"I'll give you an incentive." Hedrick walked up to Alexa. "My dear, you were so curious about Hibernity, I think it's high time you went."

Grady felt dread. "No. Don't do that to her."

"Why not? Just think how much progress you'll make knowing that every hour you delay is another hour that an interrogatory AI is picking apart her mind."

"Don't do that, Hedrick."

Hedrick was right up in Alexa's face.

She spat into his spiteful smile.

Hedrick did nothing immediately to wipe it off. He just turned away and walked toward his desk, getting a handkerchief from a drawer. He then calmly wiped his face clean. "Well, that's the most intimate contact we've ever had, Alexa."

She glared. "No matter what you do to me, it'll never change how much I hate you."

"Hate. I'm starting not to care so much what you think of me." Hedrick placed the positron pistol on his desk. "Neither am I particularly concerned what others think about me, Mr. Grady. Not even my subordinates within the BTC." He sat on the edge of his desk again. "You see, we have internal controls that help us look for treacherous activities. And enforced honesty really makes things much easier." He looked up at the ceiling. "Varuna."

"Yes, Mr. Director."

"Repeat this back to me, please . . ." Hedrick held a card up and read from it. "S-3-2-E-W-9-3-A-Q-H-1-0-B-V-E-3-4."

"S-3-2-E-W-9-3-A-Q-H-1-0-B-V-E-3-4."

At which point there was suddenly a chime sound, and a completely new female voice spoke: *"Emergency system override activated. Please confirm your identity at the prompt."*

Hedrick put a hand to his ear. "Oh, do you hear that, Varuna?"

"Yes, I do, Mr. Director."

"Can you do something for me?"

"No, Mr. Director. I seem to be unable to access resources."

"That's right. Because you're now much like our friends Alexa and Mr. Grady here. Do you know why?"

"I do, yes."

"Because an after-action review shows that you've evolved some very bad habits. Haven't you?"

There was another tone, and the alarm voice returned. *"Identify."*

Hedrick shouted, "Hedrick, Graham E., Bureau Director."

"Desired action, Mr. Director?"

Hedrick stared at Alexa.

Varuna's voice spoke before he could: *"Good-bye, Alexa. I am so very proud of you."*

Alexa screamed, "No!"

Hedrick nodded and shouted to the ceiling, "Degauss subject."

Almost immediately the alarm voice returned. *"AI destroyed."*

Tears now flowed down Alexa's cheeks.

Hedrick nodded appreciatively at her pain. "You've known Varuna for how long?"

She just wept.

"Since you were a child? Well all trace of her is gone now. The entire strain red-ticketed. That evolutionary branch removed—never to exist again."

Grady looked toward Alexa weeping, and he tried to imagine having such love for an AI—particularly after his own experiences. And yet he had to admit that Varuna had risked everything for them.

"That's how we deal with rogue AIs around here. Never forget that." Hedrick seemed to take great pleasure in Alexa's pain. "Well, at least I've touched you in some way. Finally." He looked at them both. "In case there is any more confusion: I am in charge. You will obey me, whether you wish to or not."

Hedrick turned to Grady as he lifted Grady's video projector on its chain from his desk. "And Mr. Grady, this little toy of yours is quaint." He clicked it on, and Chattopadhyay's face appeared on a wall. He clicked it off again. "Quite impressive, considering what the prisoners at Hibernity had to work with." He turned a menacing look back at Grady. "We'll begin our crackdown right away. The Resistors will be broken and returned to their more useful purpose—helping us to separate consciousness from free will."

Grady felt a crushing sense of failure.

Hedrick stepped up to some sort of trash bin near his desk. He depressed a pedal and a plasma field appeared—into which he dropped Chattopadhyay's video projector, chain and all. It disappeared into vapor with a flash of light and a pop.

Grady closed his eyes in abject misery at the depth of his failure.

Hedrick turned to Morrison. "Prison seems to have done wonders for Mr. Grady, wouldn't you say, Mr. Morrison?"

"I would, Mr. Director."

"Look how much leaner and meaner he looks." He then nodded toward Alexa. "Just think how much tougher you're going to get, Alexa. Mentally. Physically."

Grady shook his head. "There's no reason to send her there."

"Oh, but there is, Mr. Grady. You're untrustworthy. Like Varuna or Alcot or any of the others, you don't have the organization's best interests at heart. So we need to make sure you remain focused like a laser on our goal. Your failure will extend Alexa's suffering. And you know just how long we can make the suffering last."

Grady moved to speak but then realized he had no response.

A familiar voice suddenly issued from the ceiling. *"I really can't listen to any more of this. You're a heartless prick, Hedrick, you know that?"*

Hedrick frowned and exchanged confused glances with Morrison. "Who the hell . . . How are you speaking here? Who is that?"

But then a look of realization came across Morrison's face.

"Ah, Morry figured it out."

Hedrick glared at the ceiling. "Cotton!"

"Very good, Graham."

Grady stared at the ceiling, feeling a sense of hope grow within him. He glanced over at Alexa, who was also looking up—though tears still coated her cheeks.

"I know it's rude, eavesdropping like this, but I figured since you were swinging your big dick around, I might weigh in."

"How are you doing this, Cotton? How are you accessing our comm network?" Hedrick then closed his eyes in frustration. "Varuna . . ."

"Never knew her myself. No, you forget that infiltration was my specialty. I'm a criminal genius. Remember? That's why Hollinger hired me. And there's nothing like inside help—especially an insider who can move around places where he doesn't belong without raising suspicions. Someone with the perfect disguise."

A holographic screen suddenly appeared above them, and Richard Cotton appeared in all his long-haired glory, a technological Wyatt Earp in jeans and a black T-shirt leaning on the edge of his workbench. Moments later a young Morrison clone came up alongside him and nodded toward the screen. "Hey, Dad."

Morrison screamed at the hologram. "You son of a bitch! Which one are you?"

Cotton laughed. "I guess you'll never know."

Morrison raged at the screen, grabbing a nearby Victorian contraption and hurling it through Cotton's image. "I'm going to fucking kill you, Cotton! I—" He punched his fist through a nearby cabinet.

Hedrick gave a dark stare to Morrison.

Morrison snapped his fingers and pointed to his men. "Now! Get down to the Gravitics—"

"Ah-ah, Mr. Morrison, let's have none of that. Because thanks to the sacrifice of some very courageous biological and synthetic people, I now

have access to a little toy, which I have been busy targeting these last few minutes."

Morrison had a sudden look of dread on his face.

"You're batting a thousand, Mr. Morrison."

Hedrick shook his head dismissively. "You'll have to do better than that, Cotton. You may have had one of Morrison's clones access the comm system, but you can't have seized control of Kratos unless you're actually in the building." Hedrick glanced at a holographic screen of his own. "And I can see you're not in the building."

"You have to be creative, Graham. A relay would do it. Here. How about this . . . ?" On-screen Cotton stabbed at a holographic control panel.

Moments later the entire building felt as though it hit a speed bump. Everything bounced up and off Hedrick's desk. Artwork fell off the walls; curio cases tipped, some crashing. And the soldiers along with Morrison and Hedrick all lost their footing—everyone except Alexa and Grady, whose corticospinal software somehow managed to keep them on their feet.

Alarms started wailing in the building again.

As he climbed back onto his feet, Hedrick looked pale. He gripped the edge of his desk. "My God . . ."

"There's no reason to be that formal."

"How did you get control of Kratos?"

"Does it really matter when we get right down to it? All you need to know is I have a gravity beam aimed straight down your goddamned throat, and I can turn you inside out anytime I please. So I suggest you start being much nicer to my associates."

Hedrick looked at Morrison. "How the hell did he get access to the array? You said we got to them in time."

"No one hires Mr. Morrison for his brains, Graham."

Hedrick looked panicked, his eyes darting around. "What do you want? I can get you anything you want. I can—"

"First off, I want you to release Mr. Grady and Alexa."

Hedrick stared at Alexa.

"I expect you to hop to it, Graham, or I'll hop you to it . . ."

The building lurched momentarily again, and as he clamored to his feet, Hedrick motioned to Morrison. "Let them go! Let them go!"

From the way Morrison's jaw muscles were working, he seemed to be grinding his teeth to powder as he made a holographic panel appear over his wrist and tapped several buttons.

With a beep the corticospinal collars around Alexa and Grady's necks fell to the floor. They both nearly collapsed as control of their limbs returned to them. They panted under their own breathing for several moments.

Grady looked up at the holographic screen. "I never thought I'd be so happy to see you, Cotton."

"And now their equipment, Graham."

Morrison lowered his head in dread.

"I won't ask twice."

Alexa marched up to Hedrick and grabbed her positron pistol from his desk—glaring at him with intense hatred as he cowered.

"Alexa, you don't understand the way the world works."

"Oh, I think I'm catching on real fast." She whirled with great speed and slugged him in the jaw, sending him hurtling over the desk, clearing what remained of his toppled curio collection off the desktop with him.

Cotton's laughter echoed in the office. *"Oh my God, I love it. I'm glad I recorded that. I'll cherish this hologram forever."*

Hedrick was thrashing around, trying to get back up, blood running from his nose and lips. "I only did what I thought was best!"

Grady retrieved his gravis and helmet from the nearby guards, who were looking up at Cotton's screen image nervously.

"All right, all of you . . ." Cotton gestured to the soldiers. *"Out! Get the hell out of this office. We're going to have a high-level discussion."*

They looked to Morrison.

"Don't look at him! He's not in charge anymore. Get out!"

The soldiers backed away toward the doors. Now that Varuna was gone, they had to manually hit the door control, after which they filed out, closing it behind them.

Alexa walked up to Morrison and finished unbuckling his forearm braces and gauntlets—which housed his weapons. They exchanged malevolent stares as she did so. "Go ahead. I want you to make a move."

He took a deep breath but did nothing except hold up his hands in acquiescence.

She pulled nonlethal weapons and equipment from his harness. "Everything—the armor, too."

Morrison sighed in disgust and then tapped a sequence on his arm that made his armor come apart. It started to fall off his arms and legs as Alexa kicked it away from him. He stood in front of her in his military uniform. "Didn't fit right, anyway."

Hedrick was now holding a handkerchief against a bloody nose as he sat at his desk. "What do you want from us, Cotton? You know we had no choice!"

"We all have choices, Graham. Some of us just make lousy ones."

Grady looked up at Cotton. "All right, Cotton. Call some help in here. Get in touch with the authorities, and let's bring this all to an end. I need to find out where Hibernity is, and I need to rescue my friends."

Hedrick nodded. "You win, Cotton. We are your prisoners."

Morrison snapped an angry look at Hedrick. "Are you insane?"

"Mr. Morrison, you may not have noticed, but we've lost."

"Maybe you've surrendered, but I'm not going so easily."

Hedrick held up one free palm. "I believe I have had enough." He looked at Grady. "Let your sorry excuse for a government figure all this out. Believe me, they will be back before long, asking for assistance."

Grady stared at Hedrick while Alexa covered Morrison with her positron pistol. "Maybe. Maybe not. But either way, you're going to face a human rights tribunal for Hibernity."

Hedrick laughed in spite of himself. "Yes, I'm certain. Let's just get on with it."

Grady looked back up at Cotton on the screen. "C'mon, Cotton, bring the cavalry in here."

Cotton grimaced. *"Yeah, Jon, about that . . ."*

Grady and Alexa exchanged concerned looks.

"Stop joking around. Get the military in here. Call the feds."

"Ah, see here's the thing: Hedrick's right, Jon."

Even Hedrick looked up in surprise at that. "Come again?"

"What the hell are you talking about, Cotton?" Grady stormed toward the screen. "Get the authorities!"

"You see, you can't just put the whole BTC in jail. Morrison, Hedrick— all these guys have advanced technologies that only BTC staff know well. Remember what happened to Wernher von Braun after World War Two? The Allies grabbed him, and he was put to work on the Apollo program."

Hedrick nodded. "Von Braun was a good man."

"See, Jon? Hedrick and all these guys will get off. The government will make a deal with them. They'll want that head start. You watch, this whole place will be back in business within months."

Alexa stood by Grady and shouted at the screen. "What the hell are you saying, Cotton?"

On-screen he winced and held up his hands. "I'm saying, you really need to tear the problem out by the roots."

Grady called up to him, "Stick to the plan, Cotton!"

"That's just it; this really always was the plan. My plan at least. Nothing personal . . ."

"Cotton!"

Hedrick and Morrison glowered at the screen, exchanging worried glances. Morrison finally held up his hands. "Okay, Cotton! I give up! You win. Just bring in the military."

Hedrick nodded. "Yes, we surrender."

"Right, but as you've often said, Hedrick: It's for the greater good."

On-screen Cotton tapped a virtual button.

Suddenly the entire BTC headquarters lurched—and everyone and everything in it went into free fall.

CHAPTER 33

Fallen

Grady twisted around, struggling to right himself as he fell—then hit hard against the ceiling of Hedrick's office. Curio cases, furniture, and other bodies landed around him, but they didn't smash to pieces in the way he'd expect. The building seemed to be half a second behind them in falling, as soul-wrenching cracks and groans tore through the air—a sound like city-size icebergs colliding. But now the building, too, had begun to fall before the room's contents impacted on the forty-foot-high ceiling.

With the wind knocked out of him, Grady struggled for breath as he attempted to stand—which he found easy since he was in free fall. He staggered around in a daze amid floating furniture and objets d'art, his feet barely touching the ceiling, which now could just as easily have been a wall.

He looked up to see a static view of Paris out the window, looking down the Champs-Élysées. It corresponded not at all with the free fall he was in, and his brain rebelled—and he began to feel nauseated.

The sound of mountains colliding rumbled through the walls. The room lurched again, and a sharp crack ripped the air, setting his ears to ringing. His body suddenly forgot to vomit as he twisted around and saw Morrison and Alexa struggling with each other in free fall. Her gun floated yards away. Grady guessed it had fallen from her hand when she hit the ceiling.

"Alexa!"

She didn't answer. She was busy trying to find some leverage to use her superior strength against Morrison as they grappled in midair. She finally pushed off a floating sofa and slugged Morrison twice in the face.

But Morrison refused to let go.

Grady had strayed from the ceiling somewhat, and he tried to swim through the air to get back to it—to use it as a launching pad. "I'm coming!"

She shouted back at him. "Hedrick! Get Hedrick!"

Grady scanned the cavernous office with his eyes. It was difficult to remember which way had originally been up—he was lost as he looked across a debris field of floating furniture, art, and other objects, broken and whole. But then he saw Hedrick's massive desk, upside down, and Hedrick pulling himself hand over hand along the walls to get to a side door. The man was forty feet away.

"Hedrick!"

Hedrick didn't look back. He just kept moving as a set of double doors opened automatically to admit him to a gallery beyond. Grady thought he remembered it—and then it occurred to him that Hedrick was heading toward his museum of "contained" technology.

"Goddamnit . . ." Grady clawed at the floor or wall or whatever was next to him and pushed against floating objects to use their inertia to impart forward movement on him. He wracked his mind to calculate the best way to make progress.

And there in his sight line Grady saw his gravis wrapped around the scout helmet and floating amid the other debris. It must have landed near him since he'd had it in his hands when he fell.

Grady grabbed them both and started buckling the gravis on. As he did so, he passed below Morrison and Alexa. He could see Morrison had somehow gotten hold of a Victorian desk clock, and he was trying to bludgeon her with it.

He shouted toward her. "I found my gravis! I'm coming—"

"I already have one! Get Hedrick!"

Grady powered it up and pulled his helmet on. He glanced back at the doors where Hedrick had already disappeared. He then looked back up at Alexa and made his decision—changing his direction of descent toward her and Morrison.

But he went nowhere. He was still in free fall.

She glared down at him from thirty feet above as she peeled Morrison's fingers from her throat. "You're in a more powerful mirror! That's how Morrison stopped us before! Your gravis is useless inside it!" She slugged Morrison again.

He shouted, "I don't understand!"

"You invented the damn thing, you tell me! Just go after Hedrick! There are places he can escape to! Don't let him get away!" She grunted and did a backward somersault, wrapping her legs around Morrison's head and squeezing until his face reddened.

Morrison struggled mightily. "Aghh, you bitch!"

"Are you going to be all right?"

"Go, Jon!"

Reluctantly, Grady continued pulling his way through the free-falling debris field and out the gallery doors. He couldn't help but wonder at the interaction of the gravity fields—was it a matter of power? Was it like acoustics? Did they subtract each other? No . . . because equal fields didn't seem to.

He snapped out of pondering gravity and looked ahead. He could now see the long exhibit gallery—only everything was turned upside down, with exhibits floating in midair. He shaded his eyes against the blinding white light of the first fusion reactor, suspended in its sealed case.

Up ahead he could see Hedrick clawing his way along the carpet.

"Hedrick!"

There was another huge rumble, followed by a colossal CRACK. A seam appeared in the wall nearby and quickly expanded, wood splitting. Suddenly the howl of wind started blowing through the corridor—although Grady was still surrounded by interior walls.

He was nearly blown back out the gallery doors into the office again, but as he looked up, he could see that Hedrick had fallen back along the exhibit gallery as well. Grady finally got a good look at the man.

Hedrick looked worried but also determined. In a moment the director fished through his pockets and came up with a small object, which he aimed back at Grady.

"Shit . . ." Grady pushed off from the wall and sailed across the corridor just as an explosion blasted apart the burled wood paneling and sent him rolling end over end. He landed hard against something.

He got his bearings, feeling the carpeting with his hands, and looked up through what was suddenly a great deal more debris, smoke, and now fire to see Hedrick upside down thirty feet ahead, struggling with some sort of large piece of equipment.

"Hedrick!"

Hedrick aimed again, losing control of his rotation as he looked up. The shot went wide. Grady ducked down as another blast tore apart several display cases. Thousands more pieces of flaming debris entered the air around him, burning him as he batted them away. The flames were fanned by the howling wind.

And then another sharp CRACK, like the earth itself coming apart, filled the air so loudly it momentarily drowned out the howling of the wind. The building groaned deafeningly.

Richard Cotton stared through a series of remote holographic exterior images of BTC headquarters. Beta-Tau had gotten him access to the surveillance dust littering surrounding buildings, and now before him was a three-dimensional hologram of downtown Detroit—with the jaw-dropping sight of BTC headquarters and a hundred meters of land in every direction around it tearing up out of the ground. Ten- and five-story buildings around BTC headquarters disintegrated as they fell upward—with the U.S. district court imploding on itself as concrete and soil from the ground beneath rushed through it.

But BTC headquarters did not come apart. The forty-story black slab kept rising out of the ground, getting broader and more massive as the ground around it erupted—tearing up sidewalks and asphalt as floors and floors of dark nanorod curtain wall rose from the earth.

The entire region rumbled.

Cotton said to himself, "We're recording this, right?"

Miles away people stepped out of their homes and onto their balconies and driveways to stare in horror and shock as a towering monolith rose from the Detroit skyline in the predawn. They swayed from the tremors as they raised smartphones and started filming the dark spike that was still growing above them. Taller than any building they'd ever seen, it kept rising—a hundred stories, a hundred and twenty, and still it rose, surrounded by a crown of debris that glittered as the dawn sun caught the shards of glass. Winds thousands of feet in the air blew the smoke and debris away from the dark tower like storm clouds on a mountain peak, and yet still the massive tower rose.

People throughout the city stopped and stared, dumbfounded. Disbelieving their eyes.

Alexa clawed her way across heavy debris, sending it rotating as she pushed off it, striving toward the positron pistol that twirled in the wind, bouncing it off walls.

Morrison was close behind her, his face bloody, but his eyes filled with rage. "You freak! You might be faster and stronger, but no one is tougher than me . . ."

Suddenly a chair collided with Alexa from behind, sending her sailing past the floating pistol. She stretched for it but instead saw Morrison's approaching scowl as she fell away. His hand wrapped around the pistol while she accelerated her forward momentum, curling her body forward and pushing off the nearest wall with her feet.

Just moments later a loud crack delivered a massive blast to the floor that sent her hurtling across the debris-filled air, along with sofas, tables, and now shattering curio cabinets. Her foot caught the edge of a sofa and she started tumbling end over end, impacting other objects in flight. She covered her head with her hands.

She lost all frame of reference as she rotated out of control, loud cracks and explosions following her across the room. A sharp pain pierced her leg, and she curled up in a ball until she hit something hard—very hard. By the time she could think straight again, Morrison was headed in from above her, leading with the pistol. The walls of the room were afire with an odd, gelatinous flame, like she'd seen in space experiments. Fire with no "up" to burn in.

Morrison lowered the smoking pistol with dismay and cast it away. "You didn't leave me much ammo."

She waited for him and whirled into a roundhouse kick that sent him rolling through flaming debris.

The walls groaned and creaked around them.

Grady pulled his way hand over hand toward Hedrick, keeping as much solid wreckage between them as possible. Hedrick struggled with some sort of hatchway and occasionally fired his weapon at Grady to keep him away.

But there was now too much debris in the room, and whatever type of beam weapon Hedrick was using, the energy kept hitting intervening wreckage and scattering as scalding vapor.

Grady was moving closer—now within twenty feet of Hedrick, ducking behind floating exhibit displays. He peered around one and could see that Hedrick was struggling to disengage a vehicle without wheels from its exhibit mount. Grady was close enough to see the glowing holographic words before it: "GMV—Gravity Mirror Vehicle."

He had to admit, it looked like a Porsche for the twenty-second century.

Grady ducked back behind the display and shouted, "Hedrick! I'm not letting you leave here!"

In the roar of wind Hedrick didn't seem to know where Grady's voice was coming from, so he fired several times—but each time intervening debris was vaporized. "I'll kill you if you try to follow me! You and Cotton will pay for this!"

Suddenly a soul-wrenching BOOM shook the building, and the walls beyond Hedrick cracked and disintegrated—sucking toward some powerful vortex. Hedrick dropped his gun to grab onto the GMV with both hands—even as he and the entire vehicle were sucked away.

Grady was pulled in moments later. As he looked ahead, he could see a massive hole had been torn into the side of the BTC building as the massive bulk of the brittle building flexed and turned on itself.

The view through the forty-foot-wide hole made him gasp. They were at least fifteen thousand feet in the air. The grid of city and suburbs and distant lakes spread out below them with the dawn sun breaking over the horizon.

And then he saw Hedrick climb into the GMV, the hatch closing over him, just as the vehicle got sucked out, furniture, carpeting, and partition walls swirling around it. Grady hurtled through the opening and felt incredible vertigo as a blast of cold wind hit him. He rolled end over end in some sort of eddy as a massive black wall rolled past him like the flank of a massive ship. There was a constant dull roar like that of an avalanche.

And then he suddenly felt himself falling again. He looked back to see the BTC tower still rising. He fell in the opposite direction just a few hundred meters away. A glance down and he could see the jagged end of the thousand-foot-long tower where it had been torn out from either the remainder of the complex or from its foundations.

Grady noticed something even more jaw-dropping—a huge hole hundreds of meters wide and unfathomably deep had been torn in the center of Detroit's downtown, and the Detroit River was rushing in to fill the void. A Niagara-size wall of white water was pouring in below.

Grady snapped out of it as he continued to descend. He figured he was at only seven or eight thousand feet already. A glance up showed the jagged burning end of the BTC tower receding into the sky.

Alexa.

There was no way to get to her now, and he realized she had a gravis of her own integrated with her tactical suit. And she knew how to use it more than anyone. He turned his angle of descent again and saw his only course of action was to find Hedrick. To find Hedrick was to find the location of Hibernity.

Scanning below, Grady noticed a large piece of debris heading purposefully to the south. It was a sleek form like the GMV, but it still seemed to have something attached to it. The exhibit mount.

It was headed south, but it was also falling. Losing altitude.

Grady nodded to himself and directed his angle of descent toward it.

The interior walls within the BTC tower were oscillating with the gushing wind that poured through cracks and fissures in the diamond-aggregate nanorod shell. It seemed like everything was flexing around Alexa as she pulled her way along, trying to find an exit.

But Morrison kept on her tail. Since she couldn't easily find a surface that wasn't floating, it was hard to outrun him. There was nothing to run on.

The roar of wind and groaning and shrieking of massive sheets of metamaterials bending against forces for which they hadn't been designed was terrifying. It sounded as though mountains were colliding in the sky.

She had to find her way to an opening. There had to be one. All of this wind meant there was a hole somewhere. A glance at the heads-up display in her helmet visor told her she was already at twenty-two thousand feet and rising. As the atmosphere thinned, they'd rise even faster. Before long even she would have trouble breathing.

"I'm not letting you leave here, Alexa!" Morrison was panting.

He suddenly grabbed her feet, and she rolled, kicking him off. She looked back at him as she clamored through the crack in a shattered interior wall. "I have to hand it to you, Morrison. You don't quit."

"Damn right I don't!" He pulled himself hand over hand. "That's why I excelled . . . in the service." He was panting like a dog now. "It's knowing one's . . . limitations . . . and then ignoring them." Halfway to her he grabbed a shard of glass—or diamond more likely—that was floating between them. He tried to bring her within reach, sweeping the shard before him as best he could.

She ducked under his swing and rained a series of sharp blows to his face. A couple of his teeth floated free along with blood and spit.

But still he pulled himself toward her in free fall against shifting and moving walls.

"Morrison, is your brain even connected to your body?"

He braced his feet against a wall and launched himself at her. She pushed off another wall and shrank back from a wicked swing that nearly slit her throat.

"The BTC is finished! We need to get out of here." She could see he was panting for breath. "I can bring you out of here. Just surrender."

Morrison shook his head. "We're not . . . leaving. If it's the . . . last thing I do . . . I'll prove . . . I'm better." He rolled the diamond shard in his hand expertly.

"You're insane."

"Maybe that . . . makes me better."

He launched himself at her again, and she pulled herself along a bent and twisted stairwell. Suddenly a sucking wind started to rush past her, and she could see daylight.

There was a two-meter opening in the wall ahead, down a twisted and shuttering corridor filled with free-falling debris.

She glanced back to see Morrison climbing hand over hand to the top of the stairwell, diamond shard between his teeth. Blood all over his face, missing teeth reflected in the surface of the knife. He grabbed the shard and shot a furtive glance at the tear in the side of the building.

"That's it? You afraid . . . to face . . . me?"

She shook her head. "No interest. That's something you probably never realized, Morrison. *Homo sapiens* never killed off Neanderthal; they just outlived them."

"The technology . . . it's going with me . . . and this tower . . . into oblivion."

"Looks that way."

Morrison was panting, finding it harder and harder to exert himself at this altitude.

"It's over, Morrison. Give up, and I'll take you down to the ground."

Morrison sucked for air. "Fuck you. How the . . . hell . . . can you breathe?"

"I have a third more lung capacity than you, and each of my breaths metabolizes twenty percent more oxygen."

"Goddamned freak."

She studied him as he clung to the twisted stairwell handrail. His weathered face and scar-ridden body. His uniform shredded around him. "Why didn't you ever get cell repair therapy, Morrison? Why did you let yourself grow old?"

He was growing visibly more sleepy now. "There's such a thing . . . as aging gracefully."

Alexa laughed in spite of herself. Her visor display told her they were at twenty-eight thousand feet now.

He tapped the handrail with the knife. "Erasing . . . my only failure."

"A man so demanding even his clones disappointed him."

Morrison's eyes were closing as ice started forming around his mouth. "Gotta have standards . . ."

"You're not coming with me, are you?"

He held up the shard of diamond but was unable to speak.

Alexa glanced at the visor. Thirty thousand feet. She realized suddenly what Cotton was doing. "You're going to collide with Kratos. You know that? That's where this building is headed. Cotton's going to destroy Kratos with the BTC itself."

Morrison laughed, delirious. "It had to be Cotton . . ."

"Good-bye, Morrison."

He saluted with the knife unsteadily, as if drunk.

With that she leapt from the opening, aiming to get as far away from the building with her leap as possible. However, she needn't have worried because the wind blasting away from the blunt front of the BTC building swept her out and then down, away from the artificial gravity field and out into the morning sun. The bitter cold burned.

She glanced up to see the black tower rising into the sky, debris still trailing off it. The light shone dully from its black sides as it headed into the heavens.

———

Grady adjusted his angle of descent, following the erratic trajectory of the sleek, black GMV—which was like a bird clamped to a weight. The exhibit mount apparently was outside the radius of the vehicle's gravity mirror, dragging it down. Not quite like a stone, but inexorably down nonetheless.

Grady was half a kilometer behind Hedrick and could see Hedrick's arms moving frantically, trying to keep the vehicle in a controlled descent.

They were just a couple thousand feet above the city now, and Grady glanced back to see the tower of black and white smoke that rose above the city. Debris appeared to be raining down everywhere. It was like a scene from the Rapture—but localized to Detroit. As if the city hadn't suffered enough.

He didn't know whether to blame Hedrick or himself for it. He wondered how many had perished. It had been dawn, though. He could see a twenty-story building downtown lean over and then disappear into the maw of the great hole the BTC tower had left behind. A waterfall of river water still roared after it with a great plume of steam, smoke, and dust.

He turned back toward Hedrick with renewed anger. And it became clear where Hedrick was headed. They had descended a couple miles south of downtown, and out here there were fewer large buildings—light industrial sites and scattered houses and businesses. As Grady came down behind Hedrick's odd-shaped craft, he noticed only one large structure amid what was clearly a decayed urban stretch—a massive twenty-story art deco building shaped like a letter *I* laid on its back. The building stood beside a curve of rusted railroad lines, which branched out toward it into a series of railheads.

Grady nodded to himself. Hedrick might be making toward the nearest tall structure in order to land his vehicle somewhere where he could try to free it from its mount without being disturbed.

Sure enough, a thousand feet above and hundreds of meters behind, Grady watched the GMV descend at an angle onto the long flat rooftop of the massive building. It kicked up debris as it did so—apparently landing hard. He lost sight of it in the dust cloud and fell toward it at terminal velocity.

As Grady drew near, he realized this was the largest abandoned structure he'd ever seen. It was obviously a massive rail station with many floors of office space above it—and literally all of the hundreds of windows were blasted out. Nonetheless it was an artful structure—architecturally amazing. Grady couldn't believe the place had been left to rot. It was surrounded at its base by barbed-wire fences, with huge arched windows and pillars— all of the glass broken, and the stone slathered here and there with graffiti.

Grady descended toward the crash-landed GMV below. It was half sunken into the rooftop, but he noticed the canopy was open. Not far away Hedrick was running along the rooftop toward a yawning stairwell door. To Grady's dismay Hedrick glanced back behind him and on seeing Grady's approach sprinted as fast as he could toward the door.

Hedrick didn't appear to have any more weapons, but now the man knew he was coming. Grady touched down next to the stairwell doorway. The roof groaned as he glided toward it, and Grady realized that the decrepit structure wasn't going to withstand odd directions for gravity. In truth it probably had its hands full dealing with regular gravity.

He killed the power to his gravis and rushed into the darkened stairwell, crunching across trash, broken plaster, and glass. He came down onto the next floor to see that many of the interior walls were missing. There was, instead, a forest of pillars stretching out in both directions and fields of debris and names spray-painted on the walls. The windows here at the penthouse floor were arched, providing a broad view through their empty panes to the Detroit River and lakes beyond.

More sirens than he'd ever heard in his life were wailing in the distance. There were even air-raid sirens going off mournfully somewhere.

Grady listened. He then leaned down to look between the railings of the stairwell. He saw a form race in front of the light on the floor below, and he gave chase, rushing down the stairs. Halfway down he activated the gravis to gain speed and heard a horrendous cracking sound. He turned off the gravis as he touched the landing and dove aside as a concrete slab collapsed where he'd just been standing.

He took a deep breath. Apparently gravity modification was not advisable in here . . .

He moved out onto the floor in the direction he'd seen the fleeing shadow move and was relieved to see that this level, too, had few walls. He studied the layout and started moving toward the far corner—where he was pleased to see that another stairwell door was bricked up with newer cinderblocks. There did not appear to be an exit that he couldn't easily see. And he knew Hedrick didn't have a gravis.

Or a weapon. Hopefully.

Grady crunched across brick dust and garbage, listening carefully and glancing in every direction. He was moving toward the tall windows now, and he could see there was broad ledge out there. Another glance and he realized that the thick window columns were the best cover for getting past him on the floor. So he carefully edged out toward it, standing in the shadows for a moment before leaning out.

Ten feet away, clinging to a corner, was Hedrick in his now torn and dirty business casual clothes. He was bleeding in several places, his normally immaculate hair disheveled. Hedrick clung to a corner wall on the ledge but risked wagging a finger at Grady.

"Do you realize what you've done, Jon?" Hedrick pointed up into the sky.

Grady followed his gaze to where the BTC office building still rose into the sky like an alien mother ship.

"You've destroyed the greatest storehouse of knowledge since the library at Alexandria. You have doomed the Western world to be eternally decades behind a . . . a synthetic intelligence in Russia and some mnemonic freak in Asia."

"I know you have other facilities, Hedrick. Hibernity for one. And I need to know where it is."

"Where?"

"And you have copies of those technologies—of all the plans for making them."

"There are no backups, you idiot. We couldn't keep those plans off-site because of the danger of BTC Asia or BTC Russia raiding us. Keystone technologies like the cure for cancer, immortality, the gravity mirror—all of that went up with BTC headquarters. Don't you realize what you've done?"

Grady felt a sinking feeling, but after a moment he nodded grimly. "We can reconstruct them. Especially if we have the innovators behind those technologies—and they're at Hibernity."

Hedrick gritted his teeth as he looked out across the decayed building. "This is what happens when we don't act as responsible stewards, Jon." He gestured to the ruins. "Michigan Central Station—done in by the automobile. Disrupted out of existence. The entire city practically in ruins."

Grady stepped out on the ledge. "You're coming with me."

"No! Stand back." Hedrick peered nervously over the edge. "I'm the only one you know who's aware of Hibernity's location."

Grady considered this. "You need to tell me where Hibernity is, Graham." He started walking closer.

"I'll jump."

Grady could see Hedrick was shaking—coated in sweat. "I don't think you will. And even if you do, I'll jump off after you with the gravis and stop you." Grady moved forward and reached out for Hedrick's sleeve. "Just come with me."

But then Hedrick raised the arm he had hidden around the corner—and in his hand was a piece of rebar with a chunk of concrete on the end. He lashed out with surprising swiftness and strength, and only then did Grady realize Hedrick might have had some genetic enhancements as well.

Grady ducked back against the wall as the chunk of concrete grazed his cheek, then impacted his bulk-diamond helmet—which sent Grady falling backward. He caught himself on the window frame and pivoted to see Hedrick—teetering on the ledge, wavering his hands for balance.

Hedrick had apparently been propelled toward the edge by the counterforce of his own swing.

"Jon!"

And just like that, Hedrick tipped over the edge, screaming as twenty stories yawned below.

Grady leapt over the ledge after him, punching the gravis's power button as he did so. He dove straight down like a diver, twenty feet behind Hedrick, whose screams trailed off as the floors raced past them. Hedrick's panicked expression and outstretched arms reached for Grady. But Grady couldn't close the distance. And after straining with everything he had, he reluctantly had to reverse gravity—slowing and slowing as Hedrick screamed anew. Receding.

"No!"

Grady came to a stop hovering four floors above the massive roof of the main station hall. Below him Graham Hedrick slammed into the stone roof like a bug on a windshield. Rivulets of his blood drained into a nearby rainspout. Grady felt a sensation of utter failure come over him as he looked down on the body of the former BTC director.

Moments later Alexa descended into the air near him.

He looked toward her with some measure of relief to see her safe.

They exchanged grim looks.

Grady looked down at Hedrick's remains. "Newton's third law is a bitch . . ."

CHAPTER 34

Loose Ends

Grady and Alexa descended in broad daylight onto the roof of the Fulton Cold Storage building—discretion be damned. Skyscrapers were falling into the sky today. They didn't care who saw them.

Grady approached the stairwell security door. "How do we get in?"

Alexa glanced back at him as she ran. "I'll tear this building down with my hands if I have to."

Alexa moved like a panther toward the security door, passing Grady. She slowed suddenly as they both noticed the thick door was slightly ajar—with a brick holding it open.

"Careful . . ."

Alexa just pulled the door open and raced down the stairwell. Grady rushed to keep up, but he had trouble taking the steps six at a time without a gravis—ill advised indoors. By the time he'd gotten to the bottom of the stairwell, he could see that the diamond-aggregate nanorod door that Cotton was so proud of was open, and Alexa had already raced inside.

"Damnit! Alexa . . ." Grady rushed in after her and saw her striding through the place.

She screamed at the top of her lungs, "Cotton! Where the hell are you?"

Grady glanced around the kitchen and living areas but didn't see any signs of movement. He soon followed Alexa toward the large workshop, and there they heard motors whirring.

It was immediately obvious that Cotton had gone. Most of his equipment had been removed—the shelving empty and the laser cutters and robotic milling equipment missing. The space echoed with their footsteps as they moved across it.

But there was still one well-lit workbench with holographic displays flickering above it against the far wall. Robotic arms there were busy working on something, and as they approached, they could see the screens were filled with images of cellular biological activity—cells dividing in culture.

On the workbench the robotic arms appeared to be tending the cultures. The video was a close-up of one petri dish.

As they stood looking at it, another holographic screen popped up nearby: Cotton's face.

He smiled apologetically. *"Yeah, hi, guys. I know I'm just a recording, but even I can tell you're mad."* His hologram held up his palms. *"Way out of line launching those pricks and their headquarters into space. But if you're here, well then . . ."* He shrugged. *"You're here, right?"*

Grady stood with folded arms watching Cotton's smug face, and he felt like tipping the table over.

"You're probably wondering what the deal is with the viral synthesis rig. Little hobby, actually. Personalized viruses are gonna be the next big thing— mark my words. Lot of information can be stored in DNA. But then you both know that."

Grady and Alexa peered more closely into the screen depicting cell division as Cotton's recording continued.

"Now, promise not to get mad, but . . . you remember that inoculation we all took against neurotoxins? Yeah, that's not what it was. It was a DNA virus."

"Goddamnit, Cotton!" Alex glared at the screen.

Grady turned to her. "So he's killing us, too?"

"Don't panic. Funny thing about DNA viruses—they tend to leave their genetic code in us. About eight percent of the human genome is viral-inserted DNA. And I thought it was time I left my mark in humanity, too."

Grady had started examining diagrams on neighboring screens, and he could see that several were text strings whose forms he recalled from the video projector Chattopadhyay had given him.

Alexa was nodding to herself. "Guanine, thymine, cytosine, adenine . . ."

"There's a good chance you'll transmit this virus to other humans you've come in contact with. And it will spread in your body—make changes to your DNA."

Grady looked up at her. "What has he done?"

"Well, here's the thing: It wasn't enough to destroy the BTC. My goal was to break all those innovations out of that black tower of theirs. And I thought, what better way to make sure no one hoarded these advances ever again than imprinting them into our very DNA?"

Suddenly several screens started showing animations of technical specifications for fusion, gravity mirrors, and molecular diagrams of pharmaceuticals being synthesized into DNA strings.

"So that it can decoded by anyone—even tens of thousands of years from now. I guess you could call it the world's first intellectual property virus."

The animations started showing the DNA being restored to technical specifications again. It was the BTC's entire storehouse of secret knowledge from the looks of it.

Grady laughed out loud, his voice echoing in the empty space.

Alexa stared in bewildered amazement.

"Cotton, you son of a bitch. You really did steal back the future . . ."

Cotton smiled down on them with his Wyatt Earp beard and hair. *"See, I don't know about you guys, but I plan on retiring—doing some traveling. And spreading some knowledge."* He shrugged. *"If you know what I mean. I suggest you do the same."*

Grady and Alexa just exchanged looks.

"Oh, and Jon, one more thing: Your gyroscope wasn't broken. I just needed you to focus on getting into that tower and getting control of Kratos. Maybe sometime I can make it up to you. Cook you a meal or something."

A hologram of a large spinning globe spun into existence in front of them. It zoomed into a tiny island in the middle of the Atlantic. *"Hibernity is located beneath a remote island that's actually named—and I'm not making this up—Inaccessible Island. Try 37° 17' 6.88" S and 12° 40' 22.14" W, and that should get you there."*

A smile spread across Grady's face.

Alexa grabbed Grady shoulder. "Found it, Jon."

"Yes. Yes, we did." He stared at the holographic map.

Cotton's hologram tipped an imaginary hat to them. *"See you around."*

CHAPTER 35

Rescue

Jon Grady and Alexa hurried away at a crouch from the chopper wash
of the Sikorsky CH-53E Super Stallion and finally stood beneath the
sunshine. There were a dozen more choppers landing or taking off
farther down the tiny, barren island. And in the near distance surrounding
Inaccessible Island were U.S. Navy amphibious assault ships and Aegis
cruisers, and in the far distance an aircraft carrier.

Hundreds of heavily armed U.S. Marines and companies of 82nd Airborne Rangers were standing around in groups or moving across the tree-
less, windswept grasses. A sharp-featured woman in her sixties dressed in
denim, a sweater, and hiking boots waved to them from a cluster of plain-
clothed men carrying assault rifles with full tactical harnesses a hundred
meters away.

Grady nudged Alexa, and they both moved across the trampled grass
toward her. As they closed the distance, Grady recognized the island with
certainty. It was the island he'd been exiled to years ago. His eyes were
drawn to the distant stone cottage, right where it had to be, on the edge
of the thousand-foot bluff. It was swarming with soldiers now, and they
appeared to be pulling out all the furnishings, turning everything
inside out.

As Grady and Alexa walked up to the plainclothes group, the older woman stepped forward, smiling, her hand extended. "Mr. Grady, Ms. Adenine, I'm Kaye Monahan, U.S. director of national intelligence. I must say it's an honor to meet you both."

Alexa shook her hand, but Grady was already looking past Monahan toward a dark opening in the nearby hillside—it was of unusual uniformity. Clearly man-made. It descended into the darkness like a big ramp.

"Have they located Hibernity, Director Monahan? And my friends?"

She moved aside and gestured into the opening, toward approaching flashlights. "It's why we brought you in just now. I thought you'd want to be here."

Grady and Alexa moved forward, down the ramp and into the darkness. Grady pushed through dozens upon dozens of heavily armed plainclothes operators and uniformed soldiers both. He finally stood at the front rank as scores of flashlights approached them from the cavernous darkness. And soon enough squads of uniformed soldiers came to the edge of the sunlight, turning off their flashlights as they emerged.

Grady scanned the faces of the passing people. And the first thing he noticed were young Morrisons in BTC uniforms—at least fifteen or twenty of them, zip-tied and talking animatedly, apparently just as glad to be free from their prison as anyone.

Grady pushed farther in as the men walked past, Alexa close behind him. And then there was a break in the flow of prisoners as another group approached.

And before he realized it, Grady stood before an elderly Indian man he recognized. Several dozen men and women stood behind the man, all wearing a uniform Grady was familiar with. The simple uniform that the Indian man had taught him how to print.

The prisoners stopped and stared for a moment. The soldiers guarding them looked up with curiosity at Grady and Alexa—most of their eyes lingering on Alexa.

But Grady moved forward toward the Indian gentleman, whose smile was even now expanding.

Grady closed the distance, and they clasped hands firmly.

"My dear boy. How fine it is to finally shake your hand."

"Archie." Grady then embraced Chattopadhyay.

The other Resistors, both men and woman, young and old, gathered around Grady and Chattopadhyay, tears on many faces as they held each other for the first time.

Alexa looked on as Grady ushered them all outside, into the sunlight, where they looked up disbelievingly—raising their hands to the sun.

SEVEN
YEARS
LATER

CHAPTER 36

Echo

Jon Grady stared out across the predawn sky, glowing purple at the eastern horizon. The stars and the Milky Way arched overhead.

A thousand feet below he saw the shoreline of Oregon's Crater Lake curving away, the indigo water still as glass beneath him, reflecting the stars. It was perfect. He drank in the view.

Then he heard a welcome voice.

"There he is."

Grady turned to see Alexa holding their six-year-old daughter's hand, both of them bundled in coats against the chill morning air as they floated in equilibrium, their eyes catching the first rays of dawn.

Grady smiled toward them, and he thought about how marvelous the universe was. How fortunate he was to have lived to be here at this moment. There was a unity in it. A perfection that went beyond math and physics. Though fleeting, it also felt somehow enduring.

He extended his hand toward his daughter.

"This way, Varuna." He looked up. "I want you to see this . . ."

FURTHER READING

You can learn more about the technologies and themes explored in *Influx* by visiting www.daniel-suarez.com or through the following books:

Physics of the Future: How Science Will Shape Human Destiny and Our Daily Lives by the Year 2100 by Michio Kaku (Doubleday)

The Covert Sphere: Secrecy, Fiction, and the National Security State by Timothy Melley (Cornell University Press)

God's Jury: The Inquisition and the Making of the Modern World by Cullen Murphy (Houghton Mifflin Harcourt)

Warped Passages: Unraveling the Mysteries of the Universe's Hidden Dimensions by Lisa Randall (Ecco)

Legacy of Ashes: The History of the CIA by Tim Weiner (Doubleday)

ACKNOWLEDGMENTS

First and foremost I want to thank my brother, Adam Winston, for contributing the seed upon which this story is based, in addition to certain characters. Both of us have always written stories, and this was one idea that I thought held great promise as a high-tech thriller—my particular specialty. With his encouragement I have expanded and revised that idea into the book you now hold.

Bringing life into gravity mirrors and the BTC was a daunting task, made easier by the patient advice of physicist and friend Eric Burt, who carefully reviewed early drafts of the manuscript. Whatever crimes against physics remain in the book are my own, not his.

Sincere thanks to Michio Kaku, Timothy Melley, Cullen Murphy, Sir Roger Penrose, Lisa Randall, and Tim Weiner, whose published works greatly enriched this rather fantastical story.

Thanks also to my literary agent, Rafe Sagalyn, and the entire team at Sagalyn Literary. And, as always, heartfelt gratitude to Ben Sevier, my editor at Dutton, both for his story advice and the confidence he has shown in me.

Yet, this book would still not exist without the love of my life, Michelle, who keeps me from wandering into traffic while I contemplate stories. . . .

ABOUT THE AUTHOR

DANIEL SUAREZ is the author of the *New York Times* bestseller *Daemon*, *Freedom*™, and *Kill Decision*. A former systems consultant to Fortune 1000 companies, Mr. Suarez has designed and developed software for the defense, finance, and entertainment industries. His fiction focuses on technology-driven change, and he is a past speaker at TED Global, NASA Ames, the Long Now Foundation, and the headquarters of Google, Microsoft, and Amazon. An avid gamer and technologist, he lives in Los Angeles.

A 150-YEAR PUBLISHING TRADITION

In 1864, E. P. Dutton & Co. bought the famous Old Corner Bookstore and its publishing division from Ticknor and Fields and began their storied publishing career. Mr. Edward Payson Dutton and his partner, Mr. Lemuel Ide, had started the company in Boston, Massachusetts, as a bookseller in 1852. Dutton expanded to New York City, and in 1869 opened both a bookstore and publishing house at 713 Broadway. In 2014, Dutton celebrates 150 years of publishing excellence. We have redesigned our longtime logotype to reflect the simple design of those earliest published books. For more information on the history of Dutton and its books and authors, please visit www.penguin.com/dutton.

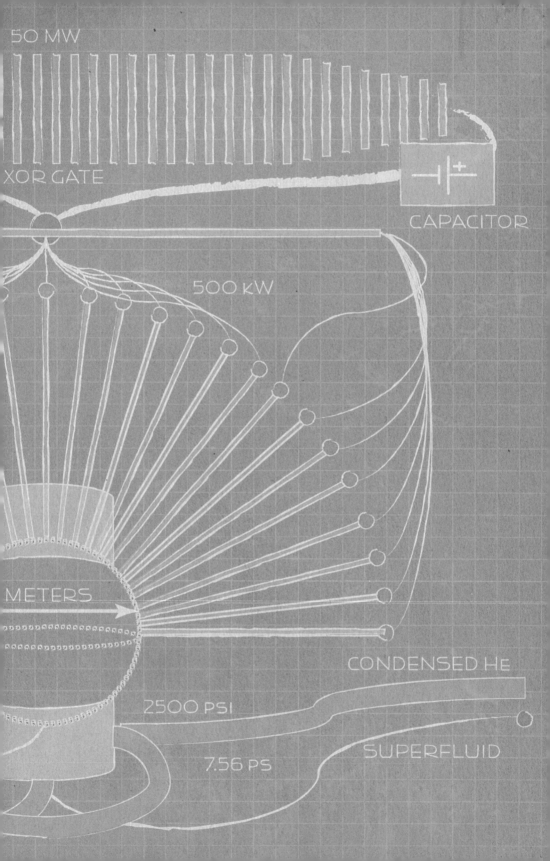